STAND YOUR GROUND

A sage hen suddenly fluttered skyward. Hardly had the bird taken wing when five riders boiled out of a ravine hidden by the rolling plains. Some fifty yards away, they spurred their horses and thundered forward, pistols popping in a ragged volley. Lead sizzled through the air with a low whining buzz.

The herd bolted, spooked by the gunfire. Jordan brought the Winchester to his shoulder, sighting on the lead rider, and fired. The impact of the slug hammered the man from his saddle, and he pitched sideways to the ground. To the rear, Poe and the other hands cut loose in a drumming tattoo with their carbines . . .

St. Martin's Paperbacks by Matt Braun

WYATT EARP
BLACK FOX
OUTLAW KINGDOM
LORDS OF THE LAND
CIMARRON JORDAN
BLOODY HAND
NOBLE OUTLAW
TEXAS EMPIRE

Coming Soon
THE SAVAGE LAND

TEXAS EMPIRE

MATT BRAUN

St. Martin's Paperbacks

TEXAS EMPIRE

ISBN: 0-312-96036-0

Printed in the United States of America

St. Martin's Paperbacks edition/November 1996

St. Martin's Paperbacks are published by St. Martin's Press, 175 Fifth Avenue, New York, NY 10010.

10 9 8 7 6 5 4 3 2 1

TO

THE ADAIRS

PAST AND PRESENT, PIONEERS ALL

AND

ALLEN, DAWN, AND BEAU

THREE OF A KIND, ALL ACES HIGH

Author's Note

Texas Empire is based on a true story. The character of Jack Jordan was patterned on the legendary Charles Goodnight. A Texas Ranger and army scout, Goodnight went on to establish one of the foremost ranching kingdoms in the Old West.

In partnership with Oliver Loving, he blazed the Goodnight-Loving Trail from West Texas to Colorado. Tens of thousands of cattle were driven over the trail in less than a decade. The herds provided beef for mining camps and stock for expanding ranches throughout the High Plains.

In 1874, following the end of hostilities with the Southern Plains Tribes, Goodnight laid claim to the mighty Palo Duro Canyon. There, in partnership with an Irish aristocrat, he established the JA Ranch, which grew to encompass more than one million acres. His partner, John Adair, was a distant ancestor of the author's.

Charles Goodnight was a trailblazer, a man of action against both the warlike tribes and white outlaws, and a visionary who carved a cattle empire from the wilderness. For this account, certain names have been changed and time has been compressed for the sake of story. Jack Jordan, a fictional character, commemorates the life and times of Charles Goodnight.

The exploits of Jack Jordan are grounded in fact. Historical characters and actual incidents, based on fact, have been presented against a panorama of the settlement of the West. As with any fictional account, literary license has been taken in the telling. Yet the story itself is true to the times.

Texas Empire depicts the saga of one man's courage and vision.

PROLOGUE

A killing mood rode with the men.

Captain Sam Ross knew they would not be restrained once the hostiles were overtaken. He led a company of forty Texas Rangers across the buff plains skirting the Pease River. Their direction was northwest, toward the distant escarpment that guarded *Llano Estacado*. Somewhere ahead was a raiding party of Comanche warriors.

Five days past, the Comanches had struck west of Weatherford, plundering and killing along the line of frontier settlements. Their goal was horses, the only wealth prized by the Plains Tribes, and they had laid waste to several ranches in less than a day. Then, turning to flee, they had overrun one last ranch on the western edge of Parker County.

Daniel Sherman, the rancher, and his son were chopped down in the first moments of the onslaught. After setting the house ablaze, the raiders staked Alice Sherman, the rancher's wife, to the ground. She was pregnant, swollen to full term, but the warriors were heedless of her condition. They raped her repeatedly, one after the other, goaded to cruelty by her shrill screams. Finally, bored with her gibbering terror, they scalped her and fired three arrows into her breast. She was left for dead.

Ross and his Rangers, ordered to pursue the hostiles, came upon the scene the following day. They found Alice

Sherman still alive, having given birth to a dead baby, the ground around her a welter of blood. Hard men, not easily shaken, they watched her draw a last breath as they tried to minister to her wounds. They buried the woman and her family in a common grave, their mouths tight with rage. The raid had claimed the lives of eighteen people; but the sight of a woman so savagely violated brought bile to their throats. Words failed as they rode out, but there was unspoken accord among the Rangers. They would take no prisoners.

Jack Jordan was of a similar mind. Though younger than the other men, not yet twenty-three, he was chief scout of the Ranger Company. For the last four years, while the Civil War raged elsewhere, he had served with the frontier battalion. The mission of the battalion was to protect settlements from hostile tribes, who raided with impunity once military posts were abandoned to fight the larger war. Jordan had seen many atrocities in his time with the Rangers, for the Comanche were the fiercest of all the Plains Tribes, merciless in their raids on *Texicans*. Yet the death of the Sherman woman was beyond savagery, beyond anything human. Like the other Rangers, he meant to exact a heavy toll.

For four days, Jordan had scouted a mile or so ahead of the company. The trail had pressed through the Western Cross Timbers, a stretch of land dense with woods, and then onto the open plains. From there, much as he'd expected, the raiders had turned northwest, into a vast wilderness known to few white men. The tracks were easily followed, for the Comanches were driving a herd of some one hundred fifty stolen horses. His greatest concern was that the raiding party might make a run for *Llano Estacado*.

Toward the headwaters of the Pease, a towering escarpment stood like a fortress wall. Above lay *Llano Estacado,* the fabled Staked Plains, thousands of square miles of flat grassland, broken occasionally by a hidden canyon. *Llano Estacado* was uncharted, with no maps or landmarks, an ancient stronghold of the Comanche, the Kiowa, and other warlike tribes. The *Comancheros,* Mexicans who had conducted trade with the hostiles for generations, traversed the Staked Plains without need of map or compass. But no white man claimed such knowledge, and those who ventured there had never returned. *Llano Estacado* was shrouded in mystery, still unexplored.

Shortly before sundown, Jordan discovered where the herd had forded the Pease to the north bank. There the trail turned in a westerly direction, toward the distant headwaters, and *Llano Estacado.* Yet the tracks were clear to read, and he noted that the pace of the herd had dropped off to a slow trot. So far west of the settlements, the hostiles clearly thought they had outdistanced all pursuit. The chances of overtaking them suddenly improved.

Jordan dismounted, studying the sign. The churned earth was still moist to the touch, not yet baked hard by the afternoon sun. Tracking at night seemed to him too risky, for the moon was down, and he would likely lose the trail. The better plan was for the Rangers to camp on the river, close to fresh water, and resume pursuit at first light. One foot in the stirrup, about to remount, he noticed a dark, squarish object beneath the shade of a cottonwood. He walked forward and picked it up with a look of surprise. He was holding a tattered copy of the Holy Bible.

When he opened it, he found an inscription on the flyleaf. The names of Daniel and Alice Sherman, and their son William, along with their birth dates, had been entered in the delicate penmanship of a woman. Staring at it, he was struck by a thought that razored his mouth in a grim line. Alice Sherman would never enter the name of her daughter, born dead only four days ago. The baby, and the family, lay cold in a shallow grave.

Jordan was struck as well by the practical nature of savages who slaughtered whole families. Over time, the Comanche had learned that paper offered great resistance to the impact of bullets. When they looted a settler's home, books of any description were considered a prized object.

Warriors packed the books inside their round, bull-hide shields, to absorb bullets fired at them in battle. A Comanche brave, perhaps the one who had scalped Alice Sherman while she still lived, had accidentally dropped the Bible from his shield. With any luck at all, Jordan told himself, it would get the bastard killed tomorrow.

A short while later, Ross led the Rangers across the river. Daylight was fading to dusk, and he agreed with Jordan, ordering the men to pitch camp for the night. As the company dismounted, Jordan handed him the Bible. He stared at the inscription a moment, his eyes cold.

"Sorry sonovabitch," he muttered. "I'd pay the price to get him in my sights."

"You'll most likely get your wish, Cap'n."

"Figger we're that close, do you?"

"Way I read the sign," Jordan replied, "we're two, maybe three hours behind. Ought to catch 'em sometime tomorrow mornin'."

Ross frowned. "They could still make a run for *Llano Estacado*."

"Well, I tend to doubt it, Cap'n. Way they slowed down, they've got no notion we're on their tails."

Ross accepted the statement at face value. Four years of working together had convinced him that Jordan was a rarity among scouts. The young Ranger possessed some infallible instinct for the wilds, and wild things, Comanche or otherwise. His gift for tracking had yet to play him false.

Nor was he any slouch as a fighter. Ross had watched him grow from a lithe youngster of eighteen to a tough, sledge-shouldered veteran who sat tall in the saddle. The other men, though older, willingly entrusted him with their lives. He inevitably led them to the hostiles, and in battle, he was fearsome to behold. Wherever the action was thickest, he was there.

"All right, Jack," Ross said now. "We'll plan to ride out at dawn."

"Cap'n, I just suspect that'll get the job done."

Ross understood that orders were unnecessary. Jordan,

forever one step ahead, would be gone before the sky paled.

The sun crested the horizon as Jordan reined to a halt. He was some five miles west along the Pease, the Ranger company not more than ten minutes behind. For a moment he sat studying the horse tracks, which still paralleled the river. Something about the tracks struck him as odd.

Then, looking closer, he spotted a single set of fresh tracks. The sign indicated that a lone rider had returned downriver, crossing the tracks of the horse herd, and ridden north onto the plains. His first thought was that a scout had been sent to check the raiders' backtrail for pursuit. He sat perfectly still, scanning the terrain off to the north.

Some fifty yards away, on a stunted knoll, he saw a stand of chittam trees. The tracks led on a beeline to the knoll, and another set of tracks appeared to turn back in the direction of the river. Several moments slipped past while he pondered what seemed a puzzle. Finally, pulling a Henry repeater from the saddle boot, he rode toward the knoll.

The puzzle was quickly solved. At the knoll, he saw that the rider had dismounted and walked along the treeline. A berry, bittersweet in taste but savored by Comanches, grew profusely on chittam trees. The rider had probably eaten his fill for breakfast, and perhaps collected more in a perfleche bag. Studying the footprints more closely, Jordan realized something of far greater import. The sign was less than an hour old.

Not far upriver a row of sand hills intersected the Pease from the north. Jordan recalled from previous scouts that a creek fed into the river on the opposite side of the hills. He looked west, every sense suddenly alert, watching as a faint tendril of smoke drifted skyward from beyond a distant ridge. Swearing softly, he whirled his horse and galloped off downriver. Some minutes later he slid to a halt before Sam Ross, at the head of the Ranger column.

"Cap'n, we've got 'em!" he whooped. "They're

camped on the other side of them hills.''

Ross looked doubtful. ''Why would they do a damn-fool thing like that?''

''Thought they'd outrun us, that's why. Probably figured to lay up a day and give the horses a breather.''

''You're plumb certain about that, are you, Jack?''

''Hell, they're over there cookin' breakfast right now, Cap'n. We caught 'em with their pants down.''

Ross motioned the column forward. With Jordan in the lead, they angled off to the north at a slow trot. As they rode, the Rangers unlimbered their carbines and checked the loads. The thought uppermost in their minds was of a woman and her dead baby, and they were spoiling for a fight. They rushed onward now toward retribution.

Some minutes later, formed on a line, the Rangers boiled over the top of the hills. On the far side of the creek, grazing on a grassy plain, the horse herd bolted westward. The Comanche raiders, thirty or so in number, gaped in stunned surprise as the Rangers charged down the slope. With no chance to mount their ponies, some of the warriors ran for the creek and others turned to fight. The Rangers pounded forward, their guns blazing in a drumming roar.

The battle was swift, and deadly. Fully half of the warriors were killed as the Rangers thundered through the camp. On the far side some of the Rangers wheeled about for another charge, while others engaged Comanches within the treeline along the creek. Jordan shot a brave who stepped from behind a tree with arrow nocked and bow drawn. The brave staggered, blood splotching his chest, and the arrow skittered harmlessly overhead. He fell backward into the creek.

Jordan whirled his horse, levering a fresh round into the chamber. Across the campsite he saw a warrior fire an ancient musket at Ross, killing the captain's mount instead. The horse went down in mid-stride, hurling Ross out of the saddle and spilling him onto the ground. The warrior pulled a knife, loosing a blood-curdling screech, and jumped Ross before he could regain his feet. The Comanche straddled him, the knife upraised.

On the instant Jordan brought the repeater to his shoulder, caught the sights, and fired. The warrior's head exploded in a mist of brains and gore, and he toppled sideways to the ground. As Ross scrambled to his feet, a final shot sounded north along the creek. Then, abruptly, a pall of silence descended over the camp. The Rangers paused, their weapons still at the ready, suddenly aware that the killing was done. Throughout the camp, and along the winding creek, lay the bodies of dead Comanches. Not one had escaped.

Later, while some of the men went to gather the horse herd, Ross and Jordan surveyed the battleground. Of the forty Rangers, only one had been wounded, a rifle ball passing cleanly through his shoulder. With a gritty grin, his arm in a sling, he assured the captain he was ready to ride. Apart from Ross's horse, the company had suffered no losses.

Jordan recovered a lance from near the body of a warrior. One among many scattered about, the lance caught his eye because of a wavy, golden scalp dangling from the shaft. He held it out for Ross's inspection.

"Look familiar?" he said somberly. "I recollect Mrs. Sherman had hair like that."

Ross glanced from the scalp to the warrior's body. "By all rights, we ought to scalp that stinkin' heathen. See how he likes it."

"Dead's dead," Jordan observed. "Don't you reckon we've settled accounts, Cap'n?"

"Yeah, I suppose." Ross was silent a moment. "Thanks for gettin' that buck, the one keen for my hair. Damn fancy shootin'."

"Hell, don't mention it, Cap'n. Glad to oblige."

"You're not half as glad as me, Jack."

Ross ordered the company to get mounted. Afterward, with the sun in their faces, they drove the horse herd east along the Pease. None of them looked back as vultures began circling the grisly killing ground. Nor was there any thought of burying the dead.

Texas Rangers never said grace over those they killed.

Part One

Chapter 1

A rainbow of colors rippled off the water from a warm July sun. Jordan reined his horse across the river in the early afternoon and rode toward town. His gaze was fixed, the look of a man troubled by time and events. He wondered if he would still own the ranch at sundown.

Pueblo was situated in the southern foothills of the Rockies. The surrounding countryside was arid, despite the proximity of the Arkansas River to the town. Eastward lay a vista of broken plains, and to the west towering summits were still capped with snow. The mountains marched northward like an unbroken column of sentinels.

By 1874, as the railway center for Southern Colorado, Pueblo had at last achieved its place on the map. The road into town crossed the Denver & Rio Grande tracks, which extended some ninety miles northward to Denver. Directly past the tracks, Pueblo's main throughfare was clogged with wagons and buggies, and the boardwalks were crowded with shoppers. The street was jammed with shops and stores, and a block away the new courthouse was in the final stages of construction. The arrival of the railroad had transformed a once isolated outpost into a bustling little metropolis.

As he rode past the Manitou House Hotel, Jordan was reminded that things were not always as they appeared. The area's outlying farmers and ranchers still brought their trade to town; but they now existed on the limited credit extended by merchants. The business district looked busy, and for the most part, shops and stores remained open for business. Yet there was a stark difference since last year's financial panic. These days no one had any cash money.

Jordan was strapped for cash himself. For a time, operating on wishful thinking, he believed he could ride out the economic collapse. But as he was forced to sell off his herd, he found himself brought face-to-face with reality. The monthly upkeep for the ranch became an intolerable burden, and though it went against the grain, there was no choice but to lay off the majority of his crew. Leigh Dyer, his foreman, and the other hands still on the payroll had been with him since the days of the trail drives from Texas. He went without in order to pay their wages.

Upstreet from the hotel, Jordan reined in before the Stock Growers Bank. He dismounted, looping the reins around a hitch rack, and stepped onto the boardwalk. As he moved toward the door, he swatted trail dust off his clothes, the bulge of a Colt Peacemaker obvious beneath his jacket. Sunlight on the bank's plate-glass window reflected his image, and he thought he looked every inch the impostor. A cattleman trying to pass himself off as a business tycoon. He steeled himself to play the part.

Inside, one of the bookkeepers ushered him into Franklin Thatcher's private office. A sturdy man, the banker's beard was dappled with gray and his hair was thinning out above a craggy forehead. George Hinsdale, their partner in several enterprises, was seated in one of the chairs ranged before the desk. A merchant by trade, he was cadaverous in build, with watery brown eyes and a reedy voice. He nodded to Jordan with solemn geniality.

"Jack," Thatcher said, motioning him into a chair. "Good to see you. I trust your ride in was uneventful."

"No highwaymen," Jordan said wryly, seating himself and placing his hat on the edge of the desk. "Country's gone plumb civilized."

"I do appreciate your wit, Jack. Where would we be

without a sense of humor? Hmmm?''

Thatcher was an urbane man, with the charm common to genteel Southerners. A native of Tennessee, he'd brought his family west following the Civil War, and settled in Pueblo in 1865. The remnants of an inheritance had allowed him to found the bank, and prosper along with the town's growth. He was shrewd and wily, a core of iron beneath the veneer of breeding.

George Hinsdale, by contrast, had established the town's first general store. From there, he expanded into a wholesale liquor business and a large grocery store. Even in hard times people needed food and whiskey, and he was rumored to be the richest man in Pueblo. Sly and crafty, a notorious tightwad, he squeezed profit from whatever passed through his hands.

When their business association began, Jordan considered himself fortunate to be involved with men of such acumen and experience. In the boomtime growth of Pueblo, their investments, at least on paper, had multiplied far beyond their original expectations. But with the crash on Wall Street, and the ripple effect westward, the attitude of Thatcher and Hinsdale had undergone a pronounced change. Jordan discovered that friendship and business, like oil and water, was a tenuous mix. He waited to hear why they had called today's meeting.

The amenities observed, Thatcher went straight to the point. ''Jack, I want you to know we value our association with you, and have the utmost regard for your integrity. That said, we are confronted with a dismal situation . . . absolutely hopeless.''

Jordan held his gaze. ''Hopeless in what way?''

''In the sense that we—George and I—have a fiduciary responsibility to the stockholders of this bank. Our mandate, by law, requires that we safeguard the bank's assets.''

''Aren't you forgetting I'm a stockholder, too?''

''A minority stockholder,'' Thatcher corrected him. ''George and I control the majority interest.''

''Way it sounds,'' Jordan said, ''we're talking about you

and George protecting yourselves. Where does that leave me?"

"I regret to say it places you in an untenable position. Unless, of course, you have some means of raising additional funds."

"You know I'm strapped for money. Hell, I've sold off my herd and fired more than thirty hands. Where would I raise more cash?"

"I have no idea, Jack. We were hopeful you might have found a solution."

There was a prolonged silence. Thatcher and Hinsdale waited for him to reply, as though he might perform a feat of magic before their eyes. Jordan had the feeling he was holding the losing hand in a high-stakes poker game. He shook his head.

"So what are you getting at?"

Thatcher's expression was sorrowful. "The Rock Canyon ranch was used as collateral for your loans in our various business ventures. Again, I regret to say those ventures are now victim to a depressed marketplace."

"Spell it out," Jordan demanded. "Are you calling my note?"

"What other choice do we have, Jack? It's simply business, nothing personal."

"When you're talking about me losing the ranch, that's personal. Goddamn personal!"

Thatcher spread his hands in a bland gesture. "We all suffer a reversal of fortune at some time in our lives. I have every confidence you'll rebound with flying colors."

Jordan gave him a wooden look. "I expected more out of you boys. Figured you'd cut me a little slack when it got down to sink or swim." He paused, glancing from one to the other. "Guess there's some truth to that old saying about fair-weather friends."

So far Hinsdale had remained a spectator. But now, in his reedy voice, he joined the conversation. "No need for you to take that attitude, not at this late date. We've carried you till the well run dry."

"George, that's hogwash and we all know it. You two haven't lost a plugged nickel on me. I paid my way right along."

"Wasn't for us," Hinsdale said sharply, "you would've folded long before now. That's the plain fact of the matter."

"Truth is, you boys could carry me till hell freezes over. Between the two of you, you've got more money than God."

"Jack, please understand," Thatcher interjected softly. "When you say sink or swim, you're asking us to go under with you. I hardly think that's a reasonable request."

Jordan's features turned sphinxlike. He saw now that they meant to take the ranch, and friendship be damned. All his life he had refused to beg favors, and he wasn't about to start. Tall and wide-shouldered, in his prime at thirty-three, his square features were set off by a thatch of chestnut hair and a brushy mustache. His eyes were piercing, a striking mix of gray-blue, and left other men with the impression he could read minds. He looked born to command a cattle outfit.

Four years ago Jordan had purchased the rights to a Spanish land grant from the last descendent of an old Mexican family. When the papers were signed, he became the sole owner of a hundred thousand acres grazeland, extending twenty-five miles along the Arkansas. The range was well watered, sheltered from plains blizzards by Rock Canyon, and covered with lush grama grass that fattened steers. At the time, he looked upon it as bounty from the gods.

By 1872 Jordan was running some ten thousand head of cattle, the largest outfit in Colorado. The civic leaders of Pueblo sought him out, and association with the town fathers quickly led to an array of business opportunities. In league with Thatcher, and a prominent businessman, George Hinsdale, he set about expanding into diversified holdings. By early 1873 he was a principal in the bank, and a joint investor in business buildings, residential city lots, and a meat-packing plant.

On paper, late in the summer of 1873, Jordan's net worth exceeded a million dollars. His wealth made him the most eligible bachelor, and certainly the prize catch, in all of southern Colorado. The woman who caught him, after a brief courtship, was Rebecca Thatcher, the daughter of Franklin Thatcher. She was twelve years younger than Jordan, considered the belle of Pueblo, and the only woman he'd ever met who was spirited enough to prove his equal. Her father still had lingering reservations about the age difference, but she had proved to be his equal as well. Their engagement had been announced in late August of 1873.

The bubble burst in late September. Jay Cooke & Company, the most prestigious financial institution on Wall Street, closed its doors. That afternoon thirty-seven banks and brokerage houses went under. An hour later, the board of governors suspended trade on the New York Stock Exchange. Before the debacle ran its course, five thousand businesses would be forced into bankruptcy.

The Panic of '73 brought the nation to its knees.

With the economic collapse, America's financial institutions crumbled into ruin. Investment capital withered overnight, and banks in Pueblo and other Colorado communities found themselves in perilous straits. Those that managed to stay afloat were forced to call in all outstanding loans, and quickly suspended activity on new loans. At the same time, the cattle market hit bottom, hovered there a couple of days, and then simply sank out of sight.

From Jordan's standpoint, it was a disaster of monumental proportions. All of his cash had gone into Pueblo investment properties, and he had mortgaged the ranch to raise added investment funds for still more business concerns. At the time, with the economy booming and Pueblo the financial hub of southern Colorado, the opportunity had seemed golden. But with the catastrophic collapse of Wall Street, all of his investments were suddenly transformed into a mountain of debt.

To Jordan, the real estate properties and business concerns were of secondary interest. His single-minded goal was to resurrect from the ashes what he had worked toward all his life, the ranch. Over the past eleven months he had slowly sold off the Rock Canyon herd, timing his sales to a gradual increase in cattle prices. But now, with the herd down to sixteen hundred head, there was nowhere left to turn. The men seated across from him had him by the short hairs, and they knew it. He nodded to Thatcher.

"Looks like I've been foreclosed. When do you want me off the ranch?"

"Oh, by all means, take your time," Thatcher said magnanimously. "Three or four months, longer if need be. There's little market for land in today's economy."

"Soon as I locate range for what's left of the herd, I'll clear out. Anything else?"

"Well, yes, there is—" Thatcher wagged his head sadly. "You realize that it's not just the ranch. We're talking about town property, the meat plant, your bank stock . . . everything."

Jordan grunted. "You cut right to the bone, don't you?"

"I've never regretted anything more in my life, Jack. I genuinely hope you understand."

"Draw up the papers and I'll sign 'em."

Jordan stood, clapped his hat on his head. He walked from the office without looking at either of them. When he emerged from the bank, his jaw was clamped in a tight line. He told himself he'd got in with fast company, where it was devil take the hindmost, and no second chances. All he'd worked for was now lost.

Yesterday a millionaire, and today out on the street with nothing to show for it. The hell of it was, he'd never seen a penny, and he never would.

He was stone broke.

CHAPTER 2

Jordan walked toward the post office. He thought he might as well collect the mail while he was in town. Then, however much he dreaded it, he would have to call on Rebecca. She had a right to hear the bad news from him directly.

Nothing was certain, but he doubted she'd heard it from her father. Thatcher would have kept it to himself, anticipating the news would draw her anger. They were already at odds over the engagement, which Thatcher had never fully accepted. With the wedding set for next month, her father probably planned to keep the matter secret until after today's meeting. Rebecca was a spitfire when she lost her temper.

A thought occurred to Jordan. He wondered if Thatcher had timed foreclosure on the ranch in an effort to forestall the marriage. Certainly, as Thatcher had admitted in the meeting, the ranch was of no immediate value to the bank. So perhaps he had played a trump card, hoping his daughter would have second thoughts about marrying a penniless man. In a way, the idea had merit, for she was accustomed to money and position, the finer things in life. Still, Jordan couldn't believe it would matter. She wasn't a person to barter her affections.

Nor could he believe that Thatcher would resort to devious tricks. In a business deal, Thatcher was ever the banker, interested only in protecting himself and his assets.

But he was a man of personal integrity, above some petty plot to spoil his daughter's wedding. Yet one thought sparked another, and Jordan suddenly realized that he might have second thoughts himself. At the moment, he had a piddling herd of sixteen hundred cows, and a crew of cowhands whose next payday would empty his wallet. Not much to offer a girl who was accustomed to the finer things in life. Hardly the basis for a sound marriage.

Wedded bliss required that a man offer his wife more. Lots more.

Jordan was still mulling it over when he entered the post office. The clerk at the window took two letters from his box, and passed them across the counter. One was for a hand at the ranch, from his family back in Texas. The other was military-issue stationery, addressed to Jordan. He recognized the bold scrawl even before he looked at the return address. It was from Colonel Ranald Mackenzie, Fort Clark, Texas.

As he opened the letter, Jordan was reminded of other times, days past. In military circles, Colonel Ranald Mackenzie was considered the foremost Indian fighter on the frontier. A Civil War hero, Mackenzie had assumed command of the 4th Cavalry at Fort Concho in 1871. Something over a year later, disgusted with chasing Comanches who routinely outwitted army scouts, Mackenzie had contacted Sam Ross, former captain of the Texas Rangers. Mackenzie requested recommendations of a scout who was versed in the far-flung regions of the West Texas plains. Ross wrote back, recommending only one man, Jack Jordan.

At the time, Jordan was in the midst of getting the Rock Canyon ranch operational. But after a series of persuasive letters from Mackenzie, he was forced to admit that any man was bound by duty when called. He agreed to serve as chief scout of the regiment for a period of one month, and no more, whatever the outcome. He reported to Fort Concho on September 1, 1872, and the 4th Cavalry rode out three days later. On September 29, with Jordan scouting the way, the regiment attacked a Comanche village of nearly three hundred lodges on the North Fork of the Red River. The campaign ended with a hostile band settled on the Fort Sill reservation, in Indian Territory.

Jordan returned to Colorado, and the Rock Canyon ranch. With typical military bungling, the army brass then transferred Mackenzie's regiment to Fort Clark, near the Rio Grande, to patrol the border with Mexico. Yet, in their brief service together, a deep and lasting mutual respect developed between Jordan and Mackenzie. Over the past two years, they had corresponded frequently, keeping one another apprised of their activities. Generally of a similar mind, they agreed that the government's war against hostile Plains Tribes was at best a joke. From the Comanches in the south, to the Sioux in the north, politicians continued to hamstring the army's efforts.

Today, scanning the latest letter, Jordan felt his pulse quicken. Mackenzie's words were little short of jubilant, relating that the War Department had finally seen the light. A campaign was even now being organized, the largest military operation ever undertaken on the Southern Plains. Though he phrased the news in a cryptic manner, for details would breech military security, Mackenzie hinted that it would be the last campaign, and an end to the hostile tribes. He urged and exhorted, and then demanded, that Jordan sign on with the 4th Cavalry. History was in the making, for the objective was the Comanche stronghold, *Llano Estacado.*

The very name made Jordan's scalp tingle. His mind went back ten years, to his days as a Texas Ranger. He recalled with vivid clarity the land two hundred miles west of the Upper Cross Timbers, where massive escarpments formed the eastern rim of the Staked Plains. A land shrouded in myth and superstition, encompassing the headwaters of the Brazos, the Colorado, and the Red. A land where no white man had ever ventured, and lived to tell the tale. The timeless uncharted sanctuary of the Comanche, *Llano Estacado.*

Jordan folded the letter with a touch of reverence. Mackenzie and the 4th, and God knew how many other commands, were to strike into the heart of *Comancheria.* Mackenzie urged him to join the campaign, what would doubtless be the last campaign. To go where no white man dared.

The challenge of it went to the very core of that old longing to explore the unknown. Deep inside he felt a rekindling of the spark to dare where other men shied away. He walked from the post office with a brisk stride, a sudden grin.

His eyes were afire with a single thought. *Llano Estacado.*

The Thatcher house was in the uptown residential district. There the wealthier families of Pueblo had built imposing homes in the Victorian style. Jordan knocked on the door shortly after three o'clock.

Rebecca appeared taken aback when she opened the door. "What a pleasant surprise!" she said gaily. "What are you doing in town?"

"Had business at the bank," Jordan said, doffing his hat. "Gave me an excuse to drop by and see you."

"As if you needed an excuse!"

Rebecca laughed, pulled him into the house. She took his arm, leading him toward the parlor. Her closeness reminded Jordan all over again of why he'd fallen for her. She was rather tall, with enormous hazel eyes and exquisite features. Vibrant and vivacious, with a sumptuous figure, she wore her dark hair upswept with fluffs of curls spilling over her forehead. Her demure day dress did nothing to hide her tiny waist and magnificent hips.

A vast Persian carpet covered the parlor floor. Sofas and settees were scattered around the room, and velvet drapes bordered the front windows. Several armchairs and a divan were arranged before a black marble fireplace. Jordan was always impressed by the lavish furnishings, wondering if he could ever provide Rebecca with anything so grand. By comparison, the inside of his log home looked like a monk's cell.

She seated herself beside him on the divan. "I'm so happy you came by," she said. "I hadn't expected to see you until Saturday night."

Jordan recalled they were to attend a dance. "Well, that's one reason I'm here. Things went to hell in a handbasket today, and we need to talk."

She was amused, rather than offended, by his casual gift for cursing. His speech was sprinkled with off-color phrases, simply part of his vernacular. But now, looking concerned, she took his hand. "What is it, Jack? Mother's out shopping, so we're alone. Go ahead and tell me. What's wrong?"

"I'm busted," Jordan said truthfully, unwilling to skirt the issue. "The bank foreclosed on the ranch, and everything else I own. I'm flat broke."

She was stunned. "Father foreclosed on you?" she said, her voice rising in anger. "Just wait till I—"

"No," Jordan interrupted. "Don't jump all over him on my account. I got myself into a fix, and business is business. I'm not owed special treatment."

"Of course you are! You're his future son-in-law!"

"Well, as to that—" Jordan suddenly looked uncomfortable. "When I proposed, I was riding high. Way things are now, I'm worse off than when I started."

She raised an eyebrow. "And?"

"You'd be marryin' a busted-down cowman. Who knows if I'll ever make a fortune. You sure that's what you want?"

"You ninny!" she said, scolding him. "I'm marrying you because I love you. Didn't you know that?"

Her Southern accent was more pronounced when she was excited. Jordan thought it was one of the reasons he'd been attracted to her. He grinned, shook his head. "You know it won't be easy. I'd understand if you changed your mind."

"Absolutely, positively not! We will be married August

twenty-first, exactly as planned.''

''Let's talk about that,'' Jordan said earnestly. ''Maybe we ought to hold off till I get squared away. Christ, I don't even have a home for you. Not now, leastways.''

She was crushed. ''You want to postpone the wedding?''

''Just till I'm on my feet again. We've got to be practical . . . don't you think?''

''You're not fooling me, Jack Jordan! There's something more to this, isn't there?''

''Well, yeah, sort of.'' Jordan hesitated, amazed that she saw through him so easily. ''The army's called me back to service.''

''Army?'' she said, astounded. ''You aren't a soldier.''

Jordan handed her Mackenzie's letter. He watched as she read it, wondering if she would again see through his flimsy reasoning. After today, he wanted time to reassess where and how to start over. The next step was critical, one that demanded consideration, and certainty. Fighting Indians seemed to him a welcome respite. A distancing from his problems.

She looked up from the letter. ''This Colonel Mackenzie is *requesting* your services. You have no obligation to agree.''

''Mackenzie's an old friend,'' Jordan observed. ''Like he says, he needs me to scout the Comanches. Besides, a man's obliged to serve when he's called. Only way we'll ever settle this country.''

''But your cattle business, have you given any thought to that? What happens if you just ride off . . . chasing Indians?''

''Hell, Becky, I'm down to sixteen hundred head. Leigh Dyer could nursemaid a herd that size with his legs sawed off.''

Rebecca hated the diminutive of her name. Jordan was the only person who had called her Becky in all her life. She forgave him because she knew he considered it a term of endearment. In a way, she thought it was sweet, part of his charm. Spoken in his voice, it somehow rang true. She searched his eyes.

"So you're determined to go. You've already made up your mind, haven't you?"

"Not by a damnsight," Jordan assured her. "Came here to talk to you first. But I have to tell you, I feel honor bound to go. I've never shirked duty before."

Rebecca knew only too well that Jordan valued his reputation, and with good reason. Across the West, despite his relatively young age, he was often referred to as a legend. At the outbreak of the Civil War, working as a cowhand in Palo Pinto County, he had been recruited into the Texas Rangers. Over the next four yours, serving as a frontier scout, he had garnered widespread renown as an Indian fighter.

After the war, Jordan returned to Palo Pinto County and went into the cattle business for himself. Tens of thousands of longhorns, left to run wild during the war, were there for the taking. Ownership was rarely in dispute, for the longhorns had bred like deer and perhaps one in ten wore a brand. The man who could hunt them down and capture them was free to claim them. Within a year he was running one of the largest herds on the Brazos.

Shorty afterward, he went into partnership with another visionary, a man named Oliver Loving. Seeking better markets for their cattle, they blazed a trail from the Red Fork of the Brazos to Fort Sumner in New Mexico, a distance of some five hundred miles. In 1867, during their second cattle drive, Loving was killed by a Comanche war party. Jordan honored his wish to be buried on home ground, and brought his body back to Texas in a buckboard. Newspapers lauded the feat, and his name took on the full-blown stature of a legend.

In the years that followed, Jordan blazed trails ever farther northward, extending through Colorado and on into Wyoming. He went where cattlemen had never dared go before, across deserts and the high plains, battling rustlers and horse thieves and hostile Indians as a matter of course.

From the Brazos to the railroad at Cheyenne, Wyoming, he marked wilderness trails of more than a thousand miles. His time as a trailblazer lasted seven years, with upwards of ten thousand cows brought north each year.

During all that time, Jordan was on the lookout for a place to settle down and sink roots. The trail drives had been immensely profitable, making him a wealthy man beyond anything he might have imagined. But the toll was heavy, for hardship carries a steep price, and his vision turned instead to establishing one of the great ranches of the West. His search ended on a cattle drive through Colorado, when he happened across the valley outside Pueblo. One look told him he'd found all he would ever want.

Today, it was gone. A dream destroyed, and a man's pride savaged, all in one blow.

By upbringing, a Southern girl was a student of male pride. Rebecca was all too aware that most men were hopeless romantics forever obsessed with valor. Certainly Jordan's response to this newest military campaign proved her point. Men loved the heroic, and it was part of the masculine role that they parade and play at war. Women saw only the suffering, while men struck postures and killed one another. Yet, for all her understanding, she saw no way to stop him. He would resent her if she tried.

She forced herself to smile. "I'll never forgive you if you run off to Texas and get yourself killed."

"Don't give it a thought," Jordan said confidently. "Never yet saw the Comanche that could punch my ticket."

"How long will you be gone?"

"I figure a couple of months at the outside. Way it sounds, the hostiles won't have the chance of a snowball in hell."

"And our wedding?" she pressed him. "What should I tell people?"

"Tell 'em the truth," Jordan said. "I got called to serve, and I went. Move things up a while, sometime in October."

Rebecca was hurt, but she nodded, smiling, revealing nothing. She understood him better than he understood himself. Today, all his dreams for the future had come crashing down. The letter from Mackenzie was merely his excuse to escape the devils of the moment. He thought to restore himself in battle, regain whatever pride he'd lost in financial ruin. She suspected that he was hurrying toward war as much for her as for himself. He wanted her to be proud of her husband.

''When will you leave?''

''Day after tomorrow,'' Jordan said too quickly, betraying a decision already made. ''Want to get Dyer and the boys squared away before I take off.''

She could have had any man in Pueblo. But of all her suitors, she had chosen Jordan for the traits she admired most. He was strong and assured, determined that his will would prevail. Still, beneath the rough exterior, there was a man of gentleness and compassion, and above all else, a man of loyalty. He gave himself completely, or not at all.

She scooted closer on the divan, put her arms around his neck. ''You're a scoundrel for leaving me at the altar just because someone sounds the trumpet. But I forgive you anyway.''

''We'll make it to the altar yet. You've got my word on it.''

She kissed him soundly on the mouth. ''Hurry home.''

Jordan grinned. ''Hell, I'm halfway back already.''

CHAPTER 3

Fort Clark was located something more than a hundred miles west of San Antonio. Fifty miles to the south lay the Rio Grande, and on the opposite bank, Mexico. In between, the rolling prairie was dotted with sand and cactus and dense thickets of chaparral. The land was populated largely by rattlesnakes and scorpions.

Jordan rode into the post the third week in August. The garrison was situated on a limestone ridge beside the waters of Las Moras Creek. To the immediate front was the parade ground, and beyond that, the regimental headquarters. Close by were the hospital and the quartermaster's depot, and farther on the quarters for married officers. Along the creek were the stables, and nearby, the enlisted men's barracks. Everything looked spruce and well tended, orderly.

Outside regimental headquarters, Jordan left his gelding tied to a hitching post. When he entered the orderly room, it took a moment for his eyes to adjust to the dim interior. Behind a desk, positioned to guard an inner office, sat a burly man with stripes covering his sleeves. Stocky and barrel-chested, he had a square, tough face and a huge walrus mustache. His mouth split in a wide grin.

"By the Saints!" he said with a thick brogue. "If it's not Jack Jordan hisself."

"Sergeant O'Meara." Jordan accepted a crushing handshake. "See the Comanches haven't gotten your hair."

"Oh, no fear of that. And yourself, you've had a pleasant ride, have you?"

"Swung down through New Mexico and then turned east. Never saw a hostile the whole time."

O'Meara clapped him on the shoulder. "You'll get your fill before we're done. There's big things brewing."

"Glad to hear it," Jordan said. "Always hated to miss a good fight."

"C'mon then and see the gen'ral. He was pleased indeed when he got the letter sayin' you'd be here."

O'Meara rapped on the door of the inner office. Upon entering, he stepped to the side and snapped to attention.

"Gen'ral, sir, beggin' your pardon. Our new chief of scouts wants to pay his respects."

Ranald Mackenzie was lean and muscular, with chiseled features and a sweeping handlebar mustache. His tunic bore the insignia of full colonel, and he gave the appearance of solidity and iron will. He rose from behind his desk.

"Well, Jack," he said, hand extended. "Good to see you again."

"Likewise, Colonel." Jordan moved forward as O'Meara went out, closing the door. "Took longer than I expected, but I'm here."

"Glad to have you with us on the campaign. I daresay we will make history this time out."

Jordan thought the remark typical of the man. A West Pointer, Mackenzie earned his first brevet during the Civil War at the Second Battle of Manassas. In all, he was wounded four times and promoted seven times in the course of the war. Under Sheridan's command, in the Shenandoah campaign, he had risen to the rank of Brevet Major General. He was twenty-five years old when the war ended.

On the western frontier, where he'd been posted after five years as a staff officer, Mackenzie had continued to make history. Possessing an innovative mind, he had adapted Civil War tactics to the treeless plains. He employed the cavalry as a long-ranging strike force, the most effective of all measures against the hostiles' guerrilla tactics. The Comanches, once acknowledged as the lords of the Southern Plains, feared him as no other horse soldier. He was relentless in the field, a commander who asked no quarter and gave none.

"In fact," Mackenzie said now, "your arrival couldn't be more timely. Our orders are to march at the end of the week."

Jordan knuckled his mustache. "Still like you said in your letter—*Llano Estacado*?"

"Indeed it is, old friend. We will hound their trail wherever it leads. Sheridan will settle for nothing less than victory."

"Way it sounds, he aims to wipe 'em out."

"Or drive them onto the reservation. The choice is theirs."

Mackenzie went on to review the reasons for a full-fledged campaign. In June, a group of twenty-eight buffalo hunters was attacked at Adobe Walls, a trading post on the fringe of *Comancheria*. The war party, some seven hundred strong, was led by Comanches, but included Kiowa, Cheyenne, and Arapaho. The buffalo hunters, losing only two men, killed over a hundred warriors with their deadly Sharps rifles. Humiliated, the Indian leaders broke off the battle, vowing revenge.

By early August, Mackenzie noted, there was a general uprising among the Plains tribes. The Kiowa and Cheyenne, as well as members of the four Comanche bands, jumped the reservation after being ordered to assemble at Fort Sill. They joined the most warlike of the Comanche bands, the Quahadi, on the Staked Plains. The Quahadi were led by Quanah, sometimes known as Quanah Parker, a chief of mixed blood. He was a formidable opponent, a military strategist who commanded respect.

The raids that followed were widespread and particularly vengeful in nature. The Arapaho and Cheyenne rode north and west pillaging Kansas and Colorado. Texans were subjected to unrelenting terror by their ancient enemies, the Comanche and Kiowa. The death toll mounted steadily, with almost two hundred Anglos butchered across the frontier. Settlers abandoned their homesteads and sought refuge at the nearest army post.

The uprising brought a backlash of public outrage. As newspapers reported on the "atrocities," army commanders sensed that the policy of peace and pacification advocated by religious organizations would shortly be reversed. Public revulsion led to political expediency, and the attitude in Washington swung full circle. The peace policy was abruptly terminated, and President Grant ordered the army to "subdue all Indians who offer resistance." Tribes caught off the reservation were to be considered hostile.

The change in policy was not limited to the southern tribes. Mackenzie remarked that the Sioux and other northern tribes were to be treated no differently than the Comanche. Never again were the Indians to be permitted to wander at will or terrorize Anglo settlers. Those who surrendered were to be considered prisoners of war and herded onto the reservations. Those who resisted were to be attacked and pursued and destroyed.

There was little opposition to what constituted a declaration of war. Editorials supported the government, and the Comanche, in particular, were vilified by the the press. Quanah and his warlike Quahadi were widely denounced for inciting the other tribes and fomenting "a summer of barbaric horror." The protests of Eastern religious factions were drowned out by the public outcry for retribution. Peace on the Western plains was to be imposed by military force.

General Phil Sheridan ordered a campaign characterized by absolute ruthlessness. At the core of his military objective was the subjugation of the Quahadi Comanche. A vast sweep of the Southern Plains was to be conducted, with army units converging from every direction on *Comancheria*. The net was to be drawn ever tighter, and for the first time, troops would penetrate deep into the unknown wastes of *Llano Estacado*. The Comanche and Kiowa were to be pursued and hounded without letup. Those who resisted were to be hunted down and killed.

Colonel Nelson Miles was ordered south from Fort Dodge, Kansas, with eight troops of the 6th Cavalry and four companies of the 5th Infantry. Colonel John Davidson was to advance westward from Fort Sill with six troops of the 10th Cavalry and two companies of the 11th Infantry. From northern Texas, Colonel George Buell was to proceed northwesterly with six troops of the 9th and 10th Cavalry and two companies of infantry. Major William Price, with four troops of the 8th Cavalry, was to sweep eastward from Fort Bascom, New Mexico.

Mackenzie, clearly delighted, observed that he'd been awarded the pivotal mission. The 4th Cavalry was designated the Southern Column, and ordered to push northward toward the headwaters of the Red River. His command was comprised of six hundred men, with eight troops of cavalry and five infantry companies detached from Fort Concho. His orders were to probe *Llano Estacado* and locate the Quahadi band. He was to kill, or capture, the war chief Quanah.

"We have the plum assignment," Mackenzie concluded with a broad smile. "Let me show you our route of march."

Mackenzie walked to a large map on the wall. He moved with a pronounced limp, which Jordan recalled was the result of a Comanche arrow. In the 1872 campaign, Mackenzie had taken a barbed shaft in the leg and refused treatment until the hostiles were dispersed. The wound healed poorly and he now lived in a state of constant pain. The example he set for those under his command was daily apparent in his game leg. He refused to acknowledge physical infirmity.

"Here's Fort Clark." Mackenzie rapped the map, using a riding crop as a pointer. "We rendezvous with the infantry from Fort Concho"—he traced a line northward

"—and then proceed to the Freshwater Fork of the Brazos. I fully expect to encounter hostiles by that time."

Jordan studied the map. "Even so," he said, "they'll scatter when we hit 'em with a regiment. Depend on them hightailing it toward *Llano Estacado*."

"I never doubted it for an instant, Jack. That's why I called you back into service."

"Somewhere up there"—Jordan moved to the wall map, indicating the vast uncharted wilderness of *Comancheria*"—I figure we'll find the headwaters of the Red. I'd wager that's where they run when they've gone to ground. Their hideout."

Mackenzie fixed him with a look. "I depend on you to ferret them out, Jack. You are the eyes of my regiment."

"I'll do my damnedest, Colonel."

The door burst open. Sergeant Major O'Meara rushed into the office, waving a telegram. "Just come over the wire, Gen'ral! The Tenth and the Sixth have engaged the God-cursed red heathens."

Mackenzie quickly scanned the telegram. "We march none too soon, gentlemen. The campaign is under way."

Upon reading the telegram, Jordan learned that the campaign had been prematurely touched off. Only yesterday, a band of Nakoni Comanche, returning from a raid in Texas, sought sanctuary in Indian Territory. Operating out of Fort Sill, Colonel Davidson and his 10th Cavalry tangled with the hostiles. The Comanche were joined by a band of Kiowa, and after a stiff fight, the combined force of hostiles broke off contact. They fled westward into *Comancheria*.

Farther north, almost at the same time, Colonel Miles and the 6th Cavalry had engaged in a running battle with some two hundred Cheyenne warriors. Finally, after five hours of bitter fighting, the Cheyenne had retreated southward onto the Staked Plains. There was every reason to believe that the Cheyenne would ultimately rejoin bands of Comanche and Kiowa known to be operating out of the distant, unmapped stronghold. The skirmishes merely underscored the need to invade *Llano Estacado.*

"Sergeant Major," Mackenzie ordered. "Advise the troop commanders to report here at 1600 hours. I'll hold a briefing at that time on this latest development."

"Yessir!" O'Meara stood rigid at attention. "Will there be anything else, Gen'ral?"

"That's all for now."

O'Meara marched out the door. Mackenzie shook his head with an amused expression. "After the war, everyone's brevet rank was rescinded. But O'Meara still insists on calling me general. The man's incorrigible."

Jordan wasn't certain what the term meant. "Well, Colonel, one thing's for damn sure. Nobody'll ever convince him you can't walk on water."

Mackenzie shrugged off the compliment. "I'll expect you at the briefing, Jack. Some of my officers aren't nearly so convinced as O'Meara." He paused, staring at the map. "They have misgivings about taking the regiment into *Llano Estacado.*"

"Understandable," Jordan replied. "We're riding into a jigsaw puzzle that nobody's ever figured out."

"You hardly seem to share their concern. You've come a long way to take the same risk."

"Guess I was born with a hankerin' to go where angels fear to tread. Hell, I wouldn't miss it for all the tea in China."

Mackenzie nodded. "Neither would I, Jack. Not for anything."

Jordan left him staring at the map. In the outer office, O'Meara was barking orders and orderlies were scurrying off to summon the troop commanders. All of it seemed to Jordan a reason to jump up and click his heels. He smiled to himself.

After years on the Plains, he was about to see it. A fabled land, ripe with legend and the stuff of dreams. *Llano Estacado.*

CHAPTER 4

Jordan rode out alone at dawn. The date was September 27 and the regiment was encamped along the headwaters of the Pease River. Their line of march had brought them at last to *Comancheria.*

The 4th Cavalry had covered more than four hundred miles since departing Fort Clark. Having sighted no hostiles along the Brazos, the column had moved northward toward the Pease. There the regiment established a base camp, with the supply train of some twenty wagons formed in a defensive square. The five infantry companies were charged with securing the camp.

Before dawn, the mounted troops were prepared to march. Jordan ranged out far ahead, looking for fresh sign, and the cavalry followed in a mile-long column. Their immediate objective was the Prairie Dog Fork of the Red River, some twenty miles north of the Pease. To the west, though the location was unknown, lay the headwaters of the Red. Somewhere along their line of march they would ascend to the high plateau of *Llano Estacado.*

Sunrise streaked the rolling prairie with shafts of gold. From his days as a Ranger, Jordan recalled the wooded creeks that fed the rivers and the general layout of the land. He opted to ride alone, for he placed little confidence in army scouts unfamiliar with the country. His solitary nature galled the three regular scouts, but Mackenzie gave him a free hand. His mission was to locate the Quahadi Comanche and guide the regiment into position for battle. He meant to do it his way, alone.

Jordan possessed a rare instinct for direction. With a destination fixed in his mind, he could find it as easily in darkness as in bright daylight. While he could never explain it, he relied on some inner compass rather than landmarks or the position of stars. Over the years he had known only a handful of scouts and plainsmen who were blessed with the same gift. Even on unfamiliar ground, on the cloudiest day, his instincts had never failed him. Whatever point he sought, he could ride to it without calculation or plan. His trust in himself was absolute.

On the march north, Jordan told himself there was little chance of entering *Comancheria* without being detected. The dust trail raised by a regiment of cavalry, not to mention the size of the column itself, was visible for miles on the open plains. Still, from the Brazos to the Pease, Jordan had uncovered no sign that the troops were being watched. The possibility existed that the regiment was under surveillance, and that he had somehow missed spotting the Indian scouts. Yet some visceral hunch convinced him that wasn't the case. He had no sense of being watched, or trailed.

All the more puzzling was the absence of fresh sign. There were old tracks of unshod horses, as was to be expected in country bordering *Llano Estacado*. Yet the bands of hostiles roaming the plains were comprised of Comanche, Cheyenne, Kiowa, and Arapaho. By rough estimate, he placed their combined numbers at a thousand or more. Likely far more including women and children known to have followed the warriors off the reservations. So he was stumped by the lack of sign and the failure to encounter war parties, let alone a single brave of any tribe. He wondered where the hell they'd all gone.

Late that morning Jordan happened upon the answer. A short distance ahead he sighted a *carreta* lumbering westward across the prairie. These oversized carts, constructed of rawhide and wood, were the principal means of transport for a brotherhood of renegade Mexicans. Drawn by yoked oxen, the *carretas* often traveled in caravans, piled high with trade goods. The cart ahead was being driven by one man, clearly an enterprising loner who had no fear of hostiles. Jordan pegged him immediately as a *Comanchero.*

The *Comancheros* were men who dealt with the horseback tribes. The trade originated with Mexican hunters who ventured onto the Plains to kill buffalo, and found instead Indians hungry for trade goods. Over the generations, they were followed by renegade New Mexicans who formed a pact with the Comanches. The commerce was principally an exchange of trade goods, often whiskey and rifles, for buffalo robes, and horses plundered from Texas ranchers. From their alliance with Comanches, the traders were known as *Comancheros.*

Jordan overtook the slow-moving *carreta* with ease. The man in the driver's seat was lynx-eyed, with leathery features shaded beneath a wide sombrero. He reined the oxen to a halt, his mouth fixed in a straight line. Jordan addressed him in Spanish.

''Buenos días, Señor Comanchero.''

''Buenos días, señor.''

Jordan gave him a cold smile. *''¿Quiere usted vivir, hombre?''*

''Sí.'' The Mexican's voice was a hoarse whisper. ''I have no wish to be killed by you, *tejano*.''

''Then listen closely. I scout for the white pony soldiers, not three miles behind. Their leader is a man who places no value on your life. *¿Comprende*?''

''Why would a *gringo jefe* kill me? I am a simple trader.''

''I will ask him to spare you—for certain information.''

''What is it you wish to know, señor?''

''¿Donde puedo hallar a Quanah?''

The Mexican paled. ''Quanah would roast me alive if I revealed his whereabouts, señor.''

"Then you have a choice." Jordan pulled his pistol and thumbed the hammer. "I will shoot you now and the pony soldier leader will give me a medal. Or you can talk and take your chances with Quanah. Which do you prefer?"

The *Comanchero* talked. His name was José Martínez, and only that morning he had finished trading with a band of Kiowa. He pointed to a stack of buffalo hides, buzzing with flies, piled in the *carreta.* The Kiowa then traveled west along the Red, where they planned to join the Comanche. Staring into the gun barrel, he revealed that some fifty miles to the northwest, high on *Llano Estacado,* there was a great canyon almost a hundred miles long. Quanah and the Quahadi band were camped in the canyon, known as Palo Duro, near the headwaters of the Red.

"This canyon," Jordan demanded, "how will I find it?"

"You will find it or ride off into it, señor. Palo Duro is many miles across."

"Let us be clear." Jordan wagged the snout of his pistol. "You cannot outrun me in your *carreta.* If you have lied, I will come back and leave you for the buzzards."

José Martínez looked in his eyes and saw death. He nodded rapidly. "By the Virgin, I tell the truth, señor."

"Vaya con Dios, Comanchero."

Jordan rode off along the backtrail. He had no reason to trust a renegade trader; but he found himself believing Jose Martínez. All through the Civil War, during his service as a Ranger, he'd heard stories of a great canyon on the Staked Plains. At the time, like the other Rangers, he had considered the tales far-fetched, the stuff of superstition. Yet today, listening to the *Comanchero,* he thought he'd heard the truth. A cocked gun was a persuasive argument.

Before noon, Jordan rejoined the regiment. He found Mackenzie near the head of the column and quickly related what he'd learned. They discussed it at length, with Mackenzie playing devil's advocate. In the end, he too agreed that the story sounded plausible. The key, he finally admitted, was that somewhere ahead Jordan would find the trail of the Kiowa band who had traded with the *Comanchero*. A trail that might be followed to the canyon stronghold, Palo Duro.

Jordan rode on to scout for sign.

Shortly before sundown, they came to the escarpment guarding *Llano Estacado*. Mackenzie halted the regiment and they sat for a time staring upward. The sight kindled a sense of awe, unimaginable wonder.

A wall of sheer cliffs rose straight up from the prairie. The plateau above was rimmed only by the sky and loomed like a vast citadel against the fading sunlight. Vertical outcroppings soared five hundred feet in the air, and the caprock, silhouetted by the fiery rays of sunset, gave the appearance of a weathered sentinel. The escarpment extended north and south beyond the vision of man, seemingly invincible. It stood like a fortress, barring their path onward.

Jordan led them into a maze of twisting ravines. The grade inclined steadily upward, and soon the regiment was strung out single file through a tortuous labyrinth. Before dark, the moon rose behind them, round and full, floating free of the earth. The silvery glow, stark as daylight, lighted their path as they struggled ever higher. Toward the end, as the winding trail steepened, the troopers were forced to dismount and lead their horses. The moon stood at its zenith when at last they topped the caprock.

On the plateau above, Jordan halted for the regiment to regroup. Mackenzie ordered a breather for the horses, and the men were given their first look at *Llano Estacado*. Nothing they had heard or imagined had prepared either Jordan or Mackenzie for the daunting sight before them. By comparison the escarpment they had just climbed was a leisurely outing, hardly more than a stroll. Overhead, the stars glittered like icy shards in a moonlit sky, creating a spectral shimmer across the earth. What they saw left them chilled.

The plains swept onward to the distant horizon. The land

was flat and featureless, absolutely empty, evoking a sense of something lost forever. There were no trees, no ridges or rolling swells, just endless space. It was as if nature had flung together earth and sky, mixed it with deafening silence, and then simply forgotten about it.

Nothing moved as far as the eye could see, almost as though in some ancient age, the land had been frozen motionless for all time. A gentle breeze, like the wispy breath of a ghost, rippled over the curly mesquite grass, disturbing nothing. The unbroken emptiness, without movement or sound, left a man feeling insignificant, somehow vulnerable. For in an eerie sense, the vast trackless barren was like the solitude of God. Distant, somehow unreal, yet strangely ominous.

Staring at the moon-washed landscape, Jordan felt himself an intruder here. He had the spooky sensation that he was looking upon something no mortal was meant to see. About the still, windswept plains there was an awesome quality, almost as though some brutally magnificent force had taken an expanse of emptiness and fashioned it into something visible, yet beyond the ken of man. A hostile land, waiting with eternal patience to claim the bones of those who violated its harsh serenity. A land where man must forever walk as an alien.

Jordan recalled stories that the vast land mass encompassed the Texas Panhandle and parts of eastern New Mexico, which lay some two hundred miles to the west. The name itself, *Llano Estacado,* was lost in the mists of time. Legend had it that the *conquistadores,* during explorations in the sixteenth century, had staked a path across the barren emptiness, to avoid becoming lost. Thus, over the centuries, the rough translation for the formidable wilderness became the Staked Plains. Looking at it now, he could understand why the Spaniards had thought it wise to mark their backtrail. A man could wander forever in a boundless sea of grass.

''Time to move out.'' Mackenzie's voice broke the stillness. ''How far to this canyon, Jack?''

Jordan motioned off to the north. "By my reckoning, about thirty miles off that way. Maybe more."

"Then we will proceed at a forced march. I want to be there before dawn."

Mackenzie ordered the troop commanders to maintain closed ranks. Even in the moonlight, the risk of becoming separated seemed magnified by the bleak landscape before them. Their voices carried on the wispy wind as the order was passed along the column.

Jordan led them north into a silent emptiness.

Far out, there was no horizon, the plains and the sky fusing one with the other. The moon went behind a cloud and for a moment the earth was cloaked in sudden darkness. Then the cloud scudded past in a glare of moonlit brilliance.

"Holy Christ!"

Jordan hauled back on the reins. His horse snorted, prancing sideways, and stopped dead. Beside him, Mackenzie and a staff officer jerked their own mounts to an abrupt halt. The three of them sat staring into a black and seemingly bottomless void. Their horses stood not ten feet from the rim of Palo Duro Canyon.

From a short distance, even in bright moonlight, the canyon was all but invisible. The earth simply dropped off into a sheer precipice, where only moments before the plains seemed to stretch onward forever. The yawning crevasse appeared to be a mile or more in width, and on either side the gorge walls rose in sheer palisades a thousand feet high. From the top, the chasm gave the impression of an inky abyss, falling off into space.

Jordan dismounted, moving forward with Mackenzie. Far below, they spotted the wink of dying campfires, telltale signs of an encampment. A stream meandered through the gorge, and along the banks; they could make out the conical shape of Indian lodges. Father upstream the canyon spread to some three or four miles wide, with lodges scattered along the winding streambed. To all appearances, there were at least a thousand hostile warriors camped in Palo Duro.

Staring downward, Jordan inspected the canyon wall. After a time, across a series of craggy ledges, he discerned an irregular break that began some fifty yards from their position. The narrow trail dropped steeply off the rimrock and followed a perilous zigzag course down the face of the cliffs. He felt a grudging sense of admiration for the Quahadi Comanche and their tactical savvy. Impregnable to swift assault, Palo Duro was a natural stronghold. All but the most determined force would be discouraged from attack.

"Well, Jack," Mackenzie said, clearly pleased. "We've cornered the rascals at last."

Jordan snorted. "Colonel, there's no way we'll make it down on horseback. Your boys are gonna have to dismount and take it single file—on foot."

"Yes, that seems a fair assessment of the situation."

"So now that we're here, what's your plan?"

Mackenzie grinned. "Quite simple, Jack. We attack at dawn."

CHAPTER 5

A gray smudge touched the horizon. The men of the 4th Cavalry quietly waited beside their horses in the sallow overcast. Nothing broke the stillness save the faint creak of saddle leather.

The regiment was arrayed in columns of companies. Behind them stretched an umber plain shrouded in the dinge of false dawn. Before them opened the colossus of Palo Duro Canyon, with the northern plain dimly visible beyond the far wall. In the early-morning chill, their horses snorted frosty puffs of air.

Jordan stood with Mackenzie at the edge of the canyon rim. Their gaze was directed downward, on the narrow, winding trail. Farther still, as though seen through a silty haze, was the Quahadi encampment. The lodges were spread along the stream, sheltered by stands of cedar and cottonwood. No smoke spiraled upward and there was no sign of movement. Even the village dogs still slept.

Westward, the canyon marched onward into infinity. A mile or so upstream was what appeared to be the outskirts of another encampment. Beyond that was yet another scattering of lodges, and far away, still another. Across from the Quahadi camp, a herd of some thousand or more war ponies grazed on an open grassland. Herds of similar size were visible opposite the villages farther upstream.

A faint blush of light tinged the sky. Mackenzie squared

himself up, nodded at the canyon. ''Lead the way down and open the fight, Jack. Hold the hostiles with our lead elements until reinforced.''

''Liable to be a long day,'' Jordan observed. ''I calculate there's Kiowa, Cheyenne, and Arapaho down there, along with Comanche. Got ourselves a regular hornet's nest.''

''The more the merrier. Let's hope they stand and fight.''

''Hell, Colonel, we'll get all the fight we want.''

''Aren't we the lucky ones? Good hunting, Jack.''

Jordan nodded, walking his horse to the rimrock. He was followed immediately by the men of A Troop, who would lead the attack. Then, with a foothold established at the bottom of the trail, Mackenzie would descend to the canyon floor with L Troop and H Troop. The balance of the regiment would file down and join the fight as quickly as possible. Troop commanders were instructed to ride where the action was heaviest.

The battle plan was dependent on surprise. Jordan went over the rimrock, all too aware that men and horses, framed against the cliffs, would soon be visible from the villages below. The trail was less than three feet wide, twisting around outcroppings as it snaked down Palo Duro's south wall. The footing was treacherous, sandy soil loosely packed between rocks and smooth stones, slick and rounded with wear. To the rear, he heard muted curses, the metallic click of horseshoes on rock, scuffling of boots in slippery dirt as men struggled to maintain their balance. The sheer drop off the edge looked like a plunge into the bowels of the earth.

Jordan kept his horse on a loose rein, trusting the gelding to find secure footholds. Watchful, picking his way downward with care, he idly wondered how many thousands of Indians had descended the narrow trail. Palo Duro was doubtless an ancient stronghold, a remote sanctuary of the Plains tribes for hundreds of years. He understood now why the Comanche considered themselves invulnerable on *Llano Estacado*. Their only enemies were the Apache far to the west, and white men. In grim amusement, he told himself the Apache were probably too smart to attack Palo Duro. Today would tell the tale on white men.

A long sweaty hour was consumed in descending the trail. To his amazement, as he emerged onto the canyon floor, Jordan realized that no alarm had been sounded. The Quahadi encampment, directly across the stream, was still and quiet, no one in sight. A lone dog barked in the distance, and the horse herd, on the south side of the stream, watched with bemused interest as A Troop spilled out onto the grassy flatland. He was struck by a wayward thought, reckoning the direction of march since scaling the escarpment onto *Llano Estacado*. Suddenly, with dead certainty, he placed the stream bisecting Palo Duro as the upper reaches of the Prairie Dog Fork of the Red. Somewhere to the west would be found the headwaters of the Red River.

Captain Nathan Beaumont, commander of A Troop, got his men mounted. His orders were to ensure that the Quahadi were left afoot when the fight commenced. The horseback tribes were fearsome warriors when mounted, but virtually neutralized when forced to fight on foot. With his troopers spread out on line, Beaumont signaled them forward and the company headed across the grazeland in a thundering charge. The Quahadi horse herd spooked, turning first toward the river, then wheeling downstream. Beaumont and his men drove them at a pounding gallop eastward along the canyon.

Across the stream, the thudding hoofbeats sounded alarm throughout the Comanche village. Quahadi warriors boiled out of their lodges, watched dumbfounded as their horses were stampeded downstream. Before they could recover, L Troop emerged onto the canyon floor, followed quickly by H Troop. The troop commanders kept their men dismounted, with horseholders to the rear, and formed a skirmish line. Gunfire became general as the soldiers poured a volley into the Quahadi tribesmen to hold them on the opposite side of the river.

Jordan rode westward a short distance, his attention fixed on the villages upstream. He saw a hundred or more warriors in the nearest village mount the night horses picketed outside their lodges. But then, in rapid order, the balance of the regiment regrouped at the bottom of the trail. Their commanders got them mounted, one company after another fanning out to the flanks of L Troop and H Troop. The warriors upstream halted, obviously wary of engaging a full regiment, and turned in retreat. Their women, thrown into panic, began dismantling lodges throughout the village.

Downstream, awaiting developments, Mackenzie saw that the threat to his left flank had been removed. He ordered a mounted charge on the Quahadi village, holding L Troop and H Troop in reserve. The regiment, formed on line, drove straight across the river, bugles blaring and guns blazing. Jordan joined the charge on the left flank, splashing through a shallow ford upstream. Quahadi warriors took cover behind trees along the shore, some firing rifles while others unleashed a shower of arrows. The regiment, troopers dropping here and there, surged onward.

On horseback, the Comanche were invincible. Yet now, forced to fight afoot, they were no match for the cavalry. Women and children began fleeing as the warriors were driven back from the stream. A tall Quahadi, shouting orders in the midst of the battle, led a step-by-step delaying action. About to be overrun, a line of troopers already mounting the riverbank, he intended to cover the withdrawal. The rattle of gunfire intensified as the companies on either flank performed a classic enveloping maneuver.

The Quahadi gave ground with stubborn courage. To their rear, the women and children retreated in a wild scramble up a trail on the north wall of the canyon. The cavalry units swept through the deserted encampment as the warriors withdrew to the base of the cliffs. Firing from behind the cover of a low outcropping, the Quahadi loosed a furious volley that halted the soldiers at the edge of the village. Jordan spotted the tall Comanche leader, still barking commands and rallying the warriors. A fleeting thought passed through his mind that this was Quanah, war chief of the band. He winged a quick snapshot, but his horse shied as he fired. The slug chipped flakes off a boulder.

The warriors suddenly bolted from cover and clambered up the sheer cliffside. They moved swiftly, their leader directing the action as they darted from rock to rock. The volume of fire from their repeaters forced the cavalry to pull back toward the stream. Some of the Quahadi died on the steep trail, brought down by the longer range of the soldiers' Springfields. But most of them made it up the north wall and disappeared over the canyon rim. A final flurry of shots ended as sunrise crested the palisades of Palo Duro.

There was no pursuit. The men and horses of the 4th Cavalry were spent, too exhausted to attempt the north trail. Mackenzie's victory was nonetheless real; nearly fifty hostiles had been killed at a loss of only seventeen troopers wounded. Of equal significance, the Quahadi had been driven onto *Llano Estacado* with no food, no shelter, and no ponies. Quanah and his band had been reduced to a collection of hungry, footsore wanderers. The cavalry units converging on *Comancheria* would soon drive them onto the reservation.

Mackenzie ordered the village burned. The horse herd was next, for to leave them behind risked the Comanche recapturing their mounts. The horses were driven to the south wall of the canyon and held there by mounted troopers. On foot, troopers supplied with extra ammunition formed a half circle and opened fire with their Springfields. The killing of over a thousand horses was a slow, grisly business; gunsmoke mixed with the stench of death spread across Palo Duro. High overhead, the buzzards began their circling wait.

Jordan agreed with the need to kill the horses. Still, however necessary, he couldn't bring himself to stand idly by and watch the slaughter. He rode west along the stream, on the pretext of scouting for the other tribes. The encampments were abandoned, lodges and provisions hauled off in hasty retreat. Some miles upstream, at the western escarpment of Palo Duro, he found a large natural spring that formed the headwaters of the Red. There, following the tracks of several villages, he discovered as well how the Kiowa, Cheyenne, and Arapaho had escaped. A trail, worn by centuries of use, ascended the north wall.

On his return downstream, Jordan took time to inspect Palo Duro itself. North and south, the walls rose a thousand feet in height, separated by distances varying between three and twelve miles in width. The river wound through the canyon, with mile upon mile of lush grazeland on either side. Jordan was impressed, silently remarking that the hostile tribes had selected the most perfect sanctuary imaginable. The canyon walls provided protection from winter blizzards, and the latticework of streams that fed the river provided firewood for warmth. The grassy flatlands provided graze for horse herds numbering in the thousands.

One thought kindled another, slowly awakening Jordan to a whole new vision. The sheltered canyon, the abundance of graze and water and trees, stretched eastward for almost a hundred miles. In total, though the calculation was beyond him without a survey, that meant thousands of square miles of grassland. However far he searched, he might never find a more suitable location for a ranch, or a more likely paradise for cows. The land itself was there for the taking, a part of Texas open for settlement once the Indians were forced onto the reservation. How long before the secret of Palo Duro leaked out to other cattlemen was anyone's guess. But for now, he was the only one who knew it was there.

Some hours later he rejoined Mackenzie on the battleground. By the south wall, the floor of the canyon was slick with the blood of dead horses, and the odor was overpowering. The regiment was formed for march, waiting in the shadows of a sun tilted westward. Thick smoke from the burned village hung on the still air.

Mackenzie was near the head of the column. He nodded as Jordan reined to a halt. "Find anything upstream?"

"Lots of sign," Jordan said. "There's another trail at the end of the canyon. Likely as not, they'll run across the Comanche somewhere north of here."

"Will they give the Quahadi any horses?"

"Probably enough to mount Quanah and his warriors. That and enough food to see them through."

Mackenzie considered a moment. "In the end, it won't matter. Their days are numbered."

"What's your best guess?" Jordan asked. "How long till they're herded onto the reservation?"

"A month at the outside, probably less. With troops converging from every direction, they haven't a chance."

"What's your own plan, Colonel?"

"We'll rejoin the supply train," Mackenzie said. "Give the men and the horses a day's rest before we turn north. I intend to hound Quanah until he begs to surrender."

"Well, I reckon you don't need me for that. Your scouts won't have any trouble north of the Pease. Trackin' hostiles up there's no big trick."

"Did I hear right?" Mackenzie demanded. "Are you quitting in the middle of a campaign?"

"All the fun's gone," Jordan said with a crooked smile. "I got you to *Llano Estacado* and found Palo Duro. What's left is just cat-and-mouse."

"Even so, the chase will have its moments. I'd prefer to have you with me, Jack."

"Time for me to get on with my business. I've got things that need tendin' back in Colorado."

Mackenzie saw that he would not be persuaded. "I take it you mean to leave now?"

"Figure I'll head west." Jordan motioned upstream. "I'll live off the land between here and home. Won't be the first time."

"I have to get the regiment out of this canyon before dark. If you change your mind, catch me along the trail."

"Not much chance of that, Colonel."

Mackenzie saluted smartly, and rode off. Jordan watched after him a moment, waiting until the regiment began the steep ascent up the south wall. Then he turned his horse into the sun, westward along the river. A single thought went with him as the shadows deepened.

One day soon he would return to Palo Duro.

CHAPTER 6

Jordan rode into the ranch the first week in October. He'd been gone slightly more than two months, and he was surprised to feel so little upon sighting the compound. Yet, as he dismounted outside the corral, he realized the Rock Canyon spread was a thing of the past. His mind was fixed on Texas, and the future.

There was a nip in the air under a bright noonday sun. On the hillsides, the trees were spotted with red and gold, a reminder of much to be accomplished before the onset of winter. He unsaddled, turning the gelding into the corral, then walked toward the main house. The cook, Mose Butler, appeared in the door of the cook shack, whiskery jaws set in a perpetual scowl. His voice was like a metal rasp on iron.

"Where in tarnation you been so long?"

"Just where you were told when I left—off fightin' the Comanche."

"Figgered you for dead," Butler cackled. "The boys about give you up."

"Sorry to disappoint you, Mose. Still got a full head of hair."

"You want some grub?"

"Fix a steak and whatever's not nailed down. I'll come over after I've had a bath."

Butler pursed his mouth. "You'll catch your death of cold, takin' baths."

"Guess that makes you the picture of health, Mose."

Jordan went into the house. He was grubby from a hard week on the trail, and his clothes felt stiff with dust and sweat. Unlike Mose Butler, who took a bath once every summer, he wanted to scald off the grime. He fired up the stove and began boiling pails of water. His clothes were dropped in a soiled heap.

Some while later Jordan emerged from the house. He wore a buckskin jacket, with whipcord pants and a striped linsey shirt. His cheeks stung from the straight razor and his mustache was neatly trimmed. He wolfed down a steak, ignoring Butler's questions, and savored his first cup of coffee in a week. Then he went out to the corral and caught a fresh horse.

On the road into town, he met Leigh Dyer coming in the other direction. The foreman at first looked startled to see him, then broke out in a jack-o'-lantern grin. He reined up short, stuck out his hand.

"Gawddamn!" he said, pumping Jordan's arm. "You've had us worried plumb to hell, and then some."

"Leigh, you boys ought to have more faith. I generally manage to get back in one piece."

"Well, boss, I'm shore glad to see you. Thatcher's so hot he could spit nails. I've just come from the bank."

Jordan frowned. "Thatcher sent for you?"

"Ordered me into town," Dyer fumed. "Chewed my ass out royally, too. All but told me to get our cows off his range."

"What was his reason?"

"Sorry scutter didn't give no reason. Just said you'd better show up quick, or he'd take matters into his own hands."

Jordan weighed telling his foreman about Palo Duro. He was bursting with the news, and wanted Dyer to hear it first. But then, on second thought, he figured it could wait until later. The situation with Thatcher sounded serious.

"I planned on seeing Thatcher myself, anyway. Guess he'll be surprised I got there so fast."

"Hope he keels over," Dyer said. "Don't have no call to talk to me like that."

"Leigh, that's one message I'll get across real clear. See you back at the house sometime tonight."

Less than an hour later Jordan dismounted outside the bank. Inside, he strode past Thatcher's bookkeeper and marched into the office. Thatcher looked up from a sheaf of documents, momentarily taken aback. Jordan slammed the door.

"Franklin, you and me have got a problem. I don't allow anyone to bullyrag my men on ranch business. That includes you."

Thatcher was livid. "How dare you barge in here without being announced. I won't stand for it."

"Stick to the point," Jordan said levelly. "You stay away from my men or you'll answer to me. Savvy?"

By now, Jordan was standing in front of the desk. His pale eyes were cold, and only the desk separated them. Thatcher tried to defuse the situation, motioning to a chair.

"Let's be reasonable about this, Jack. Calm down and have a seat."

"I haven't heard anything about my men."

"Perhaps I was overhasty. I assure you it won't happen again."

Jordan seated himself. "What's so all-fired important it wouldn't wait?"

"Jack—" Thatcher paused, collecting himself, then went on. "The whole town has been speculating about your prolonged absence. No one, including Rebecca, has heard a word from you."

"There's no postal service on the Staked Plains. I've been out of touch."

"On my word, Jack, I never heard of such a thing. Riding off like a knight in search of the Holy Grail."

"Don't get sarcastic," Jordan said. "Why'd you want to see me?"

Thatcher leaned forward. "I may have a buyer for the Rock Canyon ranch. Of course, until your cattle are off the range, I'm unable to move forward on the matter." He paused, suddenly intent. "How soon could you be out?"

"Couple of weeks, maybe a little longer. Who's the buyer?"

"An English lord of some sort. Foreigners believe there is a great future in the American West. For whatever reason, they have particular interest in cattle ranches."

"Damned smart thinking," Jordan said. "The beef market's bound to pick up, and all the cows are out here. They'll get in early and make a fortune."

Thatcher seemed unimpressed. "All I'm concerned with is selling the ranch. I want it off the books."

"How'd you like to double your money?"

"I beg your pardon?"

"Take your own advice," Jordan said agreeably. "You always told me to put money to work, let it earn more money. Whatever you get from the sale, reinvest it."

"Indeed." Thatcher eyed him skeptically. "What type of investment?"

"A solid-gold, no-way-to-lose cattle spread. A regular goddamn empire there for the taking."

"Are you serious? You're asking me to invest in another ranch?"

"Not just a ranch," Jordan corrected him. "I'm talkin' about a kingdom! Land enough for a dozen ranches."

"I think not," Thatcher said. "One ranch in a lifetime is more than sufficient. I'll feel relieved to recoup the bank's money on Rock Canyon."

"You're making one helluva mistake, Franklin. Nobody ever had a shot at a deal this big."

"Allow me to say no gracefully. I haven't the slightest interest."

"Suit yourself," Jordan said. "I'll just have to scout up another investor."

Thatcher studied him a moment. "Jack, whether you believe it or not, I felt terrible about foreclosing on Rock

Canyon. To make amends, let me suggest someone you might talk with.''

''Has he got money?''

''By all accounts, he is an extremely wealthy man. He's become the talk of Denver, just in the last few months. From what I hear, he will consider any investment.''

''Who is he?''

''Well, as I said, foreigners have come West in droves. Rumor has it he's an Irish aristocrat of some variety. In any event, he recently opened a brokerage firm in Denver.''

''Brokerage firm?'' Jordan repeated. ''Thought that was mainly stocks and bonds.''

''Apparently the man has more money than anyone west of St. Louis. Apart from the brokerage business, he has personal funds available for investment.''

''What's his name?''

''John Adair,'' Thatcher replied. ''His firm is the Denver Brokerage & Trading Company. Would you like me to write a letter of introduction?''

''You know him?''

''Only by reputation. But a letter from your longtime banker certainly wouldn't do any harm.''

Jordan gave him a look. ''All of a sudden you're keen to do me favors. What's the story?''

''To be perfectly honest . . .'' Thatcher hesitated, his ears gone rosy red. ''Rebecca gave me you-know-what over the foreclosure. As I said, I wish to make amends.''

''After a fashion, you did me a favor. I've got a hunch I'm gonna wind up richer than Midas.''

''For Rebecca's sake, I genuinely hope so. Where is this new ranch of yours, anyway?''

Jordan warmed with zest to the tale of Palo Duro.

''Texas!''

''Jesus Horatio Christ! You make it sound like the end of the earth.''

''Well, isn't it? All those Indians and . . . and buffalo!''

"C'mon, Becky, it's just a hop and skip from Colorado. Damnsight prettier than Colorado, too."

Jordan and Rebecca were seated in the parlor. Miriam Thatcher hovered unseen near the dining room entryway, her eyes round with shock. Her future son-in-law's bent for profanity often left her sensibilities in disarray. Yet today, eavesdropping on his latest daredevil enterprise, she was all but paralyzed. Her daughter's reaction seemed to her a perfect response to lunacy.

"Jack, who cares how pretty it is? What did you call it, Palo Duro? It's off in the wilds of nowhere."

"Godalmighty, what's that got to do with anything? We'll build it into something that'll make people's eyes pop."

Rebecca was exasperated. "You just refuse to understand, don't you? All my friends are here, my family, anyone who matters."

"What about me?" Jordan asked. "You always said I was the only one that mattered."

"Don't you dare do that, Jack Jordan! I absolutely will not be made to feel guilty over this. You're asking me to traipse off into the unknown like some . . . some Indian squaw!"

Jordan grinned. "The Good Book says, 'Whither thou goest, I will go; and where thou lodgest, I will lodge.' You aim to go against the Scripture?"

"Oh, please!" Rebecca's eyes were like greenfire. "The passage also says, 'Where thou diest, will I die, and there will I be buried.' Do you want me murdered by some red savage?"

"I've already told you a dozen and one times. We whipped the Comanche, drove the whole bunch to hell and gone. You've got no fears on that score."

"How on earth do you do it? You manage to make some insane adventure sound like a stroll into town."

Jordan looked hurt. "Folks thought Lewis and Clark were off their rockers, too. Way I recollect it, they found the Pacific Ocean."

"Yes?" Rebecca stared at him, baffled. "What does that have to do with this canyon in Texas?"

"Hell's bells and little fishes! The wonder of it, Becky. The puredee wonder of finding it, making it into something. I get the shivers just thinking about it."

"I'd be the first to admit that it gives me the shivers. I'm scared to death, Jack."

"No you're not," Jordan said with a sly look. "You've got more grit than a bulldog with a new bone. You'll do just fine."

"A bulldog?" Rebecca rolled her eyes. "You do have a way with a compliment. None of my suitors ever compared me to a bulldog."

"None of them offered to take you to Palo Duro, either. Once you see it, you'll never want to leave."

"Unless it escaped your notice, I haven't agreed to go. I need time to think about it, Jack."

"Tell you what," Jordan said boldly. "I'm not one to do things on a shoestring. I've got a vision of Palo Duro, and I won't settle for less."

Rebecca watched him. "What does that mean?"

"I'm off to Denver, to see this moneybags John Adair. If he turns thumbs down, we'll call it off. But if he agrees to finance it—"

"No promises," Rebecca interrupted. "You go to Denver, and meanwhile I'll sleep on it. We'll talk when you return."

"You don't fool me." Jordan gently caressed her cheek. "You've got the itch to dream big, the same as me. Just won't admit it, that's all."

"Jack, how did I ever fall in love with you?"

"Why hell, Becky, you never had a chance. I just plain swept you off your feet."

There was jest in his tone, and Rebecca knew he was trying to dampen her fears. Yet he was a persuasive man, and that was perhaps her greatest fear. She thought he might very easily talk the Denver financier into writing a blank check. Should that happen, there was no question as to the outcome. Nothing would stop him from his dream of Palo Duro.

Some deeper intuition told her that the same thought applied to her. He was a man on a quest, and were she to refuse his dream, he might very well pursue it without her. Just as he'd run off, despite her protests, to fight Indians for two months in the wilds of Texas. All of which left her in a quandary about him and about herself.

She wasn't sure that she was meant for a life in Palo Duro.

CHAPTER 7

Gold was discovered on Cherry Creek in 1859. Eastern journalists reported that nuggets the size of hens' eggs could be found strewn about the countryside. Over the next decade legions of reasonably sane men struck out for Colorado Territory. According to the newspapers, fortune awaited anyone with the daring to cross the Great Plains. Thousands came, and a few got rich.

Denver was founded on the site of the gold camp. What was once a collection of log shacks spread and grew, until finally a burgeoning metropolis arose along the banks of Cherry Creek. By 1874, Denver had become a cosmopolitan beehive, with theater, opera, plush hotels, four newspapers, three railroads, and six churches. Eastern journalists now reported that it was the richest city in the West.

The business district was located on Larimer Street. As the commercial center of the western Plains, Denver attracted banks, financial institutions, and a wide assortment of entrepreneurs. A stock exchange was formed, linked by telegraph to Wall Street, with daily trading orders humming along the wires. Western mining stocks, often a risky proposition, were traded as well. A recovery from the Panic of '73 gradually gained steam.

Jordan arrived on the noon train. He was attired in his one suit, with a crisply starched shirt, and he carried a warbag for an overnight stay. He walked uptown from the depot and checked into the Windsor Hotel, recommended to him by Thatcher. After dropping the warbag in his room, he had dinner at a cafe near the hotel. His appointment was for two o'clock, arranged by wire, and he still had time to spare. He went for a walk along Larimer Street.

On the edge of the business district, Jordan passed the Denver Club. A symbol of the city's power structure, the club was a topic of discussion throughout Colorado. Membership was restricted to those of wealth and position, the elite from the worlds of business and politics. Their numbers included bankers and merchant princes, railroad barons and financiers, and influential leaders from the nearby territorial capital. The pacts struck there often produced a ripple effect across the western Plains.

Shortly before two, Jordan entered an imposing stone building in the heart of the financial district. The ledger in the lobby indicated that the Denver Brokerage & Trading Company occupied the entire third floor. Upstairs, tugging his suit jacket into place, he gave his name to a man seated at a reception desk. Several minutes later, a young man with thick glasses approached, introducing himself as John Adair's secretary. He led Jordan down a long hallway and ushered him into a corner suite.

The office was lavishly appointed. Overlooking Larimer Street, it was furnished with wing chairs and a sofa crafted in lush morocco leather. The walls were lined with oil paintings, and at the far end of the room, framed between windows with a view of the Rockies, was a massive desk that looked carved from a solid piece of walnut. The room seemed somehow appropriate to the man who rose from behind the desk.

"Mr. Jordan," he said, with a lilting Irish accent. "How good of you to come."

"Honor's all mine," Jordan said, accepting his handshake. "I appreciate your time."

"Won't you have a chair?"

Jordan seated himself, studying the man across the desk.

Adair was in his thirties, with ice-blue eyes, strong angular features, and of slim build. His bearing was straight and square-shouldered, a posture of debonair self-assurance. He wore a frock coat with dark trousers, and a royal-blue cravat pegged by a diamond stickpin. The watch chain across his vest was woven in intricate strands of gold.

"Tell me now," Adair said with open charm. "Do you always carry a gun to your business meetings?"

Jordan involuntarily touched the holstered pistol. "Guess it depends on a man's line of work. There's times a gun comes in handy."

"Take no offense at my curiosity, Mr. Jordan. Indeed, I have a fondness for firearms of all sorts. I'm something of a hunter myself."

"What do you hunt?"

"Birds, deer, buffalo." Adair spread his hands in a grand gesture. "I've a particular taste for American buffalo."

"Like it myself," Jordan said. " 'Course, I'm partial to beef."

"As well you should be! A rancher could hardly feel otherwise."

"Not if he wants to stay in business."

"Exactly so." Adair took a letter off his desk. "Your introduction from Franklin Thatcher is one of high praise. I've not met Mr. Thatcher, but he has a sterling reputation among bankers."

Jordan nodded. "He's one of the civic leaders in Pueblo."

"Now, as to this venture of yours. Tell me something of what you have in mind."

"In a nutshell, the biggest cattle spread anywhere. I found the perfect spot, over in the Texas Panhandle."

Jordan went on to describe Palo Duro. He dwelled on the immensity of the canyon, the grazeland and plentiful water, the shelter offered by the sheer cliffs. His voice crackled with vitality.

"Nothing like it anywhere," he concluded. "Nobody'll

ever find a better place to raise cattle.''

''You've a way with words,'' Adair commented. ''From what you say, it's all but a Garden of Eden.''

''Ten years as a cattleman, I've never seen its equal.''

Adair was a shrewd judge of character. An aristocrat, heir to a large estate in Ireland, he had served briefly in the diplomatic corps. Afterward, his interest drawn to finance, he had crossed the Atlantic and established a brokerage firm in New York. Unlike many on Wall Street, he had foreseen the stock market crash of '73. He emerged from the debacle with his wealth intact.

Intrigued by America's westward expansion, he envisioned great opportunity once the economic recovery got under way. He relocated to Denver, and opened his brokerage firm in the spring of 1874. He prospered not only by his evaluation of economic cycles, but by his insights into men as well. One of the major tenets of his success was to probe a man's character before entering into a business arrangement. He decided to put Jordan to the test.

''I've looked into your record,'' he said without expression. ''You have an enviable name as a trailblazer, a vanguard of sorts for cattlemen. Most impressive, indeed.''

''Nothin' but pure necessity,'' Jordan said modestly. ''A cowman's got to find places to sell his herd.''

''Apart from that''—Adair looked him straight in the eye—''I found little to commend you, Mr. Jordan. From what I gather, you lost a ranch of sizable proportions. Not to mention several business enterprises.''

Jordan held his stare. ''You've got good sources of information, Mr. Adair.''

''Information is the difference between profit and loss. I'm no gambler, Mr. Jordan, no indeed. Perhaps that was your downfall.''

''Yeah, maybe so,'' Jordan said woodenly. ''I gambled on the investment advice of men who'd made it big in business. I should've stuck to cows.''

''Hindsight is a great teacher,'' Adair observed. ''Yet if I understand you right, you're asking me to follow the same course. Invest in something I've no knowledge of a'tall."

Jordan suddenly realized they were playing poker. He was holding a good hand—Palo Duro—but Adair had challenged with a raise. The whole purpose was to see if he could be bluffed, forced to fold. He thought two could play the game.

"While ago," he said, "you told me information was the key. How do you know which way to jump when you're still in the dark?"

"I don't take your meaning, Mr. Jordan."

"Don't take my word for it, either. Let's ride on down to Palo Duro and you have a looksee for yourself. If you're not convinced, I'll eat my hat on the spot."

"Aye, but you're talking about weeks of my time."

"What I'm talking about, Mr. Adair, is a ton of money. You got any objection to making another million?"

Adair sensed the tables had been turned. The challenge was now before him, and baited with the hook of profit, perhaps an enormous return on his investment. He liked a man with audacity, cool nerves. He considered it an admirable trait.

"Tell me, Mr. Jordan, are there any buffalo where we'd be traveling?"

"Herds so thick you could shoot for a month of Sundays. You've never seen the like, Mr. Adair."

"You don't say!" Adair marveled. "Would you be available for supper tonight, Mr. Jordan? I do believe you'd enjoy meeting my wife."

"I'd count it a privilege, Mr. Adair."

"Good, good! Now go on with your—may I call you Jack? Tell me more about the buffalo."

Jordan spun a story of great shaggy beasts beyond count.

The Adair home was a two-story stone structure with tall columns and a wide veranda. Unique to the architecture of Denver, the house commanded a sweeping view of the snowcapped mountains. The grounds were set back off a low bluff overlooking a rapid stream.

The inside of the house was even more imposing. The ceilings were high and the staircase facing the entrance rose like an aerial corridor. Large wall mirrors flanked either side of the hallway, and double French doors opened onto a room appointed with ornately carved furniture and an immense piano. Opposite was a tall-windowed study, paneled in dark wood with a fieldstone fireplace. The bookcases occupying one wall were lined with history tomes and works of literature.

Jordan was no less impressed by his hostess. Cornealia Adair was a vivacious woman, informed and refined, clearly a woman of breeding. Earlier, not above bragging about his wife, Adair had told Jordan she was the daughter of a New York banking tycoon and the sister of a United States senator. Married only three years, Adair clearly doted on her. Though they had no children, she was the wife every wealthy man sought. Attractive and sophisticated, a woman who captivated those around her.

The dining room was spacious and airy, lit by a crystal chandelier glittering with candles. Cornealia sat at one end of the table, with Adair opposite her, and Jordan in the middle. The food seemed to Jordan somehow exotic, as though he were dining in a foreign country. Oysters to begin and a swirled glace for dessert were no less familiar than the confusing array of silverware. All the while, as servants whisked in and out, Cornealia peppered him with questions about wild Indians and his life on the Plains. Finally, with the dishes cleared, coffee was served.

"Now a personal question," Cornealia said with a winsome smile. "I've been dying to ask all evening. Are you married, Jack?"

"Not yet," Jordan said, caught with his coffee cup in midair. "I aim to rectify that shortly."

"You're engaged, then. How wonderful! Will your bride accompany us on this outing to Texas?"

"Beg pardon?"

Adair laughed at his bewildered expression. "Cornealia's spoiled my surprise. I informed her this evening, before you arrived. We'll have a look at your Palo Duro."

"You will?" Jordan said, still astounded. "Well, that's fine, real fine. You won't regret it, John. Take my word."

"Understand now, I've not promised anything. We'll have our look and then decide."

"When do we leave?" Cornealia said gaily. "I can't tell you how excited I am. I've always wanted to see Texas."

"What about next week?" Jordan replied, glancing from one to the other. "Sooner we get there, the sooner you'll get your looksee."

"Marvelous," Cornealia breathed. "Oh, it sounds such a grand adventure!"

Adair sipped his coffee. "All right," he said at length. "I'll arrange things to cover my absence at the brokerage. Have you an idea of how long we'll be away?"

"You'd best allow a month," Jordan said. "Train will get us down to Trinidad. From there, it's all overland."

"A month?" Adair muttered. "I'd not planned on so long."

"Don't be silly, John," Cornealia quickly interjected. "Your staff is perfectly capable of managing things. Besides, we owe ourselves a holiday now and then."

"Do some hunting, too," Jordan added. "You said you wanted a crack at buffalo."

"Buffalo!" Cornealia trilled. "Really, John, I thought you would have learned your lesson."

"I'll thank you not to get into that."

Cornealia ignored him, her eyes dancing merrily. She related that on their train ride west, they had stopped off in Kansas. There, with Buffalo Bill Cody as their guide, they engaged in a horseback hunt on the prairie. Adair, pounding alongside a trophy bull, somehow managed to shoot his horse in the head. The horse was killed, the buffalo herd escaped, and Adair broke his arm in the fall. Tears of laughter streamed from her eyes as she finished the story.

"Well, don't you see," Adair said sheepishly, glancing at Jordan. "I'd never before hunted from atop a running horse. The trick of it eluded me, that's all."

"We'll solve that," Jordan assured him. "I'll show you how it's done when we get to Texas. Just takes a little practice."

"Will you now, Jack?" Adair said, plainly delighted. "I have to tell you, I'd count it a personal favor."

"John, you've as good as got your buffalo."

Adair beamed, nodding smugly at his wife. She simply wagged her head with an amused look of skepticism. Jordan watched the byplay, still somewhat stunned by his good fortune. Yet the trip to Palo Duro promised to be more than he'd bargained.

He thought the two of them would be a handful.

CHAPTER 8

Late afternoon shadows splayed over Pueblo. The wail of a whistle floated in on a chilly breeze out of the north. Some moments later the train slowed on the outskirts of town and chugged toward the depot. A groaning squeal racketed off nearby buildings as the engineer throttled down and set the brakes.

The engine ground to a halt, belching steam and fiery sparks in a final burst of power. Jordan stepped off the lead passenger coach, carrying his warbag. As other passengers began deboarding, he waved to the stationmaster and crossed the platform on the north side of the depot. Lost in thought, he headed uptown.

All the way from Denver Jordan had been preoccupied, staring out the window. Even now, reviewing his mental checklist, he still ticked off things that needed doing within a matter of days. After a night's consideration, he had decided to make a clean break with Colorado. The herd had to be moved off the Rock Canyon range, and there was no time, or money, to lease grazeland elsewhere. He had decided to trail them to Palo Duro.

Given the crush of time, the task before him was daunting. He first had to sell a couple of hundred head to raise cash for two or three wagons and a long list of supplies. At the very least, he needed six months' provisions to start a cattle outfit in a land where there were no stores. Tools and equipment, along with the bare minimum of furniture, would fill another wagon. Yet another wagon was needed to accommodate the Adairs on the long trek to Palo Duro. He had a lot to accomplish, and not a moment to spare.

For all that, his mind never strayed far from Rebecca. Their last conversation left small doubt that she was strongly opposed to a life in the wilds of Texas. She was a city girl, accustomed to comfort and and a pleasant life, rather than the hardship of an isolated ranch. Still, though he understood her apprehension, he was determined to prevail in the matter. He couldn't imagine life without her, but he was obsessed with the thought of Palo Duro. He meant to persuade her and marry her. The quicker the better.

Uptown, Miriam Thatcher admitted him to the house. She gave him a snippy greeting, then motioned him into the parlor and walked away. A few moments later Rebecca appeared from the kitchen, a patterned apron over her dress. Her troubled expression was one of misgiving as she kissed him lightly on the cheek. She led him to the sofa.

"Mother and I were preparing supper. Will you be able to stay?"

"Thanks all the same," Jordan begged off. "I've got to collect my horse from the livery and head out to the ranch. Just stopped by to give you the news."

She folded her hands in her lap. "Did your meeting go well?"

"I reckon it couldn't have gone much better. Adair liked the sound of it, and I think he's hooked. Fact is, I'd bet on it."

"So he didn't actually agree to provide the financing?"

"Not yet," Jordan said. "But he agreed to come have a look at Palo Duro. I'm taking him and his wife out there next week."

"His wife?" she echoed with surprise. "Why would his wife go along?"

"Hell, she's a regular stem-winder. Got as much feist as he does. Quite a lady."

"I gather you believe he will agree?"

"Yeah, I do," Jordan affirmed. "Once he sees it, how could he refuse? Like I told you, it's a once-in-a-lifetime deal."

She hesitated, watching him. "Then we won't really know until you return."

"Well, not exactly. I've got to move my herd, and I figured to have the boys trail 'em on out to Palo Duro. Something tells me Adair will come through."

"I see you've already made up your mind about Texas."

"Way it looks"—Jordan took both her hands in his—"we'll have to get married within the week. I'm not leaving without you."

"What?" Rebecca sat upright, visibly startled. "You want me to marry you now—just like that?"

"I want you to go with me as my wife. Nothing matters more to me than that."

"Apparently your precious Palo Duro matters more."

"I've got no future here, Becky. Texas is where I'll make my fortune."

"And if your deal falls through with Adair?"

"Odds are it won't," Jordan assured her. "But if it does, it's not the end of the world. We'll still be together, and that's what matters. Leastways, to me."

She lowered her head. "You know that Mother and Daddy are against this heart and soul. They think it's madness to marry you if it means running off to Texas."

"Only thing that counts is what's in your heart. You're the one that knows what's right for you."

"God, Jack." A tear rolled down her cheek. "You don't give a girl much choice, do you? If we're not married now, I may never see you again. Who knows what could happen in Texas?"

Jordan chuckled. "We'll build the goddamnedest ranch

anybody ever saw and get filthy rich. Probably raise a passel of kids, too.''

''No, not a passel.'' She wiped away the tear, managed a small smile. ''Two will do just fine. A boy and a girl.''

''Judas Priest! Are you sayin' yes?''

''I must have lost my mind. But I can't bear the thought of losing you. So yes . . . I'm saying yes.''

''I'll be double dipped,'' Jordan said quietly, enfolding her into his arms. ''You're never gonna regret it one day in your whole life. You just wait and see.''

She laughed. ''As long as we're together, I'll have no regrets. You're enough for me. You always were.''

''You won't let anybody change your mind, will you? You're liable to hear thunder and lightning over this.''

''Leave Mother and Daddy to me. Nothing they say will make a difference.''

''Figured as much,'' Jordan said, squeezing her tighter. ''Guess that's one of the reasons you rung my bell. You've got sand, and then some.''

''How gallant you are,'' she said in a teasing voice. ''Any girl would be thrilled to know she has 'sand.' ''

''All the same, you know what I mean. I never fell for anyone else.''

''Omigod!'' Rebecca yipped, shoving him aside. ''I have less than a week to plan for a wedding. I'll never get everything done!''

''Why, sure you will,'' Jordan said with conviction. ''You're a regular ball o' fire when you set your mind to it.''

''And our honeymoon!'' she exclaimed. ''What about our honeymoon?''

Jordan grinned. ''We'll have it under the stars, on the way to Texas.''

Rebecca didn't know whether to laugh or cry. Then, on second thought, she decided a honeymoon was a honeymoon, so long as they were together. She kissed him full on the mouth.

* * *

On Sunday, only five days after the wedding announcement, buggies and carriages began to arrive at the Methodist church. The ceremony was scheduled for one o'clock, and not long after the regular Sunday service ended, the church bells rang out across Pueblo.

The wedding of Rebecca Thatcher and Jackson Jordan was the most heavily attended function of the year. Invitations were ardently coveted, not unlike tickets to a new and controversial stage play. The movers and shakers of the community, despite the scandal surrounding the marriage, turned out as a group. The premier attraction was the bride.

There were rumors that Rebecca Thatcher was with child. Talk had it that her father had forced the bridegroom into a shotgun wedding. The rumors gained credence when it was learned that Jordan and his bride would depart tomorrow for Texas. At best, though everyone agreed the Thatcher girl was no tramp, the marriage had been hastily arranged. All in all, it made for delicious gossip.

By half past twelve, the streets bounding the church were clogged with carriages. On the boardwalk outside, the guests stood in lines that stretched around either corner. As they filed through the doorway, attired in finery for the occasion, they conversed in low voices and nodded to one another with smug, knowing smiles. For the most part, they felt the rumors were too titillating not to be true. There were, after all, no secrets in a small town.

Shortly before the hour every pew in the church was filled. A few latecomers hurried through the vestibule, searching for a seat. Off to one side, the bride's party was formed and waiting. Gladys Harrell, the bride's best friend, and one of the few who disdained the rumors, was acting as maid of honor. Behind her, smiling nervously, Rebecca stood with her hand tucked in her father's arm. Her cheeks were flushed with excitement.

Franklin Thatcher was torn by wildly conflicting emotions. He thought her the very image of her mother on the day he himself had been wed. Her dark hair, drawn sleekly to the nape of her neck, accentuated her exquisite features. Her veil swept the floor, and her wedding gown, hugging the curves of her body, rose demurely to her throat. There was a virginal aura about her, an overall impression of youthful innocence.

Her radiant happiness brought a lump to Thatcher's throat. Yet he was filled with anger and anguish, for he was all too aware of the rumors. Even though they were untrue, he was incensed that the family name nonetheless had been tarnished. Even worse, his daughter was being spirited away to some godforsaken canyon in Texas. He blamed Jordan for taking his daughter, and ruining her reputation among the townspeople. His arguments had been to no avail, for she was headstrong, seemingly immune to reason. He admired her spirit, and he had finally conceded to her wishes. Still, he was not reconciled to the marriage.

As the last of the guests filed through the doorway, he patted her hand. She looked around, suddenly aware of his grave expression, and her eyes went misty. He drew a deep breath.

"You look lovely."

She gave his arm an affectionate squeeze. "You and Mother have made me very happy."

"I only hope it's for the best."

"Stop torturing yourself, Daddy. Jack will make a wonderful husband."

Thatcher was silent a moment. "There's still time, you know."

"Time for what?"

"I have to ask you just once more. Are you certain about all this? Absolutely certain?"

She regarded him with a steadfast gaze. "I've never been more certain of anything in my life."

"Well—" Thatcher hesitated, searching for words. "Your mother and I thought maybe you'd reconsider before it's too late."

"Let my memory of today be a happy one." She went

up on tiptoe, kissed his cheek. "I'm marrying Jack, but I'll always be your daughter. Nothing could ever change that."

Thatcher swallowed, unable to speak. Before he could collect himself, the organ filled the church with the strains of the wedding march. Ahead of them, Gladys Harrell smiled over her shoulder, then moved off in slow-step tempo. A moment later, his face wooden, Thatcher led his daughter through the doorway.

All the way down the aisle, the guests craned for a better view of the bride. There were whispered exclamations over her gown, low murmurings as the onlookers remarked on her beauty. Rebecca heard none of it, nor was she aware of her mother weeping inconsolably in the front pew. Her gaze was unwavering, fixed on the man who awaited her at the altar.

Their eyes met the instant she entered the doorway. They remained locked together in silent communion the entire time she moved down the aisle. A quick grin lighted Jordan's features, and Leigh Dyer, acting as his best man, fidgeted nervously at his side. As Rebecca drew closer, she saw within Jordan's eyes something intensely emotional, an inner part of him seldom revealed. She thought the depth of feeling mirrored there would last her all her life.

The wedding party slowly veered away as the organ mounted to a crescendo. Her maid of honor proceeded to the rail, and her father, with a final squeeze of her hand, moved aside. Leigh Dyer held his place, managing an awkward smile, and Jordan fell in beside her. Together, they took the last step and halted before the Reverend Amos Smalley.

At his signal, they joined hands, and a hushed silence fell over the church. Then the preacher raised his arm above them in benediction.

"Dearly beloved, we are gathered here in the sight of God to join this man and this woman in holy wedlock . . ."

CHAPTER 9

Their wedding night was spent in Trinidad. Some seventy miles south of Pueblo, they arrived by train late that afternoon. After supper, in their hotel room, Rebecca found marriage to be more wondrous than any fantasy. Her husband was experienced and ardent, but nonetheless a gentle lover who led her to the discovery of passion. They clung together throughout the night.

John and Cornealia Adair arrived the following day. To Jordan's surprise, they brought clothing suitable for wilderness travel and a minimum of luggage. Rebecca and Cornealia became fast friends almost immediately, drawn together by the magnet of shared adventure. Adair was like a young boy on a lark, hardly able to contain himself until they got under way. He proudly displayed a spanking-new Sharps .50 buffalo rifle.

Mose Butler, the cook, and Hank Taylor, one of the hands, were already waiting in Trinidad. Jordan had sent them ahead by three days, with a wagon outfitted for the trek across *Llano Estacado*. Jordan's thought in bringing the cook along was to provide the Adairs with passable meals over the course of their trip. The men had also brought a string of eight horses, the gentlest of the bunch reserved for the Adairs. The wagon, loaded with supplies and camp gear, was drawn by a team of mules.

From Trinidad, the party traveled south to Raton Pass.

A natural gateway through the mountains, Raton Pass was effectively the border between Colorado and New Mexico. Some ten miles south of the pass, descending onto the plains, the wagon road intersected the Canadian River. The stream led them southeast until it gradually swung due east in a broad arc. There, flat as a tabletop, stretched the boundless *Llano Estacado*.

"By the Jesus!" Adair exclaimed, staring out across the plains. "Is there no end to it?"

"Not for a ways," Jordan said, motioning eastward. "Couple of hundred miles before we hit Palo Duro."

The small caravan halted to water the horses. Before them, the buff plains appeared to advance on into infinity. The horizon seemed beyond the reach of horse and rider, as the horizon of the sea retreats endlessly before a sailor. The vastness of the land was like a glimpse of eternity.

"Goodness," Cornealia said in a breathless voice. "It's scary and beautiful at the same time."

Cornealia was an accomplished rider. She wore a split skirt and sat her saddle as easily as a man. Beside her, also attired in a split skirt, Rebecca scanned the plains with a bemused look. Nothing Jordan had told her in any way prepared her for the limitless solitude. Yet she was taken by the majestic vista that seemingly went on forever.

"I think it's more beautiful than scary. I never imagined it would be so . . . overwhelming."

Jordan was pleased by her reaction. He had been concerned that she might be frightened by the ghostly emptiness of the plains. "Wait till you see Palo Duro," he said. "That'll flat take your breath away."

"Perhaps so," Adair interjected. "Meanwhile, where are the buffalo you promised? I see nothing but grass."

"Don't worry," Jordan assured him. "We'll find you a herd. They head south this time of year."

"Are you saying they migrate, like geese?"

"Well, not near as far. Spend the summer up around the Republican, and head down here for the winter. Likely there's a bunch that winters at Palo Duro."

"Yes, of course," Adair said with a wily smile. "All that grass and water and shelter. How could I forget?"

Jordan grinned. "What works for buffalo works the same for cows. You'll see what I mean."

"You should've been a brokerage man, Jack. You have a way of spinning dreams."

"Only when it comes to Palo Duro."

Jordan led them eastward along the river. The Canadian flowed through the upper reaches of the Staked Plains, not far north of Palo Duro. Still farther north, Leigh Dyer and the other hands were driving the cattle herd along a parallel course, following the Arkansas River. A week or so out from Colorado, the herd would be turned south, toward the Canadian. Barring any misfortune, the herd would reach Palo Duro around the middle of November.

By then, Jordan told himself, the future shape of things would have been determined. He planned to sight the westward end of Palo Duro sometime the first week in November. Once there, he was fully confident that Adair could be persuaded to finance the operation. Yet a deal was a deal only after a handshake, and Adair hadn't yet heard the far-reaching scope of his ambition. He hoped he was right about a buffalo herd having drifted south to the canyon, for Adair was intent on a kill. A successful hunt might just turn the trick.

Late that afternoon Jordan shot an antelope watering at the river. He signaled Butler and Taylor to pitch camp in a stand of cottonwoods bordering a dogleg bend in the stream. Their nightly halt was by now routine, and the men went about their chores without wasted motion. While Jordan skinned the antelope, Butler got a fire started and Taylor unloaded the wagon. Shortly before dark, with the horses picketed, everyone gathered around the fire. Folding camp chairs were set out for Rebecca and the Adairs.

Butler served antelope steaks, beans, sourdough biscuits, and coffee. For dessert, he brought out a dried apple pie fresh from a Dutch oven. The Adairs had proved to be great sports, learning to eat with tinware balanced on their knees. Jordan and the men sat hunkered on the ground, their legs crossed in cowhand fashion. Rebecca, who knew something of cowcamp etiquette, went out of her way to compliment the cook.

"Mose, your pie is absolutely delicious. I've never tasted better."

"Thank ya, ma'am." Butler beamed. "Secret's all in the crust."

"Excellent," Adair said, holding out his plate for a second serving. "Something special about food cooked over an open fire."

"Hard work and fresh air," Jordan noted. "You ride a horse all day, you're just naturally hungry come suppertime."

"Quite a shot you made on that antelope, Jack. I judged the range at two hundred yards, perhaps more."

"Guess it comes with having to shoot for your supper. First shot better count, or you're liable to go without."

"I envy you in many ways," Cornealia said. "A plainsman has a hard life, but a good one. Everything seems so uncomplicated, so elemental, out here."

Jordan chuckled. "I reckon 'elemental' is the right word. On the plains, you learn quick, or you go under."

"I must say you're to be commended. I wouldn't survive a minute by myself."

Later, the fire reduced to coals, Rebecca snuggled close to Jordan in their bedrobes. The indigo sky glittered with stars, and a brisk wind whipped across the plains. Her head nestled into his shoulder, she held her voice to a whisper.

"Your ears must be burning. I think Cornealia has adopted you as her hero."

"Feeling's mutual," Jordan said in a muffled tone. "Her and John take to the trail like old hands. For city folks, they do just fine."

"What about me?" she teased. "I'm a city girl."

"Yeah, but there's a difference between you and them. You've got some wildcat in you."

She giggled. "Are we talking about the same thing?"

"One way to find out."

Jordan wrapped her in a hard embrace. She came to him eagerly, with fierce abandon and no shame. They joined in perfect union, lost to all but the moment.

She wanted the honeymoon to go on forever.

A bright forenoon sun beat down on the plains. The wind was out of the north, and wads of cottony clouds scudded across a muslin sky. Grassy tablelands marched on with monotonous regularity to the horizon.

Rebecca rode with the Adairs, off to one side of the wagon. Jordan was on a scout, a hundred yards or so east of their position. His unerring sense of place and direction told him they were nearing the canyon. He judged the Canadian was some forty miles to their rear, and he was looking for the Comanche trail along the northern caprock. Not far away, he spotted bare ground, the earth worn hard by centuries of unshod hooves. He knew the trail was just ahead.

Jordan wheeled his horse and rode back toward the wagon. He was within hailing distance when a jackrabbit leapt from the thick grass, directly beneath the mules' noses, and bounded away. The mules spooked, taking the bit before Mose Butler could react, and bolted into a dead run. Hank Taylor spurred his horse into a gallop, trying to head the team, and Jordan barreled forward to intersect them on an angle. Butler roared a string of curses, sawing hard on the reins.

The mules suddenly slammed to a halt, slewing sideways as the weight of the wagon drove them forward. Taylor's gelding planted all four hooves, skidding past the mules, and hurled him from the saddle. He struck the ground, reins knotted in one fist, his legs dangling over a sheer precipice. The gelding scrambled backward, walleyed with fright, hauling him through the grass. Before them, not visible from a hundred yards away, was the rim of Palo Duro. Butler's eyes went round with awe.

"Gawddamn," he muttered shakily. "Would you look at that."

Rebecca and the Adairs joined Jordan near the wagon. None of them spoke, their expressions a mixture of astounded disbelief and wonder. The chasm of Palo Duro advanced onward some ten miles in width and a thousand feet deep. The canyon walls, bright with sunlight, were a spectrum of umber and scarlet and muted gold. Far below, a ribbon of water, lined with cottonwoods, wound through a broad grassland dotted with cedar and juniper. Tributary canyons, sparkling with streams, cleaved the walls of the southern rimrock.

"Jesus, Mary, and Joseph," Adair said in a dumbfounded voice. "There's a sight we'll not soon forget."

Rebecca and Cornealia merely stared, robbed of speech. Jordan laughed softly. "Told you it was big."

"Aye, you did, indeed," Adair murmured, still dazed. "I see no end to it, Jack. How far does it go on?"

"By rough calculation, I'd say a hundred miles downstream."

"God, it's grand, just grand."

Jordan rode over to the wagon. Butler and Taylor, who were staring out across the canyon, turned as he reined to a stop. "Thought we was goners," Butler said sourly. "Them gawddamn mules like to got us kilt."

Hank Taylor was a lean man, with a cheery disposition. "Quit bellyachin'," he said, grinning. "You're too damn ornery to get killed."

"Glad you boys survived," Jordan broke in. "Over to the west, there's a trail into the canyon. But it's just wide enough for a man and a horse. Want you to disassemble the wagon."

"For chrissake!" Butler grumbled. "Why don't we just shove the sonovabitch over the cliff?"

"Get busy and take it apart, Mose. Tomorrow, we'll cart everything into the canyon on the mules. Figure on supper up here tonight."

A short time later Jordan led Rebecca and the Adairs

down the trail. He planned to show them the canyon and return to the upper plains before nightfall. The grade was steep, hugging the northern palisades, with occasional switchbacks around massive outcroppings. The women were silent the entire time, but nonetheless undaunted by the sheer drop off into space. At several points, where the trail narrowed, they had to dismount and lead their horses. Something over an hour later they emerged onto the canyon floor.

From the bottom, the grandeur of Palo Duro was all the more apparent. The thousand-foot escarpments, north and south, rose like stone bastions into a sky framed against a midday sun. The cliffs, sometimes bathed in shadow, were a palette of dulled ocher and brilliant vermilion. Across miles of distance tawny grasslands were broken by the glitter of water and trees aflame with the colors of fall. The wind was constant but mild, far warmer than on the plains above.

Jordan marked the date as November 5, the day of his return to Palo Duro. He motioned with a wide sweep of his arm. "What do you think? Everything I told you?"

"Everything and more," Adair agreed. "No amount of exaggeration would do it justice."

Rebecca smiled happily. "I think I've fallen in love already. It's simply . . . magnificent."

"I wish I were a painter," Cornealia added. "All those colors beg to be captured on canvas."

Adair stood in his stirrups. He shaded his eyes against the sun, peering downstream. "Here now, do my eyes deceive me? I see something moving."

"Buffalo," Jordan informed him. "I spotted them when we were coming down the trail."

Cornealia and Rebecca followed the direction of his gaze. A mile or so downriver they saw a mass of dark brown that seemed to undulate in the shimmer of sunlight. Yet the distance was too far to make out distinct shapes.

"Are you sure, Jack?" Adair demanded. "You wouldn't joke about such a thing, would you?"

Jordan looked amused. "Got my word on it. Told you they'd hole up here for the winter."

"God love us!" Adair said, suddenly excited. "When do we start the hunt?"

"Time enough for that when we get the camp fixed up down here. How's tomorrow afternoon sound?"

"I'll not sleep a wink thinking about it."

"Oh, really, John," Cornealia scoffed playfully. "The buffalo aren't going to run off tonight."

"Not tonight," Jordan said, almost to himself. "But we'll have to run 'em off before long."

"We will?" Adair frowned at him. "Have you something against buffalo?"

"Well, the thing is, they eat grass. We're gonna need all that graze for our cows."

"Our cows?" Adair repeated, smiling. "You believe I'm sold on the proposition, do you?"

"Hell, you tell me, John. Haven't you already sold yourself?"

Adair had to concede the point. He was sold on Palo Duro, and Jack Jordan.

CHAPTER 10

The next morning was spent organizing a campsite in the canyon. Jordan selected a clearing along the river, bordered by a tall stand of cottonwoods. Butler and Taylor then made several trips down the narrow trail, the mules loaded with supplies, camp gear, and bedrolls. The disassembled wagon was hauled down in sections, the wheels alone requiring two trips.

By early afternoon the camp took on a look of permanence. Mose Butler dug a trench, with flat stones around the sides, and built a fire that would burn down to cooking embers. Rebecca and Cornealia walked downstream to a hidden copse of trees, eager for their first full bath in two weeks. Taylor hobbled the horses and mules, and turned them out to graze near the river. Then he began chopping firewood to last through the night.

Jordan and Adair waved to the women as they rode off downriver. Adair had the Sharps rifle across his saddle, brimming with excitement over the prospect of their hunt. He listened with rapt attention as Jordan explained how buffalo were killed from horseback. The thought of hooking his reins over the saddlehorn, while firing a rifle at a full gallop, gave him a moment's pause. Still, as he pondered it, he decided not to voice any reservations. He considered himself a skilled horseman.

Downstream a short way Jordan abruptly reined to a

halt. He turned in the saddle, studying the western mouth of the canyon for a long moment. Then his gaze swung southward, and he inspected the lay of the land at some length. His eyes narrowed in concentration.

"What is it?" Adair asked. "Something amiss?"

"See that creek?" Jordan replied, pointing off to the northwest. "I'll wager it's fed by a natural spring."

"Quite probably you're right. So—?"

Jordan motioned off to the southwest. He directed Adair's attention to a stretch of flat grassland, bounded on the east and west by creeks that flowed into the river. Then he gestured back toward the northwest.

"That's where I'll build," he said. "We'll put the house by that grove of trees near the creek. Lots of room for a corral and bunkhouse, even a separate mess hall." His eyes drifted upward along the creek. "And year round water from the spring."

"Admirable," Adair observed with a crafty look. "But if I finance this venture—and note my use of the word 'if'—that leaves an issue unanswered. Where will you build my house?"

"Your house?" Jordan was surprised. "You aim to live here?"

"Not on a routine basis. Of course, as your sole partner, I would visit on occasion. I'd think I deserve a home—one built of stone."

"A stone house?"

"Indeed."

"Well, there's lots of rocks around here. I reckon that wouldn't be a problem."

"Thank you," Adair said with a wry smile. "Which leaves the question of how you plan to get in and out of the canyon. That damnable goat trail hardly seems practical."

"Already thought of that."

Jordan again motioned behind them. He pointed to a small canyon that sliced into Palo Duro from the northwest, forming a notch in the northern wall. The notch broke through a sheer cliff, dropping downward in a rough but manageable grade. His plan was to build a road from the caprock that gradually descended into Palo Duro.

"Excellent idea," Adair said, thoughtful a moment. "By the bye, have you ever built a road?"

"Road sounds pretty tame to some of the things I've done. Don't worry, we'll manage just fine."

Adair accepted the statement at face value. Over the past few weeks he'd learned that Jordan was intimidated by nothing, however formidable the task. A man with the vision to tame Palo Duro would not be fazed by minor challenges. He felt confident the road would get built.

Ahead, perhaps a mile from their camp, they saw a scattered herd of buffalo. But as they rounded a bend in the canyon, the enormity of their find brought them to a halt. For miles in the distance, the floor of Palo Duro was a virtual sea of grazing buffalo. The humped, shaggy beasts spread from one wall of the canyon to the other, beyond sight. Jordan estimated there were at least ten thousand buffalo in the herd.

Adair, taken by the size of the herd, was momentarily distracted from the hunt. Ever the businessman, he noted that hides were now a commodity, harvested like wheat or corn. The slaughter began in earnest in 1870, when Eastern tanneries discovered a process for converting buffalo hides to commercial leather. Dodge City alone had shipped more than a million hides eastward during the previous hunting season. At three dollars a hide, there was a fortune to be made on the western Plains.

Jordan was all too aware of the slaughter. On trail drives, he had encountered hide hunters from Texas to Wyoming. There were hundreds of such operations on the Plains, and wagons filled with salted hides rumbled into distant railheads from early spring until late fall. Estimates of the great herds placed the count at sixty million, and that number had been reduced by tens of millions in only four years. There was profit in butchery and no dearth of men eager to take part.

Nor was the government concerned with the extermination of the herds. From a practical standpoint, Jordan explained, the army looked upon the hide hunters as allies. General Phil Sheridan, the Western military commander, applauded the hunters for destroying the Indians' "commissary." Without buffalo, the specter of starvation would soon force the Sioux and other Plains Tribes onto the reservations. The killing, with the tacit approval of the government, went on unabated.

"You've served as an army scout," Adair said. "So you support the government's decision?"

"Some people call it progress," Jordan said in a flat tone. "I suppose it's one way to get the West opened to settlement. Nothing anybody says will change it, either. Like it or not, it's a fact."

"Pragmatism always comes at a dear price, Jack. But then, as you remarked, we're not going to alter the course of things. Now, what say we get on with the hunt? I've a taste for buffalo tonight."

"Hell, it's as good as done. Just remember everything I told you."

Adair held his position as Jordan rode forward at a walk. The grazing buffalo eyed horse and rider suspiciously, and then, as he approached closer, they began drifting downstream. Jordan suddenly gigged his horse into a gallop, and on the fringe of the herd, he cut out a fat cow. Hauling on the reins, he spun around and hazed the cow back upstream. He signaled to Adair.

A beat behind, Adair urged his horse into a lope. Moments later, some ten lengths behind Jordan, he found himself enveloped in a cloud of dust. The terrified cow lumbered toward the upper end of the canyon as he spurred his horse into a headlong gallop. Slowly the gap narrowed, but the buffalo's ragged gait was deceptive, and it dawned on him that they were rapidly approaching the camp. He jabbed harder with his spurs.

Jordan dropped back as Adair at last overtook the cow. The Irishman kneed his horse alongside, matching her stride for stride on open ground north of the river. Caught up in the thrill of the chase, he had no thought for anything except the great humped beast pounding forward not three feet away from him. The cow veered toward the camp as he hooked the reins over his saddlehorn and brought the Sharps rifle to his shoulder. He aimed just behind the foreleg and fired into her chest.

In the camp, watching as the buffalo thundered toward them, everyone scattered in a different direction. Cornealia screamed, darting into the trees on the shoreline, with Rebecca hard on her heels. Taylor dropped his axe and dove for safety behind the half-assembled wagon. Mose Butler scurried away from the fire and took to the river shallows in a bounding leap. The cow, mortally wounded, collapsed in mid-stride, rolling end over end, and cartwheeled into the camp. Her nose, thick with bloody froth, came to rest a few yards from the fire.

Adair and Jordan skidded to a halt in a roiling upheaval of dust. Cornealia and Rebecca edged from behind the trees, staring at the dead buffalo, while Butler waded from the river. Taylor, flat on the ground underneath the wagonbed, slowly levered himself to his feet. Like some centaur emerging from a duststorm, Adair's mouth split in an enormous grin, and he seemed to grow taller in the saddle. He looked around at Jordan.

"By the Saints!" he whooped. "There's nothing on God's earth to equal that. Nothing a'tall!"

"You're a helluva shot," Jordan said with genuine admiration. "Drilled her square through the lights."

"By all that's holy, I did, didn't I! But I owe it all to you, Jack. You practically served her on a platter."

"John Adair!" Cornealia stormed through the camp, circling the dead buffalo. "Have you gone mad, chasing that creature in here? You could have killed us all."

"Here now, what kind of talk is that? Would you take me to task after I brought you such a grand present?"

"Please spare me your Irish charm. I've never been so frightened in my life."

"All my fault," Jordan interceded. "I got her headed in this direction and there was no turning her away. Never figured she'd beeline it into camp."

"Well, honestly!" Cornealia pouted. "You two aren't to be trusted by yourselves."

"Home is the hunter," Adair said with a flashing grin. "And we dropped her within a hop and skip of the fire. Just in time for dinner."

"I'm shore obliged," Mose Butler said with a dour grimace, eyeing the buffalo. "Never had supper delivered to the doorstep before."

Butler and Taylor harnessed the mules to a towline and dragged the buffalo some distance from the campsite. After a brief debate, it was decided that Taylor would do the skinning and Butler would butcher the cow. While Taylor began sharpening his knife, the cook led the mules back to the picket line. He was still muttering to himself about buffalo charging into the camp.

The Adairs walked off by themselves along the river. Cornealia remained in a huff, and Adair, laughing and cajoling, was trying to humor her. Rebecca joined Jordan at the fire as he poured himself a cup of coffee. There was a curious glint in his eye, and she caught his attempt to suppress a smile. She knew he was amused by the whole affair.

"You're terrible," she said. "I think you deliberately staged a show for our benefit."

"Who, me?" Jordan replied with mock innocence. "I'll admit I tried to do John a favor. Cornealia likes to rag him about the time he shot his horse in the head. After today, he'll have a little bragging room."

"Your joke almost went too far."

"Wasn't any joke to it, Becky. That buffalo might just clinch our deal."

"Are you talking about John becoming your partner?"

"Nothing else," Jordan acknowledged. "I figure tonight's the night to get down to brass tacks. I want him in a good mood."

"Why, Mr. Jordan," she said with a engaging look. "You really are a devious man, aren't you? I never suspected."

"Let's hope a dose of devious turns the trick."

The cook outdid himself at supper. He served buffalo steaks, oozing succulent juices, with wild rice and stewed apples from his horde of tinned goods. After the meal, Adair produced a bottle of aged brandy, unaware that Jordan never allowed spirits of any variety in his camps. Jordan tactfully held his silence, warning Butler and Taylor with a look, and permitted the brandy to be served. Adair raised his cup in a toast.

"As we say in Ireland, may you be in heaven a half hour before the Devil knows you're dead. And to you, Jack, all the honors for a grand buffalo hunt."

Later, with the celebration at an end, Adair invited Jordan to join him for a smoke. They walked down to the river, and Adair pulled out a leather case with thin black cigars. Jordan accepted one, though he'd never acquired a taste for tobacco, and lit up in a haze of smoke. Adair puffed for a time, studying the fiery coal on the tip of his cigar. At length, flicking an ash into the water, he gave Jordan a speculative look.

"I've a feeling you're anxious to talk business. Or do I read you wrong?"

Jordan nodded. "Now's as good time as any. I think you've sold yourself on Palo Duro."

"Indeed I have," Adair admitted. "And indebted I am for a most successful hunt. But business is business, and I've a cardinal rule for any investment. The potential return must outweigh the risk by a wide margin."

"You sound like you've already thought this out. What do you have in mind?"

"First, whatever land we acquire, we have to control it legally. I won't follow the cattle baron principle of might makes right."

"Those are my sentiments exactly. What else?"

Adair explained the structure of the deal he'd devised.

He would finance the enterprise, with sufficient funds to purchase land and operate the ranch, and stock five thousand head of cattle each year for the next five years. In return, he would receive ten percent interest on his investment and fifty-one percent ownership of the ranch. Jordan would draw a modest salary, and once a year they would divide any profits. He paused, puffing his cigar

"I think it's a fair arrangement, Jack. Do you agree?"

"On one condition," Jordan told him. "We have to be fifty-fifty partners. Otherwise you're my boss."

Adair smiled. "And you're not one to take orders, are you, Jack?"

"I'll work with you, but not for you. That's my cardinal rule."

"Done!" Adair extended his hand. "But I insist we call it the JA Ranch. Not Jordan-Adair, you understand. I'm saying John Adair. You have to allow me a certain vanity."

Jordan accepted his handshake. "Welcome to Palo Duro, partner."

CHAPTER 11

A week later Jordan rode north to the Canadian. There he found the herd waiting where the river swung in a sharp arc to the northeast. The rendezvous point was unmistakable, for it was the only spot on the river with such a pronounced bend. The cattle were gathered on a holding ground not far from the wagons.

The men were a grungy lot after the long trail drive from Colorado. They waved and shouted, greeting Jordan with looks of relief as he rode into camp. He swung down from the saddle, leaving his horse ground-reined beside one of the wagons. Leigh Dyer pumped his arm with a whiskery grin.

"You're a sight for sore eyes," Dyer said. "We was startin' to wonder if we'd found the right place."

"You couldn't miss it." Jordan motioned toward the river. "Happened across that bend back in '64, when I rode with the Rangers. Only spot like it on the Canadian."

"Well, we're here and we come through in good shape. Guess that's all that counts."

"Have any trouble?"

"Nope," Dyer said. "Didn't lose a single head and never saw the first Injun. Not like the old days."

"Old days are long gone," Jordan commented. "All the hostiles are over in Indian Territory."

"Suits me just fine. Wouldn't care if I never saw another redstick."

"Let's get this outfit on the move. We've got a drive of forty miles or so to Palo Duro."

"How's things down there?"

"Adair likes it so much he decided to stay another week. God made it 'specially for cows."

Dyer laughed. "Sounds like you made him a convert."

"Leigh, we're gonna have the goddamnedest ranch this side of Creation."

Dyer signaled the men to break camp. Within the hour Jordan led them south from the Canadian. The wagons, stocked with six months' supplies, were in the vanguard. Strung out behind, the herd of longhorns plodded onward in a column over half a mile long. Off to one side, the wrangler hazed a remuda of some sixty horses. A sense of eager anticipation spread among the men up and down the dusty column. They were at last to see the fabled Palo Duro.

Three days later, around midday, Jordan brought them to the tableland above the canyon. The hands turned the lead steers, milling the herd, and put them to graze on the broad grassy plain. The wagons were halted near the caprock, where a temporary camp would be established. Once the herd was settled down, the men were allowed to ride forward for their first look at Palo Duro. Their expressions were a mix of pop-eyed wonder and raw disbelief.

"Jumpin' Jehoshaphat!" one of the men blurted. "That's a *biiig* gawddamn canyon."

Dyer shook his head. "Any of you boys get a notion to jump across it, put wings on your horse. You'd have a ways to fly."

The men rode back to camp looking dazed. Jordan motioned for Dyer and John Poe, segundo of the outfit, to follow him. Poe was a top hand who had been promoted to segundo, second-in-command to Dyer, some years ago. Farther west along the rimrock, Jordan reined to a halt before the tributary canyon. He pointed down the slope that carved a notch in the north wall.

"We need a way into Palo Duro," he said. "Got no choice but to build ourselves a road. This notch looks to be our best bet."

The men studied the terrain, silent for a time. Finally, Dyer let out his breath in a low whistle. "That slope drops off pretty steep. Won't be no picnic party."

"Ground's rough, too," Poe added. "Take a heap of work to get it leveled out."

"All true enough," Jordan agreed. "You'll have to build three, maybe four switchbacks to offset the grade. We'll walk it today and mark the spots."

Dyer nodded. "How long you reckon this road to be?"

"I'd judge a mile," Jordan said. "Maybe a hair more."

"Never a dull moment," Poe said with a humorous smile. "You took us to Wyoming and back. We fought Injuns and blizzards and flooded rivers. Now we're gonna be road engineers. Ain't that a laugh?"

"Think of it this way," Jordan told him. "A cowpoke's a jack-of-all-trades. You're about to learn a new one."

"Well, boss, you'll get no argument there. You've showed me more tricks than a one-handed magician."

Jordan laid out the schedule. The herd would be held on the plains, guarded by a skeleton crew of two men. The rest of the hands, under the supervision of Dyer and Poe, would be put to work building the road. He wanted it completed without delay.

They walked downslope to inspect the terrain.

Adair stood sipping a cup of coffee. To the east, the sun crested the rim of the canyon in streamers of orange and gold. His gaze was fixed on the notch in the north wall, where the men were working on the road. They had been at it since first light.

For the past two days, starting at the crack of dawn, the men had tackled what seemed to Adair a herculean task. Their tools were rudimentary, comprised for the most part of shovels, sledgehammers, and pickaxes. Yet they whaled away, smashing rocks and flinging dirt with a sort of demonic teamwork. There were no shirkers in the group, and the men in charge, Dyer and Poe, labored alongside the others. The road was already three-quarters of the way down the slope.

Jordan rode out to inspect their progress early every morning and again shortly before sundown. An observer, Adair noticed that he had delegated responsibility for the project to Dyer and Poe, entrusting them to see it done properly. His orders were more often than not in the form of suggestions, and he never overrode their authority. He'd charged them with completing the job, and rather than acting the boss, he had left them to get on with it. All of the men, Dyer and Poe included, drove themselves at a brutal pace.

Watching them, Adair was reminded of a military operation. He thought Jordan had mastered the art of command, probably learned from cavalry leaders while serving as a scout. There was a sense that Jordan would not be disobeyed, and any man who failed to follow orders would be subjected to swift and harsh repercussions. Yet Jordan never raised his voice, or issued demands, and he was quick to praise a job well done. The men clearly respected him, and they seemed to look upon him as an icon of authority. Their loyalty had about it a tangible quality.

Adair was convinced that he'd made a wise decision. His investment was as much in the man as in land and cattle, the assets of a ranch. All the more so since the land was a veritable wilderness, and cattle were susceptible to harsh weather and the hazards of a trail drive. The success of the ranch would be solely dependent upon the leadership and foresight of Jack Jordan. Adair felt his initial assessment of the man, made when they first met in his office, was underscored by events of the past month. Time had proved him right.

In the distance, he saw Jordan headed back to the camp. The women were at their secret spot along the river, performing their morning ablutions before breakfast. Butler was working over the cook fire, and Taylor was tending the horses at the picket line. When Jordan dismounted, he spoke for a moment with Taylor, gesturing downstream. Then he walked toward the clearing.

"Good morning, Jack," Adair greeted him. "Your road appears to be making splendid progress."

"Better than I expected." Jordan stopped at the fire, pouring himself a cup of coffee from the galvanized pot. "The boys tell me it'll be finished today."

"I must say, I'm hardly surprised. I've never seen men work so hard."

"Wait till you see what happens at a roundup. They figure I gave 'em a holiday with this road."

Adair appeared thoughtful. "I've been meaning to ask, and your mentioning a roundup reminds me. Where do you intend to market our cattle?"

"Dodge City," Jordan said, motioning off to the northeast. "Figure it's a couple of hundred miles, maybe a little more. That makes it the nearest railhead."

"Indeed." Adair sipped coffee, considering a moment. "Being so far from civilization raises my curiosity. Who governs this part of Texas?"

"For what it's worth, we'd be part of Clay County. The county seat's in Henrietta, maybe two hundred miles southeast of here."

"What does one do if a law officer is required?"

Jordan patted his holstered pistol. "We make our own law in this part of the country. Trouble comes along, we'll handle it ourselves."

Adair nodded. "Given the circumstances, a man has to protect his own. Hmmm?"

"Out here, peace officers aren't all that much use, anyway. Never yet saw one that was johnny-on-the-spot when the shootin' started."

"Where is the nearest army post?"

"Fort Elliott's about a hundred miles to the east. 'Course, the army generally won't meddle in civilian affairs. We're pretty much on our own where trouble's concerned."

Butler clanged the lid on the Dutch oven. "Lawmen are worthless as tits on a boar hog. Like the boss says, don't you worry none about us, Mr. Adair. We got our own brand of justice."

"Yes, I've no doubt a'tall of that, Mr. Butler."

"Anybody's hungry, the grub's on. You want to wait for the ladies?"

"They'll be along directly," Jordan said. His gaze shifted to Adair. "Those buffalo have got to be run off before we move cows into the canyon. You want to join in the fun?"

"Sounds sporting," Adair said with a sudden grin. "How do you propose to drive them away?"

"John, we're gonna organize the damnedest stampede anybody ever heard tell of."

After breakfast, Jordan, Adair, and Hank Taylor rode east along the canyon. A mile or so downstream they encountered the fringe of the buffalo herd, placidly cropping grass in the early morning sun. Farther on, the density of the herd thickened, until it became an immobile wall of horns and dark brown humps. The mass of the herd extended eastward far out of sight.

On Jordan's signal, the other men fanned out, with Adair to the left and Taylor to the right. They rode forward at a steady trot, on line with one another, separated by a distance of a hundred yards. Jordan and Taylor were armed with Winchesters, and Adair had borrowed the cook's old Henry repeater. Some fifty yards away, they loosed a volley of shots, kicking spurts of red dust around the heels of the nearest buffalo. Then they charged at a gallop, whooping and shouting, firing wildly into the air.

The gunshots reverberated off the canyon walls with the staccato roar of thunderbolts. The nearest buffalo spooked, wheeling away, and took off in a ragged lope. On the instant, panic spread throughout the herd, and rank by rank, the terrified beasts were galvanized into motion. Within a matter of seconds, ten thousand buffalo were lumbering eastward, the sound of their drumming hooves almost deafening. A red cloud of dust rose in their wake, filling the canyon until it towered a thousand feet to the caprock and beyond into the sky. The shaggy herd charged downriver in a solid wedge.

A single cow emerged from the dust cloud, headed back upriver, and Jordan shot her with his Winchester. He thought to himself that the men would feast tonight on buffalo steaks, a fitting reward for their completion of the road. Then, with Adair and Taylor winged out on the flanks, his attention turned back to the stampede. Over the next hour, holding their horses to a trot, they drove the herd onward with shouts and gunfire. Some ten miles downstream, Jordan signaled a halt, the barrel of his Winchester glowing with heat. The buffalo clattered off into the distance in maddened flight.

"By all that's holy!" Adair hollered, reining his horse about. "They'll brand me a liar at the Denver Club when I tell them of today."

Jordan laughed. "Hell, John, send your rich friends on down to Palo Duro. We'll show 'em the real Wild West!"

"Jack, you've given me the story of a lifetime. All of Denver will think me nothing but an Irish braggart."

The following morning, the Adairs prepared to depart Palo Duro. John Poe and Hank Taylor, both experienced plainsmen, were assigned to accompany them back to Colorado with a wagon. There, the men would load the wagon with added provisions, and return to the ranch. By pushing along they were expected back before the first snowfall of winter.

Rebecca and Cornealia, by now confidants as well as friends, parted with tearful hugs. Jordan walked Adair to his horse, and they exchanged a firm handshake. Their time together had kindled mutual respect, and a strong sense of camaraderie. Neither of them was comfortable with the maudlin words customarily used to express shared feeling. They parted simply.

"Well, Jack," Adair said. "As we agreed, I'll open a bank account in the name of the JA Ranch. You may draw on it as you see fit."

"Good enough," Jordan replied. "Have your lawyer draft our contract, and send it to me care of Fort Elliott. I'll manage to get over there in the next month or so, and sign it."

Adair stepped into the saddle. "Cornealia and I are planning another visit next spring." He paused, nodding with a droll smile. "We'll expect to see our house—a stone house."

Jordan grinned. "I'll tend to it personally."

The Adairs reined their horses around. John Poe took the lead, with Taylor driving the mule-drawn wagon. The rest of the men loitered about camp, watching a moment, then went off to their chores. The longhorn herd had been driven into the canyon earlier that morning, and the men were now felling trees for the construction of living quarters. The ring of axes soon sounded on hard cedar.

Rebecca linked arms with Jordan. They stood a long while, waiting until the wagon and riders began the steep climb up the new road. The Adairs turned in their saddles and waved, and they waved back. Finally, when the riders disappeared from sight, Rebecca broke the silence.

"What are you thinking, Jack?"

"I'm thinking they're a matched pair, aces high."

"Yes," she said quietly. "I'll miss them terribly."

"Well, let's not lollygag around, Mrs. Jordan. We've got a ranch to build."

CHAPTER 12

Winter lay over the land like an icy shroud. By early January, a blanket of snow covered the plains north and south of the caprock. Creeks froze on the tableland above the canyon, and drifts of snow rose higher along the banks. The wind howled constantly.

Palo Duro afforded welcome protection from storms that raged down out of the north. Temperatures were higher below the rimrock, and there was seldom any great accumulation of snow. On frosty mornings ice sometimes formed along the edges of the creek, and even more rarely, along the shallows of the river. The wind, though far less frigid than on *Llano Estacado,* was nonetheless constant. The howl above became a keening moan within the canyon.

Jordan emerged from the house, clad in a mackinaw. The sky was overcast, and he stared up at the caprock a moment, watching swirls of snow tossed above by gusty winds. He often thought the Comanche had chosen wisely, centuries ago adopting Palo Duro as their winter quarters. Even in the harshest weather there was graze for horses and cattle, and never any shortage of water. The canyon was a haven from the blizzards that savaged the open plains.

All in all, Jordan was pleased with the progress thus far. Looking out across the compound, he felt that much had been accomplished in less than two months. A stout log house for him and Rebecca stood near the spring-fed creek, on the east side of the compound. To the west, separated from the main house by some fifty yards, was a combination bunkhouse and cook house. Farther north was a corral for the remuda, a blacksmith shed, and two outbuildings for storage of equipment. Closer to the river, a stone house was under construction for the Adairs.

Jordan marked 1875 as an auspicious year for the JA spread. His preliminary goal, to establish living quarters and a base of operation, was now complete. The longhorn herd, effectively contained by the canyon walls, was allowed to roam the grazelands on either side of the river. The horses were restricted to the corral at night, and driven to pasture during the day. Cougar and bear, which prowled the tributary canyons, were sometimes tempted to attack a horse. But no wild thing ever willingly tangled with a longhorn.

Still studying the overcast sky, Jordan walked toward the bunkhouse. He sniffed the air, which had the sharp, damp nip that often preceded snowfall. Since early December, four blizzards had swept across the plains, dumping enough snow to close the road along the upper section, near the caprock. The worst storm had hit on Christmas Day, during a party and dinner held for the crew in the bunkhouse. For all practical purposes, the canyon was now isolated from the rest of the world for the balance of the winter. The only way out was through the badlands at the eastern end of Palo Duro.

The crew had just finished breakfast as Jordan entered the bunkhouse. Butler was clearing a long dining table in the kitchen section, while the men got ready for work in their sleeping quarters. A potbellied stove, along with the kitchen stove, kept the place warm, even though the mix of unwashed bodies and dirty longjohns gave it the rank odor of a wolf's den. The furnishings included bunk beds, a few rickety chairs, and one washstand with a warped mirror. The men's personal belongings were stored under the beds, and their clothing hung from wall pegs. Full of coffee and flapjacks, they paired off for trips to the two-holer outhouse behind the building.

"Mornin', boss," Dyer greeted Jordan as he closed the door. "How about a cup of java?"

"Guess another cup wouldn't hurt. Pretty nippy outside."

Dyer poured, and they took a seat at the table. Jordan always had breakfast with Rebecca before walking across to the bunkhouse. Over a cup of coffee, he and Dyer went through the morning ritual of planning out the workday. He swigged at the scalding coffee.

"Might snow," he said. "Heavy clouds off to the northwest."

Dyer nodded. "I'll keep an eye peeled. Anything special you want done today?"

"Have some of the boys ride those canyons between here and the headwaters. Snow's too heavy, we'll have cows bunched in there till spring. Let's chouse 'em out."

"I'll have to pull a couple of hands off Buster's crew."

Buster Lornax was in charge of building the Adairs' stone house. A cowhand by choice, he had learned carpentry and masonry as a boy in the Texas settlements. For the most part, furniture in the main house and the bunkhouse had taken shape under his hand since their arrival in Palo Duro. Three men were assigned to his crew on the stone house.

"Take Buster if you need him," Jordan said. "That house can wait a few days. The snow likely won't."

"I'll handle it," Dyer said, blowing steam off his coffee. "Anything else?"

"Yesterday, I noticed a few buffalo have drifted back upstream. The longer we leave 'em there, the more will follow. First chance you get, have the boys run them off."

Jordan spent his days roaming the lower reaches of Palo Duro. He carried pencil and paper, and he was slowly constructing a map of the canyon. Daily operation of the ranch was in large degree left to Dyer.

"Them buffalo are a problem," Dyer said. "How're we gonna solve it for the long haul?"

"Only one way," Jordan told him. "Come spring, we'll chase them to the end of the canyon and onto the plains. Hide hunters will take it from there."

"Damn shame we gotta make them buffalo men any richer."

"The shame is there's no way for cows and buffalo to share rangeland. One's got to make room for the other."

"Guess we've got no choice but to run 'em off."

"No choice at all, Leigh. Not if we want the canyon."

Later, at the corral, Jordan roped a sorrel gelding, one of the horses in his personal string. His gaze went to the stone house as he pulled the cinch tight on the saddle. The house was in the early stages of construction, and he regretted having to pull Buster Lomax off the job. Still, there were many things that had to be completed by spring, and the house was one item on a long list. A list that would guarantee control of Palo Duro.

He rode off down the canyon.

From the house, Rebecca watched as he rode away. She saw that he'd turned up the collar on his mackinaw, and she hoped it wouldn't snow. He went off early every morning and returned long after dark, and nothing short of a blizzard could keep him at home. He was obsessed with mapping the canyon.

She ran her hand across the window glass. Every morning, when she watched him ride out, she was reminded that it was the only window on the ranch. As a surprise, certain it would please her, he had ordered John Poe to return with a window and a small cookstove from the trip to Colorado with the Adairs. The window, just as he'd planned, gave her an inordinate amount of pleasure. She knew it was a luxury in the wilderness, a very special gift.

There were so many things she had been unable to bring on their move to Palo Duro. Space in the wagons was at a premium, limited to provisions, equipment, and a few pieces of dismantled furniture. Yet, upon hearing that there were no stores within two hundred miles, she had insisted on bringing several bolts of cloth and a feather mattress. She was willing to rough it in the wilds of Texas, but only to a certain extent. A bed without a mattress seemed to her somehow uncivilized.

All things considered, she was content with their first home. The main room consisted of a kitchen and dining area, and a parlor of sorts set before a stone fireplace. Between the fireplace and the small cookstove, which seemed to her a godsend, the house stayed toasty warm even in the coldest weather. The bedroom opened off the parlor area, and the bed frame, like most of the other furniture, had been crafted by Buster Lomax. The sole exception was a rocking chair, yet another surprise, which had been dismantled and carted across the plains. She realized that the simplest of things, a rocker and a window, were sometimes the rarest of gifts.

From one of the bolts of cloth, she had fashioned curtains for her window. She held the other bolts in reserve for dresses, and a shirt she'd made Jordan for Christmas. The cookstove, though smaller than the one in the bunkhouse, gave her a degree of independence she might never have imagined before Palo Duro. Without it, she would have been forced to dine with the crew, and never share a meal alone with her husband. She knew the stove was an afterthought on Jordan's part, one that came to him only after their trek across the plains. Yet she was nonetheless thankful, for his thought was to make her comfortable, and happy. The stove, more so than the window, turned the house into a home.

The breakfast dishes washed, she began kneading bread dough on the kitchen table. In good weather, she might have asked one of the men to saddle a horse, and then gone for a ride. She was still fascinated by the canyon, a world of discovery where rock formations were layered with bands of startlingly different colors. But on cold, snowy days, she kept herself busy with household chores, and tried not to think of Pueblo. She missed the dances and the music, church socials with her friends, the times of laughter. Most of all, since Cornealia Adair's departure, she missed the everyday conversation women loved to share with each other. There was no one to talk to, no one to share her thoughts.

She loved her husband more than she'd ever imagined possible. He was at once gentle and strong, unfailingly considerate, and a man of admirable character. Yet he was quiet, a man of few words, usually lost in thoughts of the ranch even when they were together. She never questioned his love, and at night, snug in their bed, he fulfilled her in ways that left her giddy and shameless. The other times, when he sat contemplating his grand designs for Palo Duro, she felt shut out, overwhelmed by his silence. She wanted him to talk about anything, or nothing, a simple sharing of thoughts. A time when they spoke only of themselves.

Often, when she was alone, she dwelled on the thought of having a baby. As much as they made love, she was amazed that she wasn't already with child. Yet, however much she wanted a baby, the idea sometimes left her frightened. Off in the wilderness, two hundred miles from the nearest doctor, she wondered how the birth would be performed. She knew little of such things, and she felt certain her husband knew even less. Still, she supposed pioneer women had babies every day, without the help of a doctor. She told herself God would decide the time for her to become pregnant, and as for the rest, she would find a way. She was after all, a pioneer herself. The first white woman to live in Palo Duro.

She laughed softly, kneading the dough, wishing Indian women still lived in the canyon. She thought they would know all there was to know about having babies.

A light snow fell across the canyon. Jordan halted at a bend in the river, well downstream from the buffalo herd.

He judged he was some fifteen miles from the home compound.

Over the past two months, he had discovered that mapmaking was a painstaking process. The landmarks were easily committed to memory, and stored away in his mind. But committing them to paper, with any degree of accuracy, was a far more difficult task. He had never before appreciated the skill of cartographers.

The more he explored Palo Duro, the more impressed Jordan became with the land. A network of creeks, north and south of the canyon floor, fed into the Prairie Dog Fork of the Red. The creeks formed a natural irrigation system, watering an abundance of graze the breadth of the canyon. He had yet to find a section too arid for raising cows.

Jordan finished the last notation on his map. After stuffing the folded paper inside his mackinaw, he reined about and headed for home. A few miles upstream he would have to skirt the buffalo herd, and he found himself wishing they were gone from the canyon. Still, while winter persisted, the buffalo were the least of his problems. Far more immediate was completion of the map.

By early spring, Jordan felt certain his presence in Palo Duro would become known. Buffalo hunters, perhaps a cavalry patrol, would carry the word to the outside world. Before that happened, he had no choice but to undertake a land-buying program. Otherwise, when the word got out, cattlemen would be drawn to Palo Duro from across the plains. Yet the plan he'd hatched to control the canyon required an accurate map, all the more so since no map of Palo Duro existed. He decided to redouble his efforts.

The snow slacked off as Jordan rode into the compound. After unsaddling, he turned his horse into the corral and dumped the saddle in an equipment shed. A shaft of light spilled through the window of the house, and it seemed to him a beacon in the night. He was glad he'd ordered the window, for he knew it gave Rebecca great pleasure. He wondered if she knew it pleasured him as well. Simply knowing she was there, waiting, was his reward.

When Jordan came through the door, she turned from the stove. The aroma of fresh-baked bread and beef roast filled the house. She crossed the room as he hooked his hat and mackinaw on wall pegs beside the door. Before he could say anything, she took his face in her hands and kissed him on the mouth. Her eyes shone with happiness.

"Well, now," Jordan said, momentarily flustered. "You know how to welcome a man home. What's the occasion?"

"No occasion," she said lightly. "Isn't a wife allowed to greet her husband?"

"That greeting was a little warmer than usual."

"Was it?" She gave him a sloe-eyed vixen look. "Maybe you'll figure it out for yourself."

"Figure out what?"

She walked back to the stove, the swish of her hips somehow provocative. She smiled at him over her shoulder, her voice curiously sultry. "We'll talk about it after supper."

CHAPTER 13

Jordan forded the Colorado River on February 17. On the opposite bank was Austin, the state capital of Texas. His trip had been long and wearing, covering almost five hundred miles from Palo Duro. By pushing himself and his horse, he had made it in fifteen days.

Darkness was falling as Jordan rode into town. He first found a livery stable, leaving orders for his horse to have a good rubdown and then a special treat of oats. Upstreet, he located a modest hotel, and after renting a room, he took supper in a nearby cafe. He was tired but exhilarated, for Austin was where he planned to acquire control of Palo Duro. The next few days were the most critical of the entire venture.

After supper, Jordan returned to the hotel. He stripped down to his longjohns and stretched out on the bed, weary to the bone. Yet sleep was elusive, and he found himself staring blankly at the ceiling. Having planned so long and traveled so far, his thoughts should have been on the task ahead. But he was unable to shake the mental image of Rebecca, and the unpleasant scene before he'd departed Palo Duro. Her words still rang in his ears.

"You expect me to spend a month here—*alone*?"

"You're not alone," Jordan said, surprised by her anger. "Leigh and the boys are right over there in the bunkhouse. They'll look after you."

"That's not the point!" she retorted. "You're leaving me alone. For a whole *month*!"

"Becky, try to understand. I've got to make this trip. Otherwise we could lose Palo Duro."

"You could take me with you."

"I already explained that. I'll be traveling fast and light. There's no way you could go along."

"You don't want me along, that's it, isn't it?"

"Listen to me real close," Jordan said, holding his temper. "You knew I was a cattleman when we got married. Would you expect me to take you on a trail drive?"

She glared at him. "It's not the same thing at all."

"Why, hell yes, it's the same thing. There's times I'll have to be gone on business, and you've got to get used to the idea. That's all part of runnin' a ranch."

"So I'm to be content with your absence and play the part of a good little wife. Is that it?"

"You ought to hear yourself," Jordan said in a hollow voice. "You make it sound like I'll enjoy being away from you. Do you honest-to-God believe that?"

Her eyes welled with tears. "No, of course not. It's just . . ."

"Just what?"

"I feel so lost without you . . . even for a day."

"Then you ought to know it's the same for me. No place I'd rather be than here at home with you."

"Do you really mean that, Jack?"

"I never meant anything more in my life. Why else would I have married you?"

Rebecca's anger turned to resignation, and then subdued sadness. Stretched out on the hotel bed, he still remembered her brave smile when he rode off down the canyon. Even so, he knew that while she accepted the situation, that was not the end of it. Somehow, in her own mind, she would have to come to grips with their life in Palo Duro. He went to sleep troubled by the thought.

Jordan rose early the next morning. After breakfast, he found a tonsorial parlor and bathhouse, where he treated himself to the six-bit special. A haircut was followed by a shave, the mustache trim included, and then a long, steamy bath. For a quarter extra, while he was in the tub, the extra set of clothes from his saddlebags were sponged and pressed. An hour later he emerged from the establishment a new man, scrubbed clean and smelling of bay rum lotion. He walked toward the state capitol.

Jordan, like most Texans, took inordinate pride in Austin. In 1839, three years after Anglo settlers won independence from Mexico, the town had been designated the capital of the Republic of Texas. Following annexation to the United States, with statehood granted in 1845, Austin remained the capital. During the Civil War, when Jordan rode with the Rangers, Texas had seceded from the Union and fought under the Confederate flag. But in 1870, at the close of the Reconstruction Era and an end to Union occupation, Austin had been voted the permanent capital of Texas. Through war and rebellion, the town had served as the bastion of the Lone Star State.

Today, at the capitol building, Jordan made his way to the Bureau of Land Records. Like most cattlemen, he was familiar with the land laws passed by the legislature in 1873. The enactment created millions of acres of public domain, principally in the Texas Panhandle, still designated on maps as *Llano Estacado*. The law divided public domain holdings into various classes, including railroad grants and lands for private sale. Once the Panhandle was settled, the railroad grants were to be offered as an inducement to build rail lines into the region. But settlement was far in the future, and Jordan had no interest in railroad grants.

The lure that drew him to Austin was instead the lands for private sale. With the assistance of a clerk, he began poring through the records pertaining to the Panhandle. He quickly discovered that politics, as usual, made for strange bedfellows. The state legislature, by way of secret bids, had sold land certificates to individuals and companies who speculated in land. The certificates granted the holder ownership of vast tracts of land throughout the Panhandle, most of it located in relationship to rivers. The purpose was to set the free enterprise system in motion, through speculators, and bring about settlement of public domain lands. A fact lost on no one was that the bids had been rigged to favor the supporters of influential politicians.

Jordan was outraged. In effect, crooked politicians had robbed him of the chance to bid on public domain lands. As he dug further into the records, he discovered that three companies had been awarded land certificates for the whole of the Texas Panhandle. The certificates were dated July 10, 1874, only days after it became known that the army would mount a massive campaign to drive the Comanche and other warlike tribes onto the reservation. The land speculators, scenting a windfall, had waited to exercise their bids until it became apparent the hostiles would be herded off the plains. Their patience was rewarded when *Llano Estacado* was transformed into the Texas Panhandle.

A crude map was included as part of the land records. Jordan saw that the Panhandle had been lopped into three sections, and land certificates issued for each section. One was for roughly half the area north of Palo Duro, encompassing a section bisected by the Canadian River and bordered on the west by New Mexico. A second section, also north of Palo Duro, covered the other half of lands along the Canadian, bordered on the east by Indian Territory. The third land certificate, which centered on the Prairie Dog Fork of the Red, encompassed a wide swath of plains that stretched westward from Indian Territory to the New Mexico border. Palo Duro Canyon, though unmarked on the map, traversed the eastern section of the grant.

The firm awarded the certificate was the Munson Land Company, located in Austin. The company was owned by one Gunter Munson, and there was no record that any of the land had as yet been sold. Jordan breathed a sigh of relief, thinking perhaps he was not too late. He rose from the table where he'd spread the records and walked to the clerk's desk. He nodded pleasantly.

"Are those records up to date?"

"As of yesterday," the clerk said. "No land transfers have come in today."

"Let me ask you," Jordan said without expression. "You know a man named Gunter Munson?"

The clerk laughed. "Watch yourself if you intend to trade with Gunter. He's been known to squeeze blood out of a turnip."

"Drives a hard bargain, does he?"

"Hard as nails," the clerk observed. "I take it you're interested in land out in the Panhandle?"

Jordan shrugged. "Only if I could get it at a decent price. That's lonesome country out there."

"You should check into the School Lands. The state will give you a better deal than Gunter Munson."

"What's school lands got to do with the Panhandle?"

The clerk explained that the state had retained alternate sections of land within the public domain grants. These sections were designated the School Lands, and were to be leased to private individuals, in an effort to encourage settlement. The funds raised under the leasing program were earmarked to improve and expand the public education system. The clerk produced another file, unfolding a map with a checkerboard grid displaying location of the School Lands. Too many sections to count were located within Palo Duro.

Jordan scanned the map. "How's a lease work?"

"You lease by the acre," the clerk said. "Depending on the amount of land, you could get it for eight to ten cents a year. That's per acre, of course."

"A section's six hundred forty acres." Jordan performed a mental calculation. "You're saying it could be leased for a tops of sixty-four dollars a year?"

"Well, keep in mind, the minimum term is ten years. As a rule, you have to pay two years in advance."

"Who do I talk to about a lease?"

Jordan was ushered into the office of Walter Walsh, the

State Land Commissioner. An hour was spent studying the crude map, with Jordan comparing it to the far more accurate map he carried in his head. Commissioner Walsh, with no idea why anyone would settle in the Panhandle, moved to close the deal. He offered Jordan the pick of the land for six cents an acre.

From the headwaters of the Red, Jordan selected 235 sections in a patchwork design that stretched far down the river. Walsh was puzzled by the scattered selection, but he refrained from asking questions. The total came to 150,400 acres, with lease payment of $90,240 over ten years, requiring two years in advance. Jordan wrote out a draft on the Denver National Bank for $18,048.

Early that afternoon Jordan entered the offices of the Munson Land Company. There were several land agents in the outer office, but he demanded to see the owner. When he mentioned the Panhandle, their resistance melted on the instant. He was shown into a private office at the rear.

Gunter Munson was a heavyset man, with florid features and sharp, beady eyes. His office was lushly appointed, with a large desk, leather wing chairs, and a thick carpet. He rose ponderously to his feet and shook Jordan's hand. His mouth creased in a benign smile.

"Please have a chair, Mr. Jordan. How may I help you?"

Jordan seated himself. "I understand you hold the land certificates on the Prairie Dog Fork of the Red River. I'm interested."

"Are you familiar with that part of the country, Mr. Jordan?"

"I rode through there a couple of times."

Munson unfurled a duplicate of the map in the Bureau of Records. He spread it across his desk. "Where, exactly, are your interests, Mr. Jordan? Perhaps you could show me on the map."

Jordan pretended confusion, as though disoriented by the map. All the while he was gauging location and distance, comparing it to the land he'd leased that morning. He finally jabbed at the map with a finger. "Along the upper part of the river."

"I see." Munson squinted at the map. "According to army reports, there is a large canyon in that area. I hear it's called Palo Duro."

"You hear right," Jordan told him. "That's Mexican for 'hard wood.' "

"I'll have to remember that. How much land are you interested in, Mr. Jordan?"

Jordan took a pencil off the desk. He began marking a crazy quilt of land, selecting from memory sections where the canyon was several miles across. He finally paused. "That ought to do it."

Munson revised his estimate of the man across the desk. "If I calculate correctly, you're talking about something on the order of a hundred thousand acres."

"Sounds about right."

"Are you a rancher, Mr. Jordan?"

"I intend to be," Jordan said. "Whether it's there or someplace else depends on the price you're asking."

"Well, that's prime land," Munson noted. "The current market value is a dollar twenty-five an acre."

"Too rich for my blood, Mr. Munson. I could do better up on the Canadian."

"I see you've been talking to my competitors." When Jordan just stared at him, Munson went on. "Tell you what I'll do, Mr. Jordan. If you pay the full amount today, I could let you have it at a dollar fifteen."

"Still too steep," Jordan said. "I'll give you fifty cents."

"No, that's out of the question. A dollar ten."

"You ought to take what you can get, Mr. Munson. You haven't sold any of that land since you bought it. I'll go sixty cents."

Munson suddenly realized that Jordan had checked the land records. "Let's compromise," he said smoothly. "A dollar an acre."

"Sixty-five."

"Ninety-five."

"Call it six bits and I'll write you a bank draft."

"Absolutely not!" Munson scoffed. "Ninety is my best deal. Take it or leave it."

"I'll leave it."

Jordan rose from his chair with a curt nod. Munson hesitated, wondering if it was a bluff. Then, as Jordan reached the door, he decided not to risk it. "Very well, Mr. Jordan, seventy-five cents. I must say you're practically stealing it at that price."

Jordan smiled. "Glad we could do business, Mr. Munson."

Not quite an hour later they signed a sales agreement. Jordan insisted that a copy of the map be made an exhibit to the contract. Finally, with the paperwork in order, he wrote a bank draft for $75,000. Munson was still staring at it when he walked out the door.

Uptown, Jordan recorded the sale at the land office. He waited until a deed was prepared, naming himself and John Adair as co-owners. On the street, walking toward the hotel, he could hardly contain himself. The papers in his pocket were for 250,400 acres, more than he'd ever dreamt possible as a start. Yet the patchwork design of the holdings seemed to him nothing short of divine inspiration. A barrier, he told himself, to lock out others. The critical first step.

Palo Duro Canyon was now secure.

CHAPTER 14

Jordan rode north to Palo Pinto County. The county seat was Golconda, a small town located a few miles south of the Brazos River. The countryside was hauntingly familiar, a place of distant memory and old landmarks. He had the odd sensation of traveling backward in time.

Outside Golconda was the original homestead where he had grown to manhood. Farther north was Black Springs, site of the first ranch he'd built following the Civil War. His parents, who were among the first settlers in the county, had passed away shortly after the war ended. Though he had no other family, he was struck by a deep sense of homecoming. The years seemed to melt away.

Palo Pinto County was situated in the heart of the Upper Cross Timbers. A forest belt of blackjack and post oak, the Cross Timbers extended south from the Red River far into the interior of Texas. The woods varied in width from a half mile to ten miles, and to the east and west were rolling prairies of grass. The land all along the Brazos was cattle country.

Golconda was the town where Jordan had signed on with the Rangers. To the west lay the frontier where he had spent years tracking raiding parties of the Comanche and other hostile tribes. Almost ten years ago, in partnership with Oliver Loving, he'd begun blazing cattle trails that took him to New Mexico, Colorado, and Wyoming.

All that was in the past, for he had not returned since the early years of the cattle drives. Yet, upon entering town, it was as though he'd stepped into yesterday.

The courthouse square seemed to have changed hardly at all. The store names were the same, and apart from improvements on the courthouse, everything was as Jordan remembered it. The town's one hotel was on the south side of the square, a two-story structure with a high false front. Hitching his horse out front, he collected his saddlebags and rifle and crossed the boardwalk. Lon Oxnard, the proprietor, stared at him curiously as he came through the door. Then the light of recognition dawned.

"Jack Jordan!" Oxnard whooped. "How the hell long's it been?"

"Too long," Jordan said, shaking his hand. "Good to see you again, Lon."

"What the deuce brings you back to Golconda?"

"Same old thing. Lookin' to buy some cows."

"Lots of those around," Oxnard said jovially. "You organizing another trail drive?"

Jordan shook his head. "I quit the trail quite a while ago. I'm interested in breeder stock."

"We heard you had a place up in Colorado. Somewhere around Pueblo, wasn't it?"

"That's old hat, Lon. Got myself a new spread."

"Yeah, whereabouts?"

"Over in the Panhandle," Jordan said. "Place called Palo Duro Canyon."

"The Panhandle?" Oxnard repeated quizzically. "I hadn't heard there was cattlemen up that way."

"News travels slow in those parts. I reckon I'm the first to settle there."

"Looks like you're still blazin' trails, after all, Jack. Nobody but you would settle in Injun country."

"Well, it's cow country now. The Comanche are gone, and I'm there to stay."

The word spread quickly around town. Jack Jordan, the Ranger scout and trailblazer, was a legend throughout Palo

Pinto County. Everyone was amazed, but hardly surprised, that he had established a ranch in the wilds of *Comancheria.* He seemed to them the one man who could unravel the mystery of *Llano Estacado.*

For the next week, Jordan crisscrossed the county like a mounted whirlwind. The news of his interest in cows preceded him, and ranchers were waiting to show him their herds. Everywhere he went one of the first questions asked was why he had settled in the Panhandle, which was still thought to be a wasteland. He stock reply was that buffalo had thrived there for centuries, and cows would fare equally well. He began referring to it as a "kingdom of grass."

The ranchers were all men he'd known from his years on the Brazos. They were skeptical about the Panhandle, and privately thought he should have settled elsewhere. But there was no resistance to the argument he put forward about selling breeder stock. Their ranges were overcrowded with cows, the result of a cattle market that hadn't yet fully recovered from the Panic of '73. They could wait for better times, or even risk trailing larger herds to Dodge City. Or they could sell to him for cash money.

The thought of cash in hand was a persuasive argument. A cow might fetch twenty-five dollars in Dodge City, Jordan noted, assuming market prices rose and remained steady. But the perils of the trail were known to all, and there was no certainty that Eastern cattle buyers would offer top dollar. The old adage that a bird in hand was worth two in the bush made eminently good sense to the ranchers of Palo Pinto County. Jordan refused to dicker, offering what he considered a fair price on the Brazos, twelve dollars a head. By the end of the week he had bought 12,000 cows.

Jordan was all too aware that he had overstepped the bounds of his agreement with John Adair. In all, including the lands leased and purchased, and the cows he'd bought, he had written bank drafts for $237,048. But then, at the time of their agreement, neither of them had envisioned acquiring the rights to a quarter million acres the first year. He wrote a long letter and mailed it from Golconda, explaining that they had accomplished in a matter of months the goal established for their second year of operations. Based on that logic, he had every confidence that Adair would replenish the dwindling bank account. Of the original amount, barely enough remained to properly outfit the JA spread.

To that end, Jordan spent a good part of the next week hiring cowhands. The task was especially difficult, for there were two obstacles that had to be overcome. The first was Palo Duro itself, located in the middle of nowhere and not all that appealing to men who enjoyed an occasional night on the town. The thought of no town within riding distance, and even worse, no women, was too much for most men. The second hurdle was Jordan's unbending rule that there was no gambling, no liquor, and no fighting in his outfit. Those who objected were bluntly advised of his code for keeping cow camps free of trouble.

"Whiskey, cards, and cows don't mix. You work for me, you stick to the rules."

The obstacles were offset in large degree by simple economics. A legion of cowhands had been reduced to saddletramps when ranches went under during the Panic of '73. They picked up a day's work here and there, but for the most part they were eager to find a steady job. All the more appealing, Jordan offered them "forty and found," ten dollars a month over the going wages. Given the hard times, there were men willing to try a monastic life in the wilds of Palo Duro. Toward the end of the week Jordan had hired fifty hands.

The next step was to get them mounted. In the course of three days, traveling as far east as Weatherford, he purchased a remuda of two hundred fifty horses. Working night and day, he also bought ten wagons, as many teams of mules, and adequate provisions to last through the spring. When he was finished, he figured the bank account in Denver had a balance of three or four dollars. Whether

Adair cursed him or commended him was a matter of only passing thought. He'd got the ranch off to a running start.

The cows were split into six herds, two thousand head to a herd. For trail bosses, Jordan promoted the most experienced hands, and increased their wages five dollars a month. Wagons and saddle stock were distributed among the crews, and on March 7, the first herd was started west along the Brazos. One day apart, the herds would take the trail, following a route laid out by Jordan. Their course was west to the Salt Fork of the Brazos, then northwest to the Pease, and from there, due north to the plains below the Canadian. There, turning west, they would arrive at the road into Palo Duro. The drive, barring mishaps, would cover some three hundred miles in three weeks.

Over the next several days, Jordan wore out several horses riding the backtrail. He made sure the herds got under way, and slowly gained confidence in the men he'd selected as trail bosses. Finally, satisfied that all was in order, he appointed relay riders to drift from herd to herd, and keep the separated columns on course. The fifth day out, he overtook the lead herd late at night, some five miles east of the Salt Fork. When he stepped down from the saddle, he at first thought everyone had retired to their bedrolls. Then he saw two men seated in the shadows of the campfire, a bottle passing between them. One of the men quickly thrust the bottle behind his back.

"You there!" Jordan said, striding forward. "What's your name?"

"Baker," the man replied in a gruff voice. "Clell Baker."

"I told you there'd be no whiskey in my camps."

"Little nip now and then never hurt nobody. I get my work done."

"Which one of you brought that bottle along?"

Baker glanced at the other man, then shrugged. "Don't fault him none. I brung it."

"You're fired," Jordan said curtly. "Pack your gear and get out of camp."

"Tonight?" Baker climbed to his feet. "Who the hell you think you are, anyway? Nobody puts a man on the trail at night."

"Let's not have any argument. Get moving."

"You lousy sonovabitch!"

Baker suddenly launched a haymaker. The punch caught Jordan above the eye and drove him back a couple of steps. As he regained his balance, Baker waded in with a looping roundhouse right. Jordan slipped the blow and buried his fist in the other man's belly. Baker folded at the midsection, gasping for breath.

Jordan coolly measured him. Before Baker could straighten up, he unleashed a splintering left-right combination. The blows flattened Baker's nose and opened a cut over his brow. His knees buckled, and a final hard, clubbing right dropped him on the ground. He was out cold.

A rider appeared out of the darkness. Jordan turned and saw Jud Mitchell, the man he had promoted to trail boss. Mitchell swung out of the saddle and hurried forward, looking from Jordan to the fallen man. His features were squinched in bafflement.

"Mr. Jordan," he said tentatively. "What's happened here?"

The other hands, awakened by the fight, were standing in their bedrolls. Jordan rubbed the angry welt over his left eye. "Where've you been, Mitchell?"

"I was out checking the herd."

"Did you know there was whiskey in your camp?"

"No, sir." Mitchell groaned. "Honest to God, Mr. Jordan, I stuck by your orders. Baker must've been sneakin' drinks when I wasn't around."

Jordan scrutinized him with a hard stare. "We'll let it pass this time," he said. "But if it happens again, you're out of a job. I won't have a trail boss who can't control his men."

"There won't be no second time, Mr. Jordan. You can bank on it."

"Get Baker mounted and on his way. I want him out of camp tonight."

Jordan walked to the river. He squatted down, dipping a kerchief in the water, and pressed the cold cloth to his forehead. Behind him there was a low murmur as the men began recounting what they'd seen of the fight. The consensus was that it would be unwise to tangle with the man who paid their wages. Orders were orders, clearly meant to be followed.

There would be no drinking on the JA.

The first herd was trailed into Palo Duro on March 23. Jordan led the way into the canyon, with point riders holding the cows to a sedate walk. The cows were skittish at the top of the escarpment, but gradually fell into a shuffling column on the road downward. The men brought them to the bottom in a slow, smooth descent.

Leigh Dyer and the regular hands rode forward to meet them. Jordan explained there were six herds in all, being trailed one day apart. After a brief discussion, it was decided the herds would be spaced easterly along the canyon, separated one from the other by at least a mile. John Poe was sent uptrail to lead the second herd into Palo Duro.

Jordan turned the operation over to Dyer, and rode downstream. In the distance, he saw that the walls of the Adair stone house were completed, and work had started on the roof. As he approached the corral, the door of the log house flew open and Rebecca ran into the yard. He waved, reining to a halt, and stepped out of the saddle. She threw herself into his arms.

"Oh, Jack!" she cried, peppering him with kisses. "I was worried out of my mind. Are you all right?"

"Fit as a fiddle," Jordan said, his arms around her waist. "I generally manage to get back in one piece."

"But you've been gone six weeks. Six whole weeks! I began imagining the most terrible things."

"Well, I had lots to get done. Take a look at that herd

up the canyon. There's five more just like it headed this way."

"You didn't!" she said, astonished. "You bought six herds?"

"Twelve thousand head." Jordan grinned proudly. "Hired fifty new hands, too. We're on our way to big things."

"Good Lord, what will John Adair say? You were only supposed to buy five thousand cows this year."

"I wrote him a letter that'll smooth everything over. He's gonna purr like a cat."

"What was in your letter?"

Jordan spread his arms to the sky. "Becky, we've as good as bought this whole goddamn canyon. We'll own it sunrise to sunset."

She looked up at him. "You're serious, aren't you?"

"Tell you what I'm really serious about."

"Oh?"

"I need a bath." Jordan put his arm around her shoulders. "How'd you like to scrub my back?"

"Why, Mr. Jordan, I believe you missed me."

"One way to find out."

They walked toward the house.

CHAPTER 15

The Platte was at floodtide. Winter melt from an April sun sent water cascading down from the Rockies. The streets of Denver were a quagmire, ankle-deep in mud, and traffic slowed to a crawl. Springtime, eagerly awaited, was no time to venture forth afoot.

The northbound train chugged to a halt outside the depot. Jordan stepped off the middle passenger coach and walked to the end of the stationhouse. He tossed his warbag into a cab for hire and gave the driver his destination, the Windsor Hotel. The buggy moved off slowly, wheels churning mud, and he sat back in the seat. He idly pondered Adair's reaction to his telegram. The thought made him smile.

Three weeks ago, Jordan had decided that a trip to Denver was in order. The herds were settled in the canyon, and Leigh Dyer was capable of looking after the ranch. There were matters weighing in the balance, and Jordan wasn't content to await Adair's spring visit to Palo Duro. All the more so since he was in a rush to move his plans ahead, and the next step would require a considerable sum of money. He concluded there was nothing to be gained in biding his time, for sooner was better than later. He would go to Adair.

Rebecca was thrilled when he told her. The prospect of visiting her parents, and all her friends, left her giddy with excitement. They departed a few days later, accompanied by John Poe and three hands, along with a wagon. Their trek across *Llano Estacado* proved uneventful, and brought them finally to Trinidad. From there, they took the train to Pueblo, where Rebecca's parents greeted her like someone returned from the dead. Jordan stayed one night, wiring ahead to Adair, and caught a train the next morning to Denver. Poe and the hands were left to enjoy themselves in Pueblo.

Uptown, Jordan told the cab driver to wait. He checked into the hotel, leaving his warbag at the desk, and hurried back outside. His telegram had requested an afternoon appointment, and he figured the earlier the better. A short while later the cab deposited him outside the office building on Larimer Street. Upstairs, in the brokerage house, he was ushered immediately into Adair's office. He was prepared for a cool reception.

"Well, well," Adair said with an indifferent handshake. "Have you come all this way to make amends?"

"For what?" Jordan tossed his hat on the desk. "All I've done is drop another fortune in your lap."

"Have you, indeed? The last time I looked, our bank balance was in arrears. How does that improve my fortune?"

"In Dodge City, those twelve thousand cows would more than double our money. You want me to put them on the trail?"

Adair was again taken by his audacity. "You've more gall than any man this side of Dublin. The cows apart, how do you explain the debt we've incurred for land?"

"I told you all about that in my letter."

"Your letter was a tad short on details. Perhaps you could enlighten me further."

"Always glad to oblige, partner."

Jordan pulled a map from his inside coat pocket. He spread it across the desk, revealing the land bureau's checkerboard grids covering Palo Duro. With his finger, he traced darkened squares along the Prairie Dog Fork of the Red.

"These squares are called sections. Every section has six-hundred forty acres. We've bought or leased two hundred thirty-five sections—"

"Yes, I know," Adair interrupted. "I got that much from your letter. As I recall, a quarter million acres."

"Forget the acres," Jordan said. "Look at the way our sections are positioned along the canyon."

Adair peered at the map. "So?"

"We control the widest parts of the canyon. The spots with the most graze and the broader stretches of the river. Nobody in his right mind would settle on the sections in between."

"I fail to take your point."

"Why, it's simple, John. We've got the prime land, and we *own* the headwaters of the Red. Any jaybird tries to run cows in there, we could make his life plumb miserable."

"Ummm." Adair studied the map a moment longer. "You're saying these other sections are now worthless to anyone else. How were you able to put that over on the people in Austin?"

Jordan smiled. "They've never even seen the canyon. I knew it like the back of my hand. Nobody's got the least notion I took the choice parcels."

"What happens when they finally wake up?"

"We'll have them by the short hairs. With nobody else to sell to, they'll have to sell at our price. Give me a year and we'll own the whole of Palo Duro."

Adair barked a short laugh. "By all that's holy!" he said. "You've pulled off a grand scheme, Jack. I'm impressed."

"Glad to hear it," Jordan remarked. "'Course, all that's just the first step. We've got to move on to other things."

"I take it that's what brings you to Denver. Are these 'other things' going to cost me money?"

"Call it an investment in the future of the JA Ranch. I think we ought to consider buying some blooded stock."

"By blooded stock, do you mean purebred cattle?"

Jordan nodded. "I figured on Herefords. Lots of them right here in Colorado, imported from England. They're our ticket to improved bloodlines."

"Aren't longhorns adequate?" Adair asked. "Why do we need to improve the bloodlines?"

"Longhorns are tough range cows. They'll eat anything and last the course on trail drives. But they're not the future of the cattle business."

"How so?"

"Shy on weight," Jordan said. "Herefords are heavier and they're bigger boned. Cross the two breeds and you've got the best of both worlds. A cow that'll produce more meat even on open range."

"Granted," Adair agreed. "However, a breeding program of that nature requires several years. We're now discussing an extremely long-term investment."

"That's what we've been talking about all along. Neither one of us got in it for the fast kill."

"Yes, that's true, Jack. On the other hand, why invest further when a ready market exists for longhorns?"

"There's a market today," Jordan conceded. "But ten years from now people will demand higher quality beef. That's why ranchers have started importing purebred stock. We've got to look to the future."

Adair was silent a moment. "I assume you came with a proposal in mind. Tell me about it."

"I figured we'd start off slow. Maybe a hundred bulls—"

"A hundred!"

"—and a couple of hundred cows."

"Have you an idea of the cost?"

"In round numbers," Jordan ventured, "maybe thirty thousand."

"Not to mention operating expenses for the ranch. So

you're asking me to invest another hundred thousand. Correct?''

''That ought to cover it.''

Adair rolled his eyes. ''You're lucky I admire a man with brass. I'll have the bank transfer the funds.''

''By the way,'' Jordan said in an offhand manner. ''Your stone house is finished. Turned out real nice.''

''Did it, now? Cornealia and I were planning a visit toward the end of May. She'll be pleased with the news.''

''I'll have a couple of the boys meet you in Trinidad. You'd best bring along a wagonload of furniture. Lots of empty rooms to fill.''

Adair laughed. ''That will cost me another pretty penny. Cornealia never does anything by half measures.''

''Neither do you,'' Jordan said, grinning. ''Guess that's why I picked you for a partner.''

''Jack, you've blarney enough for a dozen Irishmen. Will you have supper with us tonight?''

''Hell, John, thought you'd never ask.''

Later, after Jordan was gone, Adair sat staring out the window at the Rockies. He was amazed, and not a little amused, that he'd let himself be persuaded so easily on the matter of additional funds. But then, on further reflection, he was reminded that a wise investor took the long-term view.

Jack Jordan was his investment in the future.

The journey home was slowed by the Herefords. Unlike longhorns, their tender hooves were ill-suited to the rough terrain on a trail drive. Worse, they were massive in breadth, slung low to the ground, and not built for speed. A good day seldom covered more than ten miles.

Jordan and Rebecca rode out front. Poe and two of the hands alternated between flank and drag, hazing stragglers back into the herd. The wagon, driven by the third hand, lumbered along some distance to the rear. Apart from added provisions, five windows, crated in sturdy boxes, were stored aboard the wagon. One, when installed in the log house, would give Rebecca a second view of the canyon. Three were meant for the Adairs' home, and the last would let sunlight into the bunkhouse.

Three weeks had elapsed since Jordan's trip to Denver. With Poe and the hands, he'd spent two weeks scouring Colorado for Herefords, and dickering on price. By train, the herd had been transported to Pueblo, and then trailed east along the Arkansas. Four days on the trail had done nothing to diminish Jordan's sense of accomplishment; he spent half his day turned in the saddle, admiring the Herefords. Their distinctive rusty-red coats and white faces were visible for miles across the open plains.

Rebecca likened her husband's exuberance to that of a boy let loose in a candy store. She shared his happiness, though there was a curiously mixed quality to her own feelings. She had reveled in the social whirl of Pueblo, lionized by her friends as an intrepid pioneer woman. Yet, however sad the parting from her parents, she found herself anxious to begin the return journey. Colorado seemed a pleasant interlude, but strangely lacking the vitality of wilderness life. Her greatest revelation was that she missed the canyon, and the ranch. Palo Duro was now her home.

Late that afternoon she noticed a change in Jordan's manner. All in a matter of minutes he seemed watchful, somehow on guard. His gaze continually swept the plains, and she sensed a mounting tension. The look on his face frightened her.

"Jack, what is it? What's wrong?"

"We're being followed."

Her eyes darted around in alarm. "I don't see anyone."

"They're out there," Jordan said. "I feel them."

"What do you mean, you *feel* them?"

Jordan couldn't explain it. His years on the plains, living among wild things, had instilled in him an instinct too sharp to ignore. He had survived on countless occasions by sensing something out of the ordinary, something unnatural. Today was one of those times.

"No questions," he said firmly. "Just do like I tell you.

First sign of trouble, stay close and stay behind me. Keep a tight rein on your horse.''

''Yes, of course, I understand.''

Jordan pulled his Winchester from the saddle scabbard. He stood in the stirrups, turning to the rear, and waved the carbine overhead. The signal caught the attention of Poe and the other men, put them on instant alert. A moment later they all had their carbines in hand.

Off to the north, a sage hen suddenly fluttered skyward. Hardly had the bird taken wing than five riders boiled out of a ravine hidden by the rolling plains. Some fifty yards away, they spurred their horses and thundered forward, pistols popping in a ragged valley. Lead sizzled through the air with a low whining buzz.

The herd bolted, spooked by the gunfire, wheeling away to the south. Jordan brought the Winchester to his shoulder, sighting on the lead rider, and fired. The impact of the slug hammered the man from his saddle, and he pitched sideways to the ground. To the rear, Poe and the other hands cut loose in a drumming tattoo with their carbines. A second man tumbled onto the grassy plain, then a third.

The last two riders sawed on the reins, hauling their horses about, and pounded off to the west. Jordan dismounted, motioning to Poe, who immediately jumped from his saddle. They took solid standing positions, Winchesters at their shoulders, sighting on the distant riders. The sharp crack of Jordan's Winchester was followed a split second later by the report of Poe's carbine. One of the riders threw up his arms, falling from the saddle, and the other struck the ground in a dusty heap. Their horses barreled onward across the plains.

''Crazy devils!'' Poe shouted. ''Why'd they come at us like that?''

''Make sure they're dead,'' Jordan called back. ''You and the boys check 'em out.''

Poe mounted, leading the hands forward at a lope. Jordan stepped into the saddle, still watchful, the butt of the carbine resting on his thigh. Rebecca appeared stunned, somewhat unnerved by the brutal suddeness of death. She had never seen a man killed, certainly not five in a span of seconds. Her voice was tremulous.

"Why did they attack us like that? You didn't answer Poe."

"Night raid wouldn't work," Jordan said flatly. "Herefords are slow on the trail, and they knew we'd track 'em down within a few hours. They had to kill us all."

"For a herd of cows?" she said, shocked. "Kill us just for that?"

"Word gets around about a herd worth thirty thousand on the hoof. Those bastards would've killed us for a lot less, and no second thoughts. You included."

"Was that why you shot the men trying to escape . . . because of me?"

"Yeah, partly." Jordan hesitated, then went on. "There were other reasons, too."

She looked at him. "What other reasons?"

"Becky, I've got a rule I live by. When a man tries to kill me, I don't leave any loose ends. He might try again."

There was a prolonged silence. She thought the rule he lived by was unbelievably cruel, almost barbaric in a way. But then, on deeper reflection, she saw that it was infinitely practical, perhaps the only way in a land without law. At length, amazed at herself, she decided that events sometimes dictated no other choice.

"Jack, would you teach me to use a gun?"

"I think that'd be a good idea. Might come in handy sometime."

Jordan rode off when the men finished checking the bodies. They circled south across the plains and began collecting the scattered herd. Rebecca waited by the wagon, still somewhat shaken by what she'd seen. Her eyes strayed to the distant bodies, the last two men killed. The thought occurred that her husband was not only right, but entirely justified.

They would never return to try again.

PART TWO

CHAPTER 16

Bloodgold shafts of light hovered on the western horizon. Twilight crept slowly across the canyon, and a soft breeze feathered the leaves on cottonwoods along the river. There was a stillness across the land, a time when the earth and all its creatures awaited the coming of night.

Jordan was partial to evening, in the way a nighthawk comes alive with darkness. With the day's work done, waiting for Rebecca to serve supper, he often took a seat in one of the cane-bottomed rockers on the porch. For him, it was a peaceful time of day, a time of reflection and weighing plans for the future. The challenge of the days ahead always seemed to him a logical extension of the past. He thought 1876 would be the turning point for the JA.

A year ago, almost to the day, he had trailed the Herefords into the canyon. The bulls had been placed on selected ranges with longhorn brood stock, and the cows had been bred to longhorn bulls. The initial phase of the breeding program, mixing blooded stock with range stock, would soon become apparent. Toward the end of April, less than a week away, he expected the first drop of calves.

The past year had also brought about rapid expansion of the JA spread. Jordan's original plan, designed to block others from settling in Palo Duro, had worked much as he'd predicted. Gunter Munson, the Austin land speculator, had awakened to the fact that the JA, for all practical purposes, controlled the canyon. Jordan had purchased another 125,000 acres, and leased an additional 125,000 acres of School Land. The ranch now encompassed slightly more than a half million acres.

John Adair, as good as his word, had provided funding for the expansion. Over the last year Jordan had increased the longhorn herd to more than 50,000 head. There were now almost a hundred hands on the payroll, and permanent line camps had been established nearly the length of the canyon. The camps generally bordered creeks, with log bunkhouses for a crew of five or six men, including a cook. Provisions to supply the operation were freighted from Trinidad once a month, hauled overland by a caravan of wagons.

Under Jordan's direction, the headquarters compound had been transformed into an oasis of civilization. Water was now supplied through iron pipes connected to the natural spring on the slope above the main house. A separate cook house and mess hall had been built, with two cooks feeding the twenty men quartered in the bunkhouse. Across the way, the Adairs' stone house stood in stately contrast to the log structures, and a warehouse had been built to stock provisions. The Adairs usually visited the ranch in May and again in late September or early October.

Tonight, as dusk settled over the canyon, Jordan ruminated on the months ahead. After a year and a half, the JA was at last ready to begin marketing cattle. Until now, all his efforts had been directed to acquiring land, building the ranch, and stocking the herds. But in late May, he planned to start the first of four herds on a drive to the railhead at Dodge City. Once again, though he was vaguely familiar with the country north of the Canadian, he would be blazing a trail through unsettled wilderness. The prospect of exploring new lands rekindled old fires, and left him enthused to get on with the project. He was ready to hit the trail.

Jordan chuckled to himself, thinking that John Adair

was even more eager to get the trail drives under way. By now, Adair had more than $500,000 invested in the ranch, and he was anxious to see a return on his money. Fortunately, the timing was excellent, for cattle prices were climbing steadily, driven by increasing demand for beef in Eastern markets. Jordan was convinced that the investment in time, effort, and money would soon result in a payoff of handsome proportions. He meant to get top dollar in Dodge City.

"Jack, I have supper on the table."

Rebecca stood in the doorway, an apron stretched taut over her stomach. She was seven months pregnant, and looked as though she might give birth to twins at any moment. Jordan believed her more beautiful than ever, with an aura of radiance he attributed to oncoming motherhood. He was wildly excited by the thought of being a father.

Unfolding from the rocker, he walked to the door. "How's our boy?" he said, gently rubbing a hand over her stomach. "Acting lively today, is he?"

"Kicking like a horse," she said in an uneven tone. "So I suppose you're right about it being a boy. A girl wouldn't do that to her mother."

"All depends on whether she's got her mother's spirit. 'Course, I still think it's a boy."

"Let's eat before supper gets cold."

Rebecca waddled to the table. She felt bloated and ungainly, so unattractive that she'd come to detest mirrors. Worse, she was convinced that her husband found her unattractive, perhaps even ugly. His attempts to humor her were appreciated, and he went out of his way to be attentive. Still, she was unable to put aside the thought that he no longer found her appealing.

Jordan heaped his plate with steak, and vegetables from their stock of tinned goods. His days were spent checking outlying line camps, and he was famished after a hard day in the saddle. He began larding jam on a slice of warm sourdough bread, watching as Rebecca fixed her plate and poured herself a glass of milk. Upon learning she was pregnant, he had imported a milch cow all the way from Colorado. The hands, thoroughly shamed by such a lowly chore, took turns milking the cow.

"Have to say it again." Jordan tore off a chunk of bread, chewed with relish. "You could outbake Mose any day of the week."

She smiled, pleased with the compliment. "How was your day? Anything newsworthy?"

"Just getting things squared away for roundup. Calves ought to start droppin' any day now."

"You're excited to see them, aren't you? The Hereford calves, I mean."

"Yeah, I am." Jordan munched beefsteak, suddenly grinned. " 'Course, I'm lots more excited about the little one you're carrying. How you feelin'?"

"Like one of your cows," she said with an amused expression. "I keep getting bigger and broader."

"Well, it won't be that much longer. June's not all that far off."

"You wouldn't think so if you looked like a cow. I wish it were tomorrow."

Jordan reached across the table, took her hand. "You could get big as a barn and you'd still be the apple of my eye. Don't be so hard on yourself."

She squeezed his hand. "I hope you mean that. Sometimes it just seems—"

The thud of hooves outside interrupted her. A moment later footsteps sounded on the porch and there was a sharp rap at the door. Jordan rose from the table, quickly crossing the room, and lifted the door latch. Leigh Dyer stood in the spill of lamplight, a grin plastered across his face.

"We've got neighbors!" he blurted out. "Somebody's started a ranch up on the Canadian. Met 'em myself not three hours—"

"Slow down," Jordan said, motioning him through the doorway. "Give it to me from the beginning."

"Evenin', Miz Jordan." Dyer doffed his hat, went on

in a loud voice. "I was up at the Rush Creek line camp and run acrost a strange rider. Says he works for the Circle B outfit."

"Never heard of them."

"Owned by a fellow name of Sam Bugbee. Had a ranch down south of San Antonio. Sold it off and moved his outfit up here."

"How long's he been there?"

"Near on a month," Dyer said. "Got his headquarters on the bend where the Canadian swings northeast."

"Good spot," Jordan observed. "Any idea how many head he's running?"

"Close to twenty thousand. Leastways, that's what his hand says."

"Sounds like he's here to stay. How much range does he have?"

"Way his hand talked, it's about three hundred thousand acres. Most of it east along the Canadian."

"By God!" Jordan said, clearly pleased. "I'm glad we finally got ourselves a neighbor. I'll have to ride up and meet this Sam Bugbee."

Dyer nodded. "He already knows we're here in the canyon. From what his hand says, the word's spread all over Texas."

"Wouldn't surprise me in the least, Leigh."

After Dyer was gone, Jordan rejoined Rebecca at the table. His features split in a wide smile. "What do you think? Happy we're not off by our lonesome anymore?"

"I'm thrilled," she said. "Although it's what, forty miles away? That's hardly a neighbor."

"Closest thing to it out here in the Panhandle."

"I wonder if he has a wife . . . and family."

"Honey, I'm damn sure fixin' to find out. I'll head that way first thing tomorrow."

Rebecca took a long sip of milk. Any neighbor, she told herself, was better than no neighbor at all. Even one a two-day ride from Palo Duro.

She offered a small prayer that Sam Bugbee was a married man.

A log house overlooked the Canadian. Set back away from the river, the main house was flanked by storage sheds to the east and a crude bunkhouse to the west. A herd of some fifty horses grazed on a plain shaded by cottonwoods.

Jordan rode into the compound as the sun dipped westward. For the past two days he had spotted scattered herds of longhorns ranging southward, guarded by Circle B riders working out of line camps. The ranch headquarters, well situated and stoutly built, merely reinforced his original hunch. Whoever ran the outfit knew his business.

The door of the main house opened as he stepped out of the saddle. The man who walked forward to meet him was tall and beefy, with the bowed legs and slim hips of a lifelong horseman. His features were weathered by sun and wind, and a handlebar mustache covered his mouth like a bird's nest. He nodded pleasantly.

"Howdy," he said. "Welcome to the Circle B."

"You must be Sam Bugbee. I'm Jack Jordan, from the JA, down on Palo Duro."

"Glad to make your acquaintance." Bugbee shook his hand with a firm grip. "Would've paid you a call, but we've been a mite busy gettin' things squared away. Heard about you in Austin, when I made a deal for the land."

Jordan laughed. "Some folks might say I got the best of those city boys. Hope it worked out as well for you."

"Saw what you'd done when I checked the records at the land bureau. 'Course, I was dealin' with another speculator, but I just followed what you'd laid out. Leased some School Lands, and then beat down the price on what I bought."

"What decided you on the Panhandle?"

"All this grass." Bugbee gestured out across the plains. "Beats the hell outta the place I had down on the Nueces."

"Good cow country," Jordan agreed. "I've been hoping somebody else would settle here. I'm pleased to have you as a neighbor.''

''Feeling's mutual, especially where you're concerned. Christ, I've been hearing about your trailblazing for years.''

''Gettin' ready to blaze another one, come June. Figured I'd scout the easiest way to Dodge City.''

''Damnnation!'' Bugbee cackled. ''You just took a load off my shoulders. I aim to trail a couple of herds to railhead myself.''

''I'm taking four,'' Jordan said. ''We'll lay out a path you could follow in the dark.''

''That's the best news I've had in a month of Sundays.''

''So you'd have no objection if I cross your land with my herds?''

''No objection at all,'' Bugbee affirmed. ''You bring 'em right along. Listen, how'd you like to stay the night? The missus and I'd be proud to have you.''

''I'm obliged,'' Jordan said. ''Fact is, my wife will be glad to hear you're married. She misses womenfolk.''

''Well, come on inside and meet Martha.''

Martha Bugbee was a plump woman with a quick smile and an easy disposition. She and Bugbee had four children, ages three through eight, and their manners indicated that she ruled the house with a strong hand. Over supper she drew Jordan out about Rebecca and their life in Palo Duro. His description of the canyon held Bugbee and the children spellbound.

''A thousand feet deep,'' Bugbee marveled. ''Lord, that must be a sight.''

''Door's always open,'' Jordan said. ''You folks will have to pay us a visit. Becky would be tickled pink.''

''Count on it,'' Bugbee assured him. ''Maybe after we get done with the trail drives.''

''I'd like to meet your Becky,'' Martha added. ''When did you say the baby was due?''

''Way she calculates, it'll be sometime toward the end of June.''

"Have her get word to me when the time comes. First baby and all, she might need help with the delivery."

"That's mighty good of you to offer. She'd feel easier with another woman there."

The children, three boys and a girl, listened with rapt attention. The older boy, fidgeting with excitement, waited for a pause in the adult conversation. He scooted forward in his chair, his eyes fixed on Jordan.

"Mister, how far down's a thousand feet?"

Jordan knuckled his mustache. He suppressed a smile, aware that it was a serious question for the youngster. "Son, how tall are you?"

The boy's chest swelled. "Nearabouts five feet."

"Well, if you stepped off into the canyon"—Jordan held his gaze—"figure you'd tumble over a couple of hundred times before you hit bottom."

"Goldarn." The boy gulped, eyes round as buttons. "Makes you dizzy just thinkin' about it."

Jordan chuckled. "Son, I've been dizzy since the first time I saw it."

CHAPTER 17

The Adairs arrived the third week of May. John and Cornealia were mounted, and they were accompanied by two JA hands. On the long journey across *Llano Estacado,* Cape Willingham had acted as their guide and game hunter. Jud Mitchell drove the wagon loaded with provisions and camp gear.

Their descent along the road into Palo Duro brought exclamations of wonder from Cornealia. The canyon was in the midst of spring bloom, and the land was a rainbow of nature's most brilliant colors. Sagebrush was covered with purple flowers, and yucca was clustered with yellow bells shaped like lanterns. The canyon floor was ablaze with buttercups, larkspur, bluebells, and a vast array of other wildflowers. White moths floated in dazzling, snowy clouds all along the river.

"Oh, John," Cornealia said breathlessly. "It's more spectacular every time we come here. Look at those walls!"

"Aye," Adair agreed, no less awed. "Truly a piece of God's handiwork."

Throughout eons of time nature had slowly eroded the vast fissure of Palo Duro. The walls of the canyon were layered with rock formations, stacked one on top of the other to the height of the caprock. The bottom of the palisades were a startling blend of red clays intermixed with white strips of gypsum. Higher up, shale and sandstone rose along the battlements in bands of purple, gold, and pink. The sun, dipping westward, cast orange flame across the sheer walls. The effect was a dazzling explosion of colors that left the senses reeling.

Adair shook his head, staring upward. "In many ways, I envy Jack and Rebecca. There's a touch of paradise to this place."

"Yes, there is," Cornealia said in a soft voice. "Although I have to say it would drive us to distraction to live here the year round. We are much too citified for the wilderness life."

"No, my dear," Adair corrected her. "We're too much the snobs for Palo Duro. In a word, too spoiled."

"Honestly, John, there is nothing wrong with being spoiled. I rather like it."

"All the same, I still envy our friends. What they have here cannot be valued in money alone. Some wise man once said that serenity has no price."

"Oh, for mercy's sake! You sound like a parlor room philosopher."

Adair laughed, pointing ahead to where Jordan and Rebecca waited outside the stone house. Their reunion was one of spirited cordiality and warm friendship. The house had been aired out in anticipation of the Adairs' spring visit, the furniture dusted and the hardwood floors polished to a sheen. While the hands unloaded the wagon, Rebecca linked arms with Cornealia and walked her toward the log house. Jordan fell in beside Adair.

"You're just in time for supper, John. I only rode in a few minutes ago myself."

"We're in luck, then," Adair said jovially. "Rebecca always sets a fine table."

"How was your trip?"

"Well, by now we're veterans of the trail. We managed splendidly."

The women went inside the house. Jordan motioned to one of the rockers on the porch, and took the other for himself. Adair clipped the end off a cigar, lighting it, and puffed a cloud of smoke. His eyes roved out across the canyon.

"A beautiful sight, indeed," he said, pointing with his cigar to a distant herd of cattle. "I trust our cows are thriving on all that spring grass?"

"Fat as pigs," Jordan replied. "We started roundup a week ago today. You'll like what you see."

"Have the Herefords done as well as you'd hoped?"

"Goddamnedest thing anybody ever saw. Hereford bull with a longhorn cow, or vice versa, all works out the same. We got ourselves some chunky calves, regular little butterballs."

"I'm delighted to hear it," Adair said. "Perhaps we'll realize a profit, after all."

"We're on the way," Jordan allowed. "I figure to trail eight thousand head to railhead next month. Probably double that number before the season's over."

"What sum might we be talking about? In round numbers?"

"Depends on the market. Four hundred thousand, maybe more."

Adair wedged the cigar in the corner of his mouth. "Jack, I like your way with figures. You've done a grand job, indeed."

"Told you we'd make money," Jordan said. "Hell, we've only just got started. There're good times ahead."

"My friend, I never doubted it for a moment."

Inside the house, Cornealia set four places at the table while Rebecca busied herself at the stove. The windows were open, but the heat from the wood-burning stove made the room uncomfortably warm. Cornealia noted a light film of perspiration on Rebecca's forehead.

"In your condition—" Cornealia nodded pointedly to her swollen stomach. "You really should have the cook prepare your meals and bring them over here. All this heat isn't good for you."

"Why, it's only May," Rebecca said lightly. "Wait until July or August. Now, that's hot!''

''Yes, but you're what, a month away from having the baby? Seriously, you shouldn't be slaving over a hot stove.''

''Oh, it doesn't bother me. Besides, I prefer my own cooking to what Mose fixes for the men.''

''I can understand that,'' Cornealia said. ''How are you feeling, generally?''

''So healthy it's absolutely disgusting. I just wish I weren't so big. I feel awkward as an ox.''

''Well, you look wonderful. I must say pregnancy agrees with you.''

''I know,'' Rebecca admitted. ''I must be one of those women made to have babies.''

Cornealia smiled ruefully. ''I wish I could say that about myself. John and I try—oh, how we try!—but nothing happens.''

''Jack and I went through the same thing for several months after we were married. But you musn't ever give up hope. Just keep trying.''

''Never fear, I give John no choice in the matter. I wonder he doesn't think me a hussy.''

Rebecca opened the oven to a blast of heat. She removed a fresh loaf of bread and set it to stay warm on the back of the stove. ''I wish you could stay until the baby is born.''

''Oh, I do, too!'' Cornealia said. ''But John couldn't possibly be away from his business that long.'' She paused, idly adjusting silverware. ''How will you manage out here by yourself . . . the delivery?''

''I haven't had a chance to tell you. We finally have neighbors, a rancher and his wife, up on the Canadian River. Mrs. Bugbee has four children of her own, and Jack says she's a very capable woman. She offered to help when my time comes.''

''How nice of her,'' Cornealia said. ''Although I seem to recall the Canadian is two or three days from here. How will she know the right time?''

"Don't worry." Rebecca blew a damp lock of hair off her forehead. "I'll send one of the men to get her a week before I'm due. Everything will work out fine."

"You really should allow extra time. Babies have been known to come early."

"Call it female intuition, but I somehow know there won't be any problems. I'm just so happy I'll have another woman with me."

Cornealia hoped the optimism was well placed. But then, on second thought, her concern slipped away. Over time, she had watched a demure city girl become a strong, self-reliant pioneer woman. The transformation had been remarkable, a feat that impressed her beyond words.

She thought Rebecca would manage the situation with optimism to spare.

Jordan and Adair sat their horses on a small rise watching the operation below. Older calves, the ones birthed in early spring, were cut out from the herd and roped. The catch rider then dragged the blatting calves to a small fire.

Five men, one handling a white-hot branding iron, swarmed over the calves. Within a couple of minutes they were branded and earmarked, and the bull calves were castrated. Afterward, somewhat altered in appearance but no worse for wear, they scooted off searching for their mama cows. The operation was swift, with no wasted motion.

"Highly efficient," Adair remarked. "A fine example of teamwork."

"Only way," Jordan noted. "Every man to his job and they all pull together. Otherwise it'd be a goddamn circus."

Adair had attended last year's spring and fall roundups. Yet he was all the more impressed by the sheer size of this year's operation. Their day had started at sunrise, and by late afternoon they had inspected the gathers being conducted by the crews of three line camps. The roundup was the first step to organizing the summer trail drives.

Across a wide stretch of grassland a herd of close to

five hundred head had been gathered. Some of the hands were still combing tributary canyons for range stock and spring calves, and the gather would continue for a week or so. Seven other crews were working different parts of the JA, separating breeder stock from steers and older cows intended for market. Once the roundup was completed, four herds of two thousand head each would have been assembled for the trail drive to Dodge City.

The eight line camps scattered around the JA were of particular interest to Adair. It struck him again that the overall operation resembled a military organization, with outposts throughout the canyon. "Tell me," he said. "What determined the location of your line camps?"

"Graze and water," Jordan informed him. "I blocked off sections with creeks running through good grassland. Got roughly eight thousand head under each line camp."

"How did you select the foremen of the line camps?"

"There's only one foreman, Leigh Dyer. Line camps are run by bosses, generally a top hand. 'Course, he's got to be able to manage men. Command their respect."

Adair understood by now that a "top hand" was one who excelled in all aspects of working cattle. From that, he earned the respect of the other men, and perhaps a promotion to boss of a line camp. The chain of command extended upward to John Poe, the segundo, then Dyer, the foreman, and ended at the top with Jordan. Given the size of the ranch, and the complexities of daily operation, Adair's admiration was virtually boundless. He thought Jordan had a natural genius for organization.

Their inspection of line camps that day merely reinforced Adair's view. The workday began at dawn, with the men served a beans-and-beefsteak breakfast, while the nighthawk milled the remuda near camp. By sunrise, all the men were mounted and rode out to begin gathering cattle and haze them back to a prearranged bunch ground. There, by early afternoon, branding got under way, with trail stock moved to a separate holding ground. The workday seldom ended before sundown.

"The poor little devil," Adair said, watching as a hand wielding a knife transformed a bull calf into a steer. "A quick slice and he walks away a eunuch."

"Steers make better beef—" Jordan suddenly paused, stood in his stirrups. "What the hell's that?"

Slim Johnson, one of the hands, rode out of an arroyo across the way. His lariat was snugged around the saddle horn, and at the end of the line was a black bear, squatted on all fours and being dragged along in a dust cloud. The bear was a full-grown sow, easily four hundred pounds, and fought the loop dabbed around its neck with savage snarls. Johnson rode on a beeline for the branding fire.

The men around the fire jumped back, releasing the newly castrated calf. Johnson angled downwind of the flaming logs, then swung his horse in a wide arc, and brought the bear rolling end over end to within yards of the men. Another rider spurred forward, casting his lariat, and tossed a loop around the bear's hind legs. Johnson gigged his horse in the opposite direction, and the lines snapped taut as a bowstring. The bear, roped at both ends, was stretched out to full length.

"Slap a brand on the ol' bitch!" Johnson hollered gleefully. "Gonna run our range, she oughta wear the JA."

One of the men grabbed an iron from the fire. While the others cheered him on, he cautiously circled around, wary of the bear's front claws. Then, darting forward, he raised the iron in both hands and rammed it into the right hindquarter. The bear roared, thrashing and kicking, as hair burned and smoke rose from the sizzling iron. Johnson and the other rider flipped loose their loops, charging the bear with popping lariats, and drove her away from the fire. She disappeared into the arroyo with a bold JA stamped on her furry rump.

"By the Jesus!" Adair roared with laughter. "What a story that will make in Denver. Absolutely marvelous!"

Slim Johnson and the other men broke off whooping and shouting, suddenly aware of Jordan's scrutiny. His features were stolid, and he stared at them for a long moment.

Then, with a faint smile, he nodded. "You boys rope real good," he called out. "Leave off the bears and stick with cows. Let's get back to work."

The men bobbed their heads, still grinning, and turned back to the fire. Adair sensed that the reprimand had been gently delivered, a light rap on the knuckles. He looked at Jordan. "Are you annoyed with them, Jack?"

Jordan's eyes were amused. "No harm done," he said. "Cowhands like rough sport, and nobody was hurt. But they'll think twice next time."

"And if someone had been injured?"

"I reckon Slim Johnson would be lookin' for a job."

"Probably so," Adair said. "Of course, all's well that ends well. Don't you agree?"

"One thing's certain," Jordan said. "You've got braggin' rights no other rancher can claim."

"Oh, what's that?"

"A bear with JA on her ass."

There was a moment's pause, then they both burst out laughing. As the sun heeled over in the sky, they reined about and rode west along the canyon. Adair thought it a grand joke, a classic of Western humor.

He couldn't wait to tell Cornealia the punch line.

CHAPTER 18

A starlit sky cast pale light across the canyon. They were seated on the porch of the stone house, conversing in low tones. This was the Adairs' third night at the ranch, and Cornealia had insisted on preparing supper. She readily admitted that she was out of practice in a kitchen, and the meal confirmed her statement. Everyone ate sparingly.

Rebecca was nonetheless pleased by the gesture. She knew Cornealia wanted to relieve her of cooking for at least one night, and the thought was what counted. For Jordan's part, he found it difficult to concentrate on the conversation, a lively discourse by Adair on the nation's continued economic recovery. His stomach groaned, and he kept wondering what he might find in the larder at home. He hoped Cornealia wouldn't again offer to play hostess.

Across the way, the mournful strain of a harmonica carried from the bunkhouse. The men were seated outside on benches, shadowed in a spill of lamplight from the window. The Adairs often remarked on the quaint, bucolic nature of ranch life, and rough cowhands who were seemingly lulled by soft, wistful tunes. Though he made no comment, Jordan understood that hard men were usually lonesome men, their quiet times filled with thoughts of family and sweethearts left behind. The wailful harmonica was merely an expression of memories past.

The quiet of the evening was suddenly broken by the drum of hoofbeats. A rider galloped into the compound from the east, swinging out of the saddle before the log house. He left his horse heaving, standing spraddle-legged in the yard, as he hurried toward the porch. Jordan rose from his chair and stepped into the sallow starlight. He called out in a loud voice.

"Nobody over there. You lookin' for me?"

The man whirled in mid-stride and raced across the compound. He skidded to a halt before Jordan, breathing heavily. His shirt was soaked with sweat.

"Injuns!" He gestured wildly to the east. "Whole mess of Injuns downriver. Joe Pritchard sent me to warn you!"

Pritchard was boss of the Pleasant Creek line camp, some twenty miles down the canyon. From the looks of the man, and his horse, he had covered the distance at a killing pace. Jordan placed a calming hand on his shoulder.

"What's your name?"

"Orville White."

"All right, Orville, slow down and get your breath. Did you see these Indians yourself?"

"Yes, sir," White panted. "There's a couple hundred, mebbe more. Camped on the river, mile or so below our cabin. They're killin' cows!"

Adair stepped off the porch as Leigh Dyer hurried across from the bunkhouse. Jordan kept an unruffled tone in his voice. "How many cows have they killed?"

"Dunno for sure," White said. "Mebbe ten or so. Run 'em down and filled 'em full of arrows."

"Have they attacked the line camp?"

"Hadn't done nothin' when I took off. They was busy butcherin' them cows. Acted like they ain't et in a while."

Jordan nodded. "You said a couple of hundred Indians. Were there any women and children?"

"We skedaddled when we seen 'em. But, yeah, there was women and kids in the lot."

"How were the men armed?"

"Bow and arrow," White said with a quizzical frown.

"Now that you mention it, I never seen no rifles."

"What about Pritchard?" Jordan asked. "Does he intend to try anything?"

"Not against a bunch that big. Him and the boys are holed up in the cabin. Told me to tell you he'd hang on till you got there."

"Any idea what tribe this bunch is from?"

"Comanche, I reckon," White said. "Who else'd bust out of the reservation?"

Rebecca and Cornealia hovered at the edge of the porch, their features grave with concern. Adair spoke for the first time. "I've no experience with Indians, Jack. Do you think we're in danger?"

"Hard to say," Jordan replied. "Sounds like they're after food more than a fight. 'Course, we can't afford to take chances."

"What do you propose to do?"

"Plan for the worst and hope it doesn't happen."

Jordan began issuing orders. He told Dyer to send riders to the line camps in the upper canyon. The men there, some twenty in number, were to meet him at dawn a mile west of Pleasant Creek. Half the men from the headquarters crew would accompany him, and Dyer would remain behind with the rest to protect Rebecca and the Adairs. He planned to confront the Indians with a show of force at sunrise.

"How about the other crews?" Dyer said. "The line camps in the lower canyon? What d'you think's happened to them?"

"Just a hunch," Jordan mused, "but I figure the Indians bypassed them. Otherwise we would've heard something by now. Let's get a move on, Leigh."

Dyer rushed off to dispatch riders. Adair moved to face Jordan. "I intend to go with you," he said. "After all, I am half owner of the ranch."

Jordan stared at him. "Indians aren't your game, John. You'd do better to stay here and look after the women."

"Indeed not!" Adair said, offended. "Unless you stop

them, we haven't a chance anyway. I'll ride with you."

The stubborn tone of his voice told Jordan that argument would be wasted. "Suit yourself, John. Get armed and be ready to leave at midnight."

Jordan walked off with Rebecca. Behind, they heard Cornealia berating Adair about his stubborn pride. They were halfway across the compound before Rebecca spoke. There was fear in her voice.

"You won't attack the Indians . . . will you?"

"Guess that depends on whether they'll go peaceful."

"Go where, Jack? What does that mean?"

"Palo Duro's our home, Becky. I aim to drive 'em out."

Jordan scouted the encampment at first light. The lodges, along with various trappings strewn about, were a telltale sign. A band of Comanche was camped on the north bank of the river, and a band of Kiowa was directly across the stream. He estimated there were no more than sixty or seventy warriors in both bands.

Upstream again, he rejoined Adair and the men. These were cowhands, rather than trained soldiers; but he was confident they were equal to a fight, if it came to that. He outlined the situation, then explained the plan he'd evolved from his scout. They would approach from the north, halting a hundred yards or so from the Comanche encampment. He would then ride forward alone, and try to arrange a pow-wow with the chief.

Should the situation turn sour, Jordan told them, John Adair would assume command. They were to hold their position, fighting at a distance, where the long reach of their Winchesters would have deadly effect over bows and arrows. The Comanche were to be engaged first, with no fire directed on the Kiowa until they forded the river. The outcome, Jordan assured them, was that the Indians would retreat when faced by determined men with rifles. The military would have relieved the Indians of their firearms on the reservation, and that provided the edge. Arrows were simply no match for Winchesters.

Jordan led them downriver. The sun rose as they approached the Comanche village, and he motioned them to halt and spread out on line. Satisfied with their deployment, he gave Adair a final nod and rode toward the encampment. A woman, fetching water from the stream, spotted him and quickly sounded the alarm. Warriors ran from their lodges, tugging on buckskins, and took a position some thirty strong at the edge of the village. They stood silently, watching beyond him to the mounted line of riflemen, as he reined to a halt. He held up his hand in the peace sign.

A tall warrior, unarmed except for a sheathed knife, stepped forward. Jordan recognized him immediately, recalling the brave he'd fired at and missed during the battle of Palo Duro in 1874. There was no question in his mind that this was Quanah, chief of the fierce Quahadi band. He wondered why they had jumped the reservation, particularly after all this time. Even more, he was amazed they had eluded pursuit by the army.

"*Hao,* Quanah," he said. "Anybody here speak English?"

"I talk some," Quanah said in a deep voice. "White holy man teach on reservation."

"I come in peace."

"That good, pony soldier scout. Last time we meet here, you try to shoot Quanah."

"You remember that, do you?"

"Remember good," Quanah said. "Not forget day Mackenzie kill our pony herd. Why you still here?"

"Live here now." Jordan motioned off to a cattle herd in the distance. "Those are my cows."

"Palo Duro not your land. Comanche land."

"Texas now claims all this land. Made me pay plenty to live here. Your argument is with Texas, not me."

"Ummm." Quanah considered a moment. "Food bad on reservation. My people come here to hunt buffalo. Find only your cows. Where buffalo gone?"

Jordan wanted to avoid the touchy issue of hide hunters.

"Gone north," he said. "Summer feeding grounds."

"That not good. My people hungry."

Across the stream, Jordan saw Kiowa warriors gathering along the riverbank. He chose his next words carefully. "We talk peace," he said. "I feed your people. Nobody get hurt."

"What your name?"

"Jordan."

"We kill cow and talk, Jordan. People just hungry. Not want war."

"What about Kiowas?" Jordan asked pointedly. "They talk peace?"

Quanah's mouth quirked in a faint smile. "Kiowa not wise people. Follow where Comanche lead."

There was a sense of dignity about the Quahadi leader. Jordan felt the man's commanding presence, and some deeper instinct that Quanah could be trusted. "I will send my men away," he said. "We will kill a cow and talk."

Quanah nodded. "No harm come to you in Comanche camp. Quanah give word."

Jordan rode back to the waiting cowhands. He quickly explained the situation, noting that he'd been invited to work out a truce with the Comanche and Kiowa leaders. There was a murmur of disbelief among the men, and Jordan stilled it with a sharp command, ordering them to return to their line camps. Adair spoke what was in the minds of all the men.

"These are savages," he said, waving at the lodges. "Are you so certain you can trust them once we're gone?"

"Have to start somewhere," Jordan told him. "Seems pretty obvious they're not spoilin' for a fight. They're just hungry."

"How will you convince them to leave Palo Duro?"

"Quanah strikes me as a man of good judgment. I think he'll see the light."

Adair scowled. "I've no liking for this plan a'tall."

"Guess you'll just have to trust my judgment, John."

"And what do you expect me to tell Rebecca?"

Jordan smiled. "Tell her to keep a lamp in the window. I'll be home tonight."

Still apprehensive, Adair reluctantly led the men upstream. Upon returning to the village, Jordan found that the Kiowa chief, Tapedeah, had been summoned by Quanah. The sun was high by now, and the three men were served a meager breakfast of stewed beef and river water. Jordan slowly became aware that, apart from wild berries and the cows killed yesterday, neither of the tribes had any rations. Except for the beef, they were one step away from starvation.

The three men retired to Quanah's lodge. There they met in council throughout the morning and all that afternoon. Jordan learned that hopelessness and desperation had caused them to flee Indian Territory. The monthly food allotments, dispensed by the government, were woefully inadequate and often of substandard quality. Quanah and Tapedeah had led their people off the reservation not to raid or kill, and with no thought of outdistancing the army. Their return to Palo Duro was a search for the buffalo, for food.

Jordan was taken by their plight. He knew that government contractors, who supplied the reservations, were notorious for delivering goods of the poorest quality. Yet, until today, he had been unaware that the food allotments were insufficient, never enough to last a full month. Given the same circumstances, he would have jumped the reservation himself, and to hell with the consequences. Toward late afternoon, he proposed a compromise, which hinged on their return to the reservation. The middle of every month, to feed their people, his men would deliver ten cows to the eastern edge of the canyon. The Comanche and the Kiowa, for their part, would never again return to Palo Duro.

Tapedeah, suspicious throughout the day, seemed amazed by the offer. He asked Quanah, who had translated during the discussions, to speak his words. "Tapedeah say," Quanah repeated, "*tejanos* always his enemy. Now, a *tejano* become friend."

Quanah extended his hand. "I think same way, Jordan. We shake like white men do."

Jordan accepted his handshake. "Old enemies often make good friends. I'm glad I could help your people."

The opportunity to assist them came sooner than Jordan might have expected. An hour or so before sundown, a troop of cavalry suddenly appeared downstream. At a shouted command, the troopers maneuvered on line, facing the lodges, prepared to charge. Alarm spread through the villages as an officer and a guidon bearer rode forward under a white flag. Jordan went to meet them.

"Captain Edward Nolan," the officer said crisply. "Commanding a troop of the Tenth Cavalry. May I inquire who you are, sir?"

"Jack Jordan's the name, Captain. I own Palo Duro Canyon."

"Your name is familiar, sir. I believe you served under Mackenzie in the campaign of '74."

"Yeah, I did." Jordan jerked a thumb over his shoulder. "I take it you're trailin' this bunch."

"For the past three days," Nolan affirmed. "We cut their trail south of Fort Elliott. Our orders are to return them to the reservation. By force, if necessary."

"Won't require a fight, Captain. They'll go peaceable."

Jordan explained the treaty he had negotiated on behalf of the JA Ranch. Nolan was impressed, and more than a little relieved at the peaceful resolution. By sundown, Nolan had met with the tribal leaders and worked out an orderly transition. The Comanche and Kiowa, escorted by the cavalry, would depart for Fort Sill at sunrise.

Shortly after dark, Jordan mounted his horse. Quanah, who was standing nearby, raised his arm in farewell, and friendship. They somehow knew they would meet again.

Jordan waved and rode toward home.

CHAPTER 19

Dusk settled over the canyon as the men trooped up to the log house. Their faces were freshly scrubbed and shaved, their hair slicked back, for the meeting was to be conducted in the presence of the women. They removed their hats as they halted on the porch.

"C'mon in, boys," Jordan said, holding open the door. "Find yourselves a seat at the table."

Leigh Dyer led them into the house. The men appeared awkward in mixed company, bobbing their heads in unison to Rebecca and Cornealia, and finally to Adair. Dyer, Poe, and Cape Willingham took chairs on the far side of the table. Jud Mitchell and Deacon Walsh got themselves arranged on the side nearest the door.

Jordan took a chair at the head of the table. He waited until Adair seated himself at the opposite end. "You boys want some coffee?" he said, looking at the men. "Ladies won't mind if you smoke."

Rebecca and Cornealia served coffee in china mugs. The men murmured their thanks, and all five pulled out tobacco sacks, began rolling cigarettes. Adair lit a long cigar, and within moments the dining area was enveloped in a pall of smoke. The women retreated to chairs in the parlor.

"You all know why we're here," Jordan said. "Today's May 26 and we start the trail drive tomorrow. I aim to sight Dodge City by June 9."

The men exchanged quick glances. Jordan had selected Poe, Willingham, Mitchell, and Walsh as trail bosses for the four herds. Dyer, much to his chagrin, was to remain behind and oversee ranch operations. He envied the other men their trip to the fabled cowtown, the saloons and dance halls. Still, as foreman of the JA, he was forced to agree with Jordan's decision. Someone with authority had to stay behind.

"That's pushin' it, boss," Poe said, voicing what the others were thinking. "I recollect you sayin' it's nearabouts two hundred miles to Dodge."

"Fifteen miles a day," Jordan acknowledged. "I allowed an extra day just in case anything goes haywire."

"What John's sayin'," Dyer interceded, "is that fifteen a day is the best we ever managed on long trail drives. That's a tough pace to hold for two straight weeks."

Jordan had personal reasons for setting a fast pace. Rebecca was due to deliver the last week in June, and he fully intended to be with her when the baby was born. By reaching Dodge City on June 9, and allowing three or four days to sell the herds, he figured his return to Palo Duro somewhere around June 20. Barring any mishaps, that was still cutting it close, with little time to spare. He refused to justify his personal affairs to the men.

"Let's not bandy words," he said, looking around the table. "I picked you boys because you've got the most experience on trail drives. I expect you to hold whatever pace I set. Understood?"

The men understood. Jordan would brook no interference, and he would tolerate no one questioning his orders. Even so, none of them took his hard tone personally, for they had unstinting faith in his judgment. The drive might be punishing on men and cattle, but one thing now seemed certain. He would get them to Dodge City in the time allotted.

"We'll trail four herds a day apart," Jordan went on. "Cape, you'll take the first herd, and I'll ride with you. Jud, you've got the second herd, and Deacon's got the third.'' He nodded to Poe. ''John, you'll take the last herd. I reckon you know what I want.''

''I reckon so.'' Poe puffed his cigarette, exhaled smoke. ''Keep pushin' things along from the rear, and collect any stragglers. I'll handle it.''

Jordan glanced from man to man. ''You boys assign relay riders between your herds. Give 'em fast horses, so they'll make good time back and forth. I want a report every night from all of you.''

Deacon Walsh was a lean man with gnarled features. He shifted in his chair. ''What happens if there's trouble, stampedes or such? Do we stop to let that herd catch up?''

''Get word to me,'' Jordan said. ''I'll make the call when, and if, it happens. All right, Deacon?''

''You'll be with the lead herd the whole time?''

''That's the general idea. I'll range out ahead by half a day and scout the easiest route. Ought to rejoin the lead herd by sundown every day. Any trouble, let me know *muy pronto*.''

''Ain't expectin' none,'' Walsh said slyly. ''Leastways, not with my herd. It's these other boys you gotta worry about.''

The men hooted him down with laughter. Jordan listened to their banter a moment, then quieted them with an upraised hand. He ordered the first herd, already in position at the head of the canyon, to be driven up the road onto the plains at sunrise. The other herds, a day apart, would follow in order.

Jordan spread a hand-drawn map across the table. ''Here's our general line of march,'' he said, pointing with his finger. ''We'll head northeast to the Salt Fork of the Red, and on up to the North Fork of the Red.'' His finger traced a line to the Canadian, and northward to the Cimarron, in Indian Territory. ''We'll end up here, on the Arkansas, outside Dodge.''

''That stretch through Injun country,'' Poe said. ''I've heard tell they collect fifty cents a head toll over on the Chisholm Trail. Do we pay it?''

''No,'' Jordan said shortly. ''Offer them one cow, take it or leave it. They're not lookin for trouble these days. So hold the line.''

''What about rustlers?'' Mitchell asked. ''Once't we cross the Kansas border, we're liable to tangle with night riders. Anything changed there?''

''Jud, our rule's the same as always. We don't take prisoners, whether it's cow thieves or horse thieves. Find yourself a tree and hang them.''

There was a startled gasp from the parlor. Cornealia sat rigid, her eyes wide with shock, staring at him in disbelief. Adair, who appeared equally dismayed, hitched forward in his chair. His features were grim.

''Jack—'' He waved his cigar in a nervous motion. ''I've no qualms with summary justice here in Palo Duro. After all, as you've said, we must enforce our own law in the wilderness.''

He paused, wary of sounding too much the outsider. ''But that sort of thing in Kansas seems to me an altogether different matter. Wouldn't that place us at odds with the authorities?''

The men looked at him as though he had sprouted a wart on his nose. Never before had they heard anyone address Jordan in a lecturing tone, and they awaited a reaction. Adair toyed with his cigar, waiting as well, aware that both Cornealia and Rebecca were now intent spectators. Jordan's expression was unreadable, but he stared down the table with a level gaze. He was clearly unaccustomed to having his orders challenged.

''From here to here''—his finger traced an arc from Indian Territory to Dodge City, and westward across the plains—''it's the same as Palo Duro. No law within a day's ride, and rustlers do as they damn well please. Unless we protect ourselves, we could lose a whole herd in one night. How would you feel if somebody robbed us of sixty thousand dollars?''

''In Kansas,'' Adair replied, ''the law would send them to prison.''

''In Kansas,'' Jordan countered, ''the law would never catch them. They'd drive that herd over to Colorado, or down to New Mexico, and find ready buyers. We'd still be the losers.''

''You're saying there is no alternative to hanging them. Is that it?''

''I'm saying rustlers have to believe it's certain death to mess with the JA. Until the law solves the problem, we have to look to our own. That's the alternative.''

Adair looked down at the table. ''How many men have you hanged, Jack?''

''Too many,'' Jordan said. ''But they tried to kill me, and my men, and they tried to steal my livelihood. They're the kind of bastards who'll take a life to rustle a cow. I figure they got what they deserved.''

''Let us hope the situation improves with time. I'm sure you would welcome that change.''

''Welcome it with open arms, John. Hanging a man's a sorry spectacle, and it stays with you. Not a thing you forget.''

''I daresay.'' Adair popped the cigar into his mouth. ''Excuse the interruption, and please continue with your meeting. I'll defer to your judgment in these matters.''

''Thank you, John.'' Jordan glanced around at the men. ''Think that about covers it. Unless somebody's got questions.''

''We're all set,'' Poe said with a wide grin. ''Dodge City, here we come!''

''You boys better get yourselves some shut-eye. I'll see you in the morning.''

The men nodded to Rebecca and the Adairs, and filed through the door. Jordan excused himself and followed them outside. He caught up with Dyer in the yard, waiting as the others walked toward the bunkhouse. His voice was pitched low.

''Leigh, I need a favor.''

''Name it, boss.''

Jordan looked back at the house. ''The missus is due

late next month. I'm gonna bust my butt to be here, but things don't always work out.'' He hesitated, his gaze fixed on Dyer. ''I'd count it a personal favor if you'd watch over her.''

''You rest easy,'' Dyer said. ''I'll look after her like she was my own sister.''

''Sam Bugbee's wife promised she'd come down when it's time. Get word to her if I'm not here.''

''Don't worry your head, boss. I'll take care of it.''

''I'm obliged, Leigh.''

''Honor's all mine. She's a pretty special lady.''

Rebecca stepped through the door. Dyer waved and strolled off toward the bunkhouse. She halted at the edge of the porch, framed in a shaft of lamplight from the window. Jordan crossed the yard, aware of an odd expression on her face. She put a finger to her lips.

''Keep your voice down,'' she said. ''I had to leave them alone.''

''Why's that?''

''Cornealia doesn't understand your attitude toward rustlers. John is trying to explain it to her.''

Jordan grunted. ''What's her problem?''

''In my opinion—'' She stifled a small laugh. ''I think it's because she has never been shot at. The sound of bullets tends to give you a whole new perspective on things.''

''That the voice of experience talking?''

''Well, I'd hardly forget the day those men tried to steal our Herefords. I was never so frightened in my life.''

Jordan stepped onto the porch, took her in his arms. ''I think you're tellin' me fibs.''

She looked at him in surprise. ''What do you mean?''

''Way I remember it, you weren't scared that day. You were mad as hell.''

''As a matter of fact, I was. So?''

''So you got me to teach you to shoot. I pity the robber that shows up here when you've got a gun handy.''

''Well—'' Her eyes brightened with amusement. ''A lady does have to protect herself.''

"My sentiments exactly."

Jordan kissed her. They stood locked in embrace for a long time, her arms around his neck. When they parted, there was a strange look in his eyes, somehow luminous. For a moment, she thought perhaps it was the reflection of starlight. Then she saw something deeper, far stronger than words.

She knew few women had ever been so loved.

The herd topped the road onto the plains. Jordan rode to the edge of the caprock, and peered down into Palo Duro. Far below, outside the stone house, he saw Rebecca standing with the Adairs. He removed his hat and waved it high overhead.

From the canyon floor, Rebecca waved back, her eyes moist with tears. On the caprock he was limned in the scarlet flare of sunrise, too distant to make out his features. Yet she knew it was him, and as he whirled his horse northward onto the plains, a lump formed in her throat. She would remember him that way, until he returned. His grand gesture of farewell.

The Adairs were prepared to leave. Their departure had been delayed only until the herd was out of the canyon. The wagon was already loaded, with one of the headquarters hands assigned as the driver. Hank Taylor, who would guide them across *Llano Estacado,* waited nearby with their horses. Cornealia turned as the rider they all knew to be Jordan wheeled away from the northern caprock. She looked at Rebecca.

"Try not to be sad. Before you know it, he'll be back."

Rebecca smiled through her tears. "I just never get used to seeing him ride off. I suppose I never will."

"Every woman knows that feeling." Cornealia hesitated, glancing at Adair, who nodded. "Before we go, I have something to confess. I misjudged Jack last night, all that talk about rustlers. I simply lacked the courage to tell him myself."

"We talked about it, and believe me, he understood. He

would never think badly of you.''

''I hope not,'' Cornealia said. ''I admire him so, and you too, my dear. John and I are so proud of you both.''

''God's truth,'' Adair added. ''You and Jack were made for each other. I've never seen your equal.''

''Oh, you will!'' Rebecca said brightly. ''When you return in the fall, you'll find a little Jordan here. I just know it's a boy.''

''I can't wait!'' Cornealia said, her eyes merry. ''Of course, you know I expect to be his godmother.''

''And I his godfather,'' Adair said adamantly. ''I'd not allow another the honor.''

Rebecca swiped at a tear. ''We wouldn't dream of anyone else.''

Cornealia wrapped her in a hug. ''Take care of yourself until we see you next. You're never out of my thoughts.''

She hurried toward her horse, dabbing at her eyes. Adair enfolded Rebecca in his arms, and kissed her on the cheek. ''God bless all in the Jordan house. Look for us again in September.''

Taylor got them mounted, and led the way out of the compound. Leigh Dyer walked across from the cook shack and joined Rebecca. They stood watching as the wagon and riders slowly faded into the distance. She waved when the Adairs began ascending the road to the plains. Dyer saw a tear roll down her cheek.

''Anything I can do for you, Miz Jordan?''

''No, Leigh,'' she said. ''I'm just fine, thank you.''

Unbidden, she heard again the parting words of John Adair. She thought it not so much a sentiment as a benediction already come true.

God bless all in the Jordan house.

CHAPTER 20

The herd was driven hard the first day out. Longhorns were contrary creatures, wary of unfamiliar range, and the purpose was to trail-break them within a couple of days. Jordan rode ahead on a northeasterly course, planning to halt the first night on the Salt Fork of the Red. The distance was slightly more than twenty miles.

The marching order was one established by Jordan many years ago. In the lead was the chuck wagon, driven by the cook, with provisions, assorted equipment, and the hands' bedrolls. The wrangler and his nighthawk followed close behind with the remuda, some sixty head of horses. The job of the nighthawk was to guard the remuda during the hours of darkness. The cattle herd trailed along a mile or so to their rear.

Two point men rode at the front of the herd. Their job was to keep the longhorns on the northeasterly course set by Jordan. Off to either side, swing and flank riders kept the cows in line and hazed bunch quitters back into the herd. To the rear, a drag rider choused stragglers into the fold and pushed the herd along. Cape Willingham, the trail boss, constantly circled the herd, watchful for any problems.

The lead steer, known to everyone as Old Blue, was a veteran of the trail. Bought many years ago by Jordan, he had been kept in service because of his natural bent for setting the pace. A leader rather than a follower, Old Blue took it upon himself to move to the front of the herd every morning. He marched off at a steady stride, with a brass bell around his neck, and the other longhorns followed along, as though lulled by the clang of the bell. An oddity among longhorns, Old Blue liked to travel, and clearly enjoyed long, arduous trail drives. He set a blistering pace, daily claiming his position in the vanguard.

The herd covered twenty-three miles the first day, arriving shortly before sundown at the Salt Fork of the Red. The longhorns were so worn out they could barely stay awake to graze, much less attempt to return to their home range. In the days to follow, with Old Blue leading the way, work would begin early and end late. The hands saddled by starlight each morning when the air was still crimpy and their ponies were full of fight. Once they got the herd strung out and moving, the steers were allowed to graze along a mile or so in a northerly direction. Then they were hazed steadily until noon, when Willingham brought the outfit to a halt for the midday break.

The chuck wagon was generally nearby so the men could wolf down a meal of cold beef and biscuits. Still, there was no time to rest, for after a quick meal the men got busy saddling fresh mounts from the remuda. When the steers started lying down Willingham knew they had grazed long enough, and gave the signal to resume the drive. Toward sundown, at a spot selected by Jordan during his daily scout, the hands drove the herd onto a bedground for the night. If everything went according to plan, the men were usually unsaddled and ready for supper by dark. Yet their workday was far from over.

Every hand, old or young, rode night guard in four-hour shifts. As seasoned trail hands were quick to note, longhorns were temperamental beasts, easily offended and prone to spook. Without someone to keep them company during the night, a strange noise, even a high wind, might start a stampede that would scatter cows for miles in every direction. To stay awake during guard, some of the hands used a home remedy called rouser—a dab of tobacco juice under the eyelid. Even though a man had spent fourteen hours in the saddle since morning, rouser was a surefire cure for drowsiness. One dose was generally enough.

Still and all, the hands managed to get their sleep, sometimes as much as three or four hours a night. Then, as it seemed they had just closed their eyes, the cook would rout them out of their soogans and blast them awake with six-shooter coffee. The name derived from the fact that most trail cooks considered coffee passable only when it was thick enough to float a loaded six-gun. After a hurried breakfast, the hands barely had time to stow their bedrolls in the wagon before the nighthawk drove the remuda in for saddling. The workday had begun again.

The horse herd was the wheel around which any trail drive revolved. Every man in the outfit had six mounts in his string, which meant the wrangler and his nighthawk had the full-time chore of shepherding over sixty cow ponies. While the remuda consisted solely of geldings, Willingham had brought along a bell-mare as a safety measure. Should the horses get scattered in a stampede, or somehow wander off, the crew would be out of business. But so long as the horses could hear the mare's bell, there was little fear of them straying too far. Even though gelded, they still had an affinity for the mare.

Jordan ordered that the herd be pushed hard on the second day as well. He planned to halt on the North Fork of the Red, something more than twenty miles from their camp the first day out. The pace was rough on men and cows alike, but he saw it as insurance of sorts. Experience had taught him to trail-break a herd at the outset, thoroughly wear them down, and thus eliminate problems in the days ahead. Longhorns were stubborn, never to be trusted, and had to have their resistance broken by driving them to the point of exhaustion. Later, farther up the trail, they would be allowed to graze longer and restore lost tallow. For now, he meant to sap their will to run wild.

That night, with the herd bedded down near the North

Fork, the hands began collecting around the campfire. The area surrounding the chuck wagon was considered the domain of the cook, in large degree a kingdom ruled by a tyrant. Even Jordan watched his manners around the chuck wagon, for cooks were a notoriously capricious lot. More than one trail drive had been brought to a standstill because the chief pot-walloper had gone on strike with a case of hurt feelings. Bumpus Moore, the cook for Willingham's crew, was typical of the breed.

A pugnacious man, short of temper and sharp of tongue, Moore governed his chuck wagon by an inflexible code of rules. He had to be supplied with wood and water, and woe unto the man who expectorated tobacco juice into his cook fire. These were absolutes, never to be profaned, or the crew would rapidly find themselves on meager rations. The cardinal rule was that there were to be no complaints, spoken or otherwise implied, about the quality of his cooking. Those who didn't like it didn't have to eat it, but they were forewarned to keep their mouths shut. Moore's revenge—a dose of castor oil surreptitiously administered to the offender—resulted in a case of the running trots. For men who spent their lives in the saddle, this represented the ultimate threat.

Hard as it was to keep from bending the rules, there were certain advantages. Tonight, having been acknowledged as King around his chuck wagon, Moore concocted a favorite among cowmen. When the hands lined up with their tin plates, he served son-of-a-bitch stew, which consisted of loins, sweetbreads, liver, and heart simmered in a spicy gravy. To complement the stew he ladled out Spotted Pup, a combination of rice, raisins, and brown sugar, along with sourdough biscuits and molasses. Having outdone himself, Moore looked on as the hands dug in with an assortment of loud slurps and appreciative belches.

After scraping his plate clean, Willingham rolled himself a smoke. He lit the cigarette with a stick from the fire, and looked up with a wide smile. "Bumpus, I have to hand it to you. That's damn fine grub."

The men voiced their agreement, and Moore beamed. "Anybody wants seconds, come and get it. I'm fixin' to close down for the night."

There was a rush to be first in line. Jordan watched with amusement for a moment, then nodded to Willingham. "I think you've got him euchred, Cape. We'll eat good all the way to Dodge."

"Had a good teacher," Willingham said, grinning. "Watched you sweet-talk Mose Butler all those years."

"Well, Mose is in his glory now. Lord and master of the headquarters cook house."

"All the same, I'd bet he misses the trail."

Before Jordan could reply, one of the relay riders from Jud Mitchell's outfit rode into camp. He dismounted, moving around the fire, and halted before them. "Evenin', Mr. Jordan," he said. "Jud told me to tell you our herd's at the Salt Fork. Deacon Walsh's relay man brought word his outfit's outta the canyon and on the trail."

"You're just in time for supper," Jordan said. "Get yourself a plate before those boys finish it off."

The man ducked his head, turning toward the chow line. Willingham smiled. "Looks like things are comin' together the way you planned. We're off to a good start."

"Long ways from here to Dodge, Cape. We'll take it one day at a time."

Sam Bugbee was as good as his word. The JA herds were allowed to cross Circle B range with the full cooperation of his outfit. A wide corridor was established through his lands along the northeasterly route selected by Jordan. His men moved Circle B herds east and west to create open, unimpeded passage for the longhorns. The plan came off without a hitch.

On the fourth day, shortly before noon, Jordan's lead herd pulled up before the Canadian. The river was running wild, still flooded by spring rains and snow melt off the distant mountains. The turbulent waters splashed over the shoreline, so foamy and full of silt that it looked as though a cow could walk from one bank to the other. The crossing promised to be a dicey proposition.

Bugbee was waiting on the south bank. Jordan reined to a halt, exchanged a greeting, and sat watching the roiling waters. For a moment he considered holding the herd south of the Canadian until the next morning, then just as quickly discarded the thought. The river might remain at flood for another week, and he didn't have time to spare. Today or tomorrow made no difference.

"What d'you think?" Bugbee asked. "Looks pretty bad, don't it?"

"Bad or not," Jordan said, "we'll have to cross. God only knows when it'll go down."

"You're liable to lose some cows."

"Guess that's the risk we run, Sam. There's other rivers between here and Dodge. I can't let one hold me back."

Bugbee nodded. "Maybe it'll slack off before I start my herds north."

"Possible." Jordan sounded unconvinced. "You've got three days before my last bunch comes through. You might catch a break."

"I suppose anything could happen between now and then."

"Hell, that's the wonder of it, Sam. Every day's a new dawning."

"For a fact," Bugbee agreed. "I wanna thank you again for layin' out a trail to Dodge. Takes a load off my shoulders."

Jordan shrugged. "Least I could do for you letting me cross your range. Out here, we've got to stick together."

"Say, I almost forgot to ask. How's your little woman doing?"

"She's getting along just fine. Looking forward to meeting your wife when her time comes."

"Martha's already plannin' on it. She's got the gift when it comes to birthin' babies."

Cape Willingham reined in beside them. He nodded to Bugbee, then looked at Jordan. "What'll I tell the boys?

We gonna get our feet wet today?''

''No need to hold off,'' Jordan said. ''I'll take the lead and you bring up the rear. Let's get it done.''

''I'll move 'em right along.''

Willingham reined about, waving his hat, and signaled the men riding point. Jordan shook hands with Bugbee. ''See you up the trail somewhere, Sam.''

''Good luck to you, Jack.''

Jordan rode to a wide defile along the shoreline. The point riders quickly got the lead steers strung out and walking briskly in his direction. With Old Blue out front, they choused the herd toward the river in a pie-shaped wedge. The swing and flank riders moved in from the sides, hazing the longhorns into a narrow file as they approached closer to the south bank. Jordan drove his horse into the swift current directly ahead of the lead steers. He gave the gelding a loose rein as they struck out for the opposite shore.

The point riders began yelling and popping their lariats. Driven onward, following Old Blue, the longhorns plunged into the water before any of the lead steers had time to mill and form a bottleneck. The hands riding swing and flank kept the herd moving steadily forward, crowding those in front into the river with constant pressure from the bawling, wild-eyed steers just behind. Willingham and the drag rider held their positions at the rear, shouting and whistling, gradually easing more cattle into the funnel. The stream of longhorns plowed endlessly into the river.

Late that afternoon the last of the herd scrambled ashore on the north bank. The wrangler and his nighthawk drove the remuda across next, followed closely by Bumpus Moore in the chuck wagon. Jordan and Willingham agreed that, all things considered, it hadn't been a bad crossing. They had lost only three steers to the Canadian.

''What now?'' Willingham said. ''Keep 'em movin'?''

Jordan studied the angle of the sun. ''We'll make camp here tonight. Give the boys a chance to get dried off.''

''Yeah, I guess they're due a break anyway. I calculate we've come about eighty miles in four days.''

"From here on, we'll hold it to fifteen a day. I want those cows fat and sassy when we hit Dodge."

"Just like old times," Willingham said. "Give them cattle buyers an eyeful of good Texas beef. Make 'em pay through the nose!"

"Cape, you never get a second chance to make a first impression, and that's a fact of life. Tell Bumpus to lay on a big spread for the boys tonight. I'll see you about sundown."

"Where you headed?"

"Still a couple of hours of daylight left. Think I'll scout north of here a ways."

Jordan rode off, sopping wet from fording the river. Willingham thought it typical of the man, concerned about the crew but heedless of his own welfare. The hands were to be rewarded for a good job, with a special supper and a few hours of loafing around camp. The man who paid their wages allowed himself no such respite, one eye always on the task ahead. He meant to squeeze the last drop of sunlight from the day.

Willingham turned to getting the herd settled for the night. As he watched the crew mill the longhorns onto a bed-ground, he caught sight of Old Blue. The other steers, famished from the day's march and swimming a river, immediately started cropping grass. But Old Blue stood gazing off into the distance, as though pondering why the drive had been halted. Willingham told himself that Old Blue and Jack Jordan were birds of a feather.

Their gaze was forever fixed on the horizon. Tomorrow.

Chapter 21

Rebecca finished the breakfast dishes. There was little cleanup after a meal, since she was cooking only for herself. Nor were meals an occasion to be anticipated, something to look forward to and plan around. With Jack gone, her appetite had diminished day by day.

She dumped the dishwater into the slop pail, which one of the hands emptied each day. Drying her hands, she moved to a large calendar, tacked to the wall in the dining area. She marked the day, crossing it out with a pencil, noting that it was June 3. Eight days since Jack had departed on the trail drive.

The thought struck a spark of loathing. She was feeling sorry for herself, and she'd always detested people who wallowed in self-pity. Yet she was lonely and bored, lonesome despite a bunkhouse full of cowhands and the attentive, considerate manner of Leigh Dyer. She knew Jack had instructed him to look after her, but it made little difference. She was still trapped in her own solitary world.

Her mind focused more and more on the baby. Every morning, when she marked a day off the calendar, she wished it were a week instead. She desperately wanted the time to pass, the month to end. For she was due the last week of June, and the arrival of the baby seemed to her some magical fountainhead of a new beginning. Something to occupy her mind, and someone who would truly need her, every minute of every day. Someone to relieve the desperate sense of loneliness.

She reread again the latest letter from her parents. Twice a month a rider was sent to Fort Elliott, to collect mail from the outside world. She reveled in the news from her parents, and this time the letter had accompanied a small box bound with twine. At her request, her mother had sent along packages of seeds for a wide variety of garden vegetables. She dropped the letter on the table, and stood looking for a moment at the seed packages, which had arrived yesterday. She decided to start planting today.

A light knock sounded at the door. Dyer stood there, smiling pleasantly, hat in hand. "Mornin', Miz Jordan," he said. "I'm fixin' to ride out to some of the line camps. Anything you need before I leave?"

"Why, yes, Leigh. Could you arrange for a couple of men to help me? I want to start a garden."

"Ma'am?"

"A vegetable garden." Rebecca held up one of the packages. "Carrots, turnips, cabbages, all sorts of things."

Dyer looked skeptical. "Pardon me askin', Miz Jordan. But are you sure them things will grow down here in the canyon?"

"Flowers seem to thrive in this soil. I think vegetables will do just fine."

"Lot of work raisin' turnips and such. Garden's got to be watered and weeded real regular. Who's gonna tend it?"

"Some of the men," Rebecca said. "I'll work with them to make sure it goes right."

"Well, don't you see—" Dyer faltered, clearly at a loss. "Cowhands don't take to such work, Miz Jordan. They didn't hire on to be . . . uh . . . farmers."

"Oh, really now, that's nonsense, Leigh. Think how wonderful it will be to have fresh vegetables. A little gardening won't hurt them."

"I doubt the boys would see it that way. Did you talk to the boss about this?"

"No, I did not." Rebecca's eyes flashed. "And whether it's beneath them or not, we're going to plant a garden. I want you to assign two men to the job today. Is that clear?"

Dyer knew when he was outmatched. He'd been ordered to look after her, and if it took a garden to keep her happy, then there was no way around it. He wondered how the hell he would explain it to the hands.

"Whatever you say, ma'am," he conceded, backing away from the door. "I'll find you a couple of men."

"Thank you very much, Leigh."

The men Dyer sent over were reluctant workers at best. They obviously felt they'd been drafted into performing the menial chores of a sodbuster. Rebecca laid out a garden plot east of the house, and got them busy with shovels. She was pleasant but firm, and they followed her directions with the abashed look of men unaccustomed to taking orders from a woman. She knew they would never hear the end of it in the bunkhouse.

Late that afternoon the garden began to take shape. The men carefully, if slowly, removed weeds and tufts of grass, and left behind fresh upturned soil. The work would have gone faster with a hand plow, but they labored away under a hot sun with shovels. Separate rows were dug, some fifty feet in length, for the various varieties of vegetables, with the earth formed into mounds. The men rarely spoke, though it was clear that they took pride in doing any job well. They made a special effort to keep the rows uniform and straight.

Rebecca periodically came down from the house to check their progress. She had just started across the porch when a wagon approached from the west and rolled to a stop in the yard. The man who jumped down from the driver's seat was a stranger, but dressed in the garb of a cowhand. He moved forward, glancing at the men in the garden, and halted a short distance from the porch. He doffed his hat.

"Howdy, ma'am," he said. "Would you be Miz Jordan?"

"Yes, I am."

"I ride for the Circle B. Miz Bugbee sent me to bring you some goods."

"How nice of her," Rebecca said with surprised delight. "What sort of goods?"

The man appeared embarrassed. "Well, ma'am, it's mostly chickens. Got some eggs, too."

"Are you serious? Live chickens?"

"Yes'am, they're live all right. Miz Bugbee's got herself a whole henhouse full."

Rebecca followed him to the wagon. He unloaded a wire crate with three brown hens and a feisty rooster. Then, with gingerly care, he lowered a wooden box to the ground. Inside were two dozen eggs, packed securely in handfuls of dried grass. He stood back as though released from a heavy burden.

"I can't believe it!" Rebecca exclaimed. "All those eggs, and the chickens. How will I ever thank Mrs. Bugbee!"

"I 'spect you'll get your chance, Miz Jordan. She's waitin' word when to come down here for your baby. Said to tell you to send a man to fetch her."

"Oh, I will! I most certainly will."

The Circle B hand was invited to spend the night. He walked over to the cook shack for a cup of coffee, and related a tale that left Mose Butler aghast. According to him, Martha Bugbee kept chickens, raised hogs for ham and bacon, and ruled her husband and kids with a viper's tongue. She was hell on wheels, he said, nobody to tangle with. Butler could only shake his head in sympathy.

When Leigh Dyer rode in that evening, he was greeted by yet another shock. Rebecca called him over to the house, pointing to the crate of chickens and the box of eggs sitting on the porch. Holding out one egg for herself, she told him the rest were for the men, a special treat for tomorrow's breakfast. Then, after complimenting the men who had worked on the garden, she informed him that their next project was to build her a chicken coop. She wanted it completed first thing in the morning.

Dyer walked toward the bunkhouse in a daze. A garden and chickens, all in one day, seemed more than he could bear. Next thing, she'd want him to build a pigpen.

The old days, he told himself, were gone forever.

Jordan sat his horse on a swell of prairie overlooking the Cimarron. The river was wide and swift, but flood season was drawing to a close, and the water level looked manageable. There was a good ford along a stretch of flat ground, with a rocky streambed free of quicksand. He thought it would be an easy crossing.

All day as he scouted ahead of the herd, he'd calculated time and distance. They were four days north of the Canadian, and still averaging fifteen miles a day. On the other side of the Cimarron, at some unmarked boundary, they would cross into Kansas. By dead reckoning, he figured they were five days out from Dodge City. His original estimate, barring any mishap, would be met.

Still, as he waited on the herd, Jordan warned himself against overoptimism. So far, the trail drive had been without incident, a grueling but nonetheless smooth journey across the plains. On their passage through the western strip of Indian Territory, they had encountered none of the horseback tribes. There had been no stampedes, no lightning storms or violent winds, nothing to mar their steady march northward. From past experience, he knew that trail drives were never simple, or without hazard. He was wary of too much good luck.

Their one problem had been the bones of dead buffalo. For the past three days, the plains had been covered with the bleached grayish bones of tens of thousands of buffalo killed in previous years. The herd had to be guided through the wasteland of bones, for longhorns were skittish around anything with the scent of death. Only this morning Jordan had begun encountering the carcasses of recent kills, stripped of hides and rotting in the sun. He surmised the hide hunters had followed the herds farther north, to the summer feeding grounds along the Republican. The enormity of the slaughter sickened him, for there were no settlers clamoring for land on the vast buffalo ranges. Hides were the sole reason for the slaughter, and he saw in the bones the passing of an era. The buffalo herds would soon be wiped out.

Off to the south, Jordan spotted the column of longhorns. The sun was dipping westward, and he decided to hold the herd on the south side of the Cimarron. Early tomorrow, after a night of rest and graze, the river crossing would be more easily managed. Longhorns, even at the best of times, were intractable creatures, and there was no need to push them too hard this close to Dodge City. He rode out to meet the herd.

Willingham was in the lead. To his rear were the point riders, Josh Pilcher and Alvin Rickard. As Jordan approached, he saw movement on the ground directly in front of Rickard's horse. A diamondback rattlesnake was coiled not a foot away, broad head weaving and rattles buzzing loudly. The horse spooked, rearing sideways in a violent lunge, and tossed Rickard from the saddle. He hit the ground on his back, arms and legs awry, momentarily stunned. The rattler struck in a blurred motion, burying its fangs in an outflung arm. Rickard screamed as the snake coiled to strike again.

Jordan rammed the spurs into his gelding. Out of the corner of his eye he saw Josh Pilcher draw a pistol, then hold off as he crossed into the line of fire. The rattler struck a second time, fully five feet in length, as his horse closed to within a few feet. He leaned down out of the saddle, grasping the saddlehorn with his left hand, and grabbed the snake by the tail while it was still stretched to full length. He whirled the rattler in a back-and-forth motion, and popped it in midair like a bullwhip. The snake's head snapped, its neck broken, and he flung it onto the ground. He swung down from the saddle.

"Mind those cows!" he shouted at Willingham. "Get 'em turned!"

The longhorns were wall-eyed with fright, startled by the sudden commotion, on the verge of bolting into a stampede. Willingham and Pilcher rode into the herd, forcing Old Blue and the lead steers in a gradual, rolling turn eastward. Within moments, the column swung back into itself and the herd milled to a standstill. Jordan dropped to his knees beside Rickard, who held his arm clutched in a vise-grip. His eyes were stark with terror.

"I'm bit," he choked out. "Oh, Jesus have mercy, I'm bit."

"Listen to me!" Jordan commanded. "Let go of your arm so I can have a look. You hear me, let go!"

Rickard loosened his grip, slumping back on the ground. Jordan pulled his sheath knife and deftly slit the shirtsleeve from cuff to shoulder. There were two sets of puncture wounds visible, one on the upper biceps and another on the forearm. Working swiftly, Jordan unknotted the bandana around Rickard's neck and fashioned a tourniquet above the upper wound. By then, Willingham was at his side, pinning Rickard to the ground.

Jordan quickly sliced a broad X across each of the fang marks with his knife, and began sucking venom from the wounds. The taste was vile, but he ignored it, spitting blood and poison whenever his mouth filled. He kept at it until the flow of blood slowed to a trickle, only then aware that Rickard had passed out. He wiped a smear of blood from his face, and sheathed his knife. He nodded to Willingham.

"Get Bumpus to bring the wagon. We'll carry him down to those shade trees by the river."

"You think he'll make it?"

"Cape, that'd be anybody's guess."

Underneath the cottonwoods lining the Cimarron, they arranged a pallet of blankets for Rickard. Bumpus Moore, who as cook also served as the camp doctor, put together a poultice of salt and river mud, and wrapped the wounds.

There was nothing else to be done, and the other men gathered a short distance away while Moore went about preparing supper. By sundown, Rickard's arm was swollen to three times normal size, his face flushed with fever and his body wracked by chills. Added blankets were used to cover him, and the men took turns bathing his forehead with cool river water. He drifted in and out of consciousness.

Supper was a somber affair. There was little talk, and none of the usual bantering that went on after a day on the trail. The hands sat grouped around the campfire, their features shadowed by the flames, listening to Rickard moan. Finally, one of the men pulled a harmonica from his pocket, and began playing an old, familiar tune. Another man, his voice a clear tenor in the still night, picked up the melody.

A ten dollar horse and a forty dollar saddle
Off on the trail a punchin' Texas cattle
I awake in the mornin' long fore daylight
And before I sleep the ole moon shines bright
No chaps, no slicker, and it's pourin' down rain
I swear I'll never ride night-herd again
It's beef and beans for me most ever' day
Lord, I'd as soon be eatin' dry prairie hay
Feet in the stirrups and my seat in the sky
I'll quit punchin' cows in the sweet by and by

The men stared into the fire as the last refrain drifted to a close. They seemed unable to look at each other, and the sudden stillness was broken by one of them clearing his throat. Bumpus Moore walked to the nearby pallet and knelt down to check on Rickard. When he climbed to his feet, his expression was grave, and he walked back at a slower pace. He glanced at the harmonica player.

"You know any hymns?"

"Yeah, I know a couple. You want me to play 'em?"

"Never be a better time. Maybe somebody's listenin'."

"You talkin' about somebody in the sweet by and by?"

Moore nodded. "Alvin ain't long for this world."

The wail of the harmonica silenced a bullfrog along the river. The men sat in stony silence, listening to the mournful strains of "Amazing Grace." No one sang this time.

CHAPTER 22

By late evening, the herd was through grazing. One by one, the cows began lying down, legs folded beneath them, their heads nodding in a wakeful half-sleep. Longhorns were essentially creatures of the wild, not unlike deer or mustangs. Their sleep was guarded, broken by the slightest sound.

The men on night guard worked four-hour shifts. There were two men to a shift, and the first shift went on duty when the day's drive was halted. The guards rode the perimeter of the bed-ground, one on either side of the herd. Their patrol brought them together about once an hour, north or south of the herd.

The primary duty of the night guard was to prevent a stampede. Longhorns were prone to run at the slightest excuse, and the guards were constantly on the alert for anything out of the ordinary. Lightning and rain squalls were of particular concern; but a strange noise, the odor of a skunk, even a keening wind could make the herd restless. Cowhands were of the opinion that longhorns often ran just for the hell of it, no excuse needed.

The threat of rustlers was yet another concern. All of the men had been on trail drives, mostly along the Chisholm Trail through Indian Territory. Some of the older ones had driven to Abiline or Wichita, or other Kansas railheads, before Dodge City became the reigning cowtown. To a man, they knew that no herd was safe from rustlers until it had been delivered intact to a railhead. Thieves had been known to stampede a herd within a day's drive of Dodge City.

Tonight, the longhorns were unusually restless. Cows throughout the herd kept standing, staring suspiciously into the starlit darkness, only to collapse into watchful sleep. The hands riding the eight-to-midnight detail were watchful as well, their nerves put on edge by the constant movement. A few cows disturbed from slumber was to be expected; a couple of hundred moving about was cause for wary caution. The men came together at the south end of the herd around ten o'clock.

"Don't like it," one said in a low voice. "They're actin' awful spooky."

"I got a feelin' the bastards are gonna run. You seen anything to set 'em off?"

"Nothin' to put 'em on the prod like this. You think we ought to warn Willingham?"

"Let's wait a while longer. Him and Jordan have been taking turns lookin' after Alvin. Mebbe these critters will get cooled down."

There was a moment of silence. "You figger Alvin'll pull through?"

"Ain't likely. You see the size of that gawddamn rattler? Probably squirted Alvin with a quart of juice."

"Nothin' I hate worse'n a snake. Scares the bejesus outta me ever' time I run acrost one."

"How you think Alvin feels? Hope he's ready for the Pearly Gates."

"Never yet met a man who was ready to die. Hell, that ain't natural."

"Well, we'd best quit jawbonin' and get back to work. I don't want these sonsabitches runnin' on my watch."

"See you on the next go-round."

The men separated and rode off in opposite directions. Down by the river, sparks flared as Jordan fed more wood into the fire. Flames provided the only light in his vigil over Alvin Rickard, and he'd kept the fire stoked all evening. He and Willingham alternated caring for the dying man, allowing the cook and the hands a decent night's sleep. He walked back to the bed pallet beneath the trees.

Rickard was conscious. The chills had passed, but he still burned with fever, and the top blankets had been thrown aside. For the past few hours he'd faded in and out of consciousness, slowly losing ground as the venom spread through his system. But now, his eyes were clear and he seemed fairly lucid. He licked his lips.

"How long've I been out?"

"Couple of hours." Jordan bathed his forehead with a damp cloth. "How do you feel?"

Rickard grimaced. "Like I'd been run over and stomped. Hurts like a bastard."

"I've seen men snake-bit before. Wish there was something to do, but there's not."

"You ever seen one get well?"

"Why, sure I have. Happens all the time."

"Quit funnin', Mr. Jordan." Rickard swallowed, took a shuddering breath. "I'm fixin' to die, ain't I?"

Jordan saw nothing to be gained with a lie. "Alvin, I reckon your luck ran out. That's just the hard truth."

"Well, no use squawkin' about it. I've had my day, now and then."

"Sorry it worked out this way. Anybody you want me to get word to?"

"Nobody that'd care to hear."

Rickard's gaze drifted off. He stared into the starlit sky, as though searching for something not visible. After a time, he looked around. "You ever think about God?"

"How do you mean?"

"Life in the hereafter. Heaven and hell."

Jordan realized that he hardly knew Alvin Rickard. There were over a hundred men on the JA payroll, and he sometimes had trouble keeping their names straight. Yet now, like a minister at a deathbed, he was being asked to guide one of them into the unknown. He decided to say what he himself would like to hear.

"The Scripture says a man who repents his sins will know everlasting life. I always took that to mean he'd live in a place where there's just peace and happiness. All his worldly troubles behind him."

"Sounds pretty good," Rickard said. "Maybe I won't hurt so bad when I get there."

"Alvin, you won't hurt at all. That's strictly for this world."

"Heard preachers talk lots about the Promised Land. Wonder where it is just exactly."

"I always wondered myself," Jordan said honestly. "Guess it's someplace special that God put aside during the Creation."

"Guess so." Rickard considered a moment. "You figger that's where the soul goes . . . when a man passes on?"

"Well, the way I read the Good Book, that's the general idea. The spirit of a man lives on forever, sort of eternal."

Rickard tried to smile. "Trouble is, I might not get sent to heaven. Might wind up in hell."

"Tend to doubt it," Jordan said easily. "You talk like you've already repented your sins. That's your ticket to the Promised Land, bought and paid for."

"Yeah, and it's a one-way ticket, too. Express train to the end of the line."

"You'll like it when you get there, Alvin. Hold me a spot for when my time comes."

"I'll get Saint Peter to greet you with a brass band. Think I'll take myself a little nap. I'm feelin' tired."

"We'll talk more when you wake up."

Rickard closed his eyes. His breathing was uneven and labored, as though his body had suddenly given up the fight. Jordan's throat clogged with admiration, for he sensed that the man had purposely tried to cover his fear with a note of humor. No man could go out with greater dignity than to jest about his one-way journey into the hereafter. Looking down at the still form, he sensed something else as well.

Alvin Rickard would never wake up. The express train he'd joked about was waiting.

There were five men. They were hidden in the trees along the Cimarron, not a hundred yards upriver from the camp. After dark, covered by the sound of the harmonica, they had moved downstream, into a concealed position. Their eyes were fixed on the herd.

The leader of the bunch was short and bearded, a man of foxlike cunning. All evening, while his men waited deeper in the trees, he had watched the night guards patrol the herd. Again and again, he had counted in his head the time that elapsed on their back-and-forth patrol, north to south. He now knew the raid had to be completed in under an hour.

Greed was not a factor in his plan. Any attempt to rustle the entire herd would almost certainly result in a pitched battle. His men were outnumbered more than two to one, and he knew the trail hands would fight to defend the herd. Instead, his plan was to quietly steal a hundred head and slip away undetected into the night. The payday was not so large, but the risks were reduced to an acceptable level. He and his men would live to steal another day.

Shortly after ten o'clock, when the night guards turned to patrol along a southern line, the gang leader signaled his men forward. They moved out of the trees into the starlight, their horses held to a slow walk. The longhorns nearest the river awoke, watching warily as the riders fanned out, circling left and right. The men eased into the herd, working stealthily, and cut out a wedge of cows on the northern end. Their voices low, clucking softly, the gang got roughly a hundred head up and walking. They drove the longhorns westward from the herd.

Off to their rear, Old Blue awoke with a start. The riders were plainly visible in the starlight, and he saw part of his herd being hazed at a walk toward the river. He scrambled onto all fours, goaded by some protective instinct for the herd, and the bell around his neck clanged like a temple gong in the still night. On the instant, longhorns throughout the herd responded to the sound of the bell, and lurched erect. Old Blue took off at a lumbering trot toward the riders.

The night guards wheeled and spurred their horses into a gallop. Their first thought was that the herd had spooked, and they pounded north to head off a stampede. But to their front, angling westerly from the herd, they saw shadowed riders driving a bunch of cows toward the river. The man on the west flank of the herd whooped a warning at the top of his lungs, alerting the camp. The guard on the east, driven by an urge to overtake the rustlers, recklessly attempted to force a shortcut through the massed longhorns. Old Blue trundled on toward the distant riders.

The gang leader whirled his horse, any attempt at stealth now forgotten. His plan abruptly changed from rustling cows to escape, and for that he needed a diversion. He'd lost the rustled stock in any event, for the longhorns had turned on his men and charged back in the direction of the bell. He pulled his pistol and thumbed off five shots at the herd, the fiery muzzle blast lighting the darkness. The roar of gunfire echoed in the night like rolling thunder.

Old Blue spun away from the staccato blast of the pistol. He broke into a headlong run, the bell flapping and clanging, driven onward by some atavistic sense of survival. The longhorns to his direct front bolted, panicked by their leader's flight, spreading terror to those behind them. The herd suddenly wheeled around, two thousand strong, and barreled off in a maddened surge to the southeast. The night guard on the far side, caught in the midst of the stampede, went down aboard his thrashing horse. The longhorns' sharp hooves hammered them into the ground.

The other night guard savagely gigged his horse into a gallop. He circled the herd on the south, searching for what had now become the lead point of the stampede. His thoughts were no longer on the rustlers, who were fleeing westward along the river. Nor was he aware of the commotion in the camp, Jordan shouting orders as men jumped from their bedrolls. Awake, swigging a last cup of coffee, Jordan was the first to reach the picket line, where saddled night horses were stationed for the crew. He jerked the cinch tight, bounding aboard his gelding, and reined out of camp. Willingham was only a step behind.

Jordan raked his horse, bending low in the saddle. The herd was no more than a minute ahead, and he urged his horse onward, passing the rear of the column at a dead lope. Longhorns were fleet as deer, but no match for a horseman, and he steadily gained ground as the cattle veered off across the plains. The earth shook beneath thousands of hooves, and though the cows were clearly visible in the starlight, he skirted the eastern flank at a distance. The danger lay in his horse stumbling on the uneven terrain, or breaking a leg in a prairie dog hole. Men thrown into the onrushing path of a stampede rarely lived to tell the tale.

Some ten minutes later Jordan overtook the lead steers. Willingham was only a few lengths behind, and on the opposite side of the column he saw one of the night guards. He motioned off to the west, then slowly edged his horse into the wedge of cows at the point. Still at a gallop, he loosened his lariat, and began popping the cows leading the charge. Close behind, Willingham shouted and waved his hat, crowding the longhorns to Jordan's rear. A quarter-mile farther along the steers at the point began a gradual, sweeping curve westward, forced to slow their pace as Jordan pressed them into a tighter turn. The column curled, doubling back on itself, and the stampede dropped off to a shuffling turnabout. The herd was milled into a mass of bawling, wild-eyed longhorns.

Willingham quickly got the hands stationed around the herd. Jordan reined in beside the night guard, a man named Homer Bolton. "What the hell happened?" he demanded. "Was it you firing that gun?"

"Not me, boss!" Bolton said hurriedly. "Rustlers was makin' off with a little bunch, and they commenced shootin' when I spotted 'em. Herd took off like scalded cats."

"How many rustlers were there?"

"Don't rightly know, for sure. Everything happened pretty fast."

Willingham rode up, nodded to Bolton. "We're missing Joe Hyde. Wasn't he on night guard with you?"

"Awww, Jesus," Bolton said in a hollow voice. "Thought I saw him and his horse go down when the cows spooked. Hoped my eyes was just playin' tricks."

"Maybe they were," Jordan said. "Go have a look for him."

When Bolton rode off, Willingham grunted sourly. "All he's gonna find is a greasy spot. Hyde would've caught up by now . . . if he was alive."

"Likely so," Jordan observed. "When the herd's calmed down, pick out a couple of grave diggers. Way it looks, we've got two boys to bury."

"Alvin passed on?"

"Yeah, just before the stampede started. We'll hold funeral services at first light."

Willingham stared at him in the pale starlight. "You aim to go after the rustlers?"

Jordan nodded, his eyes like iron. He rode toward the river.

CHAPTER 23

A dinge of light brushed the eastern sky. The men were standing beneath the cottonwoods, gathered around two graves hollowed from the earth near the river. The bodies were wrapped in blankets, woolen shrouds fastened with strands of rope.

The men were somber, their eyes rimmed with fatigue and sadness. All night, digging graves and moving the herd back toward the river, there had been little time to reflect on the permanence of death. But now, staring down at the bodies, they were forced to consider the mortality of man. Any one of them, except for the luck of circumstance, could be lying there wrapped in coarse blankets. Life no longer seemed so certain.

Jordan was positioned at the head of the graves. He removed his hat and the other men quickly followed his lead. There was something barbaric about committing men to the ground in such rough fashion. But there was no lumber to build coffins, and no practical way of carting the bodies to Dodge for a proper funeral. On a trail drive, where the ordinary was often impractical, most men accepted that things had to be managed in the best way possible. A funeral was no different.

"Joe Hyde and Alvin Rickard," Jordan said in a tight voice, "were damn good men. They always pulled their weight when there was work to be done, and they were good company around a campfire. We'll miss them." He paused, glancing around at the sober faces. "Any of you boys want to say a word about Alvin and Joe?"

The men stood silent, their heads lowered. Jordan waited a moment, allowing them a chance to speak, finally nodding to Willingham. The trail boss and three others stepped forward, clapping their hats on, positioning themselves at the ends of each shrouded form. They grabbed the head and foot of the blankets, and gently lowered the bodies into the ground. Then, removing their hats, they again took positions beside the graves. Jordan looked once more at the men.

"Any of you boys recollect your Scripture? Alvin and Joe ought to be sent off with the proper words."

None of the men responded. "All right, I'll do my best from memory." He stared out across the plains. " 'The Lord is my shepherd; I shall not want. He maketh me to lie down in green pastures; He leadeth me beside the still waters.' "

Bumpus Moore sniffed, wiped his nose with a dirty kerchief. All the men were taken by the words, for they stood beside the waters of a river and before them stretched the green of the plains. Jordan hesitated, struggling to remember the passage from the Bible, then went on.

" 'Yea, though I walk through the valley of the shadow of death, I will fear no evil. Thou art with me, and Thy mercy shall follow me all the days of my life. I will dwell in the house of the Lord forever.' Amen."

There was a muttered chorus of "Amens" from the hands. After a strained moment, two of the men began shoveling dirt into the graves. The others, their eyes averted, moved toward the camp in a solemn knot. Jordan walked off a short distance with Willingham.

"We'll need markers," he said. "See what Bumpus can rig with their names on it."

"I'll knock a couple of slats out of the wagon."

Jordan nodded. "I'll be taking three men with me. Hold the herd here till we get back."

Earlier, at first light, Jordan had inspected the riverbank for tracks. He knew there were five rustlers, with a lead now approaching seven hours. Willingham looked at him. "How long you figure to track them?"

"Till we find them," Jordan said flatly. "However long that takes."

"Deacon Walsh oughta be along with his herd late today. What if you're not back?"

"You and Deacon get both herds across the river. Afterward, you take some of Deacon's hands to fill out your crew. Head due north and you'll hit the Arkansas."

"That's five days from here," Willingham said, concern in his voice. "Think it's gonna take you that long?"

"Don't know," Jordan told him. "Depends on how far and how fast those rustlers traveled."

"What if they're headed for Colorado? Or New Mexico?"

"Cape, you know the rule. Nobody kills one of our men and gets away with it. One way or another, we settle the account."

"Yeah, I know," Willingham said. "But what if you're still gone when we hit Dodge? What'd we do with the herd?"

"Find a holding ground," Jordan replied. "Sit tight till I get there. Tell the cattle buyers I'll be along."

"Hope you catch the bastards *muy pronto*."

"There's bound to be a fight when we do. I'll need the steadiest men in your crew once the shootin' starts. Who would you pick?"

Willingham thought about it. "I'd take Ray Wilson and Ben Thorn. Josh Pilcher, too. Nothin' much rattles them."

"All right," Jordan said. "Tell them it's strictly volunteer. No hard feelings if they want out."

"Not a man in the crew that wouldn't volunteer. They'd all jump at the chance."

"Let's get a move on, then. I'm ready to pull out."

Ten minutes later Jordan led the men out of camp. Behind them, the first rays of sunrise broached the horizon and spread across the land. The tracks along the shoreline were easy to read, the earth churned by five horses at a hard gallop. Jordan signaled his men into a steady trot. They rode west along the Cimarron.

The trail angled southward a few miles west of camp. Ahead lay the strip of Indian Territory that abutted the borders of Texas, New Mexico, and Colorado. Jordan followed the tracks all morning, aware that the rustlers had gradually slowed their pace from a gallop to a trot, and finally to a walk. From the sign, they were not expecting pursuit.

Twelve miles or so south of the Cimarron lay the North Fork of the Canadian. Toward noon, with the sun high overhead, Jordan spotted the treeline along the river. Even from a mile away, he could make out a faint tendril of smoke drifting through the trees. He turned sharply away from the tracks, followed by his men, and veered off to the southeast. A few minutes later, hidden within the treeline, they reined to a halt.

Jordan got them dismounted, their horses firmly tethered. Armed with six-guns and carbines, the men gathered around him on the riverbank. "I figure they're about a mile upstream," he said. "From the looks of that fire, they're not expecting company."

"Must be idjits," Pilcher snorted. "Oughta known we'd come after them."

"Tend to doubt it," Jordan said. "They didn't get away with any cows, and there's no way they'd know about Joe Hyde being killed. Probably thought they got away safe."

"Too bad for them," Thorn said, grinning. "How you plan to jump 'em, Mr. Jordan?"

"We'll move upstream slow and easy. Keep a sharp lookout in case they've got a guard posted. We'll try to take them without a fight."

"And if that don't work?" Pilcher asked.

"Shoot anybody that makes a wrong move. We've not taking prisoners."

Jordan led the way upstream. The men trailed him in single file, their carbines at the ready. Some twenty minutes later he motioned them to a halt in a stand of cottonwoods. Ahead, he spotted horses tied to a picket line, and a short distance beyond, the campsite itself. Smoke spiraled skyward from a small fire, where one of the rustlers tended to a coffeepot. The others lazed around the camp, yawning and scratching, still half asleep. They were stretched out on the ground, heads propped against their saddles.

To all appearances, the gang had slept late, with never a thought to pursuit. After satisfying himself that all five rustlers were accounted for, Jordan signaled his men. He waved his arms, spreading them out in a line abreast of him, then gestured toward the camp. At a measured pace, their carbines cocked, they advanced through the trees. One of the horses at the picket line suddenly rolled its eyes, snorting loudly.

The man at the fire looked around, his features etched with amazement. But the shock lasted a mere instant, and he jackknifed to his feet, clawing at a pistol on his hip. Jordan took deliberate aim, sighting as he rose from the fire, and shot him in the chest. He stumbled backward, knocking the coffeepot over, and dropped to the ground. The other rustlers, stunned awake, watched with dumbfounded stares as Jordan and his men materialized from the trees. Jordan wagged the barrel of his Winchester.

"Nobody move!" he barked. "Get those hands up!"

The rustlers raised their hands overhead. Jordan moved into the clearing, flanked by his men. His gaze swept the startled faces of the gang members. "Who's in charge here?"

There was no response. Three of the rustlers batted their eyes, darting sideways glances at the fourth man. He was short and muscular, with tousled dark hair and a full beard. After a moment, aware that his men had given him away, he shrugged. "I guess I've been elected."

"What's your name?"

"Who's askin'?"

Jordan sighted on his forehead. "Give me a name or get shot. Take your choice."

"Lon Blanchard," the man said. "What's the idea of bustin' into our camp and shootin' that boy dead? You're gonna answer for this."

"No, it's the other way round, Blanchard. Last night you and your gang tried to rustle my herd."

"You'll play hell provin' that."

"Got all the proof we need," Jordan said. "We followed your tracks south from the Cimarron. You left a trail plain to read."

"So what?" Blanchard said with a wolfish grin. "I don't see no cows around here, and nobody to say we're rustlers. It's your word against mine."

Jordan looked around at Pilcher. "Get their guns. Stay out of my line of fire."

Pilcher leaned his carbine against a tree. He circled behind the gang, pausing only long enough to take each man's pistol from its holster. With two guns stuffed in his waistband, and one in either hand, he crossed the clearing on the opposite side. He stopped beside Jordan.

"What'd I do with these?"

Jordan shifted the Winchester to the crook of his arm. He pulled a pistol with gutta-percha handles from Pilcher's waistband. Hefting it, he looked at Blanchard. "Any question this is your gun?"

Blanchard appeared puzzled. "You seen him take it off me. What kinda game we playin' here?"

Jordan thumbed the hammer to half-cock, opened the loading gate, and spilled cartridges onto the ground. He smelled the cylinder and barrel, then smiled at Blanchard. "Freshly fired," he said. "You must've reloaded after you rode off last night."

"I dunno what you're talkin' about."

"Last night, you fired five shots at my herd. One of my hands was killed in the stampede."

The other gang members went pale. Two were in their

thirties and the third appeared scarcely more than twenty. Their heads turned involuntarily toward Blanchard. "You got nothin' on us," he blustered, glaring at Jordan. "Just a gawddamn accident, that's all it was."

"No accident," Jordan said in a cold voice. "You and your boys murdered my man."

"That's the biggest crock of shit I ever heard!"

Jordan motioned to Pilcher. "Take one of their ropes and cut it in lengths. Tie their hands behind their backs."

"Like hell!" Blanchard started to his feet. "We're not gonna be hung!"

"Yeah, you are." Jordan pointed the carbine at him. "Sit still or I'll plug you in the leg. Either way, you'll hang."

Blanchard dropped back on the ground, and the other men sat frozen in place. Pilcher cut a rope into three-foot lengths, and bound their arms behind their backs, their wrists cinched tight. At Jordan's order, he then gathered ropes from the other saddles, tossed them over a stout limb, and snubbed them firmly around the trunk of a cottonwood. Wilson and Thorn, meanwhile, led four horses from the picket line and halted them below the tree limb. Jordan nodded toward the gang members.

"Get 'em mounted."

The rustlers were hoisted aboard their horses, and positioned beneath the dangling ropes. Pilcher rode forward on the fifth horse, and one by one fitted a noose around the men's necks. Jordan and the JA hands then cut switches from a nearby sapling, and moved to the rear of the horses. Directly behind Blanchard, Jordan fixed the doomed man with a look.

"You boys got about ten seconds to say your prayers."

Blanchard gazed stolidly into the distance. The men on either side of him seemed resigned, their eyes dull and empty. The youngest rustler wet his pants, tears streaming down his face. His lips moved in a monotone chant.

"Ooo Jesus! Lord God Jesus!"

Jordan raised his arm, hesitating a moment, then nodded. The switches cracked across the horses' rumps, and the animals bolted forward. The rustlers were jerked into the air, then swung back as the ropes hauled them up short. When the nooses snapped tight, their eyes seemed to burst from the sockets, growing huge and distended. They thrashed and kicked, their legs dancing, as though trying to gain a foothold. Their gyrations spun them in frenzied circles.

A full minute passed while they vainly fought the ropes. Then their faces purpled, slowly turned a ghastly shade of blackish amber. One by one their mouths opened, swollen tongues flopped out like onyx snakes. Their bodies went limp, necks crooked at a grotesque angle over their shoulders. The only sound was the creak of ropes.

"Christ," Wilson muttered, staring up at them. "Never seen a man hung before. Shore ain't no easy way to die."

"Tell it to Joe Hyde," Pilcher said. "He got tromped to death by a herd of steers. I'd take a rope any day."

"We're through here," Jordan informed them. "Let's get back to our horses. We've got a long ride."

Pilcher turned. "Ain't we gonna bury 'em?"

Jordan walked off downstream. The men took a last look at the bodies, then hurried along behind. The message, though unspoken, was clear.

The murderers of Joe Hyde were to be left for the buzzards.

CHAPTER 24

Dodge City sweltered under an early afternoon sun. The trailing season had only just begun, but the vice district was jammed with Texans. A carnival atmosphere permeated the streets, with saloons, whorehouses, and gambling dives catering to the rowdy nature of cowhands. A combination of wild women and popskull whiskey quickly separated most of them from their wages.

Jordan was surprised by the crowds. Dodge City billed itself as "Queen of the Cowtowns," but it was larger and livelier than he'd expected. He was surprised as well by the number of herds on the holding grounds outside town, along the plains bordering the Arkansas. From the looks of things, ranchers throughout Texas got an early start on the drive to railhead. He wondered how that would affect cattle prices.

Late that morning he had guided Willingham's herd onto the holding ground. Deacon Walsh was half a day behind, and expected to arrive sometime before nightfall. After getting the herd settled, he had bathed in the river, given himself a shave and mustache trim, and changed into fresh clothes stored in the chuck wagon. Only then had he felt prepared to set off in search of cattle buyers. He'd ridden into town shortly after the noon hour.

Fort Dodge, the nearest army post, was situated five miles east along the Arkansas. Until 1872, with the arrival of the railroad, Dodge City had been a windswept collection of log structures devoted to the buffalo trade. But now, hammered together in the middle of nowhere, it had sprung, virtually overnight, into the rawest boomtown on the Western Plains. A sprawling hodgepodge of buildings, the town was neatly divided by the railroad tracks.

The vice district, known simply as the South Side, ran wild night and day. There, the trailhands were allowed to let off steam in a no-holds-barred pursuit of drunkenness and depravity, gunplay excepted. But at the railroad tracks, locally dubbed the Deadline, all rowdiness ceased. The lawmen of Dodge City, reportedly the toughest in the West, rigidly enforced the ordinance. Anyone who attempted to hurrah the town north of the tracks was guaranteed a stiff fine and a night in jail.

The moment Jordan crossed the tracks he sensed a remarkable change. On the other side of the Deadline, it was like passing from a three-ring circus into a sedate churchyard. There were no drunks, no fistfights or raucous crowds, almost no Texans. Everyone conducted themselves in an orderly fashion, and while the plaza was filled with wagons, the only disturbance came from cursing muleskinners. North of the tracks people appeared to have their minds on business.

The dusty plaza along Front Street was clearly the center of trade and commerce. Down at the end, flanked by several smaller establishments, were the Dodge House Hotel, Zimmerman's Hardware, and the Long Branch Saloon. Up the other way were a couple of banks and the newspaper, bordered by cafes and shops and varied business places, including a mercantile emporium. Farther north, beyond the plaza, was the residential district of town.

Jordan thought it a highly sensible arrangement. The wages of sin on one side of the tracks and the fruits of commerce on the other. The neutral ribbon of steel in between served as a visible, and clearly effective, dividing line. To the benefit of all concerned, it seemed to work uncommonly well.

Skirting the train station, Jordan held his gelding to a walk. Toward the west end of town, he spotted the cattle pens and the loading yard. He scanned the buildings on the plaza, wondering where he might find the cattle buyers. Often as not, they headquartered in one of the better saloons. He reined up before the Long Branch.

After hitching his horse, Jordan crossed the boardwalk and went through the door. The saloon was a model of decorum, unlike the dives he had seen on the South Side. A mahogany bar fronted one wall the length of the room, with an ornate gilded mirror centered on the backbar. Directly opposite were gaming tables, offering a choice of faro, roulette, dice, and chuck-a-luck. Toward the rear of the room were tables reserved for poker.

Jordan saw a familiar face at the bar. Will Bascom, a rancher from the Upper Cross Timbers, stood with one boot heel hooked over the brass rail. A man of some girth, he was dressed in range clothes, sipping a whiskey. He spotted Jordan in the mirror, and turned with a broad smile. He extended a hand the size of a horseshoe.

"By God!" he said loudly. "Good to see you again, Jack."

"Hello, Will," Jordan said, shaking his hand. "How're things down on the Brazos?"

"Better'n they've been in many a year. Hit Dodge day before yesterday, and sold my herd this mornin'. Here, lemme buy you a drink. I'm celebratin' good times."

"Little early for me, Will. I take it you got a fair price."

"Top dollar." Bascom lowered his voice with a sly look. "Milked the bastards till they was dry. Got twenty-nine a head."

Jordan laughed. "Hell's bells, I guess congratulations are in order. You think the price will hold?"

"Lemme tell you, them buyers are plumb hungry for cows. They'll take anything on four legs that's got horns."

"Sounds like the beef market back east is booming."

"Gospel truth," Bascom observed, tossing off his drink.

"Folks back there must purely love beefsteak. Never seen anything like it."

"I just pulled in," Jordan said. "Who are the main cattle buyers?"

Bascom ducked his head toward the rear of the room. "Them two jaspers sittin' right over there. Both outta Chicago."

"Which one bought your herd?"

"The taller one, Dave Thompson. Other feller's name is Lloyd Meecham. They rep for the biggest meat companies in the business."

Jordan studied the men a moment. "How come they sit together like that? Aren't they competitors?"

"Double whammy," Bascom told him. "Already got the prices fixed, but they'll try to beat you down. Take turns on which one gets the herd."

"So they both get all the cows they want?"

"None of the other buyers are in their league. Work it right, and they'll outbid anybody."

Jordan nodded. "Where do the other buyers hang out?"

"Mostly the Dodge House," Bascom said. "Thompson and Meecham got this here saloon staked out for themselves."

"I reckon I'll test the waters. Talk to you later, Will."

Jordan walked to the rear of the room. He stopped before the table, nodding to the men. "I understand you gents are the top cattle buyers in town. I'm Jack Jordan and I've got cows for sale."

Thompson was tall and angular, with a waspish expression. Meecham, by contrast, was a portly man with fuzzy muttonchop whiskers. After a round of introductions, they got Jordan seated at the table and offered him a drink. He declined, lounging back in his chair, and waited for one of them to open the discussion. Meecham finally took the lead.

"What part of Texas are you from, Mr. Jordan?"

"Palo Duro Canyon," Jordan said. "That's over in what's called the Panhandle."

''Yes, that would be western Texas, wouldn't it? I've not heard of your canyon, Mr. Jordan. Is it large?''

''Thousand feet deep and a hundred miles long. Large enough for me.''

''I would think so,'' Meecham said. ''How much of the canyon do you control?''

''All of it.''

Jordan let them digest that for a moment. Finally, after exchanging a glance with Meecham, Thompson idly waved his hand. ''How many cows do you have in—what was it—Palo Duro Canyon?''

''Fifty thousand,'' Jordan said casually. ''Sixty thousand, maybe more, next year.''

Thompson regarded him narrowly. ''How many are you trailing to Dodge this year?''

''I'll have four thousand on the holding grounds by dark. Another four thousand will be here in the next couple of days. Likely trail eight or ten thousand more in September.''

''Really?'' Meecham said, somewhat astounded. ''That's quite an operation, Mr. Jordan.''

''Yes, isn't it,'' Thompson remarked. ''Odd we haven't heard of you before. What is your ranch called?''

''The JA,'' Jordan said, poker-faced. ''Stands for the initials of my partner and co-owner, John Adair. Maybe you've heard of him.''

''Adair.'' Thompson steepled his fingers, thoughtful. ''I seem to recall something about a John Adair from New York. Something about Wall Street, the stock market.''

''Same man,'' Jordan said. ''Relocated his brokerage firm to Denver. We're partners now.''

''Of course!'' Meechan blurted. ''Adair sold out before the market crashed in '73. His name even made headlines in Chicago.''

''Wouldn't doubt it,'' Jordan commented. ''John's pretty shrewd when it comes to the economic climate. That's why he got into the cow business.''

"Does he think there's another fortune to be made in cattle?"

"Knows it for a fact," Jordan said confidently. "Easterners like their beef, and the market gets bigger every day. We've even started a breeding program to improve the stock."

"Oh?" Thompson's look was sharp and impenetrable. "What sort of breeding program?"

"Hereford purebreds crossed with longhorns. Before long, we'll deliver cows pudgy as pigs."

The perception slowly dawned on Thompson and Meecham that they were not dealing with a hardscrabble Texas rancher. Jordan's relationship with John Adair impressed them, and they sensed he was a man who understood the subtleties of negotiation. A man who could finesse a situation to his own advantage, just as he had now put them on notice. His disclosures about the JA Ranch, though seemingly guileless, had been dropped into the conversation with clever purpose.

"Let me ask you," Thompson said. "Would you be interested in a long-term arrangement? Delivering cattle on a contract basis?"

"Anything's possible," Jordan said, avoiding a direct answer. "Today, I'm looking to sell what I've got on hand. You interested?"

"By all means," Meecham chimed in. "Of course, we'll have to inspect your cows before we can talk a deal."

"First herd's already on the holding ground. What about right now?"

"Fine with me." Meecham glanced at Thompson, who nodded. "Would you like to ride along in our buggy?"

"I'll lead you out on my horse."

Meecham pulled out a roll of bills and dropped money on the table. They shoved back their chairs and stood, following Jordan toward the door. Will Bascom, still sipping whiskey, glanced up at them in the backbar mirror.

Jordan winked at him as they went past.

* * *

The holding grounds stretched for miles along the banks of the Arkansas. Far to the south, separated by varying distances, some twenty herds of longhorns were spread across the verdant prairie. The cows were held there until sold, then moved to the loading chutes at the railroad. Smoke from campfires lifted in dusky spires against a cloudless sky.

Jordan rode alongside the buggy. He led Thompson and Meecham past the chuck wagon, where Willingham and most of the crew stood swigging coffee. A short distance ahead, the herd grazed under the watchful eyes of two outriders. With close to forty thousand longhorns on the holding grounds, the cowhands took nothing for granted. A single mishap might start a stampede that would scatter cows for fifty miles.

Meecham was bathed in sweat, his corpulent frame roasting under the afternoon sun. Thompson, who was driving, appeared unaffacted by the blast of heat. Some thirty yards from the herd, Jordan reined in and motioned the buggy to a halt. He waved in a sweeping gesture.

"Two thousand here, and six thousand more on the trail. All prime stock."

The cattle buyers gazed out across the herd, noting the JA brand. The longhorns were rangy but nonetheless fattened out from being slowly grazed northward the past five days. After a while, Thompson nodded judiciously, turning to Jordan. "Fairly decent cows," he said. "How do we know the other three herds are as good?"

"I guarantee it," Jordan assured him. "Otherwise you're not obligated."

"What price did you have in mind?"

"Some better than what you've been paying."

Thompson looked indignant. "We top anybody's price in Dodge."

"Yeah, that's the trouble." Jordan motioned across the prairie. "You're robbing these outfits blind by buying in big lots. Keeps the prices depressed.''

Meecham snorted. ''Are you really concerned with what other men are paid, Mr. Jordan.''

''Nope,'' Jordan said simply. ''They're full grown and I didn't take 'em to raise. I speak just for myself.''

''So what price are you after?''

''Thirty-one dollars a head for all four herds. Meet my price and we'll likely do business in the future.''

''Will we indeed?'' Thompson demanded. ''Have we your assurance of that . . . or it is merely an empty promise?''

''Money talks,'' Jordan said bluntly. ''Give me a fair price every time and I'll bring you more goddamn cows than you can stuff into boxcars. Like they say, one hand washes the other.''

''Suppose we compromise and settle on thirty?''

''You gents are in this for the long haul, and so am I. Thirty-one a head or no dice.''

''A man who bargains too hard often loses the deal, Mr. Jordan.''

''Not near as often as a cheapskate, Mr. Thompson.''

Meecham sat forward, his weight jostling the buggy. ''Gentlemen, please, let's not spoil a good thing. You have yourself a deal, Mr. Jordan. Thirty-one a head.''

''Glad to hear it.'' Jordan decided to soothe ruffled feathers. ''You boys dicker harder than the buyers up in Cheyenne. You're quite a team.''

Thompson allowed himself a tight smile. ''You hold your own as well, Mr. Jordan.''

''Jack Jordan!'' Meecham suddenly spluttered. ''I thought I knew your name from somewhere, and it just came to me. You're the cattleman who blazed the trail from Texas to Cheyenne.''

Jordan grinned. ''Guilty on all counts, Mr. Meecham.''

After they sealed the pact with a handshake, Thompson and Meecham drove off. On the way back to town, they wondered that the name had escaped them from the beginning. But then, all the talk about John Adair abruptly made sense. They agreed, with grudging admiration, that Jordan had deliberately distracted them from himself. A fox in the henhouse, he chose to deal in cows.

CHAPTER 25

Old Blue led the way into the stockyards. The longhorns were skittish, eyeing the train and nearby buildings with fright, ready to run at the slightest excuse. But Old Blue marched forward, calm and undaunted, the clang of his bell beckoning them to follow. The crew, whistling and shouting, lariats popping, choused the steers into the cattle pens.

Jordan sat his horse off to one side of the pens. He watched as Willingham got the crew positioned and began issuing orders. A veteran of many loading operations, Willingham knew his business and went about it with no wasted motion. Later, when the other herds were driven into the stockyards, he would oversee those operations as well. He was the one man Jordan trusted to get the job done.

Loading chutes were dropped into place, and the men began hazing cows up the ramp and into boxcars. It was a hot and dirty business, mostly cursing and prodding, worse than the trail drive itself. The longhorns sometimes balked at the head of the chute, stubbornly bunched in a knot, and refused to budge. All too often a steer would spook halfway up the ramp, rearing backward in the chute, and start a stampede in the wrong direction. The operation was hard on men and cows alike.

As the morning wore on every member of the crew became grime-streaked and sweaty and thoroughly out of sorts. Most of them were skinned and bleeding from scrambling to safety atop fences, and their curses became louder and viler with each new mishap. But as the sun rose higher, nearing the noon hour, the last boxcar was loaded. Willingham slammed the door shut, threw the latch, and moved back onto the boarding ramp. Wiping his face with a filthy bandana, he jumped to the ground and walked down the tracks. He joined Jordan at the east end of the cow pens.

"Guess we're ready to roll," he said. "Feel like I've been in a brawl."

"Good job," Jordan said, rewarding him with a smile. "You and the boys go back to camp and get cleaned up. I'll meet you in a couple of hours in front of the Lady Gay saloon. Tell the boys I'll pay them off then."

"They'll be mighty glad to hear that. They're ready to cut loose and see the elephant."

The term was common among trailhands. At the end of a long drive, their sole interest was a night on the town, seeing the elephant. Their wages would be squandered in large degree on rotgut whiskey and soiled doves, who worked the town's many whorehouses. Few of them would return to Palo Duro with anything left from their pay.

The men rode off as Lloyd Meecham approached the cow pens. Old Blue, trailing behind on a rope, would be used to lure the other herds into the stockyards. Jordan made a mental note to reward Old Blue with a bucket of beer, the rangy steer's drink of choice. Unlike the rest of the herd, Old Blue would return to Palo Duro, and live to trail another day. Jordan smiled, thinking about it, as he stepped from the saddle to greet Meecham.

"All loaded," he said, jerking a thumb at the boxcars. "They're your cows now."

"Well, that's fine," Meecham said. "They'll be on their way to Chicago within the hour."

"Which leaves the matter of settling accounts. Our deal was you'd pay me for each herd as it's loaded."

''Exactly why I'm here, Mr. Jordan. Do you want it in cash, or do you plan to open an account at the bank?''

''Three thousand in cash,'' Jordan replied, ''and a draft for the balance. I'll send it along to our bank in Denver.''

''However you prefer,'' Meecham said. ''Suppose we walk up to the bank and complete the transaction. Afterward, Dave Thompson and I would like to buy you a drink. Celebrate the start of a long and mutually profitable association.''

''A cool beer doesn't sound bad. I'm not much for hard liquor.''

''You're a rarity indeed, Mr. Jordan. A Texan who avoids acquaintance with John Barleycorn.''

''Some men like it, some don't. I never developed the taste.''

They walked uptown to the bank, Jordan leading his horse. There, after Jordan gave him a bill of sale, Meecham withdrew three thousand in cash and signed a draft for $58,907. By rough calculation, Jordan figured the four herds would net a sum just over $247,000. A profitable venture, he told himself, one that would please John Adair. He folded the bank draft and slipped it inside his hatband for safekeeping. The cash would go toward wages and a long list of supplies for the ranch. All four chuck wagons would return to Palo Duro loaded to the gunnels.

From the bank, they walked back down the street to the Long Branch. Thompson was seated at his usual table, and rose to shake hands with Jordan. A waiter took their orders, and soon returned with two whiskies and a beer, cooled with winter ice chopped from the river and stored in an icehouse. Meecham raised his glass in a toast.

''Here's to a long and prosperous alliance!''

''I'll drink to that.'' Jordan sipped his beer. ''Prosperity beats the alternative.''

''We've made an excellent start,'' Thompson said. ''Our arrangement will work to the advantage of all concerned in the years ahead.''

''Out of curiosity,'' Jordan said, looking from one to

the other. "How do you gents divvy things between yourselves? Who decides who gets which herd?"

The two men swapped a glance. Whatever passed between them, Thompson was apparently designated the spokesman. "We've been competitors for years," he said. "All the way back to '67, when Abilene became the first cowtown. We finally got tired of butting heads."

"Only hurt ourselves," Meecham added. "We were in a constant bidding war with each other and all the other buyers."

"So we joined forces," Thompson went on. "Simply put, Lloyd takes one herd and I take the next. We end up with the same number of cows."

Jordan swigged beer. "How do the other buyers feel about that?"

Thompson made a dismissive gesture. "We bid higher, and we're entitled to the best stock that comes up the trail. The others choose not to match our prices."

"Why so?"

"To be perfectly frank, they're satisfied with inferior beef. We deliver the cream of the crop, and our companies are known for quality. Our beef commands higher prices all across the East."

"Never could stand scrub cows," Jordan said. "A man who runs poor stock ought to take up farming."

"Our opinion exactly," Meecham remarked. "Whatever you do in that canyon of yours, it shows in your longhorns. They're top-notch stock, far above what we usually see."

"No big mystery," Jordan said with an expansive grin. "Palo Duro's got the best goddamn grass this side of China."

The men chuckled appreciatively, and there was a moment of silence while they sipped their drinks. Jordan turned the conversation to another matter of curiosity. "You mentioned Abilene," he said. "Guess you must've known Bill Hickok?"

"Yes, indeedy," Meecham said with a sly chortle.

"Wild Bill, prince of the pistoleers. A dead shot, drunk or sober, and mostly drunk. I heard he's become a cardsharp in one of the Dakota mining camps."

"How would he compare with the lawmen here in Dodge?"

"A different breed altogether. During his time in Abilene, Hickok was a killer with a badge. The lawmen here are more on the order of policemen. Wouldn't you agree, Dave?"

"No question," Thompson affirmed. "Not that they aren't handy with a gun, you understand. But the deputy sheriff here is a perfect example. Bat Masterson—"

"Masterson?" Jordan interrupted. "There was a Bat Masterson who fought at Adobe Walls. He's a lawman now?"

"And a good one," Thompson noted. "Not at all like Hickok. He might bust a cowhand over the head with a gun and cart him off to jail. But he hasn't killed anyone since he came to Dodge."

"I heard the law's pretty tough here. Who's the town marshal?"

"A political hack of no consequence. The one you're referring to is the assistant town marshal, and a very tough man, indeed. His name is Wyatt Earp."

"Never heard of him," Jordan said. "How long's he been a lawman?"

"Quite a while," Meecham commented. "When Wichita was the main railhead, he served there with some distinction. Dodge City hired him away just last month."

"What makes him so tough?"

"Mostly because he won't tolerate disrespect for the law. Anyone who resists an order from a peace officer almost certainly gets buffaloed."

"Buffaloed?"

"A technique Earp introduced here. Cracking a lawbreaker over the head with a Colt revolver. People say they drop like a shot buffalo."

"An apt analogy," Thompson said. "Earp was a buffalo

hunter before he became a peace officer. Perhaps he coined the term.''

''That's a new one.'' Jordan shook his head. ''You're saying he draws a gun and clubs a man before the man can defend himself? Earp must be damned fast.''

''I've seen them all,'' Thompson said, nodding. ''Hickok, Bully Brooks, Tom Carson, Mike McCluskie, all the cowtown peace officers. Earp is by far the fastest of the lot.''

Jordan glanced at a clock mounted on the wall. ''Say, look at the time.'' He pushed back his chair. ''I've got to meet my crew and pay them off. Thanks for the beer.''

''Our pleasure,'' Meecham said. ''We'll see you at the stockyards tomorrow. Enjoy yourself on the South Side.''

''I've got an idea my boys intend to cut the wolf loose. You hear any commotion tonight, it's likely the JA.''

Outside, the plaza baked under a brassy midday sun. Jordan mounted his horse and rode toward the railroad tracks. The noise from the vice district carried across town, a calliope of hurdy-gurdy pianos mixed with boisterous shouts and an occasional Rebel yell. He was reminded of the curiously practical code that prevailed in Dodge. Anything went below the Deadline.

The South Side, despite the early hour, was wide open and running wild. As Jordan crossed the tracks, the boardwalks on both sides of the street were packed with carousing trailhands. Directly ahead lay the Lady Gay and the Comique, the favorite watering holes of Texas cowmen. Within easy walking distance was a thriving infestation of saloons, gaming dens, dance halls, and parlor houses. A rough-and-ready form of free enterprise reigned in the vice district.

The idea was to separate the Texans from their wages, and send them back down the trail with empty pockets. The sporting element had perfected it to a near science, and they provided all the temptation necessary. Wicked women, pandemic games of chance, and enough distilled spirits to ossify even the strongest men's gizzard. It was bizarre and ribald, oddly irresistible. Sodom and Gomorrah on the plains.

Jordan found Willingham waiting with the crew outside the Lady Gay. The men were shaved, their hair slicked back, some of them decked out in fresh duds saved for the fling in Dodge. They watched the riotous parade on the street like eager young boys ganged up before the window of a candy store. Jordan thought half of them would be in jail before the night was out.

Willingham stepped forward as he dismounted. "We've been waitin' on you, boss. The boys are about to pop a cork."

"From the looks of you, your cork's about ready to pop too, Cape."

"Well, hell." Willingham ducked his head. "I ain't had a woman in nigh on six months. Time to get the pole greased."

Jordan dismounted as the men crowded around. He pulled a roll of greenbacks from his pocket and began thumbing bills. As a bonus for getting the herd through safely, he gave each man an extra half month's wages. The men beamed at their sudden wealth.

"Listen close now," he said, looking around the circle of faces. "Try your damnedest to behave and not get crosswise of the law. I won't have you make a bad name for the JA."

"That's good advice," a voice called out. "A night in the pokey would spoil your boys' fun."

Two men, both wearing badges, stood on the boardwalk. One was lithe and tall, with cold blue eyes and a handlebar mustache. The other was a solidly framed man of medium height, his brushy mustache neatly trimmed. The taller one fixed the men with a hooded stare.

"Pay attention to your boss and don't try to hoorah the town. All it'll bring you is grief."

Jordan gave Willingham twenty dollars. "Go ahead and take the boys inside, Cape. First drink's on me."

Willingham led the men into the Lady Gay. Jordan

stuffed greenbacks into his pocket, mounted the boardwalk. "I'm Jack Jordan, owner of the JA."

"Deputy Marshal Earp," the taller one said. "This here's Deputy Sheriff Masterson."

"Glad to meet you," Jordan said. "I understand you gents keep the lid on things around here. Must be a full-time job."

"Night and day," Masterson said pleasantly. "Wish there were more herd owners like you. That'd make our job lots easier."

"I'll try to keep my boys in line. They're not troublemakers."

"We appreciate it," Earp said. "Enjoy yourself in Dodge, Mr. Jordan."

As they walked away, Jordan thought their manner fitted their reputation. Neither of them looked like a man overly bothered by the prospect of trouble. He moved across the boardwalk and pushed through the batwing doors of the saloon.

A band was blaring away on the upper balcony. Toward the rear, whooping cowhands whirled girls around the dance floor like a gang of acrobatic wrestlers. The bar was lined three deep, with an even more dazzling array of girls mingled among the drinkers. All fluffy curls and heaving breasts, they were decked out in spangles and warpaint. Their gowns were short at the bottom and peck-a-boo on top.

Jordan elbowed his way through the crowd. A trailhand keeled over, glass in hand, and toppled to the floor as he approached the JA crew. He quickly filled the hole at the counter, where Willingham stood with his arm wrapped around a girl who looked like a painted doll brought to life. Willingham's mouth split in a lusty grin.

"Boss, I want you to meet Ruby Sue. I think we're in love!"

Jordan smiled, ordering a beer. The girl batted her eyelashes, and though there was no resemblance, he was somehow reminded of Rebecca. He sipped the beer, lost in his own thoughts, wondering how things were at Palo Duro. Another couple of days, he told himself, and the herds would be sold. His business in Dodge at an end.

He suddenly wanted to be on the trail for home.

CHAPTER 26

A brooding loneliness hung over Palo Duro. Somewhere in the distance a squirrel chattered, and a bluejay, sounding a scolding cry, took flight. Within moments, an empty silence once again settled across the canyon.

Rebecca sat in one of the rockers on the porch. The house was warm in the midday heat, and she welcomed a breeze rolling in from the south. Across the way, she heard Mose Butler's voice from the cook shack, berating his kitchen helper for some offense. She listened a moment, amused by his vituperous tone and his choice of words. She thought he enjoyed his reputation as a salty, bad-tempered curmudgeon.

For all his bombast, she found him to be a man of unflagging consideration. Butler saw to it that the milch cow was milked daily, and had even devised a way to store the milk in a sealed crock and keep it cooled in the natural spring. He regularly stopped by the house to inquire about her condition, and make sure she was drinking milk with her meals. His concern was touching, almost fatherly, and completely out of character with his tyrannical manner in the cook shack. The crew never suspected that there was a gentler side to his nature.

Leigh Dyer was even more attentive. He dropped by the house before riding out every morning, and again when he returned in the evening. His concern for her welfare was genuine; but he was awkward in her presence, and acted somewhat like a soldier operating under strict orders. Which was in large degree the case, for she knew he'd been assigned to look after her in Jack's absence. Still, she appreciated his daily visits, and went out of her way to assure him that all was well. She sometimes thought he was more worried than she was herself.

Not that she dwelled on the matter to any great extent. By her calculations, she was two weeks away from delivery, and felt disgustingly healthy. The baby was active, kicking harder every day, clearly ready to be brought into the world. She expected Jack to return by the end of the week, and that would leave plenty of time to send for Martha Bugbee. Somehow, upon learning that another woman had settled in the Panhandle, all her worries had been pushed aside. She knew her baby would be born with a knowledgeable midwife in attendance.

The southerly breeze brought with it the scent of wildflowers. She enjoyed warm afternoons, seated in her rocker, looking out across the canyon. There was a time, particularly in the first year, when she thought she would never come to grips with the isolation of Palo Duro. In those early days, she desperately missed the company of other women, and the solitude made it all the worse. But now, after more than two years, she was comfortable with what she once considered the wilds of Texas. Palo Duro was her home.

Her days were regulated by the cycles of ranch life. The men rode out in the morning not long after sunrise, and usually returned as sundown gave way to dusk. In between, a quietude settled over the compound, and she'd even learned to judge midday by the position of the sun. She no longer regulated her day by clocks, but rather by events. The saddling of horses, the clang of the dinner bell, even the talk and occasional laughter from the bunkhouse in the evening. She was a part of all this, and she felt content and secure when she went to bed at night. She belonged here.

From her conversations with Dyer and Butler, she knew that the men themselves were anticipating the birth of the baby. Apparently, from hints dropped here and there, there was considerable discussion in the bunkhouse as to whether it would be a boy or a girl. She suspected they were betting on it, and it amused her to think that most of them probably favored a boy. Buster Lomax, unasked, had crafted a wooden cradle on rockers, the outside bordered with intricate carvings of longhorns and prancing horses. Simply by the look of it, she knew Lomax expected a boy.

Her eye was drawn to the garden. Dyer had permanently assigned one of the hands to tend the garden, care for the chickens, and milk the cow. The man's name was Floyd Studer, and he had become the butt of endless jokes in the bunkhouse. At first, badgered unmercifully by the rest of the crew, he'd threatened to quit. But within a few days he had fallen under Rebecca's spell, and afterward followed her instructions like a moonstruck calf. By now, he had appointed himself her guardian, constantly watching over her as he went about his chores. He bore the gibes of the crew with stoic good humor.

Rebecca pushed herself out of the rocker. She moved to the edge of the porch, holding on to the central beam, and lowered herself to the ground. So close to full term, she was ponderous and ungainly, fearful of falling and hurting the baby. She walked toward the garden, certain that the weight she carried made her look like a spraddle-legged duck. In her mind, she often pictured herself on the day of her wedding, svelte and trim and attractive. She meant to regain her figure once the baby was born.

Studer looked up from hoeing weeds. He was a thin man, all knobs and joints, with bony features. His face seemed in a perpetual state of blush whenever he was in her presence. He knuckled the brim of his hat. "How you feelin', Miz Jordan?"

"Just fine, Floyd." Rebecca shaded her eyes against the sun. "Keeping up with those weeds is a job, isn't it?"

"Never seen nothin' like it, ma'am. Dig 'em up one day and they're back the next."

"I suppose it's all this good soil. Wildflowers certainly thrive here in the canyon. Apparently, weeds do, too."

"Hadn't give it much thought," Studer said, studying on it. "I just suspect you're right, though. Shore lots of flowers hereabouts."

"And soon we'll have vegetables." Rebecca looked out across the garden. "Turnips and carrots, all sorts of things. Won't that be wonderful?"

"Yes'um, I was sorta thinkin' the same thing. Haven't had grub like that since I was a kid."

"Did your mother have a garden, Floyd?"

"Oh, shore," Studer said, bobbing his head. "She set powerful store by her garden. Always used to say she had a green thumb."

Rebecca smiled. "I wouldn't doubt that it runs in the family. You've certainly done a nice job with our garden."

"Well, that's good of you to say, ma'am. Fact is, I was gonna ask you about buildin' a fence. You give any thought to that?"

"A fence around the garden?"

"Wouldn't be a bad idea, ma'am. Deer and critters are gonna start raidin' this patch once things commence to grow. Figgered to build a fence that'd keep 'em out."

"Yes, you're right," Rebecca said. "We can't have all your hard work go for nothing. Build us a fence, Floyd. A tall one."

"Get on it tomorrow," Studer said, blushing under her approval. "Won't take no time once I get started."

Rebecca abruptly stiffened. A sudden gush of fluid soaked her underdrawers and skirt, and flooded down her legs. Her face paled, and she looked down at a widening puddle spreading around her feet. For a moment she was dumbfounded. Then the realization struck her with instant clarity. Her water had broken!

Studer stood with his jaw agape. He looked from her to the puddle around her shoes, and back again. "Miz Jordan?" he said in a tinny voice. "You awright?"

Rebecca shook her head. She swayed, suddenly unsteady and faintly dizzy. "Help me into the house. I'm going to have the baby."

"*Now!*" Studer felt his own legs wobble. "You're gonna have it now?"

"I don't know. Please, Floyd, help me."

Studer took her arm in a firm grip. She tottered, supporting herself on his arm, as he slowly walked her toward the house. At the porch, he assisted her up one foot at a time, and led her through the doorway. Inside, they moved past the dining area and parlor, and into the bedroom. He lowered her onto the bed and she stretched out, all the color leached from her face. She drew a deep breath, tried to compose herself. Tried to think.

"Listen to me, Floyd."

"Yes'um," Studer muttered shakily. "I'm listenin'."

"Go get Mose Butler," she said. "Tell him to come here right away. Then go find Leigh Dyer."

"Don't you worry." Studer turned toward the door. "I'll fetch him myself."

"Wait!"

"Yes'um?"

"Send someone to get Mrs. Bugbee. The lady at the Circle B ranch."

"You just rest easy, Miz Jordan. I'll tend to it."

Studer hurried out of the room. Rebecca lay back against the pillow, her head spinning. She tried to remember what she'd heard from her mother, and other women in Pueblo, whenever the talk turned to women having babies. She recalled that the first sign of impending birth was when a woman's water broke. Something about a sac of fluid surrounding the baby that split apart when the time was near. But she couldn't remember any set length of time from the water breaking to the onset of labor. She vaguely recalled that it could be an hour, or several hours. Even a day or longer.

However long, she realized now that Martha Bugbee

would never make it in time. From Palo Duro to the Canadian, and back again, was at least five days. For whatever reason, she was two weeks early, and her baby would be born without a midwife. Her mind reeled at the thought, and she cursed the day she had ever come to such a godforsaken wilderness. But then, drawing deep breaths, she confronted the immediate problem, put her mind to work on what she knew of birthing babies. What she knew was very little, all of it based on sewing-circle gossip, brief snippets of conversations from long ago. Too little, too late.

She murmured a prayer for her baby. For the courage to do what must be done.

Mose Butler burst into the room. His features darkened when he saw her on the bed. "You feelin' poorly, Miz Jordan? Floyd says your time's come."

"I think it has, Mose. Although I don't feel anything yet. Labor pains, I mean."

"Floyd's gone off to find Leigh. I sent my swamper to get Miz Bugbee. But godalmighty, she's a far piece off, Miz Jordan. Can you hold out that long?"

Rebecca forced herself to remain calm. She had to depend on Butler, and perhaps Leigh Dyer, and men knew even less about having babies. Any sign of panic would panic them even more, and she needed their help. She managed what she hoped was a serene smile.

"We'll have to do this without Mrs. Bugbee. The baby will decide when it's time, and we have to be ready. I'll need your help, Mose."

"Me?" Butler shrank back. "Miz Jordan, I dunno nothin' about babies. What could I do?"

"Just follow my instructions, and listen to your common sense. I can't do this without you, Mose."

"I'll do whatever you tell me, Miz Jordan. You just gotta understand—"

Rebecca winced as the first contraction hit her. Her hands involuntarily went to her stomach. "The baby just decided it's time." She smiled bravely. "Start boiling water and get some clean bedsheets out of the cabinet. Will you do that for me, Mose?"

"Yes, ma'am. Water and sheets. I'll get on it."

Butler went to work, firing the stove and hauling water. Rebecca closed her mind to the sounds, willing herself to relax. She dimly recalled that the time between contractions determined how soon a baby would be born. Once the contractions became faster, and steady, the birth was imminent. She began counting, mentally gauging how much time elapsed until the next contraction. She barely reached eight minutes before the pain ripped through her insides.

The afternoon passed with excruciating slowness. Butler came in to check on her every few minutes, but there was little he could do. Finally, as the sun dipped westward, Rebecca knew she was running out of time. The contractions were now scarcely a minute apart, and she sensed everything would move quicker now. She told herself to forget modesty, put shame from her mind, and think only of the baby. All afternoon she had delayed the inevitable, and it could be delayed no longer. She called Butler into the bedroom.

"Listen to me, Mose," she said. "The baby's almost here, and I know you're going to be embarrassed. But neither one of us has any choice about this. You have to help me get undressed."

"I can't do no such thing, Miz Jordan. Why, godalmighty—"

"You do as I tell you! Help me right now!"

Butler edged warily toward the bed. He kept his eyes averted, his face beet-red, as he assisted her out of her dress, then removed her shoes and stockings. She kept her petticoat on, but berated him into helping her out of her underdrawers. The next contraction struck a hammer blow, and beads of perspiration popped out on her forehead. She lifted her petticoat, spread her legs. Her eyes drilled into him.

"You have to look!" she ordered in a shrill voice.

"You have to help the baby out. Do you hear me, damn you!"

Leigh Dyer walked into the room. His jaw dropped at the sight of her, and he seemed rooted to the floor. Butler grabbed his arm. "Jesus Christ, am I glad you're here. You know anything about birthin' babies?"

"No," Dyer said lamely, unable to take his eyes off her. "All I've ever done is help deliver calves."

"Then you're the doctor!" Butler shoved him forward. "Just pretend like this here's another calf."

The contractions abruptly quickened. Rebecca stifled a shriek and gulped a shuddering breath, imploring him with her eyes. Dyer crouched between her knees, began massaging her widened vulva, just as he'd done with cows in trouble at calving time. He kneaded the flesh, drawing it outward, gently forcing it to stretch. Rebecca puffed, gasping air, and strained harder.

The baby's forehead appeared and Dyer stretched the folds of the vulva wider still. Then, with a sudden rush, the head emerged cradled in his hand. He gingerly worked the shoulders free and a moment later lifted the newborn infant from the bed.

"Gawddamn," he said with a dopey grin. "It's a boy."

"Cut the umbical cord." Rebecca's voice was weak. "Tie it in a knot."

"Yeah, sure thing, Miz Jordan. You all right?"

Her eyes closed before she could reply. She drifted into sleep.

CHAPTER 27

The river was molten with sunlight. Overhead a hawk floated past on smothered wings, scanning for prey. Nothing moved along a shoreline studded with cottonwoods.

The JA outfit crossed the Canadian the third week in June. Jordan and Willingham splashed through the ford at the head of a long column. Behind, strung out one after another, were the four crews and their remudas. The chuck wagons sagged beneath the weight of provisions and equipment bound for the ranch.

Jordan set a blistering pace. The column was four days out of Dodge City, having departed the day after the last herd was loaded into boxcars. The men were by now recovered from their hangovers, following a monumental binge in the cowtown. Only three of them had spent a night in jail, which was thought to be a record for civilized behavior by a Texas outfit. The others were broke but filled with memories of drunken nights and the exotic mating habits of Kansas whores. Their stories were told again and again around campfires.

The men would have preferred a more leisurely pace on their return journey. Some of them, having served in the army, spoke of it as a forced march. But their grumblings were kept to themselves, never voiced within earshot of Jordan. There were few secrets in a cattle outfit, though he never spoke of personal matters to anyone. The men were aware that his wife was expected to give birth sometime the last week in June, and understood why he pushed the column southward from sunrise to sunset. He was determined to be there when the baby was born.

Jordan was nonetheless in high spirits. He had delivered four herds to railhead, and his deal with Dodge's leading cattle buyers boded well for the future. After taking care of payroll expenses, and purchasing supplies, he had forwarded drafts totaling $242,000 to the bank in Denver. That exceeded what he'd thought to clear by some forty thousand dollars, ample proof for John Adair that the JA was a profitable operation. Still, with that behind him, his mind focused all the more on Rebecca, and he continued to set a brutal pace. He felt some curious sense of urgency to reach Palo Duro.

After fording the Canadian, Jordan spotted a trail herd off to the west. He figured it was Sam Bugbee's second herd, the one thought to be delayed, or lost. Only two days ago, south of Dodge City, he had come across Bugbee and the first Circle B herd. At that time, Bugbee had expressed concern that he'd received no word by relay rider from the second herd. He intended to push on, since he was so close to railhead, and worry about the other herd later. But now, as a man rode forward to meet them, Jordan felt relieved for Bugbee. The missing herd was missing no longer.

"Howdy," the rider said as he reined to a halt beside Jordan and Willingham. "You the JA outfit?"

"I'm Jack Jordan. You the trail boss for Circle B?"

"Joe Dorsey," the man identified himself. "We got off to a late start."

"Guess you did," Jordan said dryly. "I saw Sam Bugbee on the trail a couple of days ago. He was worried you'd gotten yourself lost. What happened?"

"Rustlers," Dorsy said with a furious expression. "Hit us night before last and got away with better'n two hundred head. We killed one of the bastards. Shot him dead."

"Well, that is news, bad news. I figured it'd be a while before rustlers got around to the Panhandle."

"Sorry sonsabitches done found us now. Scattered my herd plumb to hell and gone. Finally got 'em on the trail this mornin'."

"These cows you lost?" Jordan said. "Which way were they driven after the raid?"

"Haven't got the least notion," Dorsey admitted. "We had ourselves a helluva mess just collectin' the herd. Wasn't time to go off lookin' for tracks."

"One thing's for goddamn sure where Sam's concerned. He'll bust a gut when he hears how many cows you lost."

"I wish to Christ it wasn't me that had to tell him. He's gonna skin my ass."

"You learned a lesson," Jordan observed. "Always track rustlers down and settle their hash. Otherwise they'll figure you're a soft touch. Hit you time after time."

"Yeah, you're right," Dorsey conceded. "One dead thief don't hardly make up for two hundred beeves."

"Any idea who he was? Where he's from?"

"There wasn't no papers on him. From his rig, he could've been an ordinary cowhand."

"Was his horse wearing a brand?"

"Never saw hide nor hair of his horse. Guess it got run off in the stampede."

"Watch yourself on the trail to Dodge. Cow thieves are thick up that way."

"Yessir, I will." Dorsey's face suddenly brightened. "Say, all this talk about rustlers, and I plumb forgot. Guess you haven't heard you're a daddy."

"What?" Jordan appeared rocked by the news. "My wife's had the baby?"

"I'd just suspect so, Mr. Jordan. Three days back one of your men come to fetch Miz Bugbee. He said your missus's time was on her."

"So you don't know if she's already had the baby?"

"Dunno anything more'n I told you. Miz Bugbee lit out in a buggy lickety-split. Never saw her move so fast."

Jordan was silent a moment. At length, he turned to

Willingham. "Cape, go pick out four horses from the remuda. I want fast ones."

Willingham nodded. "You gonna make a run for home?"

"I'll change mounts as they tire out. You'll find them where I leave them between here and the canyon. Likely they won't stray too far."

"Not if they're run that hard."

Willingham wheeled his horse back toward the remuda. Joe Dorsey wished Jordan luck, and rode off to rejoin his herd. Lost in his own thoughts, Jordan merely nodded, judging time and distance. With roughly eighty miles to cover, and several hours of daylight left, he planned to ride through the night. Without killing the horses, he figured he could make it to Palo Duro by early tomorrow morning. He told himself he had to make it.

Ten minutes later Jordan rode south across the plains. He gigged his gelding into a steady lope, the spare horses trailing behind, their halters attached to a rope around his saddlehorn. The thought uppermost in his mind was that the baby had come early, Rebecca had been there alone. Martha Bugbee could never have arrived in time.

He urged his horse to greater speed.

The battlements of Palo Duro stood rimmed against the flare of sunrise. Jordan rode into the compound as the men trooped down from the bunkhouse to the corral. He was mounted on the last of the four horses, and he ignored the stares of the men, reining to a halt before the main house. He left his horse lathered with foamy sweat in the yard.

Martha Bugbee stepped through the door of the house. She crossed the porch as Jordan swung down from the saddle and lurched forward. His face was wreathed with exhaustion, and the look of a man crazed with worry. He stared straight into her eyes, searching for some message of what awaited him inside. She stopped him at the edge of the porch.

"Simmer down," she said with a gentle smile. "You

don't want Rebecca to see you looking like a wild Indian."

Jordan caught his breath. "She's all right?"

"She lost a lot of blood and she had a hard time. But God knows it could have been worse. She's doing just fine."

"And the baby? Were you able to save the baby?"

"You have yourself a son, Jack. Healthy and hungry, and all the parts in the right places."

"A son."

Jordan spoke the word in a hushed voice. His eyes glistened, and for a moment she saw the core of tenderness behind the rough exterior. But then he seemed to regain himself, and swallowed around the lump in his throat. He shook his head with a bemused smile.

"Thank God and thank you, Martha. I'm in your debt."

"God maybe," she said lightly. "By the time I got here, it was all over. A couple of your men are the ones who deserve a medal. They delivered the baby."

"Men?" Jordan appeared confused. "What men?"

"Leigh Dyer and Mose Butler. The two of them together made a dandy midwife. I couldn't have done better myself."

"What went wrong? How'd they get involved?"

"Nothing went wrong especially," she said. "Your son just got tired of waiting, and picked his own time to be born. That turned out to be about two weeks early."

"I'll be damned." Jordan sounded slightly dazed. "And Leigh and Mose delivered him?"

"Count your lucky stars they did. Of course, when I got here they were both nervous wrecks. I'm not sure they still believe it themselves."

"You're sure Becky's all right?"

"She will be with the proper rest. Now that we've got you calmed down, come on in and see for yourself. She's been on pins and needles waiting for you to get here."

Jordan followed her into the house and through the parlor. At the bedroom door, she stepped aside and motioned him forward. "Rebecca, honey," she said in a cheery voice. "Look who's come home."

Rebecca was propped up against a bank of pillows. The baby was cradled in her arms, greedily nursing on her swollen breast. She saw Jordan standing in the doorway, and something beyond words passed between them. A sudden rush of tears streamed down her cheeks.

"Oh, Jack!" she cried. "We have a son. A darling little boy. Just look at him!"

Jordan moved to the bed. He looked down on the suckling baby with an expression of awed wonder. His eyes were fierce with pride, and for a brief instant, moist with emotion. He cleared his throat, but words failed.

"Isn't he precious?" Rebecca said. "Have you ever seen anything so wonderful in your life?"

"Nothing even close," Jordan said with a sudden grin. "Hard to put it in words."

"And he's so big!" she burbled. "He has your features, too. He looks just like you."

The baby let go of her breast with a smacking sound. He yawned, tiny fists clenched, then dropped off into a contented sleep. She laid him at her side, and he popped a thumb into his mouth. She laughed, covering her breast, and held her arms out to Jordan.

Martha Bugbee moved into the parlor as they embraced. Jordan held her tightly, her arms wrapped around his neck. She kissed him on the cheek, then a longer kiss on the mouth.

"You feel so good," she murmured. "I'm so thankful to have you home again."

"Wish I'd got here sooner," Jordan said. "Never would've left if I'd known there was any chance of trouble."

"Now don't start blaming yourself for that. Leigh and Mose got me through it just fine."

"Yeah, that's what I heard. Martha told me all about it."

Jordan had seen thousands of cows drop calves. He knew all there was to know about gaping birth canals, the welter of blood, and the sharp smell of afterbirth. Without asking, he knew as well that Dyer and Butler had seen the spread of his wife's legs, put their hands on her. They had seen her naked, cleansed the blood from her body, removed her afterbirth. They knew her more intimately than he himself.

Yet he would never speak of these things. Not to Rebecca, certainly not to Dyer or Butler. These men had brought his son from the womb, and likely saved his wife from an agonizing death. Except for them, their courage to act, he might be burying his wife, perhaps a baby born dead. He would say nothing of this, for there were no words to express what he felt for these men, the debt he owed them. Instead, he would offer some token of his gratitude. A gesture stronger than words.

Holding Rebecca, he decided to give each of the men a hundred cows. They would own the cows, and the cows' calves, and be allowed to raise them on the JA. All of which violated the unwritten law that no hand was permitted to run stock on the ranch where he worked. They would understand the significance of the gesture, and understand as well that he would never speak of what went on in his wife's bedroom. Nor were they to speak of it, either.

Martha Bugbee appeared in the doorway. "Your foreman's outside," she said. "Asked me to tell you it's important."

Rebecca moaned in protest. Jordan kissed her on the nose, got to his feet. "Don't you go away," he said. "I'll be right back."

"Oh, believe me, I'm not going anywhere. Just don't be too long."

"I'll be back in a jiffy. Promise."

Dyer was waiting on the porch. He nodded, grinning as Jordan emerged from the house. "Congratulations, boss. You've got yourself a fine boy."

"Thanks, Leigh." Jordan accepted his handshake. "I'm under orders to hurry back. What's so important?"

"One of the boys just brought word. Thought you ought to know we had some stock rustled last night."

"Where?"

"Over by Tule Creek," Dyer said. "Got off with about fifty head."

Jordan scowled. "What about tracks?"

"I'm gonna go have a look. Should be back by dark."

"Guess the thieves have found us, Leigh. I figured it would take them longer."

"There's something else," Dyer said. "We've got ourselves a new neighbor. Feller by the name of Earl Stroud. Bought land over in Tierra Blanca Canyon."

"How'd you find out?"

"One of our line riders run across one of his boys. I let it go, waitin' till you got back. Thought you'd want to pay him a call yourself."

Jordan considered a moment. "Funny we never got rustled till this Stroud showed up. Maybe it's more than a coincidence."

"Yeah, maybe so," Dyer agreed. "What d'you want to do?"

"Well, one thing's for damn sure. We're fixin' to meet Mr. Stroud. We'll talk about it tonight."

Jordan walked back into the house. Bad news would spoil his homecoming for Rebecca, and he decided to keep it to himself. He put on a broad smile as he entered the bedroom.

"Time to meet my son! Let's wake him up."

Rebecca told herself he was going to be an impossible father.

CHAPTER 28

To the west, the caprock of Palo Duro rose against a backdrop of limitless sky. Pleasant Creek curved in a graceful bend where it flowed through the grazeland and joined the Red. Far to the south, the majestic palisades of the canyon were rimmed with cottony clouds.

Jordan rode off to one side of the tracks. Leigh Dyer, John Poe, and Hank Taylor followed close behind in single file. The trail was almost two days old, and virtually invisible to anyone in the party except Jordan. From the tracks, he knew there were three men driving the rustled stock.

The tracking party had departed the headquarters compound at dawn. Jordan felt disgruntled about leaving Rebecca and the baby, particularly since he had returned home only yesterday. But the credo he'd lived by for so many years had prevailed even in his personal affairs. Thieves were to be hunted down and dispatched, without regard to the consequences. Personal matters would have to wait.

By mid-morning, Jordan and the men had reached the Tule Creek line camp. A mile or so south of the camp, Dyer had pointed out the tracks he'd uncovered late yesterday. From there, they had followed the trail in a westerly direction, crossing Pleasant Creek around noontime. The tracks at that point slowly veered off to the southwest, into a stretch of badlands at the head of the canyon. The terrain gradually became rougher, the ground baked hard as flint. Jordan finally signaled a halt.

''I've lost the sign,'' he said to the other men. ''Not sure I would've found it when it was fresh. Somebody knows his business.''

''Why?'' Dyer asked. ''You figure they brought 'em this way on purpose?''

''I'd say it's pretty goddamned certain. Ground's so hard it won't hardly hold a track.''

''Sounds like they know the layout of the JA.''

''Yeah, it does,'' Jordan remarked. ''I just suspect they scouted things real good beforehand. Too tricky to be otherwise.''

''Helluva note,'' Dyer said disgustedly. ''Hate to lose fifty head of cows.''

''Maybe we haven't lost them.''

''What d'you mean?''

Jordan motioned off to the southwest. ''Think we'll scout around ourselves. Tierra Blanca Canyon's over that way.''

Dyer exchanged a glance with Poe and Taylor. He looked back at Jordan. ''You thinkin' this Stroud feller stole the cows?''

''Like I said yesterday, I'm not much on coincidence. Stroud stakes out Tierra Blanca and rustlers start workin' the Panhandle. Case I forgot to mention it, the Circle B got hit four nights ago.''

''I'll be go to hell,'' Poe interjected. ''How many'd they lose?''

''Couple of hundred,'' Jordan said. ''Circle B hands killed one of the thieves. Shot him.''

''And two nights later,'' Poe said, ''we got hit. Starts to sound a little strange, don't it?''

''Coincidence on coincidence,'' Dyer said thoughtfully. ''Maybe Stroud's our man, after all.''

''Let's have a looksee,'' Jordan said, reining his horse around. ''Find out what's what with Mr. Stroud.''

Far off in the southwest corner of Palo Duro there was a fissure in the canyon wall. The passageway was abutted by the badlands, and extended a mile or more through a rocky gorge. On the opposite side, the gorge opened onto Tierra Blanca Canyon, which was bisected by a narrow stream. The land was harsh and arid, sparse on graze.

Jordan was familiar with Tierra Blanca. In 1875, while surveying Palo Duro, he had come across the gorge leading southwest. A brief inspection had convinced him that he was not interested in the distant canyon. The terrain lacked sufficient grass, and water, to be included as part of the JA. Tierra Blanca was less than a tenth the size of Palo Duro, with small tributary canyons extending east and west. Here and there, shallow creeks fed into the central stream.

Early that afternoon Jordan spotted bunches of cows in the distance. He led the men into the shade of a rocky outcropping, and signaled them to dismount. From his saddlebags he removed a small brass telescope, and climbed to the top of the ledge. He extended the telescope to its full length and scanned the terrain below. The cows were longhorns, much as he'd expected, scattered in bunches the length and breadth of the canyon. He estimated their number at no more than a thousand head.

Some three miles down the canyon Jordan caught the faint outlines of a structure. The range of the telescope prevented him from bringing it into focus; but through the haze, he thought it had the look of a log house. Something bothered him about the longhorns, and he again scanned the floor of the canyon. As he swept back and forth, it occurred to him that there were no riders in sight, no one working the cattle. He wondered what kind of spread let its herd run loose, without at least one rider on routine patrol. On the nearest bunch of cows, he saw that the brand was a Rocking S.

Jordan collapsed the telescope. He worked his way down the face of the outcropping, and jumped the last few steps to level ground. The men were seated in the shade, smoking cigarettes, their horses ground-reined. Dyer gave him an inquisitive look.

"What's the word, boss? Anything interesting out there?"

"Not much of an outfit," Jordan replied. "Sorriest bunch of scrub cows I ever saw. Look thin as rails."

"Don't surprise me none," Dyer said. "There ain't much for a cow to eat in Tierra Blanca. Damn poor country."

"You could double that in spades. Makes me wonder why anybody would want to settle here."

"Maybe they got other business besides raisin' cows."

"Maybe so," Jordan said. "What I saw wouldn't be worth trailin' to railhead."

Poe ground his cigarette underfoot. "How many head they got?"

"I'd judge a thousand, give or take. Funny thing, there's nobody riding herd. Not a soul in sight."

Poe chuckled. "Maybe they figure it's not worth the trouble. Nobody's gonna steal scrub cows."

"What about our bunch?" Dyer said. "Spot anything with a JA on its rump?"

"Nope," Jordan said, shaking his head. "All I saw was Stroud's brand. Appears to be a Rocking S."

Dyer got to his feet. "You're fixin' to brace Stroud, ain't you? I can tell just by your look."

Jordan nodded thoughtfully. "I spotted a house down the canyon three or four miles. Figured we'd drop by and meet our new neighbor."

"You gonna put a bee in his ear about our cows?"

"That's the general idea."

"What if he don't take kindly to the notion?"

"I reckon you know the answer to that, Leigh."

"Tell him to stick it where the sun don't shine?"

"We'll start there and see where it goes."

Jordan walked to his horse, stepped into the saddle. The men got themselves mounted and followed him from the shade of the outcropping into the hazy sunlight. There was no question in their minds of what he intended.

His rule was to hang any rustler caught in the act. A suspected rustler got only one warning.

The cabin was situated near the western wall of Tierra Blanca Canyon. A log structure, it was a crude affair thrown together with haste and no great pride. Off to the south was a corral with some twenty head of horses.

Jordan led his men into the compound. His first impression of the Rocking S was that it looked like a fly-by-night outfit. The cabin and the corral, with a one-hole privy off to the rear, comprised the ranch headquarters. There was a sense that it could be abandoned overnight, and no great loss. He'd seen line shacks with a more substantial look of permanence.

There were five men loafing around the front of the cabin. One stood in the doorway, a thickset man, hard-faced with muddy eyes, in his early thirties. The other four flanked him, two on either side, idly leaning against the front wall. They were a tough-looking lot, all of them armed with pistols, their faces watchful and belligerent. Their manner gave every appearance that they had been carefully positioned. They were clearly expecting visitors, and prepared for trouble.

Jordan was prepared as well. There was nothing random about his selection of the three men who rode with him today. They were seasoned veterans, no strangers to gunfire, men he could depend on in a tight situation. Over the years, fighting outlaws and Indians, he had come to trust their instincts for the right move at the right time. As they rode into the yard, Dyer fanned out to his right, with Poe and Taylor on his left. They reined to a halt on line, some ten feet from the cabin. Jordan nodded to the man in the doorway.

"I'm Jack Jordan, owner of the JA. I understand this outfit's owned by Earl Stroud."

"That's me," Stroud said. "What can I do for you?"

The tone of Stroud's voice bordered on arrogance. There

was no offer tendered for the four riders to dismount. Custom dictated that a horseman never dismount on another man's land unless an invitation was extended. The message, clearly delivered, was that Jordan and his men were not welcome.

"Looking for some cows," Jordan said. "Somebody rustled fifty head night before last."

"What's that got to do with me?"

"We trailed 'em into the badlands at the upper end of Palo Duro. Figure they had to come through Tierra Blanca."

"How about it, boys?" Stroud turned a quizzical glance on his men. "Seen any JA cows lately?"

The men shook their heads in unison. Stroud lifted one hand in an elaborate shrug. " 'Fraid we can't help you, Mr. Jordan."

"Damn peculiar," Jordan said levelly. "Three riders and fifty cows came through here, and nobody saw them. Hard to believe."

Stroud bristled. "You callin' me a liar?"

The men on either side of Stroud started to separate, moving to outflank the riders. Dyer reined his horse sideways at one end of the line, and Taylor brought his horse around at the other end. Their maneuver effectively neutralized any advantage, and brought Stroud's men to a standstill. Jordan sat his horse stone-faced and immobile, his cold stare drilling into Stroud.

"Liars and rustlers," he said, "are generally one and the same. I'm here to find out what you are."

Stroud held his gaze. "Sounds like you're callin' me something without saying it outright. You've got a fancy way with words."

"Mister, when I call you something, you'll hear it real plain. I've been told I say 'son of a bitch' clear as a bell."

"So now I'm a liar and a rustler and a sonovabitch. Have I got it right?"

"You'll be the first to know once I decide."

A glint of mockery touched Stroud's eyes. "You run a

mighty big outfit. I hear you've got better'n fifty thousand head." He paused, still leaning against the doorjamb. "What's so important about fifty cows?"

"I've got a rule," Jordan said bluntly. "I won't tolerate a thief. One cow or fifty, the penalty's the same."

"Yeah, what's that?"

"I hang rustlers, Stroud. No excuses, no exceptions."

Stroud regarded him evenly. "Guess I've got nothin' to worry about. Me and my boys are pure as the driven snow."

"That reminds me," Jordan said. "Are you missing one of your men?"

"What makes you ask?"

"A man was killed up near the Canadian. Circle B riders shot him dead."

"That a fact?" Stroud said absently. "What'd he do?"

"Got caught rustling one of their herds."

"Go out of your way to insult a man, don't you? I think you came here lookin' for a fight."

"I came here to give you a warning."

"What sort of warning?"

Jordan's mouth hardened. "You and your men stay off my land. Don't let me catch you in Palo Duro."

Stroud cocked one eyebrow. "Set yourself up as the law around here, have you?"

"I'm the law on the JA. Do yourself a favor and stay clear. That's good advice."

"Sounds more on the order of a threat."

"Take it either way," Jordan said. "You butt heads with me, you'll lose."

Stroud stiffened. "Think so, huh?"

"I'd bet your life on it, Stroud."

Their eyes locked in a moment of tense silence. Then, as though amused, Stroud wagged his head with a sardonic look. "You've done wore out your welcome. I'll thank you to get off my land."

"Just remember that works both ways. Keep out of Palo Duro."

Jordan wheeled his horse away from the cabin. The other men reined about and followed him from the yard. They felt the stares of Stroud and his crew on their backs as they gigged their horses into a trot. Four abreast, they rode north through the canyon.

A mile or so from the cabin they forded the stream. Until now, none of them had spoken, silently replaying the encounter in their own minds. But as they gained the far bank of the stream, Dyer was unable to contain himself any longer. He looked across at Jordan.

"Stroud's got some gall, don't he?"

"Yeah, he does," Jordan said. "Too much for his own good."

"You think him and his boys will hit us again?"

"Leigh, I'd wager my bankroll on it."

"So what're we gonna do to stop him?"

John Poe burst out laughing. "What d'you think we're gonna do? We're gonna hang the bastard! Right, boss?"

Jordan's mouth curled in a tight smile. He led them toward Palo Duro.

CHAPTER 29

Late one afternoon in early September, John and Cornealia Adair arrived in Palo Duro. They were accompanied by Hank Taylor and another hand, who drove the supply wagon. Their arrival was timed to coincide with the start of fall roundup.

Jordan was working at a small desk positioned near the entrance to the parlor. The desk, like the baby's cradle, had been built by Buster Lomax. A self-trained bookkeeper, Jordan hoped to have the books in order before Adair's arrival. He was working on the final entries as Rebecca busied herself in the kitchen. The balance sheet was even better than he'd expected.

"They're here! Cornealia and John are here!"

Rebecca turned from the window as the Adairs rode into the yard. She tossed her apron on a kitchen chair and ran to the front door. Jordan closed the record book, then rose from the desk and followed her outside. The Adairs were dismounting as they came through the door and hurried across the porch. Laughing happily, Rebecca swept Cornealia into a warm hug.

"Welcome home!" she said gaily, pausing to peck Adair on the cheek. "I've missed you both so much."

"Look at you!" Cornealia smiled radiantly, holding her at arm's length. "You've already got your figure back. Was it a boy or a girl?"

"A boy," Rebecca proudly informed her. "Ethan Butler Dyer Adair Jordan!"

"Good heavens," Cornealia said, startled. "Why so many names?"

"Oh, that's a story in itself. Come on, let's go inside. I can't wait for you to see Ethan."

Jordan and Adair trailed the women into the house. Adair slapped him across the back. "Well, now," he said heartily. "How's it feel to be a father?"

"Damnedest thing," Jordan said. "I feel like clicking my heels every morning. I'm proud as punch, John."

"And why wouldn't you be? I'd think a man's firstborn would be a highwater mark in his life."

"We'll have to have a celebration, now that you're here. You'll recollect you're Ethan's godfather."

"Yes, I noticed you'd included my name. Quite a moniker you've given the little fellow. What's with all those names?"

"Like Becky said, that's another story."

Inside, they gathered around the cradle, which was on the floor near the kitchen. Rebecca scooped the baby up in her arms and turned to display him with a joyful smile. He gurgled, waving his chubby arms, and stared up at them with bright blue eyes. His features were clearly similar to those of his father.

"Ooo, my God," Cornealia marveled. "Have you ever seen anything so darling in your life? He's adorable!"

"Stout lad," Adair said admiringly. "A chip off the old block, Jack. Looks just like you."

Jordan beamed, obviously pleased by the comparison. Cornealia insisted on holding the baby, and Rebecca gently shifted him into her arms. She cooed, tickling his tummy, and his mouth ovaled in a dimpled smile. The women moved into the parlor, and Cornealia sat down in a chair with the baby. The men watched for a moment, then exchanged a glance and walked out to the porch. Cornealia seemed mesmerized by the small bundle she held.

"What a precious little angel you are! Is he always so happy, Rebecca?"

"Except when he's hungry. He raises a terrible fuss if he has to wait. And he eats like an absolute pig."

"Well, of course he does!" Cornealia leaned down to kiss his chubby cheek. "A growing boy needs lots of milk. The rancher's wife—I've forgotten her name—she must have been a big help when he was born."

"No, not really," Rebecca said. "Ethan arrived two weeks early. He was already three days old when Mrs. Bugbee got here."

"Was Jack here?"

"No, he was on his way back from Dodge City."

Cornealia's jaw dropped. "You delivered this baby yourself? Alone?"

"Not alone." Rebecca glanced toward the porch, then lowered her voice. "Two of the men came to my rescue. They delivered the baby."

"Cowhands!" Cornealia stared at her, aghast. "Cowhands performed the . . . the delivery?"

"Actually, it was the foreman, Leigh Dyer. And the cook, Mose Butler. That's how Ethan got all his extra names."

Cornealia was momentarily nonplussed. She took a moment to recover her wits. "Are you saying those men—well, you know—*saw* you?"

"All of me," Rebecca said with a giggly smile. "And I have absolutely no shame about it. They saved Ethan, and they probably saved me, too."

"I've never heard anything so bizarre in my life. A ranch foreman and a cook! What did Jack think about that?"

"We've never discussed it, not in detail anyway. But he must have felt very thankful toward Leigh and Mose. He gave each of them a hundred cows."

"Well, I'd think so!" Cornealia said firmly. "They deserve a world of gratitude. Not many men would have that much gumption."

Rebecca laughed. "You wouldn't know it to see them. They're so shy around me it's painful. Neither of them can look me in the eye."

"Perfectly understandable, given the circumstances. I mean, after all, my dear, that is rather intimate. I shouldn't wonder they feel embarrassed."

"Well, whatever they feel, they certainly take pride in Ethan. They ask about him at least once a day."

Cornealia looked down at the baby with a loving expression. "Mercy, you're just a small miracle, Ethan. What a story you can tell your children."

On the porch, Jordan studiously avoided the story of his son's birth. He distracted Adair's attention, instead, with the financier's favorite topic. Quickly turning to the matter of business, he related details of the deal he'd made with the Chicago cattle buyers. When he concluded, Adair took a moment to light a cigar. Then he nodded with a wily smile.

"You're a shrewd one, Jack. A bird in the hand, as the old saying goes. I couldn't have done better myself."

"We're in good shape," Jordan said confidently. "By the end of October, we'll have trailed another eight thousand head to Dodge. Least we'll get is thirty-one a head."

Adair performed a quick mental calculation. "For the year, then, we will have grossed four hundred ninety-five thousand. Am I correct?"

"We might lose a few head on the drive to Dodge. But that's close enough."

"So we're looking at profits of how much?"

"I'll show you the books later," Jordan said. "Way I figure, we'll clear two hundred and three thousand."

"Marvelous!" Adair grinned, puffing his cigar. "A handsome return indeed, Jack. That's splendid, just splendid."

"Yeah, I suppose it's pretty good. 'Course, I think we could do better."

"Do you now? And what would you call better?"

"Higher gross," Jordan said casually. "Higher profits."

Adair wedged the cigar in the corner of his mouth. His eyes narrowed in speculation. ''You have that crafty look about you, Jack. I've seen it before when we were talking money. Have you hatched some new scheme?''

''Let's just say more of the same. I want to expand the operation.''

''You're a bold one, you are. But then, I knew that from the start. All right, let's hear it.''

Jordan outlined an ambitious plan. He suggested that neither of them take any profits, and that the initial investment capital remain on the books. A part of the money would be used to acquire added land, solidify their control of Palo Duro from end to end. The balance would be allocated to the purchase of additional cows over the next year. He wanted to increase their herds by fifty thousand head.

''Are you serious?'' Adair said when he finished. ''Double the size of the operation in one year?''

''I'm dead serious,'' Jordan told him. ''Hell, all it takes is brass balls and a little hustle.'' He paused, smiling. ''And money.''

''Yes, of course, there's always the money. You want to reach for the sun, go for it all. Is that it?''

''Neither one of us went into this for the fast dollar. Let's do it right. Go all the way.''

Adair tapped the ash off his cigar. He considered a moment, then abruptly laughed. ''You're a born rascal,'' he said. ''But half of it's your money, so why not? We'll go all the way, Jack.''

''Glad we're of a mind,'' Jordan said. ''You won't regret it, and you've got my word on that. 'Course, there is one other thing.''

''Jesus, Mary, and Joseph! What now?''

''I plan to buy some more Herefords. The breeding program works, and we'll speed things along with more blooded stock.''

''I've only one question. Will it require added investment?''

"Nope," Jordan said. "What's in the kitty will cover it."

Adair waved his cigar. "As you say, the breeding program works. How many will you buy?"

"Three hundred bulls and a couple hundred cows."

Leigh Dyer rode into the yard. He dismounted, walked to the porch, and shook hands with Adair. During the exchange of pleasantries, Jordan noted that the foreman was forcing himself to smile. He could read Dyer after all their years together, and he knew there was trouble of some sort. At an opportune moment, he broke into the conversation.

"You're back early," he said. "Anything wrong?"

Dyer frowned. "Rustlers hit us up on Rush Creek last night. Got away with about fifty head."

"Sorry bastard," Jordan swore hotly. "Waited damn near three months before he pulled another raid. He's a slick one."

"Rustlers?" Adair interrupted. "Someone's stealing our cattle?"

Jordan briefly explained the raid in June, and the proximity of Tierra Blanca Canyon to Palo Duro. "The head man's Earl Stroud," he went on. "I warned him to stay clear of the JA. Guess he didn't take me at my word."

"Way it looks," Dyer said, "he figured we'd drop our guard after all this time. You pegged him as a cool hombre."

"Which way do the tracks run?"

"Same as last time. On a beeline for the badlands."

Jordan considered a moment. The Rush Creek line camp was some five miles northwest of the headquarters compound. He judged the distance from there to the badlands to be ten or twelve miles. By now, the rustled cows were already secreted somewhere within Tierra Blanca Canyon.

"Damnedable outrage," Adair rumbled. "What do you intend to do?"

"Try to track them," Jordan said. "Too close to sundown to leave now. We'll start first thing in the morning."

"I'll ride with you," Adair informed him. "And we'll not argue about it, either. I've no doubt Cornealia will provide all the argument I care to hear."

Jordan smiled. "I just suspect she will. You're liable to be sleeping in the bunkhouse tonight, John."

Adair won the argument. At sunrise, with Cornealia and Rebecca looking on, they rode out to the southwest. Adair appeared game for the hunt, armed with a pistol and a rifle. They were accompanied by Dyer, Poe, and Taylor.

By late morning they were well into the badlands. Once again, Jordan was unable to pick up tracks on the rough, flint-hard terrain. He was frustrated, growing angrier the farther they traveled, but forced to a grudging admiration. Earl Stroud had selected the perfect dodge to throw off pursuit. The badlands left no trace of the rustlers' passage.

The sun was high overhead when they emerged from the gorge leading to Tierra Blanca. Jordan led them to the rocky outcropping he'd used as a vantage point on their previous foray. He was none too confident that spying on the Rocking S would uncover anything that might incriminate Stroud. At best, he estimated that thirty-six hours had elapsed since the raid on the Rush Creek camp. The stolen cows were by now probably hidden in one of the many tributary canyons that sliced into Tierra Blanca. But he still felt compelled to have a look.

The men waited while he and Adair climbed to the top of the ledge. Jordan expanded his telescope and slowly glassed the length of the canyon. Just as before, he saw bunches of Rocking S cows scattered here and there, but no riders. He scanned the mouths of the nearest tributary canyons, as well as the distant cabin, and saw nothing unusual. Finally, with a muttered curse, he collapsed the telescope.

"Sure rubs me raw," he said harshly. "I know our cows are out there somewhere."

Adair looked perplexed. "Out where?"

"One of those smaller canyons. Wouldn't be hard to hide fifty head."

"Why not ride down there and find them?"

"I've got no proof," Jordan said. "Stroud and his crew would try to stop us, and that'd end up in a shootout. I won't kill a man just on suspicion."

"I see." Adair was thoughtful a moment. "Have you any idea of how Stroud disposes of the cows?"

"Alters our brand and likely drives them across the line into New Mexico. Lots of ranchers over that way turn a blind eye to rustled stock. All the more so if it's from Texas."

"Fifty cows every three months or so could get expensive. In a year's time, we'll lose a considerable sum."

"Stroud will lose more," Jordan said in a flat voice. "One day his luck will run out, and I'll catch him. That's the day he gets hung."

"The grim reaper, eh?" Adair chuckled softly. "I'd not steal cows from you, Jack. Not at any price."

"Thieves are a different breed, smart but dumb. Never yet met one who thought he'd get caught."

"What measures will you take now? Have you something in mind?"

"We'll post night patrols out of every line camp. Maybe we'll sour Mr. Stroud's luck. The dirty sonovabitch."

Adair was not surprised by the hard tone, or the invective. He knew by now that Jordan took the theft of livestock as a personal affront. An offense that was inevitably settled by summary justice.

He thought Earl Stroud was a walking dead man.

Part Three

CHAPTER 30

A blustery November wind swept over Palo Duro. Already there was a brittle smell of approaching frost, and the grasslands along the river had taken on the tawny look which signals oncoming winter. High overhead a vee of ducks, fleet silhouettes against the midday sky, winged their way southward.

Jordan was three day's ride east of the headquarters compound. He turned in the saddle, watching as the ducks battled heavy winds in their flight to warmer waters. Fall was one of his favorite times, for the trees took on brilliant colors that blazed against the spectrum of the canyon walls. Even winter had its appeal, though the frigid cold seeping off the high plains was harder on men and cows. But the snow, particularly raging blizzards out of the north, gave him an excuse to stay home. He got to spend more time with Rebecca and Ethan.

Once a month Jordan toured the line camps. The operation was now so large that it required a full two weeks to visit every camp in the outfit. On a daily basis Leigh Dyer oversaw the spread from one end of the canyon to the other. Directly under him, John Poe was responsible for the western half of the JA and Cape Willingham was segundo for the eastern division. Still, for all his trust and confidence in them, Jordan continued to make his monthly rounds. There was no substitute for a firsthand inspection, and his unannounced visits kept the men on their toes. He sometimes felt like a general inspecting his troops.

There was a personal exhilaration to it as well. Throughout the latter half of 1876, and now into the fall of 1877, Jordan had acquired land at a dizzying pace. The ranch had grown to encompass 1,135,000 acres, including sections he'd purchased outright and those he had leased under the School Lands program. The expansion had resulted in separating the ranch into two divisions, with Poe and Willingham reporting directly to Leigh Dyer. There were now eleven line camps, from Timber Creek in the east to Rush Creek in the west, with a twelfth crew quartered at the home compound. From end to end, the JA was a five-day ride.

In all, there were more than a hundred men on the payroll. One line camp might have six men and another seven or eight, based upon the extent of range to be covered and the number of cows in a given herd. Simply stocking the camps with provisions had become a logistical operation comparable to the military supplying far-flung outposts during the frontier era. At the beginning of every month, a caravan of freight wagons, drawn by six-hitch teams of oxen, rolled into the canyon from Dodge City. The supplier was Rath & Company, engaged by contract, and fair weather or foul, the wagons rattled southwest to Palo Duro. From the quartermaster depot at the home compound, the provisions were then transported to the line camps.

The greater problem, in Jordan's opinion, was in maintaining a full crew. Over the course of 1877 he'd kept a log, and on average the JA had a turnover of seven hands a month. Some were fired for violating his unbendable rule of no drinking, gambling, or fighting anywhere on the ranch. Others quit because of the isolation, and the monastic life without women, in Palo Duro. To replace them, Hank Taylor rode east the middle of every month, recruiting new hands from the western settlements of the Upper Cross Timbers. The job still paid forty a month and found, ten dollars more than the going wage on the Brazos. The extra money was usually inducement enough to lure men to Palo Duro.

Jordan often reflected that the problem was compounded by his own good fortune. The JA stood as testament to the fact that the old *Llano Estacado* was a paradise for cows. The Circle B, though on a smaller scale, had prospered under the guidance of Sam Bugbee. He was followed by another rancher in late 1876, and two more in the spring of 1877. One of the cattlemen settled near Indian Territory, and the others on the western reaches of the Canadian, their outfits now stretching almost to the border of New Mexico. Jordan was pleased by the growth, for it meant the Panhandle would one day have a railroad for shipping cattle. But at the same time, he was forced to compete with the other ranchers for cowhands, and the four spreads, taken together, employed far more men than the JA. Progress, he told himself, often came with a whole new set of headaches.

Still, he took justifiable pride in what he and John Adair had achieved in just three years. From a raw and desolate wilderness, they had carved out an empire of more than a million acres, with a hundred thousand cows wearing the JA brand. Only last month, he had trailed eighteen thousand head to Dodge City, and he planned to put at least that many on the trail in early summer of 1878. The JA was the largest ranch in Texas, perhaps the entire world, bigger even than the King ranch down near the border of Old Mexico. The operation had grossed over a million dollars for the year, and after all expenses, plus the interest on Adair's initial investment, his share of the profits had exceeded one hundred thousand dollars. He was living every cattleman's dream.

Yet the dream was not without some loose threads. During the past year, three ranches had been organized along the eastern end of Palo Duro. The outfits were small, hardly more than thirty thousand acres each, settled on sections he hadn't bothered to buy or lease. The land was surrounded by JA holdings, and he'd thought no one would be foolish enough to start operations in country controlled by a larger spread. But they were there, shirttail outfits with scrub cows, and he found them to be an infernal nuisance. He considered them outsiders, and their lands limited his absolute control of Palo Duro. He meant to buy them out one by one.

The first of the three ranchers to settle in Palo Duro had begun operation in late March. His name was Harlan Woodburn, and his spread was located some five miles west of the Timber Creek line camp. His outfit consisted of three cowhands, a couple of thousand slab-sided longhorns, and a remuda of perhaps twenty horses. He had a wife and two children, and they lived in a squalid log cabin with a dirt floor. His wife did all the cooking, and the cowhands bunked in a log hut attached to the rear of the cabin. The operation was one of hand-to-mouth existence.

A week ago Jordan had received a message from the boss of his Timber Creek camp. Apparently, in an effort to raise cash money, Woodburn and one of his hands had attempted to drive a herd of five hundred steers to Dodge City. The herd had stampeded on them twice, and what was left had been lost to a gang of rustlers north of the Cimarron. Upon returning to Palo Duro, the hand had quit, asking for work at the Timber Creek camp, complaining that Woodburn was unable to pay his wages. The story was one of poverty and despair, all too typical of hardscrabble operations. The hand reported that Woodburn couldn't afford a sack of flour, or other basic essentials.

Jordan rode into the yard in the late forenoon. A mangy hound circled his horse, barking and snapping, as he reined to a halt before the cabin. The door opened, and Woodburn stepped outside, shushing the hound to silence. He was a gawky man, stoop-shouldered and weather-beaten, with sad eyes. Jordan had treated him in a neighborly manner, and they were on speaking terms if not friends. Woodburn managed a lame smile.

"How do, Mr. Jordan," he said. "Step down and come in out of the cold. The wife's just fixin' dinner."

"Thank you kindly." Jordan dismounted, looping the reins around a hitching post. "Sure I'm not putting your wife to any trouble?"

"One more don't hardly matter. We ain't eatin' high off the hog anyhow."

"Word's around you lost your herd. That's rough luck."

"Stupid's more like it. I shouldn't 've tried that drive with only me and one man. Just plain dumb."

Jordan suspected he needed the money from the trail drive for a land payment. As he followed Woodburn inside, it occurred to him that his hunch was on the mark. He thought he'd never seen a man who looked so whipped.

Sally Woodburn was a small, frail woman. She greeted Jordan listlessly as he hooked his hat and mackinaw on wall pegs by the door. The children, a boy and a girl, were already seated at the table, their manner subdued and somehow sickly. Jordan took a chair beside Woodburn, and saw that the reports of their poverty were all too accurate. The noon meal consisted of tough beefsteak and weak coffee, Nothing else was served.

"Plenty to go around," Woodburn said without intended irony. "The rest of my hands quit yesterday and took off. Likely over at your Timber Creek camp lookin' for a job."

Jordan cut into his steak. "How will you work your herd by yourself?"

"I been askin' myself the same question. Things have gone to hell in a handbasket, all in a hurry. Don't rightly know what's next."

"Have you thought of selling out?"

"Who's buyin'?" Woodburn said morosely. "You got all the land you need, and then some. I don't see nobody else knockin' on the door."

Jordan took a swig of tasteless coffee. "Let's suppose I was in the market. What would be your askin' price?"

Surprise registered on Woodburn's features. Then his expression dissolved into a cynical scowl. "Heard I was in trouble and you come here to rob me, didn't you? Always figgered you for a hard man."

"Harlan!" Sally Woodburn admonished him. "For the love of God, act your age. Talk won't cost you nothin'. Hear the man out."

"Your wife's right," Jordan said. "I'm not here to steal your land. I'll make you a fair offer."

Woodburn still looked skeptical. "What kind of offer?"

"Depends on your situation. Do you own the place free and clear?"

"Own the stock." Wordburn glanced at his wife, and she encouraged him with a nod. He went on. "Financed the land with that Austin speculator, Gunter Munson. Owe him seven thousand come the first of the year."

"What'd he charge you for the land?"

"Our deal was a dollar an acre, and five thousand down. Gave me a five-year loan on the rest."

Jordan thought he'd already been robbed. The total for the land, including interest, was forty thousand dollars. "I'll assume your mortgage," he said, "and give you five thousand cash. You'll break even on the land."

Woodburn blinked. "What about my stock?"

"Your cows are a poor lot. I'll give you fifteen a head, cash money."

"They're worth more'n that in Dodge."

"Yeah, but they're here, not Dodge. I'll have to winter them and trail 'em north next summer. Fifteen's a fair price."

"Guess it is, at that," Woodburn said. "I got near about fifteen hundred head left."

"I'll accept your count," Jordan said. "Twenty-five thousand for your stock, including cows and horses, and five thousand for a quitclaim on the land. Do we have a deal?"

"Thirty thousand." Woodburn's mouth split in a yellow-toothed grin. "That'll give us a stake to start fresh somewheres else. Yessir, we got ourselves a deal."

Jordan knew he could have haggled, gotten the price down. But he felt sorry for Woodburn's family, particularly the children. After finishing the meager dinner, he took a quitclaim deed and a bank draft from his mackinaw. Once the deed was made out and signed, he filled in the draft for thirty thousand dollars. Woodburn stared at it with wonder.

"Tell you the truth," he said slowly. "You saved our bacon, Mr. Jordan. We was in a mighty bad fix."

"Glad it all worked out."

Jordan shrugged into his mackinaw. At the door, Sally Woodburn took his arm. "God bless you," she said, her eyes moist. "You're a good man."

"Nice of you to say so, ma'am. I wish you folks luck."

Outside, Jordan mounted and rode upstream, toward the Tule Creek line camp. He told himself the Woodburns were not all that unusual, always teettering on the edge of disaster. Like the other two ranchers in the canyon, their outfit was too small, too susceptible to misfortune. A hard winter, or bad luck during a trail drive, constantly threatened to wipe them out. When it happened to the others, he planned to be overly generous, just as he had been with the Woodburns. Their hard luck was his good luck, and he could afford to pay whatever price they asked. All of Palo Duro would soon belong to the JA.

Later that afternoon, east of Tule Creek, Jordan spotted one of the horse herds. Over the past year, he had bought a hundred brood mares and imported five thoroughbred stallions. With the horses scattered around the ranch, twenty mares to a stallion, he had begun a selective breeding program. By culling, continually breeding up, he planned to fuse the stamina and catlike agility of range mares with the speed and intelligence of thoroughbred studs. His goal was to breed the ultimate horse for working cattle.

The idea sprang from the success of his breeding program with cattle. There were now three hundred Hereford bulls on the JA, and twice that number of blooded cows. The breeding program was into its third year, and the mix of longhorn with Hereford was slowly spreading throughout all the JA herds. The result was a cow with the hardy qualities and survival instincts of a longhorn, and the heavier, robust conformation of a Hereford. The breed packed more weight, but still had the stamina for the long trail drives to Dodge City. Eastern cattle buyers clamored for cows from the JA.

For all the gains, Jordan thought success brought with it certain drawbacks. As he skirted the horse herd, headed toward Tule Creek, he was reminded that rustlers were drawn to JA livestock as well. The problem had grown worse with time, bands of rustlers and horse thieves snipping away at the ranch from all directions. Within the last year, one raider had been killed in a running gunfight, and four others had been tracked down and hanged. Yet there was no practical way to safeguard an operation as large as the JA. More got away than were caught.

The one who got away most often, and with infuriating regularity, was Earl Stroud. By now Jordan knew the trademark pattern of Stroud and his gang. A raid every month or so, always at night, and a quick retreat into the badlands to elude pursuit. For almost a year and half, Jordan had been unable to obtain proof against Stroud; it had become such a sore point that no one spoke of it in his presence. But he operated on the old adage that cautioned: beware the fury of a patient man. He waited with a certainty that fed on his anger. Stroud's first mistake would be his last.

Until then, like a watchful spider, Jordan bided his time and got on with what needed doing day by day. He rode into the Tule Creek camp as the cook clanged the supper bell.

CHAPTER 31

A wind mourned through the branches of the cottonwoods. Hazy sunlight rippled across the waters of the river, reflecting off shards of ice along the banks. Umber grasslands, blanketed with snow, swept onward to the battlements of the southern wall.

Christmas had come to Palo Duro. The night before, on Christmas Eve, a storm had layered the countryside with several inches of fresh snow. But now, in the early forenoon, sunshine filtered through an overcast sky. The canyon floor was bathed in a white, spectral glow.

Jordan declared it a holiday. A week earlier he'd sent word that the men in the line camps were to be given the day off. Wild turkey were plentiful in the canyon, and every cook was ordered to prepare a traditional Christmas dinner. Certain chores, such as splitting firewood and tending horses, were unavoidable even on Christmas Day. But otherwise the men were to have the day to themselves.

Rebecca stood at the kitchen window, looking out across the compound. She saw Jordan, bundled in his mackinaw, talking with Leigh Dyer outside the corral. She suspected they were talking business, for neither of them ever fully set their work aside. The JA was too large, and their responsibilities too great, for them to devote a day to doing nothing. Over time she had come to accept it, but there were still times she resented the demands of the ranch.

Christmas Day was one of those times.

"Señora."

She turned from the window. Juanita Morado waited by the kitchen counter, where a three-layer angel food cake was tiered on a serving dish. Rebecca moved to the counter, inspecting the cake. "Isn't it gorgeous, Juanita? Mose Butler never baked a cake that fluffy."

"Yes, señora."

"Do you know how to make sugar icing?"

"Icing?" Juanita slowly shook her head. "I no think so, señora."

"Well, let me show you. It's really very easy."

Juanita watched as she began adding sugar to the egg whites in the mixing bowl. She was still trying to teach her housekeeper the mysteries of Anglo cooking. A Mexican woman, originally from Pueblo, Juanita believed any dish was improved with chili peppers. Rebecca nonetheless looked upon her as a godsend.

Last fall, to her amazement, the Adairs had arrived at the ranch with Juanita. Jordan had engineered the surprise through a letter to the Adairs, mailed from Fort Elliott. His purpose was to provide female company for Rebecca, and to ensure that she was never again left alone without another woman being present. Cornealia Adair, working in concert with Rebecca's mother, had located Juanita in Pueblo. She seemed perfect for the job.

A plump, good-humored woman, Juanita was in her forties, and recently widowed. She spoke passable English, and the thought of caring for a *gringo* mistress and a baby boy was enormously appealing to her. All the more so since she was barren and had been unable to have children of her own. She was not in the least daunted by the trek across the plains, or her new life in Palo Duro. A bedroom was added onto the back of the house, and before long, she seemed like one of the family. She doted on Ethan, and went out of her way to spoil Rebecca.

Looking back, Rebecca often thought her husband had purposely planned it. She was with child again, two months pregnant, and eagerly hopeful that it would be a girl. The memory of Ethan's birth was still sharp in her mind, and not an experience she wanted to risk the second time around. She instinctively believed that Mexican women were natural midwives, somehow gifted with a knowledge of babies and rearing children. The fact that her housekeeper was childless did nothing to temper her belief. She was thankful merely for Juanita's presence.

Once the icing was mixed, she spread it over the cake in thick swirls. Finished, she stepped back to admire her handiwork. "There!" she said. "Have you ever seen anything so beautiful?"

"Never." Juanita dabbed icing from the bowl and tentatively licked her finger. She smiled. "Is very good, señora."

"Every cowhand on the place has a sweet tooth. They'll just love it! Now, let's see about the ham."

A large ham rested in a cooking pan on the counter. Martha Bugbee, notorious among Panhandle cattlemen for raising hogs, had sent it along as a Christmas gift. Rebecca considered it the perfect touch, a complement to the turkey being prepared by Mose Butler. A party was planned that night in the bunkhouse, a festive occasion for the headquarters crew. She thought the ham would provide a rare delicacy for the men.

For the past week, Rebecca and Juanita had spent every spare moment in the kitchen. They had baked twenty-four fruitcakes, two for each line camp, and cooked and boxed forty-eight pounds of fudge. The cakes and candy had then been dispatched by wagon, in time to reach the line camps for Christmas. Rebecca wanted every man on the JA to have something special for the holiday, and the best gift of all was to satisfy a cowhand's sweet tooth. She often thought that their craving for sweets stemmed from their celibate way of life. The only women they saw were in Dodge City, on trail drives. Or on rare occasions, the women in Tascosa.

Last spring the news arrived that a town had been

founded in the Panhandle. At first, Rebecca had been excited, for Tascosa was located on the Canadian, some sixty miles northwest of Palo Duro. She had visions of a trade center, with stores and business establishments, and an occasional shopping trip to the new town. When she kept after Jordan to arrange a visit, he'd finally told her the truth. Tascosa was a rough and rowdy collection of saloons and brothels, situated to capture the trade of cowhands from the four outfits along the Canadian. Afterward, she had lost all interest, apart from the titillating revelation it provided. She now knew why the JA hands relished their infrequent trips to Tascosa.

Rebecca finished with the ham. She had scored it, pricked it with cloves, and smeared it with a baste of honey and brown sugar. She explained to Juanita that they would put it in the oven three hours before the party, and wrap it to keep it warm on the trip to the bunkhouse. As she turned from the counter, Jordan walked through the door. His cheeks were red from the biting wind.

There was a loud squeal from the parlor. Ethan appeared around the corner, toddling forward on unsteady legs, arms waving to keep his balance. He was big for eighteen months, with a mop of sandy hair and chubby features that glowed with health. His bright blue eyes were fixed on his father, and he lurched onward at a stiff-legged gait, laughing loudly with happiness. Jordan caught him just as he toppled over.

"How's my boy?" Jordan lifted him high in the air and he squealed with giddy delight. "By God, Becky, he'll be walkin' any day now. We'll have to get him fitted for a pair of boots."

"Honestly, Jack," she said with a teasing lilt. "If you had your way, you'd already have him on a horse."

"Why, hell yes, we'll put him on a horse. You're gonna be a regular buckeroo, aren't you, Ethan?"

Jordan juggled him overhead, moving into the parlor. Rebecca watched as he dropped into a rocking chair, holding Ethan by the arms, and began bouncing him on his knee. She never ceased to marvel at the bond between them, the pure enjoyment that father and son took from one another's company. She felt warm inside, blessed to have the man and his manchild. And before long, she hoped, his daughter.

Her eyes went to their small Christmas tree in the corner. That morning, when they opened their presents, she had felt blessed as well. Jordan's gift to her was a new dress, one he'd bought in Dodge City and kept hidden since October. Her gift to him was a handsome pair of boots, brought from Denver by Cornealia in September. For Ethan there were toys and clothes, and a fine shawl for Juanita. Simple things, nothing elaborate, but great joy in the giving.

Their fourth Christmas in Palo Duro was by far the best yet. She felt warm and secure in their home, and more secure still in the love of her husband. But her greatest gift was his boundless love, so openly displayed, for their son. A gift he had no idea he'd given, and yet the most wonderous gift of all to her. The gift of love.

She thought to herself that a child truly brought joy to the world. A joy beyond measure in Palo Duro.

A livid moon hung high in the sky. The overcast had cleared shortly before dark, and the snow-covered canyon now seemed flooded with a spectral light. Out of the north a chill wind swept across the plains, lending an eerie, moaning whisper to the night. Then the moon went behind a cloud, and somewhere in the distance an owl hooted.

The bunkhouse windows glowed as the moon played hide-and-seek with the clouds. Rebecca carried the baby, swaddled in a woolly blanket against the cold. Jordan carried the ham, and a step behind, Juanita followed with the cake. There was no sound from the bunkhouse, and Rebecca thought it strange that the hands were so quiet. She had expected more noise on a night of celebration.

Jordan moved ahead to open the door. Directly opposite the entrance, the men were ranged along the far wall. They were scrubbed and shaved, their hair slicked back, attired in their best clothes. The bunks had been shoved to the far end of the room, and a Christmas tree, decorated with strings of popcorn and brightly colored cloth, stood in the corner. Off to one side was a table loaded with food, and nearby were a fiddler, a harmonica player, and a third man with a guitar. Rebecca stepped through the door, wearing her new dress, and Leigh Dyer cued the men. Their voices rang out in greeting.

''*Merry Christmas!*''

Rebecca stopped, taken completely by surprise, as the musicians broke out in a Yuletide tune. She glanced around at Jordan, and saw him watching her with a sly grin. She suddenly realized that he and Dyer had conspired with the men to surprise her with a festive greeting. Her eyes glistened with happiness, and she smiled gaily, nodding wordlessly to the men. Mose Butler and his assistant cook moved forward to relieve Jordan of the ham and Juanita of the cake. Dyer took a step forward from the men.

''Boss. Miz Jordan,'' he said with a broad smile. ''All the boys wanted me to thank you for layin' on this spread.''

''And *we* thank you.'' Rebecca finally found her voice, looking across at the men. ''We wish each and every one of you a very merry Christmas.''

''Goes double,'' one of the men called out. ''We shore 'nuff appreciated that fudge candy and them cakes. Best darn Christmas on any outfit we ever rode for.''

''Everybody's thanked everybody,'' Jordan said, moving toward the table, briskly rubbing his hands together. ''I don't know about you boys, but I'm plumb starved. Let's eat!''

The fiddler hit a chord and led the guitar and harmonica into a sprightly number. The men swarmed around the table, with Jordan in their midst, as Butler and his assistant began carving turkey and ham. Dyer led Rebecca and Juanita to chairs positioned against the wall. He peered down at the baby with a lopsided grin.

"How's the little feller?" he asked. "Looks like he growed some."

Rebecca peeled the blanket aside. "He's doing fine, Leigh," she said. "Before long he'll be walking all on his own."

Dyer tickled his tummy. Ethan looked up with a dimpled laugh and took hold of his thorny finger. "Got a grip on him," Dyer said. "Gonna be just like his pa."

"Yes, I'm sure he will," Rebecca agreed. "They're so much alike it's frightening sometimes."

Mose Butler appeared at Dyer's side. He was carrying two plates loaded with ham, turkey, bread stuffing, and stewed apples. "Here you go, Miz Jordan. You and Juanita better dig in before them boys clean us out."

"Oh, Mose, thank you." Rebecca glanced at the plates, shifting the baby to one arm. "I should have brought Ethan's cradle."

"Lemme hold him," Dyer offered. "I'd consider it a powerful honor."

Rebecca gingerly transferred him to Dyer's arms. Butler handed her a plate, pulling silverware from his shirt pocket. He extended the other plate to Juanita, nodding with a broad wink. "Hope you like that stuffing, señorita. It's my own personal recipe."

"Gracias, señor," Juanita said shyly. "Smell very good."

Butler eyed her rounded figure with an appreciative glance. Then, clearly out to impress her, he jerked a thumb at the baby. "Mebbe the missus already done told you. His name's Ethan Dyer Butler Adair Jordan. I'm right proud to have my name in there."

"That is a great honor, señor."

Butler squared his shoulders. "Mebbe you and me could have a dance later. I've been told I'm light on my feet."

Juanita smiled demurely. "I would like that, señor."

"Whyn't you call me Mose? Most everybody does."

Later, after the meal, Buster Lomax took an intricately

carved hobby horse from behind the Christmas tree. The men quieted as he crossed the room and stopped in front of Rebecca. ''Me and the boys—'' He faltered, groping for words. ''Well, we wanted to give little Ethan his first horse. Mite big for him now, but he'll grow into it soon enough.''

The hobby horse had been rubbed to a high gloss with beeswax. Rebecca was touched by the gesture, and her eyes shone with tears. ''Thank you, Buster,'' she said, looking from Lomax to the other men. ''Thank you all so much. You've made it a wonderful Christmas.''

The fiddler led off in a rollicking tune. Leigh Dyer seemed content to hold the baby again, and Jordan escorted Rebecca onto the area that had been cleared as a dance floor. Hovering about, Butler beat the other men to Juanita, and offered her his arm. They caught the beat of the music, and Butler, true to his word, proved to be light on his feet. The rest of the men, looking on, were not to be denied by the shortage of females. Laughing and bowing, choosing their partners, they paired off in a spirited, boot-stomping hoedown.

Jordan swirled around the dance floor, Rebecca held snugly in his arms. Her eyes sparkled with merriment, and deeper still, an inner well of emotion. She looked up at him with a joyous expression.

''You've made Christmas very special this year, Mr. Jordan.''

''Hell, that's the least I could do. You've made *life* special.''

She kissed him to the rousing cheers of the men.

CHAPTER 32

Far in the distance, thunderheads roiled over the southern rimrock. Bolts of lightning crackled across the sky, then flashed down to strike the earth. A sheet of rain pelted the canyon floor.

Jordan emerged from the house. He was wearing a rain slicker, and he stood for a moment watching the downpour. The river was running high, and the heavy, drumming torrent obscured his view across the canyon grasslands. He was reminded that April inevitably brought hard rains to Palo Duro.

Winter had come and gone, only to be replaced by a spring deluge. The thunderstorm made things all the more miserable, and created rough working conditions for the men. But Jordan was nonetheless in a chipper mood, and eager to get on with the myriad of chores that preceded spring roundup. He planned to start roundup early next month, and send the first herds up the trail in June. He was convinced that 1878 would be a banner year for the JA.

Rebecca stood at the kitchen window, holding Ethan in her arms. She tapped on the windowpane, and Jordan looked around, nodding as she made a face about the weather. He waved, turning up the collar on his slicker, and stepped off the porch into the pounding rain. The sky was shrouded by thick clouds, the dawn as dark as night, and lamplight framed the windows of the bunkhouse in a misty glow. He splashed across the compound.

Dyer was waiting as he came through the door of the mess hall. He removed his slicker, hooking it on a wall peg, and slapped water off his hat. His boots squished, leaving wet rings on the floor, as he moved forward and took a seat at the table. The crew had already finished breakfast, and Dyer and the cooks were the only ones in the room. Mose Butler silently handed him a mug of coffee.

"Little sloppy out there," Dyer said. "Think it'll ever stop?"

"Christ only knows, Leigh. No sign of clearing yet."

"Well, rain or shine don't make no nevermind to cows. We still got a day's work to do."

Jordan swigged the scalding coffee. "Liable to find some Herefords bogged down. Not exactly their kind of weather."

"That's a fact," Dyer acknowledged. "All that weight and them stubby legs ain't made for mud. I'll have the waterholes checked out."

"What's the latest from John and Cape?"

John Poe, in charge of the western division, headquartered at the Dinner Creek line camp. Cape Willingham, segundo of the eastern division, worked out of the Pleasant Creek line camp. Twice a week riders brought their reports to Dyer.

"They're on top of things," Dyer said. "Some early calves are startin' to drop. But that's to be expected."

"Send word," Jordan told him. "I want them here a week from today. Time to start planning roundup."

"I'll have 'em here. Anything special you—"

The door burst open. Bob Farwell, a hand from the Pleasant Creek camp, stepped into the room. He was sopping wet, rivulets of water streaming off his slicker and hat. Hurrying across to the table, he doffed his hat, water puddling around his boots. He nodded to Dyer and Jordan.

"Cape sent me to fetch you. We got hit by rustlers last

night. He wants you to came straightaway.''

''Goddammit!'' Jordan growled. ''How many did we lose?''

Farwell flinched at the tone of his voice. ''Hard to get a count in the dark, Mr. Jordan. Cape figures maybe a hundred head.''

''Where the hell was the night patrol?''

''Stumbled across the rustlers up by the south wall. They took a shot at him and he lit out for camp. Wasn't for him we wouldn't've knowed till this mornin'.''

''Which way were they headed?''

''West,'' Farwell said. ''Cape figures it was Stroud's gang.''

''Probably right,'' Jordan remarked. ''How many rustlers?''

''No way of tellin'. Dark as pitch and raining like a cow pissin' on a flat rock.''

Jordan was thoughtful a moment. He looked around at Dyer. ''Maybe we played into luck, Leigh. All this rain likely softened the ground over in the badlands.''

''Yeah, likely so,'' Dyer said. ''You're thinkin' they might've left tracks this time?''

''There's damn sure one way to find out. No need to start tracking them from Pleasant Creek. We'll head straight for the badlands.''

''They'll have made it into Tierra Blanca by now.''

''No matter,'' Jordan said with a hard grin. ''All I want is tracks that lead to Stroud's backyard. That'll be proof enough for me.''

''Suppose it's so,'' Dyer said. ''We ride in there and brace him, we'll most likely kick over a hornet's nest. Stroud don't strike me as a quitter.''

''I never expected him to go without a fight. Pick out seven men that know how to use a gun. You and me and Hank Taylor will make ten. That betters our odds.''

''Helluva note, chasin' rustlers in a goddamn gullywasher. Dumb bastards picked a fine time to steal cows.''

''Get the men ready and saddled.'' Jordan turned back

to Farwell. "You ride back to camp and tell Cape we're headed for Tierra Blanca. I'll let him know how it works out."

"You reckon I could get fed, Mr. Jordan? I ain't et since yesterday supper."

"You heard the man, Mose. Start cooking."

Jordan grabbed his slicker and walked out the door. Butler motioned Farwell to the table, and banged a black iron skillet onto the stove. He glanced around as Dyer gathered his gear from a wall peg.

"You'll wish you was a fish before this day's over."

Dyer snorted. "Only cooks get to stay warm and dry. No goddamn justice to it."

He slammed out the door.

The storm slacked off toward midday. In the distance, the line of thunderclouds drifted steadily southward, swept onward by high winds. The horizon was still darkened by gusty rain squalls.

Jordan rode at the head of the column, his eyes on the ground. They were deep in the badlands, and much as he'd expected, the rough terrain had been loosened by the jarring downpour. The hard earth submitted to the elements only by degree, but the sign was there to read. He was following the tracks of five riders and almost a hundred cows.

The trail led through the gorge that opened onto Tierra Blanca Canyon. Here too, even though the ground was as rough as the badlands, the sign was still faintly visible. The metallic clang of horseshoes on rock reminded him of the last time he'd ridden through the gorge. That was nearly two years ago, and he had been frustrated at every turn since then, with no solid proof leading to the gang in Tierra Blanca. But the heavy rains, an unforeseen ally, had at last brought him full circle. He thought today was the day Earl Stroud would swing. A perfect day for a hanging.

The men were riding single file behind Jordan. Early that afternoon they emerged from the gorge into Tierra

Blanca. The tracks were still visible at first, on a line southward into the canyon. But the ground became steadily softer, muddy and sloppy, the sign more difficult to read. A short distance from the gorge the tracks abruptly disappeared.

Jordan signaled the men to a halt. He sat for a moment studying the terrain, and then rode forward alone. His eyes on the ground, he stayed east of where the tracks had petered out, hoping the westward sun would reveal shadows from hoofprints in the earth. Finally, unable to spot any tracks, he began quartering the canyon floor. Some distance farther on, he stopped, scanning the sparse grazeland ahead. He turned and rode back to the men.

Dyer and Taylor were at the head of the column. Jordan reined up beside them, his features wreathed in disgust. "Lost the trail," he said dourly. "All that rain washed the tracks out."

"Just gone?" Dyer asked. "Ain't no sign at all?"

Jordan briefly explained. The driving rain had been an assist in the badlands, loosening the flint-hard earth sufficiently to hold tracks. But the soil in the canyon was far softer, and hours of pounding rain had obliterated all sign. The tracks had been washed away by the torrential downpour.

"Way I figure it," Jordan concluded, "there was three or four hours of rain after they drove the cows through here. Hard storm like that just wiped out the trail."

"Ain't that a helluva note," Taylor said. "You reckon we'll cut their sign farther down the canyon?"

"I'd tend to doubt it," Jordan said. "They probably got the cows hidden in one of those side canyons before the rain stopped. We're not likely to find any tracks."

"Christ on a crutch!" Dyer said, motioning out across the canyon. "We know they gotta be in there somewhere."

Taylor snorted. "Look at all them damn little canyons runnin' ever' whichaway. It'd be like huntin' for a needle in a haystack."

"How about it, boss?" Dyer said, glancing at Jordan.

"We gonna call it quits here?"

"No," Jordan said shortly. "We're long overdue for another talk with Stroud. We'll start there, and see where it leads."

"Why not just go ahead and search them canyons? We might get lucky and find the cows the first one we try."

"We will, after I put Stroud on warning. I want him to know we're searching his land."

Dyer tugged at his earlobe. "You think Stroud's gonna agree to that?"

"Doesn't matter," Jordan said. "I don't aim to give him a choice."

"Suppose he starts trouble? How d'you want to handle it?"

Jordan signaled the other men forward. When they were gathered around him, he quickly outlined his plan. Four men were assigned to ride on his right, and three on his left, as they crossed the canyon. Dyer would anchor the right end of the line, and Taylor the left, positioned to alert the others should trouble develop on the flanks. The men were instructed to ride with their rifles across their saddles.

"Keep your eyes on me," Jordan told them. "I don't want anybody getting trigger-happy and starting a war. Just follow my lead."

"Suppose they start it?" one of the men asked. "Are we on our own, or do we wait for you?"

"You're on your own," Jordan said. "Anybody on their side pulls a gun, you're free to cut the wolf loose. Don't stop till they're all down. Understood?"

The men bobbed their heads in unison. Jordan wheeled his horse around, waiting until they were in position, and led them across the canyon. The sky began to clear, clouds scudding off to the southeast, as they forded the stream bisecting Tierra Blanca. A short while later they rode into the yard of the Rocking S headquarters. To the west, a mid-afternoon sun appeared through the clouds.

Earl Stroud stepped through the door of the log cabin. The riders were spread out beyond the corners of the cabin, and his gaze swept from end to end, then shifted to Jordan. ''Long time no see,'' he said with a sardonic expression. ''Thought I told you to stay off my land.''

From within the cabin, there was shadowed movement behind the door, which had been left ajar, and beside the far corner of the open window. Jordan thought it was probably no more than two men, likely armed with rifles. ''Listen close, Stroud,'' he said bluntly. ''Anybody inside shows a gun, you're a dead man. Take it as gospel.''

''You're a big one for threats, Jordan. What gives you the right to ride in here like you owned the place?''

''Same thing that brought me here last time. Somebody stole about a hundred head last night. Tracks led straight to Tierra Blanca.''

''Do tell?'' Stroud said in a voice laced with sarcasm. ''I don't see no cows around here with JA on their ass.''

Jordan stared at him. ''Lots of places to hide cows in those little canyons. I plan to have a look for myself.''

''What if I don't agree?''

''You could always try to stop me.''

Stroud laughed out loud. ''Hell, look till you go blind. I ain't got nothin' to hide.''

Something told Jordan it was not a bluff. He knew Stroud had at least three other men, besides the two watching from the cabin. He played a wild hunch. ''Where are the rest of your boys? Already on the way to New Mexico?''

A pinpoint of light flickered in Stroud's eyes. But he recovered himself, dismissed it with an offhand manner. ''Never been to New Mexico,'' he said with heavy irony. ''Heard folks over there aren't to be trusted.''

Jordan caught the startled look, heard the lie in Stroud's voice. He knew then the stolen longhorns were no longer secreted in Tierra Blanca. Instead, the cows were somewhere to the west, lost in the vastness of *Llano Estacado,* headed toward New Mexico. A search of the tributary canyons would be futile.

''You're slick,'' Jordan said at length. ''But not slick

enough, Stroud. You'll hit the JA once too often.''

''Think so?'' There was cold amusement in Stroud's eyes. ''Even if I was a thief—which I'm not—I wouldn't be too worried. You're not much at catchin' rustlers.''

''I'll catch you,'' Jordan warned him. ''Ought to shoot you and have it done with. But I'd rather hang you.''

''Fat chance of that.''

''Only a matter of time, Stroud. You've got my word on it.''

Jordan reined sharply about and rode off. Dyer and the men wheeled their horses from on line, following him back toward the stream. Some distance from the cabin, Dyer gigged his horse and moved up alongside Jordan. His features were wrinkled in a quizzical frown.

''Why'd we pull out?'' he said. ''Thought you meant to search the place.''

''Our cows are long gone, Leigh. Headed for New Mexico.''

''So what're we gonna do about Stroud?''

''Wait,'' Jordan said. ''Wait and watch.''

''I don't take your meanin'. Wait for what?''

''The day we hang Earl Stroud.''

CHAPTER 33

Spring roundup got under way the last day in April. By the early part of May every cow camp on the JA was operating on a schedule of organized bedlam. The hands ate breakfast and supper in the hours of darkness, and more often than not missed the noon meal. Their workday was from dawn to dusk.

All up and down Palo Duro herds were being gathered on open grasslands. From Timber Creek on the east, to Rush Creek on the west, branding fires burned throughout the day. Cows with calves were held briefly at the branding fires, and then released on their home range. Older cows, those past their prime, and grown steers were separated and moved to holding grounds. The trail herds for the summer season slowly began to take shape.

Jordan was up before dawn and in the saddle by first light. He roved the canyon from end to end, inspecting the gather and new calves, and generally stopping over at a line camp for the night. Along the way he got reports from John Poe and Cape Willingham, and every third or fourth night he met Dyer at the headquarters compound. Rebecca, who was now eight months pregnant, saw him only briefly, and usually late at night. She jestfully referred to him as her will-o'-the-wisp husband.

On his daily inspections, Jordan was encouraged by what he saw. The calf crop was larger than expected, and the Hereford bloodlines were now even more apparent in selected herds throughout Palo Duro. He often found himself wishing that John Adair was there to see the progress, the rapid growth of the operation since fall roundup. But in late April a letter had arrived from Adair, brought with the mail collected every couple of weeks from Fort Elliott. Adair expressed regrets that he and Cornealia would miss their first roundup since the ranch was organized over three years ago. Cornealia's brother was being married in New York, and family obligations required that they attend the wedding. Adair promised a visit sometime in the fall.

By then, Jordan fully expected the JA to reach new benchmarks. After a hard winter, he'd been able to buy out one of the two remaining small ranchers in the canyon. He was confident that the last one, who was barely making ends meet, would agree to sell before the onset of another winter. The JA would then control the whole of Palo Duro, over 1,200,000 acres, adequate rangeland to accommodate the natural increase in a herd of more than a hundred thousand cows. Jordan sometimes wondered what he would do with himself when there were no worlds left to conquer. But the thought was fleeting, for the days, and the nights, were already too short. He had all he could handle.

From a financial standpoint, Jordan was wealthy beyond anything he might have dared imagine. His partnership with John Adair had enabled him to build a ranch far larger than either of them had envisioned at the start. He calculated the operation would gross upward of $1,200,000 for the year, based on a modest increase in cattle prices over last season. After all expenses, and barring unforeseen problems, he and Adair should split something on the order of $300,000. Their net worth, including landholdings and livestock, would be in the neighborhood of $5,000,000. But the money was only a gauge, a yardstick of worth, for in his mind the land was what counted. Even if someone offered to buy him out, he would never sell. Palo Duro was where he had planted roots, a thing beyond value. His legacy.

Jordan was not alone in the view. Rebecca shared his passion for the land, his vision of the future. Once a city girl, she now loved the grandeur of Palo Duro, considered it her home. They could easily have afforded a palatial house, a mansion of stone, but she was deeply attached to their log house. They continued to expand, adding rooms, and she was forever in the midst of refurbishing and ordering furniture from St. Louis or Chicago. Twice in three years she had visited her parents in Pueblo, quickly tiring of crowds and what seemed to her now the frantic pace of city life. Like Jordan, she missed the splendor of their canyon, and hurried her return. She was content with her life, all they had built together. She longed for nothing more.

For Jordan, her happiness was no less rewarding than the ranch itself. Today, approaching the Pleasant Creek line camp, he was reminded that her presence alone made the JA a home, rather than a roughshod cow outfit. Joe Pritchard, who rode forward to meet him, was a case in point. The boss of the Pleasant Creek camp, Pritchard was coarse and unkempt, and barely able to write his own name. But he was reliable, and he knew cows, and he had a knack for getting the most out of his crew. His crude manner was secondary to what really counted with men and cows. He got the job done.

''Howdy, Mr. Jordan,'' Pritchard said, reining to a halt. ''Things're movin' along purty good.''

''Glad to hear it, Joe,'' Jordan replied. ''Your boys still working the canyons?''

''Yessir, they shore are. We're gonna flush out ever' shit-tailed cow there is. Don't aim to miss a one.''

Pritchard was responsible for more than eight thousand longhorns. The seven men in his line camp spent their days searching tributary canyons for strayed cows, and hazing cows with calves to the branding fire. On a nearby stretch of grassland Jordan saw men stamping the JA brand on new calves. He looked back at Pritchard.

''How's it going on your trail herd?''

''We'll be ready,'' Pritchard assured him. ''Have them

goddamn cows itchin' to move out come June."

Jordan had ordered a mixed herd to be drawn from the Pleasant Creek camp. The trail drives, with nine herds altogether, were to start in early June. He knew Pritchard would meet the deadline.

"Any idea how many head you lost over the winter?"

"No sir, not just yet," Pritchard said. "Take a while for the boys to comb all them little draws and such. Surprise me if it was more'n thirty head or so."

A shout attracted their attention from the direction of the branding fire. They saw a rider emerge at a full gallop from a tributary canyon off to the west. He spotted them, and as he spurred forward, Jordan recognized him as one of the Pleasant Creek hands, Bob Farwell. He reined his horse to a halt in a cloud of dust.

"Bear!" he yelled in a shaky voice. "Sonovabitch killed a calf. You never seen—"

"Slow down," Jordan ordered. "Catch your wind and start over."

Farwell took a deep breath. "I was chousin' cows through the canyon back there. Gawddamn bear the size of a outhouse jumped out of a ravine and grabbed a calf. Like to spooked my horse from under me."

"The bear got away with the calf?"

"I dunno, Mr. Jordan. Cows spooked ever' whichaway, and my horse took off like he'd been goosed with a hot iron. I got the hell outta there."

"Let's have a look," Jordan said. "Show me where it happened."

"Uhhh," Farwell stammered, his eyes wide with fright. "You fixin' to go after that bear, Mr. Jordan?"

"I'll decide when we get there. Lead the way."

Farwell obeyed, but he was clearly apprehensive about another encounter with the bear. He led Jordan and Pritchard across a wide stretch of grassland, to the mouth of a narrow canyon that angled off to the southwest. Some of the cows gathered by Farwell were bunched outside the canyon, and the others had apparently stampeded back into the wilderness. Halfway down the canyon, Farwell's horse turned skittish, tossing its head and dancing backward. He sawed at the reins.

"There!" he said, pointing his finger. "Over by that gully."

A shallow ravine intersected the canyon from the west. Several yards from the top of the ravine, a gout of wet blood was splashed across the canyon floor. Jordan dismounted, handing the reins to Pritchard, and pulled his Winchester from the saddle scabbard. He walked forward, levering a shell into the chamber, and scanned the bottom of the ravine. Then he studied the ground at his feet.

"Boar," he said, as though thinking aloud. "Looks like a big one."

"Don't like he-bears," Pritchard said. "Sonsabitches always spoilin' for a fight. How big is he?"

Jordan pointed with the muzzle of his rifle. A clear track on the ground appeared slightly larger than a horseshoe. "From the size of that paw print"—he paused, considering a moment—"I'd judge he'll run five hundred pounds. Maybe six hundred."

"Told you!" Farwell blurted. "Gawddamn monster, that's what he is."

Jordan cut a sideways glance at him. Some men feared certain things over others, and bears plainly threw Bob Farwell into an agitated state. On the spur of the moment, he decided Farwell would be a hindrance in what had to be done. He nodded to Pritchard.

"Bring your rifle," he said, then looked at Farwell. "You stay here and hold the horses. Wait till we get back."

"Sure thing, Mr. Jordan." Farwell sounded relieved. "I'll be waitin' right here."

Jordan led the way into the ravine. From the sign, he saw that the bear had dragged the calf into rougher terrain. Some distance ahead, the ravine ended in a pile of boulders that fronted an incline. To the side of the boulders, drag marks and splotches of blood indicated the bear had hauled his kill up the slope and into a dense stand of trees. The wooded area was thick with patches of undergrowth.

For a moment, Jordan stood and surveyed the trees. He thought the bear had probably dragged the calf into the undergrowth, and bedded down for a meal. A finger to his lips, cautioning silence, he motioned for Pritchard to take a position off to his right side. The line boss nodded, indicating he understood, and Jordan sensed that this was not his first bear hunt. When he was in position, Jordan signaled for him to move out. Some yards apart, they started up the slope.

On the high ground, still separated, they moved warily into the trees. The sign was clear to read, a meandering path where the bear had dragged the calf through the brush. They were downwind, and as a warm breeze drifted through the woods, Jordan got the rank scent of bear fur. He halted, motioning Pritchard to a stop, and peered into the shadowed timber. Pritchard skirted a tree, his eyes fixed directly ahead, and stepped on a dead branch. A sharp crack splintered the stillness.

Not ten yards away, a black bear suddenly rose from the undergrowth. His muzzle was covered with blood, and his beady eyes darted from man to man. He reared upright, six feet or more on his hind legs, and roared a challenge that shook the woods. Pritchard fired too hastily, and a puff of dust kicked up high on the bear's shoulder. His head jerked around, jaws snapping at the wound, long yellowed fangs exposed in a snarl. He dropped to all fours with an enraged roar, and hurtled toward Pritchard.

Jordan took a broadside shot. The slug drilled through hide and muscle, centered behind the foreleg, and exploded the bear's heart. For a mere instant the bear staggered, then continued its charge on a direct line for Pritchard. The line boss fired, rushing the shot and missing wildly, as the bear crashed through the undergrowth. Jordan caught his sights, holding a bead on the bear's nose, and feathered the trigger. The bear collapsed in mid-stride, shot through the head. He dropped dead at Pritchard's feet.

Jordan levered a fresh shell into the chamber. He walked forward, halting a step away, and poked the bear with the muzzle of his rifle. When there was no reaction, he turned to Pritchard, whose features were drained of color. "All over, Joe," Jordan said quietly. "He's dead as a rock."

Pritchard couldn't take his eyes off the bear. "Gawd-damn close," he said in a hollow voice. "Thought I was a goner."

"You've got sand, Joe. Most men would've run rather than take a second shot."

"Shit, my legs was froze plumb solid! How the hell'd you drill him through the head? He was movin' faster'n scat."

"Just lucky," Jordan said. "Happens now and then."

"Lucky for me," Pritchard mumbled. "Never seen such shootin'."

"Let's head back to the horses. I want to make it to Tule Creek by nightfall."

A short while afterward they found Bob Farwell waiting beside the ravine. Even before they were mounted, Pritchard began telling Farwell the story. When they reached the branding fire, he told it all over again. He was still telling it when Jordan rode eastward along the river.

Late that night Jordan dismounted outside the Tule Creek line camp. He unsaddled, turned his horse into the corral, and walked to the cabin with his rifle. As he stepped through the door, the men inside went deathly silent. Two of them were seated at the table, playing poker, while the others watched from their bunks. His face congealed in a scowl.

"You there," he said to the card players. "What's your names?"

"I'm Bob Ryan," one replied, nodding at the other. "This here's Vince Sanborn."

"You're both fired," Jordan told them. "You knew the rule against gambling when you signed on. Collect your gear and get out."

"Hold on now!" Ryan yelled. "You can't put us out in the dead of night."

"I just did." Jordan looked across at Dave Reed, the line boss. "You're fired, too. I won't tolerate a man who doesn't enforce my orders."

"C'mon, Mr. Jordan," Reed said, rising from his bunk. "Nothin' wrong with a little penny-ante poker. Not even real gamblin'."

"Don't make me repeat myself. Stop by headquarters and collect your pay from Dyer. I want you out of Palo Duro."

"You're a regular sonovabitch, ain't you?" Reed growled. "I think me and these boys'll just clean your plow."

Reed started forward, as Ryan and Sanborn moved away from the table. Jordan thumbed the hammer on his Winchester, brought it to hip level. "Don't try it," he said in a cold voice. "I guarantee you'll lose."

The three men stared at him a moment. Something in his eyes told them that they were dead if they jumped him. Reed muttered an unintelligible curse, and began getting dressed. Jordan moved off to the side, waiting while the men crammed gear into their saddlebags. He kept the rifle trained on them as they went out the door.

"No way you heard the last of this," Reed called over his shoulder. "Ain't no way to treat a grown man. You're gonna be sorry."

"Do yourself a favor," Jordan warned him. "Get on your horse and keep riding. Don't come back."

Some minutes later the men rode out of the clearing. Jordan waited outside the cabin until the sound of hoofbeats faded into silence. He considered Reed's parting comment an idle treat, and let it go at that. Some men were all wind and no whistle.

Today, he thought to himself, had been a helluva day. He'd lost a calf and killed a bear and fired a line boss. Tomorrow looked to be a better day all around.

He turned back into the cabin.

CHAPTER 34

A brassy June sun stood high overhead. Dust rose in a billowing column as the trailhands drove a herd up the road from Palo Duro. Just before noon the last of the longhorns topped the rimrock onto the plains.

Jordan sat his horse off to one side. He watched as Deacon Walsh, the trail boss, emerged from the roiling dust, shouting commands to the drag riders. The men popped their lariats, hurrying stragglers along, and Walsh circled the rear of the herd. He reined to a halt beside Jordan.

"Howdy, boss," he said, his face streaked with dust and sweat. "What's your tally?"

"Two thousand and twelve," Jordan replied. "How's that square with you?"

"Dead on the money. Got the exact same count."

The herd was the first of nine that would be trailed to Dodge City. Deacon Walsh, one of Jordan's more seasoned trail bosses, had been selected to point the way north. The other herds would be driven from the canyon a day apart, following the pattern Jordan had established in 1876. He expected the last herd to reach railhead by the end of June.

Yet he had qualms about this year's drive. For the first time, he would not accompany the lead herd. He was determined to be on hand for the birth of his second child. Rebecca was due any day, and he'd promised her he wouldn't leave until the baby was born. Despite his confidence in Walsh, and the other trail bosses, he still had some misgivings. From Palo Duro to Dodge City, any number of problems could arise, from flooded rivers to raids by rustlers. He sensed that Walsh shared his concern.

"You know the drill," he said now. "Drive 'em hard until they're trail broke. Couple of days ought to do it."

"No worries there," Walsh said, though he himself seemed worried. "Any idea when you'll catch up with us?"

"Look for me when you see me, Deacon. I'll head out once the baby's here."

"What if we hit Dodge before you show?"

"Not likely," Jordan told him. "But if I'm delayed too long, I'll send Dyer in my place. You just look after your herd."

"Hell, boss, I ain't never lost a herd yet. You can count on me."

"Never thought otherwise, Deacon. Go on and head 'em north."

Walsh grinned, knuckling the brim of his hat, and rode off. Jordan watched as he overtook the drag riders, and vanished into the dust of the herd. There was a moment of apprehension, but Jordan quickly set it aside. His older hands, Deacon Walsh among them, were veterans of countless trail drives. He told himself not to borrow trouble. The herd would get through.

Jordan reined his horse back down the road. Off in the distance, the breadth of Palo Duro was ablaze with wildflowers. Entire patches of grassland were blood-red with prairie roses, and others cerulean with sun-spangled bluebells. The bright colors somehow buoyed his mood, and turned his thoughts from Walsh and the herd. His mind centered on Rebecca.

The baby was due sometime before the middle of June. Three days ago, not quite a week into the month, Martha Bugbee had arrived by buckboard. As a precaution, remembering that Rebecca had delivered early last time, she had made the trip from the Canadian well in advance. Her presence alone gave Jordan a welcome feeling of security, and a newfound comfort. All the more so since she would be assisted in the childbirth by Juanita, who herself had experience in such matters. Two midwives were better than one, and certainly better than the circumstances under which Ethan was born. This time, Jordan assured himself, women rather than cowhands would deliver his child.

Still, though he counted it a blessing, Jordan would have preferred a doctor, someone with medical training. But that was a luxury as yet unavailable, apart from an army sawbones at Fort Elliott who was three days' ride away, and knew little of birthing babies. One day the Panhandle would grow and attract sufficient people to warrant a real doctor establishing a medical practice. Until then, women would have to depend on midwives, and he thought Rebecca was luckier than most. Taken together, Martha Bugbee and Juanita were a godsend.

Rebecca took it all in stride. Jordan considered it an everlasting wonder that she had so thoroughly adapted to the hardships of ranch life. She was a woman of backbone and spirit, and seemingly indomitable no matter how severe the problem. At times, Jordan thought that women, far from being the weaker sex, were the strongest of the lot. Rebecca had taught him that women could endure and prevail in situations where most men were quick to call it quits. The ordeal of having Ethan, and the courage she'd shown, were a legend around the JA. Every man in the outfit looked upon her as a force of nature. Equal to any task.

Jordan rode into the compound early that afternoon. As he dismounted at the corral, he noticed Mose Butler seated in one of the porch rockers, holding Ethan. The youngster was watching raptly as Butler formed a cat's cradle with his hands and a piece of string. Jordan moved across the yard, wondering why Butler was looking after the boy in the middle of the day. The absence of the women set off a note of alarm.

When he stepped onto the porch, Ethan saw him and quickly squirmed out of the chair. He scooped the boy up in his arms, nodding to Butler. "Mose," he said. "What's going on here? Where are the women?"

"Inside," Butler said in a low voice. "Way it looks, your missus's time has come. Juanita fetched me to tend to the boy."

"What did she say about my wife?"

"Didn't say much of anything. Just told me to keep Ethan amused."

"I'd better have a word with Mrs. Bugbee."

The boy squealed in protest when Jordan passed him across to Butler. Entering the house, Jordan halted in the kitchen as Martha Bugbee emerged from the bedroom. She was a formidable woman, accustomed to taking charge and issuing orders, the equal of any man. Jordan often thought she would have made a good trail boss, or perhaps a drill sergeant. She bustled toward him.

"Glad you're back," she said. "Rebecca's water broke just after you rode out this morning."

Jordan wasn't sure what that meant. He knew it was a preliminary to birth, but he felt awkward about asking for details. "How's she doing?"

"Jack, I swear to God, she's fast as a bunny rabbit. Went into labor hardly an hour after her water broke. Your Rebecca doesn't waste any time."

"She's early again, same way she was with Ethan. Does that mean anything?"

"Nothing special," Martha reassured him. "Some women are early, some women are late. Babies don't arrive on a set schedule."

Jordan nodded. "I'd like to see her."

"Just don't dally around. Her contractions are pretty regular now. I doubt it'll be much longer."

Martha led him across the parlor. When he entered the bedroom, Juanita gave him a shy smile and slipped through the doorway. Rebecca lay propped against a bank of pillows, covered by a sheet. The women had changed her into a gauzy nightgown, but her forehead was beaded with perspiration. She held out her hand.

"I heard your voice," she said with a faint smile. "I knew you'd get back in time."

" 'Course I'm back." Jordan seated himself on the edge of the bed, squeezed her hand. "Way Martha talks, I timed it just right. She says you're a regular bunny rabbit."

"I'm not sure it's me so much. I think your daughter wants to be born."

"You sound mighty certain of yourself. What makes you think it'll be a girl?"

She gave him a smug look. "The same thing that made me think Ethan would be a boy. Call it a mother's intuition."

Jordan saw it in her face, that inner unshakable serenity. He managed a lopsided grin. "I suppose you've already got a name picked out."

"I've always been partial to the name Laura. Laura Jordan. I think it sounds just perfect."

"Yeah, that's mighty pretty. 'Course, you could be wrong. Suppose it's a boy?"

"Oh, fiddlesticks! If it's a boy you can name him anything you please. I'm right, though. You just wait and see."

Her cheeks glowed with a healthy apricot tint. She spoke as she always spoke, strong-willed and slightly impudent. Then, in the next moment, a contraction hit with sudden force. Her eyes widened with pain, and she gripped his hand in a viselock. Her features glistened with sweat.

Jordan's massive self-control deserted him. He'd seen men hurt and killed, but this was altogether different. He couldn't bear to watch her suffer. "Martha!" he called out. "You'd better get in here."

The contraction passed, and Rebecca sank into the pillows. She patted his hand, as though comforting a small boy in the dark of night. "Don't worry. Everything will be all right. You'll see."

Martha Bugbee hurried into the bedroom, followed by

Juanita. They quickly shooed him outside, and closed the door. Juanita flipped the sheet aside as another contraction brought a low moan from Rebecca. In a soothing voice, Martha calmed her, and took a position at the foot of the bed. The intensity of the labor, and the jolting contractions, suddenly alerted her fears. Something was wrong.

Martha lifted the flimsy nightshirt and laid it across Rebecca's swollen abdomen. Gently she spread the vulva, probed deep into the birth canal with her fingers. She encountered the baby's buttocks rather than its head, which would have been presented in a normal delivery. She withdrew her fingers, silent a moment, then darted a nervous glance at Juanita. Gesturing rapidly, she inverted her hands over Rebecca's stomach, confirming what she'd found. The baby was in a breech position.

"Madre de Dois!" Juanita whispered. "What will we do?"

"There's not too many choices. One way or another, we have to move him."

A contraction shuddered through Rebecca, and her jaws clenched against the stabbing pain. Martha waited for the contraction to subside, and then, holding the vulva apart, she inserted her hand into the canal. Ever so gingerly she attempted to rotate the baby, working to turn its shoulders. When that failed, she tried to maneuver the legs into a downward position. At last she withdrew her hand and stood. Her eyes were grim.

"Damn!" she said in a hoarse tone. "I can't turn him."

"But you must," Juanita said anxiously. "Surely there is a way, señora."

"I only know one other thing to try."

Martha quickly explained the procedure. She directed Juanita to help Rebecca over on her stomach. Working together, they then managed to raise the girl onto her knees and elbows. Rebecca groaned, fighting the pain while trying to cooperate, barely able to hold the position. Juanita supported her by the shoulders, and kept her head lowered on the bed. From behind, Martha stabilized her bent knees and elevated her buttocks. Straining to maintain their holds, they kept her there for a full ten minutes. Finally, at Martha's command, they rolled her once more onto her back.

The procedure was meant to rotate the baby as the mother was turned. Once before, when Martha had assisted an experienced midwife, the baby had revolved sufficiently to allow a normal delivery. But now, as she performed another examination, she held her breath. Her face suddenly split in a horsey grin.

"Hallelujah!" she whooped. "We did it!"

Juanita crossed herself. *"Gracias a Dios."*

The contractions abruptly quickened. Rebecca uttered a stifled shriek as the pain mounted in intensity. Martha crouched at the foot of the bed, spread Rebecca's legs, and began massaging the widened vulva. She commanded Rebecca to bear down, and the girl puffed, gasping air, and strained harder. The baby's forehead appeared and Martha stretched the folds of the vulva wider still. Then, all in a rush, the head emerged and Martha gently worked the shoulders free. A moment later she lifted the newborn infant from the bed.

"It's a girl," she said, laughing. "A perfect little girl."

Rebecca strained for a better look, tears flooding her eyes. Unable to speak, she slumped back on the bed, exhausted by the ordeal. Martha slapped the baby on the rump and brought forth a loud squall of outrage. She cut the umbilical cord, deftly tying it off, and turned the baby over to Juanita. When the afterbirth emerged, she wrapped it in a cloth, and set it aside. Humming to herself, she began cleaning Rebecca with water from a washpan.

A short time later she stepped from the bedroom into the parlor. Her eyes were bright with happiness and she nodded to Jordan. "Congratulations," she said. "You have yourself a daughter."

"A girl." Jordan beamed. "I'll be damned. How's Becky?"

"Doing just fine. Let her rest a spell and then you can

go in. She's pretty much tuckered out."

"Whatever you say." Jordan turned toward the front door with a dopey grin. "Godalmighty, isn't that something! Ethan's got himself a little sister."

Outside, Mose Butler rose from the rocking chair. Jordan took Ethan from his arms and playfully jiggled the youngster overhead. "You hear that, sprout? You've got yourself a sister." He laughed, glancing at Butler. "Doesn't that beat all, Mose?"

"Shore does," Butler said jovially. "Your missus done you proud, boss."

Ethan screamed gleefully, waving his arms and legs as Jordan jounced him high in the air. Butler stood back, watching them, thinking he'd never seen Jordan so openly jubilant. A moment passed, and then, from the direction of the river, the clatter of hoofbeats broke the spell. They turned as a rider thundered into the yard and jumped from the saddle. He hurried toward the porch.

"Joe Dobbs, Mr. Jordan," he said, huffing for breath. "John Poe sent me to fetch you. Somebody raided the horse herd down by Dinner Creek."

"When?"

"Last night," Dobbs panted. "Got away with about thirty head."

"Mose, see that he gets some grub and a fresh horse. I'll want to pull out come dark, Dobbs."

"Yessir, Mr. Jordan."

Jordan hefted Ethan in his arms, and walked back into the house. He refused to let the news darken his mood, or spoil the day. Horse thieves were a dime a dozen, and never in scarce commodity. A daughter came along maybe once in a lifetime.

On his way inside, he wondered if she would favor Rebecca. He thought it likely, and he swelled with pride. All of a sudden it was real, all of it. A baby girl and her name.

Laura.

CHAPTER 35

A brooding loneliness hung over Palo Duro. Somewhere in the distance an owl hooted, and a squirrel, chattering with alarm, scampered to safety. Within moments, an empty silence once again settled across the canyon. Off to the east, sunrise topped the rocky battlements.

Jordan walked forward, searching the ground. To the rear, still mounted, Poe and Dobbs waited with his gelding. A short way upstream, where Dinner Creek flowed into the river, a herd of some fifty horses stood cropping grass in the early light. He abruptly stopped at a shallow ford, scanning the churned earth along the other side of the river. The sign was there to read.

All through the night Jordan and Dobbs had ridden east by a full moon. Sometime before dawn, they had awakened John Poe at the Dinner Creek line camp. After a hasty breakfast, they'd swapped for fresh horses and turned north along the creek, accompanied by Poe. A few minutes before sunrise, they had halted back from the river, not far from the horse herd. Up ahead, Poe had indicated, were the tracks of the horse thieves.

After a moment of scrutiny, Jordan signaled the other men forward. He mounted, reining his horse into the ford, and led them across the river. On the opposite bank, more from habit than need, he put the tracks between himself and the blood-gold shafts of sunrise. The trail was easily followed, for thirty shod horses left sign apparent to all but the rawest greenhorn. Yet the easterly sun cast a shadow across the hooved imprints, and Jordan stuck to the cardinal rule from his days as a Ranger scout. He kept the sun on the far side of the tracks.

A short distance from the river, the trail angled off to the northwest. From the sign, Jordan could judge the length of the stride, and he saw that the raiders had held the horses to a slow trot. He signaled a halt with an upraised hand, and sat for a moment studying the tracks. With a full moon last night, the landscape had been clearly lighted, and the thieves had obviously quickened the pace. But that left the question of why they had turned northwest, and all the more puzzling, how they meant to get the horses out of the canyon. His gaze went to a palisades of the north wall, some five miles away.

"Three men," he said, as though thinking out loud. "Way I read the sign, they turned off in that direction night before last. Not pushing the horses too hard, either."

Dobbs looked perplexed. "Whyn't they take all the herd? Could've had the whole bunch just as easy."

"Too sharp for that," Jordan said. "Three men can handle thirty head with no problem. A smart thief never gets greedy."

"You think it's Stroud?" Poe interjected. "Maybe they're trying to throw us off. Head thataway, and then double back to Tierra Blanca."

"I'd tend to doubt it, John. Stroud's always stuck pretty much to cows. Never shown any interest in horses."

"Then there's something funny here. Why would they take off toward the northwest? No way out of the canyon over there."

"There's one way," Jordan said. "Not the best way, but it's a way out."

Poe frowned. "You talkin' about that old Indian trial? Hell, boss, that's not hardly fit for goats."

"Comanches used it for a hundred years or more. They never had any trouble with horses."

"Yeah, but nobody's used that trail since we come to Palo Duro. How'd anybody know about it?"

"You know," Jordan corrected him. "Not any big goddamn secret, John. Most everybody on the JA knows."

"Well, yeah—" Poe hesitated, comprehension flooding his features. "You talkin' about some of the hands? Somebody that rode for the outfit?"

"Let's just call it a hunch. If I'm right, these sonsabitches figured a new way to skin the cat. We'll find out directly."

Jordan led them northwest across the canyon. Up ahead, a section of the northern wall jutted southward, placing it closer to the river. His mind went back to that day in 1874, when he'd scouted a way into Palo Duro for Mackenzie and the 4th Cavalry. The battle had ended with the Comanche fleeing up a steep trail along the northern wall. A trail of no practical value to the JA operation, and unused now for nearly four years. Unless his hunch proved to be correct.

One thought prompted another. From the campaign against the Comanche, his mind went forward in time to establishing the JA, and bringing Rebecca to Palo Duro. Then, because the memory was still fresh, his mind jumped ahead to yesterday, the birth of his daughter. He was proud beyond reckoning, and prouder all the more of Rebecca. Last night, when he'd told her he must leave, she had accepted it without argument or rebuke. Her words were with him even now . . .

"Jack, you shouldn't look so glum. I understand. I really do."

"Hope you mean that. I figured to stay a day or so longer with you and the baby. But some things—"

"Horse thieves are not to be tolerated. Isn't that what you're trying to say?"

"Yeah, more or less. You know how I feel about that sort of thing."

"And I feel the same way. Besides, even without this,

you'd be leaving for Dodge City anyway, wouldn't you? I really do understand."

"I've told you before, but I say it again. You've got sand, Mrs. Jordan."

"Oh, honestly, spare me your flattery. I'd much prefer a kiss."

Their parting kiss still lingered. But Jordan's wool-gathering was suddenly broken as the northern wall loomed ahead. He shook off the thoughts of last night, and got back to the business at hand. The tracks of the stolen horses, just as he'd suspected, led straight to the base of the towering palisade. There, reading the sign at a glance, he saw that the horses had been driven single-file up the old Comanche trail. Someone clearly knew the ins and outs of Palo Duro.

For a moment, staring upward, Jordan recalled the day he'd winged a shot at Quanah Parker, the Quahadi leader. Hindsight improved a man's perspective, and he was glad, given the passage of time, that the shot had gone astray. But now, in a flight of idle speculation, he wondered if the Comanche had reverted to their old ways. Once the greatest horse thieves on the plains, a raiding party could easily slip off the reservation for a moonlit sortie into Palo Duro. To many Texicans, a full moon was still thought of as a Comanche Moon. Thousands of horses had disappeared under moonlit skies.

On second thought, Jordan put the notion aside. The Comanche were entirely capable of a raid, and he in no way discounted their willingness to filch a few Texican horses. But some inner voice, an instinct often more reliable than reason, told him that his hunch was correct. The raid somehow smelled of white men, thieves on the owl-hoot who were content to make off with a few head and live to steal another day. All the more so since the three men he was tracking rode shod horses. In that respect, reason merely bolstered his instinct. There were no blacksmiths among the Comanche.

Jordan led Poe and Dobbs up the steep trail. The path

was narrow, climbing at a steep grade for a thousand feet, and they were forced to proceed in single file. Hardly a quarter of the way up the wall, the footing became so treacherous that he dismounted and ordered the men to lead their horses. Dobbs, who was at the rear, hugged the wall, cursing roundly every time a dislodged stone tumbled over the sheer drop-off. The sun rose steadily toward its noonday zenith as they approached the rimrock, laboring for breath. By the time they emerged onto the plains, they were drenched in sweat.

A wind warmed by the sun drifted in from the south. Jordan ordered a breather for the horses, and walked forward to scout on foot. With the sun directly overhead, there was no way to rely on shadows in spotting tracks. But the dry earth nonetheless revealed the telltale signs of passage. The scuff of hoofprints, and clumps of buffalo grass torn from the ground, told a story all its own. Some while later, satisfied with what he'd found, he walked back to the rimrock. Poe and Dobbs were seated in the shade of their horses.

"Headed due north," Jordan said, motioning across the plains. "Once they got up here, they put the horses into a dead gallop. Likely figured to switch mounts now and then, and make better time."

"Sorry bastards." Poe finished rolling a cigarette, worked up the spit to lick the seal. "Where you reckon they're headed?"

"I'd guess they made a run for the Canadian. We'll just follow along and see what's what."

Dobbs cleared his throat. "Them boys are two days ahead with a runnin' start. You think we're gonna catch 'em, Mr. Jordan?"

Jordan walked toward his horse. "Tell you when we get there, Dobbs. Let's get mounted."

He led them north into the shimmering heat waves of distant plains.

* * *

Late the next afternoon they sighted the Canadian. The river was running swift, the strong current pushed along by spring floods. The tracks of the stolen horses went straight to the shoreline along the southern bank. There the trail stopped.

Jordan knew the men were tired. He'd paused briefly last night, allowing them to catch a few hours' sleep on the open plains. Their supper consisted of a jackrabbit shot before dark, with nothing more than branch water and beef jerky since then. But now, staring out across the river, he felt compelled to press on with the hunt. The sign told him that they were gaining on the horse thieves.

By rough estimate, Jordan figured they were hardly more than a day behind. The trail had never deviated, on a line due north from Palo Duro. Toward sundown last night, they'd found a burned-out campfire where the thieves had stopped the night before. Horse dung along the trail, hard on the outside but still moist deep inside, indicated they were slowly closing the gap. Another day might easily end the hunt.

The tracks along the shoreline convinced Jordan that the thieves had forded the river. Still, he'd learned never to take anything for granted, and he quickly outlined a plan to Poe and Dobbs. They watched as he gigged his horse into the water, fighting the current all the way across, and finally emerged onto the opposite shore. There he dismounted, leaving his horse ground-reined, and walked the bank in both directions. To his consternation, he found no tracks, nothing to indicate the horses had come ashore. After pondering on it, he thought perhaps they had been swept farther downstream. He motioned Poe and Dobbs eastward.

Jordan rode the north bank for a mile downriver. Opposite him, Poe and Dobbs kept pace along the southern shoreline. He scoured the ground, pausing here and there to inspect groves of cottonwoods, and found nothing. At a loss, he finally signaled the men and turned back in the direction they'd come. From their original starting point, he then scouted westward for a mile upstream. By now thoroughly baffled, he called off the search and rejoined the men on the opposite bank. He swung down from the saddle with a look of disgruntled anger.

"Not a single goddamn track," he said gruffly. "You boys find anything?"

"Nothin' over here," Poe said. "How the hell'd they pull it off?"

"Wish to Christ I knew, John. They're trickier than I gave 'em credit for."

"Thirty head of horses don't just go up in a puff of smoke. They gotta be somewhere."

Jordan stamped water from his boots. "Only one thing occurs to me. They could've taken to the river, herded the horses along in the shallows." He shook his head. "Not impossible, but it would've been tough going. That current's pretty fast."

"Like you said, they're tricky," Poe replied. "Question is, would they've gone downstream or upstream?"

"That's anybody's guess. Indian Territory is one way, and New Mexico's the other. Take us a week to ride the river in both directions."

Joe Dobbs kicked at a clod of dirt. "You give any thought to Tascosa, Mr. Jordan?"

"What makes you ask?"

"Damn town's rough as a cob. Last time I was there, the place was overrun with hardcases. Horse thieves might find it a likely spot."

Jordan studied on it a moment. He placed Tascosa some forty miles upstream, on the north bank of the Canadian. The town's reputation was that of a sinkhole of iniquity. Saloons, gaming dives, and cathouses catering to the raw tastes of cowhands.

"Worth a try," he said at length. "We're at a dead end here."

"Cutthroats from all over come there, Mr. Jordan. You never seen a place like it in your life."

"I heard Mick McCormick bought a saloon there. Anything to it?"

"Yeah, him and his wife," Dobbs said, nodding. "How'd you come to know Mick?"

"Dodge City," Jordan remarked. "Met him there on last fall's trail drive. One of the boys told me he'd moved to Tascosa."

"How is it you've never been there, Mr. Jordan?"

"Not my kind of place, Dobbs. Not till now, anyway."

"The boys like it," Poe said with a crooked smile. "Only place in a hundred miles with poon-tang and busthead whiskey."

"So I hear," Jordan observed. "All I'm interested in is horse thieves."

"We're gonna head that way, are we?"

"I figure we're about ten miles from Sam Bugbee's place. We'll stop there tonight and have ourselves a hot meal. Sound good?"

"You got my vote!" Poe whooped. "I'm plumb wore out on jerky."

"Say, Mr. Jordan," Dobbs broke in. "You said you know Mick. How about his wife, Frenchy? Have you met her?"

"I had the pleasure in Dodge City."

"Ain't she a looker, though? Cute as a gawddamn button!"

Dobbs went on about the woman as they mounted and rode west. Jordan ignored the monologue, his thoughts focused instead on horse thieves. The ones whose trail had ended at the Canadian.

He wondered what they would find in Tascosa.

CHAPTER 36

Jordan and his men rode into Tascosa early the next evening. All that day, while following the Canadian westward, they had checked the riverbank for sign of the stolen horses. There were tracks of cows and horses everywhere, for several ranches were now operating along the Canadian. But none of the sign offered clearcut proof of the horses they trailed.

Upon entering the town, Jordan found it neither more nor less than he'd expected. Tascosa was located on the north bank of the river, a ramshackle collection of buildings thrown together in the middle of nowhere. The New Mexico border lay some thirty miles farther west, and the nearest lawman in Texas was a ten-day ride to the southeast. All in all it looked to be a haven for men whose faces appeared on wanted dodgers.

The main street was roughly parallel with the river. Crowded together, hastily erected from ripsawed lumber, the buildings were a squalid testament to the allure of vice. Along one side of the street were two saloons, a whorehouse, and a blacksmith shop. On the other side was a third saloon, flanked by a general store, a mercantile, and a livery stable. There was no newspaper, no post office, no bank, and no streetlamps. Off to the north, there were a few houses scattered about like a handful of old dice.

Joe Dobbs pointed the way to the Exchange Saloon,

situated next to the general store on the south side of the street. Outside the saloon the men dismounted and draped their reins around a hitch rail. The street was dark, apart from light spilling through the windows of the saloons and the whorehouse, the only establishments still open. Jordan noted horses tied wherever there was a splotch of light, and he heard a woman's laughter from somewhere down the street. He was reminded of a dozen raw, windswept trail towns he'd seen from Texas to Wyoming.

The inside of the saloon was brightly lighted by coal-oil lamps. Several cowhands stood hunched over a bar that stretched the length of the room. The bartender was a large man, with flaming hair and a square jaw, and a brushy mustache. Opposite the bar were three tables devoted to poker, and not an empty seat in the house. At the far end of the room, a svelte woman with auburn hair riffled cards at a faro layout. Four cowhands, eager to test their luck, waited for her to deal.

Jordan, with Poe and Dobbs at his side, halted at the front end of the bar. The bartender finished serving a drink, placed the bottle on the back shelf, and turned in their direction. He hesitated in mid-stride, as though he'd seen a ghost, and his mustache rolled upward in a wide grin. He hurried forward.

"Jack Jordan!" he said with an outthrust hand. "By all that's holy, it's you, isn't it?"

"In the flesh." Jordan took his hand in a firm grip. "How's life been treating you, Mick?"

"Marvelous, just marvelous! And I hear you've been doing nicely your own self. I've kept up with you through your men."

"What brought you all the way out here from Dodge?"

"Opportunity," McCormick said with a wry chuckle. "Less competition here than there was in Dodge. Especially if a man sells uncut whiskey."

Dobbs involuntarily smacked his lips at the word. Jordan glanced at him, remembering that the ban on drinking stopped at the JA boundary. "Tell you what, Mick," he said, smiling. "Give my boys a shot of your best. They've earned it."

"And yourself?"

"I'll have a beer."

McCormick ambled back to the bar. Jordan's gaze strayed to the faro table, and he watched Frenchy deftly work the layout. He thought she and her husband were typical of the sporting crowd. Vagabond wanderers always chasing a greater lodestone. McCormick, with his Irish charm, was an itinerant gambler who had drifted into the more profitable occupation of operating saloons. In Dodge City, he'd met and married Frenchy, whose nickname stemmed from her girlhood in Louisiana Cajun country. She later appeared on the burlesque stage in St. Louis, and somehow found her way to the Kansas cowtowns. McCormick had transformed her from a dancer into a feature attraction at the faro table. Her sensual good looks provided temptation for a generation of cowhands.

McCormick returned with the drinks. "On the house," he said grandly, setting out brimming shot glasses and a mug of warm beer. "Now tell me, Jack, for it's curious I am, indeed. You've never before set foot in our little oasis of iniquity. What brings you to Tascosa?"

"Horses," Jordan said, pausing to sip his beer. "Four days ago, somebody stole thirty head off my place. We tracked them to a spot downriver and lost the trail. Figured we'd have a look around here."

Poe and Dobbs knocked back their drinks, awaiting a response. McCormick looked from one to the other, then chortled softly. "Ah, Jack," he said, wagging his head. "I should've known it wasn't a social call. You're after information, aren't you?"

"Well, a saloonkeeper generally hears all the local dirt. Anything come over the grapevine lately?"

McCormick darted a quick glance over his shoulder. "Listen to me, Jack," he said, lowering his voice. "I've no wish for an early grave. Whatever I say didn't come from me. Agreed?"

"Agreed," Jordan assured him. "I recollect you don't scare so easy, Mick. Who's got you worried?"

"A lad named Bonney. Known to some as Billy the Kid."

Jordan raised an eyebrow. "You're saying the Kid's in town?"

"That I am," McCormick affirmed. "Drops over from New Mexico on a regular basis. Deadly little booger, as you may have heard."

Everyone in the West had heard. William Bonney, alias Billy the Kid, was reputed to have killed a dozen men or more. A sometimes cattle rustler and horse thief, he was currently a gunman in the Lincoln County War. The hostilities revolved around rival factions battling for rangeland, and political control, in southwestern New Mexico. Only two months ago, the Kid had ambushed and killed the sheriff of Lincoln County. He was a wanted man, with a price on his head, dead or alive. No one as yet had attempted to claim the reward.

"The Kid's a killer," Jordan said now. "But he's made his reputation in the Lincoln County War. What's that got to do with stolen horses?"

"Filthy lucre, money," McCormick said, rubbing the tips of his fingers together. "Clever devil that he is, Mr. Bonney steals horses in New Mexico and drives them over here. Some people, as you are well aware, pay no mind to brands. Or God forbid, a legal bill of sale."

"Who's he sell these horses to?"

"I've no idea, really. Word has it that he deals in rustled cattle as well. Apparently, he has a secret holding ground somewhere outside of Tascosa."

Jordan shrugged. "All that's real interesting, Mick. But it's got nothing to do with my stock."

"Perhaps," McCormick conceded. "On the other hand, a man rode into town today to meet with Bonney. You can imagine the word spread like wildfire."

"So?"

"From what I gather, he has a ranch somewhere near

yours. You may know him. Goes by the name of Stroud.''

''Earl Stroud?'' Jordan demanded. ''He's meeting with Billy the Kid?''

''At this very moment,'' McCormick said. ''Bonney and his gang arrived late yesterday. Stroud and his men rode in early this afternoon. They've had their heads together ever since.''

Jordan looked like he'd had a revelation. His mind spun with the possibilities of an alliance between Stroud and Billy the Kid. Maybe they were arranging a swap of stolen livestock, making it easier for them to sell in their own territory. Or perhaps they were working out a bolder plan, the movement of large herds back and forth between New Mexico and Texas. Whatever the purpose of their meeting, no good would come of it. The JA was certain to suffer even greater losses in the future.

''This meeting?'' he said after a moment. ''Where's it being held?''

''Across the street,'' McCormick informed him. ''Dunn's Saloon is home away from home for Bonney. His kind frequent the place.''

''Men on the dodge?''

''Bandits, rustlers, pistoleros of every description. A watering hole for anyone outside the law.''

''How many men with Stroud and the Kid?''

''Well, just offhand, I would say ten or twelve. Why do you ask?''

''Thought I might have a word with them.''

''You're joking!'' McCormick saw that he was serious. ''Good God, Jack, you'd be courting certain death. Bonney's been known to kill men just for the sport of it.''

Poe and Dobbs exchanged a look. Dobbs hawked a wad of phlegm, swallowed hard. ''Mick's got a point,'' he said. ''You sure you wanna tangle with that bunch, Mr. Jordan?''

Jordan was stone-faced. ''Not your obligation to go along. Or yours either, John. You boys stay here.''

"I've come this far," Poe said in a dry voice. "Might as well play out the hand."

Dobbs sighed heavily. "Guess my mama must've raised a fool. I'll tag along, too."

"You're all crazy!" McCormick rumbled. "You'll get yourselves killed."

"Don't bet on it," Jordan said. "I remember you used to keep a scattergun under the counter. Mind if I borrow it?"

McCormick muttered an unintelligible curse. He reached under the bar and pulled out a double-barrel sawed-off shotgun. When he passed it across, Jordan broke it open and checked the loads. He snapped the breech closed.

"Much obliged," he said. "I owe you one, Mick."

"You're a man of brass balls, Jack Jordan. I hope it doesn't get you murdered."

"Why, hell, Mick, I thought you knew. I'm hard to kill."

Jordan turned from the bar. Poe and Dobbs fell in behind, and followed him through the door. Outside, Jordan instructed them to collect their carbines from their saddle scabbards. When they were ready, he explained what he had in mind, and ordered them not to fire unless he fired first. Hefting the shotgun, he led them across the street.

The horses hitched outside Dunn's Saloon stood hipshot, dozing in a shaft of light from the window. There was a low murmur of voices from inside, and the click-clack of dice rattling in a chuck-a-luck cage. Jordan pushed through the door, searching the room for Earl Stroud, and brought the shotgun to hip level. Poe and Dobbs fanned out on either side, the carbines cocked and tucked into their shoulders. The saloon went silent as a tomb.

"Nobody move!" Jordan commanded. He earred back the hammers on the shotgun, and men around the room froze. "I'm here with a message for William Bonney."

Stroud sat at a table near the far wall. Several men were ranged along the bar, and out of the corner of his eye, Jordan caught three faces. Dave Reed, Bob Ryan, and

Vince Sanborn, the three hands he'd fired from the Tule Creek line camp. Their presence here told him that they had gone over to the other side, onto Stroud's payroll. Their presence also told him how the thirty horses had been rustled from the canyon. All three knew of the old Comanche trail out of Palo Duro.

The man seated beside Stroud was betrayed by his age. Though grown, he was still a youngster in years, not yet twenty. He was short and slight of build, with lopsided features and a lantern jaw, his mouth ajar with a row of buckteeth. Yet, despite his odd appearance, there was something about him that commanded attention, wary respect. His eyes blazed with the strange, maddened glint of someone devoid of fear. He raised one hand in an idle gesture.

"I'm Bonney," he said in a piping tenor voice. "You got a name?"

"Jack Jordan. I own the JA, over in Palo Duro."

"Heard of you, Jack. Folks say you've got more cows than God."

"Folks are right," Jordan said levelly. "I intend to keep 'em, too."

"Good for you." Bonney regarded him evenly. "So what's the message you brought me?"

"Don't go partners with Earl Stroud. You'd be making a big mistake."

"Why's that, Jack?"

"For one thing, he's stupid." Jordan's eyes touched on Stroud, the shotgun steady. "I warned him off my land, and he keeps coming back. You don't want a stupid partner."

Bonney looked amused. "That's it?"

"No, there's one other thing. When I catch him—and I will—I'll kill him. Then you'd have a dead, stupid partner."

"Well, maybe not, Jack. Suppose Earl manages to get you first? Or maybe I'll do it myself."

"Never work," Jordan said flatly. "Stroud's too stupid

to pull it off. You're too smart to try."

Bonney thought on it a moment. "All right, you've spoke your piece. So where's that leave us?"

"You tend to New Mexico and I'll tend to Palo Duro. No need for us to get crosswise of one another."

"You got style, Jack. I have to hand it to you. Nobody's ever offered me a truce at the end of a shotgun."

"Hope I don't see you around, Billy."

Jordan backed toward the door. He waited until Poe and Dobbs were outside, still covering the room with the shotgun. Then, with a tight smile, he nodded to the Kid and stepped into the night. The door swung closed.

A tense silence hung over the saloon. Around the room, everyone kept their eyes fixed on Bonney, awaiting his reaction. He stared at the door for a long while, his gaze inward and reflective. Finally, with a bucktoothed grin, he shook his head. His eyes glittered with a strange, impenetrable look.

"No bluff there," he said to the room at large. "You boys just seen a man with grit. Told it straight."

"Told what straight?" Stroud blustered. "What's that supposed to mean?"

"Why hell, Earl, it means our deal's off. I don't want no stupid partner."

"You tellin' me you bought that crock of horseshit?"

Bonney laughed a mirthless chuckle. "What I bought was between him and me. That part about you."

"Yeah?" Stroud said dully. "What part's that?"

"I think the man's gonna kill you, Earl."

CHAPTER 37

The sun was a fiery ball lodged in the sky. There were no clouds to temper the heat, and a shimmering haze hung like threads of spun glass over the plains. Jordan and John Poe topped a swell in the verdant prairie, a mile south of the Canadian. They rode toward the Circle B headquarters compound.

For the JA, the summer trailing season was past. Jordan had trailed 18,000 cows north, with losses of less than three hundred head. The market held steady, and Eastern cattle buyers were in a frenzy of competition, offering top dollar. Lloyd Meecham and Dave Thompson, still loyal to the deal they'd made in 1876, outbid all the others. The nine JA herds had brought almost $600,000.

A letter from John Adair was filled with superlatives. He lauded Jordan, for the bank drafts, forwarded to their Denver account, indicated a record year in the making. In a moment of exuberance, he went on to state that the JA, and Jordan, were the best investments of his life. His outlook for the future was equally rosy, and he expressed the sentiment that the years ahead would bring untold wealth. He promised that he and Cornealia would visit Palo Duro in early October.

Jordan was no less optimistic. With a new daughter, and a strapping son, life for him and Rebecca was all they had envisioned those many years ago. Toward the end of June he had bought out the last of the small ranchers who had settled in the canyon. What had seemed a far-fetched goal, the stuff of dreams back in 1874, was finally a reality. The JA, through purchase or lease, now controlled the whole of Palo Duro. From the headwaters of the Red, to the eastern reaches of the canyon, every cow wore the JA brand. His empire was secure at last.

By the middle of July, Jordan's attention turned to other matters. An empire, however secure on paper, still had to be protected from outsiders. Despite every precaution, the JA continued to suffer regular losses from the depredations of cattle rustlers and horse thieves. Some were caught and hanged, but a great many escaped because the ranch, simply by its sheer size, was impossible to patrol. Hard as it was to admit, Jordan slowly came to the realization that it was a fight he would never win so long as he fought it alone. Other measures were needed.

From the home compound, Jordan dispatched riders across the breadth of the Panhandle. The messengers carried letters to all the ranchers who had settled along the Canadian. The rustlers and horse thieves, he wrote in the letter, were a plague upon the land, a threat to every outfit. Worse, there was a contagious aspect to it, one that infected other men and drove them into a life outside the law. The pay was good and the hours were short, and every thief who lived to brag about a raid merely lured other men into the trade. His letter set July 20 as the time for a summit meeting of all the Panhandle ranchers. The place for the meeting, centrally located to all concerned, was Sam Bugbee's home.

From a personal standpoint, Jordan's main thorn in the side continued to be Earl Stroud. He still had no proof that Stroud rustled cows, or that the band of horses stolen in early June was Stroud's handiwork. In fact, when another band was stolen in late June, and once again herded up the old Comanche trail, he began to have doubts that Stroud had switched from cows to horses. For one thing, the trail led north onto the plains, in the opposite direction from

Tierra Blanca Canyon. For another, Mick McCormick had sent word that Billy the Kid, heeding the warning, had passed on a partnership deal with Stroud. While Jordan still had Stroud pegged as a rustler, he now suspected that someone else was raiding the horse herds. He was fighting a battle on two fronts, running himself and his men ragged in the process. He thought there was a better way.

When he and Poe rode into the Circle B compound, the other ranchers were already there. Martha Bugbee met him at the door, inquiring about Rebecca and the new baby, and then led him into the house. Sam Bugbee and the ranchers were seated around the dining table, having just finished a noon meal prepared by Martha. Jordan and Poe helped themselves to the fixings, exchanging greetings and holding the conversation to cow-talk while they ate. Once they finished, Martha cleared the dishes away, setting a fresh pot of coffee on the table, and left the room. The others fell silent, some rolling cigarettes and one lighting a pipe, waiting for Jordan to get on with it. They figured the man who had called the meeting should speak first.

Jordan was acquainted with all of them. A couple were friends, and the others he saw perhaps once a year. Harry Cresswell and George Littlefield were seated on his left, with Bugbee at the head of the table, and Ben Langham on his right. He found it curious that Langham had brought along his foreman, a young toughnut named Luke Starbuck. But he let it pass, and focused instead on how to bring them together in a common cause. Cattlemen were by nature independent, opinionated, and strong-willed, and generally resistant to any leadership but their own. To make it worse, some of them were quietly resentful of Jordan, envious of a spread that ran nearly as many cows as all of them combined. He cautioned himself to proceed with tact.

"We all know why we're here," he began. "Everybody at this table has lost stock to rustlers and horse thieves. I brought you together in the hope we can work together—and put an end to our losses."

"Got that from your letter," Bugbee said, in an effort to help him break the ice. "We're all damn tired of raisin' cows just to watch 'em be stole. What'd you have in mind, Jack?"

"A cattlemen's association," Jordan said forcefully. "Get ourselves organized, pitch in together, and pool our efforts. Drive the thieves out of the Panhandle."

The men stared at him. Littlefield, whose attitude toward the JA was one of wary suspicion, finally took the lead. "This association," he said. "Cost anything to belong? Dues, or such?"

"There'd have to be, George. You can't operate an organization without a war chest."

"How much we gotta kick in to the kitty?"

"Not all that much," Jordan said. "Maybe a hundred-dollar reward on every thief. We'll divide the cost."

Littlefield eyed him. "Divide it how?"

Jordan saw where he was headed. "We'll divide it according to the size of the outfit. I was thinking half from the JA, and you boys split the other half."

"Only one trouble." Cresswell, who was an ally of Littlefield's, hitched forward in his chair. "You're twice as big and you've likely got twice as many thieves. We'd be payin' half your rewards."

"For chrissake," Ben Langham growled. "Jack would be payin' half your rewards. It'd all even out."

"What if it didn't?" Cresswell insisted. "Big outfit draws more rustlers than a little one. We'd wind up on the short end."

"Maybe not," Jordan said. "I've got a hundred men on the lookout in Palo Duro. Most thieves don't like those odds." He paused, waved around the table. "I'd wager you gents have lost more stock than the JA. Anybody care to take the bet?"

No one spoke out. After a moment, Littlefield broached another sore point. "Who's gonna run this association? You got somebody in mind?"

Jordan immediately saw the trap. "George, so far as I'm

concerned, we've all got an equal vote. Whoever gets nominated, the majority rules. You want the job?''

''Nooo,'' Littlefield said slowly. ''I'm not lookin' for extra chores.''

''Only one man fits the bill,'' Bugbee chimed in. ''Jack's the best gawddamn scout in the whole of Texas. Caught more rustlers than the rest of us put together. He's the man for the job.''

''Hold on a minute,'' Cresswell said in a raspy voice. ''I don't cotton to taking orders from somebody just because his outfit's the biggest.'' He hesitated, looked at Jordan. ''Don't take offense, Jack. Nothin' personal.''

Jordan spread his hands. ''Harry, you've got the wrong idea. Like I told you, we'll all have an equal vote. Nobody's obliged to take orders.''

''Listen to yourselves!'' Langham scolded them, glaring at Cresswell and Littlefield. ''Here's the man who brought you the idea, and you're gonna nitpick it to death. Quit pissin' and moanin', and let's get down to brass tacks. You wanna catch thieves or not?''

'' 'Course we do,'' Littlefield said defensively. ''No call for you to start hurlin' insults.''

''Everybody simmer down,'' Jordan interrupted smoothly. ''We've got to learn to work together, and trust one another. What we do here today ought to be for the long haul. Ten, twenty years down the line.''

''Twenty years?'' Cresswell gave him an odd look. ''What the samhill you talkin' about, Jack?''

''I'm talking about the future,'' Jordan said. ''We need towns in the Panhandle, and a railroad. We need our own county, and elected lawmen to keep the peace.'' He stopped, glanced from one to the other. ''Weeding out rustlers is just the first step. We've got a lifetime of work here.''

The ranchers were reduced to silence. They stared at him as though spellbound by a vision far beyond their comprehension. ''Damn right!'' Bugbee finally said in a vigorous outburst. ''Towns and trains, and all them things.

But like Jack says, first things first."

Langham nodded. "I nominate Jack Jordan for . . . for what—what the hell we gonna call this thing, Jack?"

"How about the Panhandle Cattlemen's Association?"

"Sounds good to me," Langham said. "Jack Jordan for president of the Panhandle Cattlemen's Association. Anybody second the motion?"

"I will," Bugbee volunteered. "Motion seconded."

"All in favor say aye."

Bugbee and Langham voiced their approval. Jordan abstained, refusing to vote for himself, simply by saying nothing. A prolonged moment slipped past before Littlefield finally voted in the affirmative. Cresswell reluctantly nodded his head.

"Unanimous," Langham announced. "Looks like you've got the floor, Jack. What's our first order of business?"

"Stock detectives," Jordan said without hesitation. "The cattlemen's association over in Colorado used them with good results. I think it's the place to start."

Cresswell frowned. "What the hell's a stock detective?"

"A man who devotes his full time to running down rustlers. First qualification is that he's got to know cows backwards and forwards, inside and out. Takes an experienced man to spot a brand that's been altered with a running iron."

"Sounds reasonable." Littlefield looked interested. "How's this stock detective find the rustlers?"

"Usually the hard way," Jordan said. "Most times, his work begins after the cows, or the horses, have been stolen. So he's got to be a damn good tracker, and stubborn, too. A man who'll stick to the trail."

"Anything else?" Langham prompted. "How about good with a gun?"

Jordan nodded soberly. "Anybody who's squeamish won't make it as a stock detective. Keep in mind, we don't have any jails out here. No courts, either." He paused, his features grim. "We don't take prisoners."

"Let's call a spade a spade," Langham added. "Jack's sayin' the association—the men at this table—authorizes our detectives to kill ever' rustler caught. Don't make no nevermind whether they're hung or shot. That about cover it, Jack?"

"Yeah, I think so," Jordan affirmed. "We have to set an example that will discourage rustlers from operating in the Panhandle. Everybody here agreeable with that?"

Littlefield shifted in his chair. "One time or another, we've probably all hung a cow thief. But we're talkin' about ordering it in advance, ordering men to their death. What if the law comes after us?"

"What law?" Jordan said firmly. "Until we've got ourselves a county, we're the law. Any lawman shows up asking questions, send him to me. I'll straighten him out *muy* goddamn *pronto*."

Littlefield nodded, glancing at Cresswell. After a moment, Bugbee rubbed his hands together. "Let's get it started," he said vigorously. "Where we gonna find these stock detectives?"

"Way I see it," Jordan said, "we ought to start off with two men. I brought John Poe along because he fits the ticket. He knows cows and he's a pretty fair tracker."

Everyone looked at Poe. "I sorta volunteered for the job," he said with a wry smile. " 'Case anybody's wonderin', I got no problem with hanging rustlers. Bastards deserve whatever they get."

"Damn right!" Langham woofed. "Figured where we was headed when Jack called this meetin'. So I brung along another volunteer. You boys know Luke."

Starbuck stared back at the men. He was corded and lean, all rawboned muscle, with a square jaw and faded blue eyes. Throughout the Panhandle, he was known to be quick with his fists and handy with a gun. Jordan held his gaze.

"How about it, Luke?" he said. "You willing to quit as foreman to take the job? We'd need you on it full time."

"That's why I'm here," Starbuck replied. "Mr. Langham and me talked about what's needed. I'm ready to sign on."

Jordan sensed that he was right for the job. Some men were merely hard and tough, while others were dangerous. Starbuck fell into the latter category. "Unless there are objections," he said, "we've got our stock detectives. John Poe and Luke Starbuck."

"Two enough?" Cresswell asked. "These rustlers run in packs. Same as wolves."

"Depends on the situation," Jordan said. "John and Luke figure they need help, they'll ask. We've got plenty of men."

Poe and Starbuck exchanged a look. Something passed between them, and one, then the other, smiled. The ranchers caught the byplay and knew they had picked two of a kind. A matched pair.

"Got a question," Langham said. "How do these boys operate? The Panhandle covers a lot of territory."

"We let 'em roam," Jordan said. "Their job is to be Johnny-on-the-spot whenever there's trouble. Anybody's herd gets rustled, send for them."

"Sounds like it oughta work."

"Ben, we'll make it work. Make rustling a hazardous occupation. That's the key."

"Well, we elected you president. What's your first orders for these boys?"

Jordan looked at them. "Keep it quick, clean, and final. No prisoners."

Poe and Starbuck needed no further instructions. They understood.

CHAPTER 38

A second town took root in the Panhandle. Nothing grand, it was called Mobeetie and sprang up on the outskirts of Fort Elliott. There was a general store, three saloons, and a log cabin whorehouse, all catering to soldiers from the post. Once again, the sporting crowd was in the vanguard of western settlement.

Jordan took note of Mobeetie only in passing. He knew that the town, like the army post, was some thirty miles west of the line with Indian Territory. The closet rancher was Ben Langham, whose land abutted the Indian reservation and curled around Fort Elliott. But the primary point of interest for Jordan had to do with another government agency. Mobeetie had a post office.

The owner of the general store was the postmaster, and the mail, formerly handled through Fort Elliott, was now dispatched from a cubbyhole at the rear of the store. Jordan nonetheless saw it as a sign of progress, for it was the first official post office to be designated in the Panhandle. In his mind, every new town, and especially a post office, was a step forward in luring the railroads westward. One day, rather than the long trail drives to Dodge City, he envisioned shipping JA cows from a railhead not too distant from Palo Duro.

For all that, Jordan was aware that progress too often

carried a price. Before, in the vast wilderness of the Panhandle, he and the other ranchers had operated much like the feudal lords of ancient times. But in late July, shortly after they'd formed the association, their stock detectives had struck a blow for cattlemen. Poe and Starbuck, after a running gunbattle with rustlers, had captured two members of the gang. The thieves were promptly hanged from a tree on the North Fork of the Red, which snaked through Langham's land. Some of his men, on their next trip to Mobeetie, were quick to brag on the detectives' handiwork. The news soon found its way to Fort Elliott.

Colonel James Thorton, commander of the 10th Infantry, sent word that he had been apprised of the incident. His message, delivered to Jordan as president of the Cattlemen's Association, was a stinging rebuke. Before, though he'd suspected the cattlemen of performing summary justice, he had never had proof. But now, with the story attributed to Langham's men, he branded the hangings a barbaric practice. Further, he accused the ranchers of entering into a conspiracy to commit illegal acts, not the least of which was murder. Though the military had no control over civilians, he promised to bring the matter to the attention of the proper authorities. The sheriff of Clay County, he warned, would be duly advised.

Jordan ignored the message. The colonel, in his view, sounded like a pompous windbag, with more concern for rustlers than law-abiding cattlemen. The military had no jurisdiction over ranchers, and he refused to concern himself with hollow threats. But the first week in August, when a JA rider returned from Mobeetie with the mail, he got a surprise. Colonel Thorton had been as good as his word, forwarding a report of the incident to the sheriff in Henrietta. That evening, when Jordan went through the mail, he found a letter addressed to him, as president of the Panhandle Cattlemen's Association. He read it with mounting anger.

Dear Sir,

I have this date received communication from Colonel James Thorton, commander of Fort Elliott. Colonel Thorton states that unnamed men, acting on orders of your association, hanged two suspected cow thieves sometime in July.

If such is the case, you are herewith put on notice that vigilante acts are contrary to Texas law, and will not be condoned in Clay County. Should an occurrence of this nature happen again, I will send a deputy there with a warrant for your arrest.

You are advised to disband your association, and henceforth cease vigilante actions. The law extends to the Panhandle, even though you may think otherwise. I order you to desist, or face the threat of arrest and prosecution.

Sincerely,
J. B. Arnold
Sheriff
Clay County

"Sonovabitch!" Jordan roared, waving the letter in the air. "Would you look at what this mealymouthed bastard wrote me."

"Jack, your language!" Rebecca admonished him. "I've asked you before. Not in front of the children."

Juanita turned from the kitchen stove. Ethan, who was playing in the parlor, watched his father as though awaiting lightning to follow thunder. Rebecca quickly checked the baby, who was asleep in the cradle, then hurried from the parlor. She walked Jordan out onto the porch.

"Honestly!" she said, facing him. "Ethan has big ears, you know. Do you want him cursing like a cowhand?"

"Here." Jordan thrust the letter at her. "See for yourself."

Rebecca scanned the letter. She shook her head, then

read it more slowly, her eyes wide with concern. She finally looked up at Jordan.

"Is it true?" she asked. "Were these men really hanged?"

" 'Course it's true. The sorry devils were caught red-handed. Even tried to shoot Poe and Starbuck."

"Why didn't you tell me before now? Why do I have to learn about it in a letter from the sheriff?"

"C'mon, Becky, I told you about the association. Never figured you'd want every little detail when a man gets hung."

"Actually . . ." She averted her gaze. "Well, you're right, I prefer not to hear of such things. But that doesn't change the situation, does it?"

"What situation?" Jordan said quizzically. "You talkin' about the sheriff?"

"Yes." She handed him the letter. "You should read it more carefully, Jack. He's accusing you of murder."

"Hell with him! Got that holier-than-thou attitude of people that don't know beans from buckshot. Probably more politician than he is lawman."

"That's hardly the point, is it? In so many words, he's saying the law sends rustlers to prison. Hanging them violates the law."

"What a crock," Jordan grumbled. "Only law out here is what we make for ourselves. Nothing's changed."

"Yes, it has," she said earnestly. "Times have changed, and this letter proves it. You may call Poe and Starbuck stock detectives, but the law doesn't see it the same way. The sheriff all but calls them hired killers."

"I don't give a damn what he calls them. Doesn't change a thing."

"Doesn't it, Jack? Suppose he charged John Poe with murder? Would that change anything?"

"Won't happen," Jordan said. "What's he gonna do, charge everybody in the association with murder?"

"Yes," she said quietly. "You called him a politician, and you're probably right. How can he ignore it when the army has officially lodged a complaint? That wouldn't look good at election time . . . would it?"

"You're saying he might pull some damnfool stunt just to get himself reelected?"

"I'm saying you and John, and all the other members of the association, might be charged with murder. Even if the warrants were never served, you'd still be wanted men. No better than any other outlaw."

Jordan walked to the edge of the porch. He stood staring out across the canyon for a time, wrestling with what he'd heard. "You're right," he said, finally turning back. "Thumbing my nose at him won't turn the trick. Something's got to be done."

"What does that mean?" she said, searching his face. "Are you going to write the sheriff a letter?"

"No letters," Jordan told her. "I aim to have a talk with this J. B. Arnold. Quicker the better."

"You're going to Henrietta?"

"Leave first thing tomorrow. No sense putting it off."

"What about roundup?" she said. "I thought you planned to start the trail drives in early September."

"Still do," Jordan observed. "Leigh knows what has to be done between now and then. I'll be back in plenty of time."

"Jack, are you sure about this? What if the sheriff takes it into his head to arrest you?"

"Don't get yourself all bothered. Nobody's gonna arrest me."

"How do you know? You can't be certain of that."

"Trust me, Becky, it'll never happen. C'mon, let's have supper."

Later, when the children had been put to bed, Rebecca raised the matter again. Jordan humored her, still evasive, and never gave her a solid reason. She went to bed on the verge of tears, unable to sleep despite his assurances. She worried that he was too confident, too cocky.

She was still worried when he rode out the next morning.

* * *

Henrietta was a small but thriving trade center, located on the fringe of the settlements. The town's chief claim to fame was that it served as the county seat, with thousands of square miles under its jurisdiction. Clay County officials were responsible for a land mass that rolled westward through the Staked Plains and ended at the New Mexico border.

The town revolved around the courthouse. All four sides of the square were jammed with shops and business establishments, and even on weekdays, the streets were crowded with horsemen and wagons. In recent years, farmers had settled on what was formerly open rangeland, and the frontier ways had slowly given ground to a more civilized life. These days, churches outnumbered saloons in Henrietta.

Joshua Arnold, the county sheriff, was a respected member of the community, and a staunch Democrat. A portly man, with the girth to match his prosperity, he was one of the most influential politicians in Clay County. On a bright, sweltering morning in August, seated behind his desk, he gazed out the window across the courthouse square. Apart from collecting delinquent taxes, and arresting an occasional drunk, he seldom found himself at odds with his constituents. His principal preoccupation was keeping people happy, and running a clean town. He fully expected to hold office for the rest of his life.

The door opened from the central courthouse hallway. Arnold swiveled around in his chair and saw a tall man, dressed in range clothes, with a brushy mustache and several days' growth of beard. The jingle-bobs on his spurs chimed with a faint musical sound as he crossed the room. He halted before the desk.

"Sheriff Arnold?" he said. "J. B. Arnold?"

"I'm Sheriff Arnold. How can I help you?"

"The name's Jack Jordan. Got your letter and figured we ought to talk. Rode over from Palo Duro."

"Letter?" Arnold appeared confused, then suddenly sat upright. "Oh, that Jack Jordan! You came all the way from the Panhandle?"

"Yeah, I sure did," Jordan said. "Not often I get threats from a lawman."

"Have a seat." Arnold motioned him to a chair. "Understand, the letter was more on the order of a warning. We cannot tolerate vigilante justice, Mr. Jordan."

"Got any proof I hung anybody?"

"Only the letter from Colonel Thorton, at Fort Elliott. Are you denying it?"

"Not the point," Jordan said gruffly. "You all but convicted me on what a court would call heresay. Where's your proof?"

"Well—" Arnold was momentarily flustered. "You're overplaying your hand, Mr. Jordan. I could always send a deputy out there and get the proof."

"Now, by God, you've made the point! We need law in the Panhandle, need it bad. How about posting a deputy out there?"

"No, that's impossible at the moment. The county budget couldn't afford another deputy."

"That a fact?" Jordan said. "We're overrun with rustlers and horse thieves and killers. Got ourselves a goddamn mecca for bad men. Where's the law to protect us?"

"All in good time," Arnold temporized. "One day you'll have all the law you need, and more."

"So what are we supposed to do in the meantime? Let 'em steal us blind and kill off a few here and there?"

"I have limited resources at my disposal, Mr. Jordan. I do what I can."

"Tell you what," Jordan said. "You post a deputy out there and we'll give him all the business he can handle. Till then, we'll just have to dispense our own brand of justice."

Arnold leaned forward. "You do that and you'll regret it. Then a deputy would show up—to arrest you."

"Sheriff, I won't be arrested for protecting what's mine.

You send a man out there with a warrant and he won't come back."

"Are you threatening an officer of the law?"

"I'm explaining the facts of life to you. Hell, I was a Texas Ranger before you ever pinned on a badge. So don't try to lecture me on the law."

"We seem to be at loggerheads." Arnold studied him across the desk. "A lawman and a former lawman ought to be able to find a solution."

"That's why I'm here," Jordan said. "There's five ranchers and over two hundred cowhands in the Panhandle. We've got our lifeblood and our sweat invested in those cattle spreads. You try to arrest anybody out there and we'll fight. You know why?"

"To be frank about it, no. But go ahead and tell me. Why?"

"You'd be threatening all we've worked for. You'd be defending rustlers and horse thieves when you refuse to protect us—"

"Not so, Mr. Jordan."

"—and you'd be taking food out of the mouths of our wives and kids. How do you think that'd look come November?"

"November?" Arnold repeated. "What are you talking about?"

"That's election time," Jordan said bluntly. "Think how that story would sound in the newspapers. You'd look like a first-class horse's ass, Sheriff. I seriously doubt you'd get reelected."

"I have the support of every newspaper in the county."

"Sheriff, I may not look it, but I'm worth a ton of money. I'd spend every nickel on advertisements to tell the voters about J. B. Arnold, 'Defender of Outlaws.' You get my drift?"

Arnold winced at the thought. "Well, now—" He hesitated, his eyes suddenly bright with a sly gleam. "Maybe your money could be put to a better use, Mr. Jordan. Let's say a modest donation to my campaign fund."

"How modest?"

"Something on the order of . . . five thousand?"

"Stay out of the Panhandle and we've got a deal."

Arnold smiled. "I must have a faulty memory, Mr. Jordan. Where's the Panhandle?"

Jordan rode west that afternoon. He was five thousand poorer, but richer for the experience. He had a license to hunt rustlers and horse thieves.

Dead on delivery.

CHAPTER 39

Jordan ranged out ahead of the herd. After four years, the trail northward from Palo Duro was clearly marked. Tens of thousands of longhorns, their hooves pounding the earth flat, had cut a permanent swath through the Panhandle grasslands. For the most part, it was like following a road.

The fall trailing season was under way. As usual, though it was more habit than necessity, Jordan rode with the lead herd. Deacon Walsh was the trail boss, and by now he knew the way to Dodge City as well as Jordan. His herd was the first out of the canyon, topping the rimrock on September 4. Behind, waiting to follow a day apart, were eight more herds.

Off in the distance, Jordan spotted a line of cottonwoods bordering the Salt Fork of the Red. The first day out, as was customary practice, the skittish longhorns had been driven hard. A few days farther along, once they forded the Canadian, the herd would be trail broke and pushed northward at a slower pace. From there, crossing a latticework of rivers one by one, the drive to Dodge would settle into a daily routine. Barring any mishap, the last of the herds would arrive at railhead within a couple of weeks.

The start of a trail drive was always chaotic, for men and cows alike. But within a day or so the excitement wore off, and Jordan found himself on the edge of boredom. There was no urgent need to scout ahead, particularly with river crossings and bed grounds long ago established all the way to Dodge. Apart from dealing with the cattle buyers at railhead, he sometimes felt he was along just for the ride. His trail bosses were experienced and reliable, and the trek northward across the plains soon took on a dulling monotony. His mind often wondered onto other matters.

Today, with the sun dipping westward, Jordan's thoughts centered on the Cattlemen's Association. His trip to Henrietta, and his deal with Sheriff J. B. Arnold, had eliminated unwelcome scrutiny by the law. John Poe and Luke Starbuck, operating with virtual impunity, had become the scourge of outlaws throughout the Panhandle. Within the last three weeks, they had killed one rustler in a shootout, and hanged two more who were caught on Harry Cresswell's spread. The stock detectives were resourceful, quick to cut the trail of thieves, and quicker still to impose the extreme penalty. Their reputation for swift, harsh justice made rustling a dangerous trade.

By comparison, their record against horse thieves was off the mark. Horses were stolen in a seemingly random pattern, and all of the ranchers were suffering serious losses. The one constant was that the horses, wherever they were stolen, were trailed toward the Canadian. The thieves were slippery, masters at eluding pursuit, and the tracks were always lost somewhere along the river. Poe and Starbuck were made to look the fools, for no matter how dogged their search, the horses simply disappeared. The stock detectives readily admitted that they were stumped.

Jordan was baffled as well. Every raid was hauntingly similar to the time he'd trailed a stolen band of cow ponies out of Palo Duro. The tracks inevitably led to the Canadian, and there, as though by sorcery, it was as if the horses had taken wing. On the last raid, only a week past, he had joined Poe and Starbuck in the chase. He found nothing to fault in their tracking methods, and in the end, like them, he'd stood scratching his head on the banks of the Canadian. The trail simply vanished.

But now, approaching the Salt Fork of the Red, Jordan

pondered it from the vantage of hindsight. Horses weren't known to take wing, or walk on water, and he was forced to assess it in a different light. His mind went back to the raid on JA stock, when the thieves used the old Comanche trail out of Palo Duro. The thieves' mounts were shod, as were those in subsequent raids, and that led him to think in terms of white men. Though it was a reasonable assumption, he now began to doubt his own logic. The raiders were too skilled, too elusive, far more clever than any he'd ever tracked. The lone exception, a vivid memory of years past, brought him to thieves of a different breed. The Comanche.

The thought set him off on a new tangent. For more than four years, the Comanche had been confined to the reservation, and he'd heard that they now followed the white man's path. Word got around, and talk had it that the Comanche had been converted from horseback warriors to farmers. Some people ridiculed the notion, but there was always a germ of truth in any rumor. A Comanche farmer, he told himself, might also have adopted the white man's practice of shoeing horses. For that matter, maybe all the Comanche, farmers or otherwise, now rode shod horses. Were that true, it might well explain the mysterious raids into the Panhandle.

There was one way to find out. The Salt Fork of the Red was on an easterly line with Fort Sill, the army post that kept watch over the Comanche. By quick calculation, he figured he was a two-day ride from the border with Indian Territory, and less than three days farther on to Fort Sill. Once there, by turning back northwest and cutting overland, he could easily make the Cimarron crossing in five days. Ten days away from the drive seemed no great loss, for a blind man could follow the trail to Dodge City. But he would have ample time to rejoin the herd, and perhaps locate the missing horses in the bargain. Even if he was wrong, he would be able to renew acquaintance with Quanah Parker. On the spur of the moment, he decided it was worth a try.

He rode back to the herd to tell Deacon Walsh.

* * *

Fort Sill was located along the palisades of Medicine Bluff Creek. Three miles south were the agency buildings, headquarters for those charged with the welfare of the Comanche and the Kiowa. The horseback tribes, once the terror of the Southern Plains, were now wards of the government.

West and north of the fort, the Wichita Mountains jutted skyward, wrapped in a purple haze. The red granite slopes were craggy and foreboding, dotted with scrub oak and cedar. Blackjack trees covered the foothills, while cottonwood and elm bordered the lowland streams.

The terrain sweeping away from the foothills was rolling prairie, lush with native grasses. Bounded on the north by the Washita River and on the south by the Red, the reservation spread westward toward the Texas Panhandle. By treaty, some 3,000,000 acres had been ceded to the warlike tribes.

Jordan rode in from the west. He dropped down out of the mountains and followed a rutted wagon road toward the agency. The reservation was operated by the Bureau of Indian affairs, and the agent was a man named Hazen. His principal task, well-intentioned though somewhat misguided, was to transform horseback warriors into farmers. He greeted Jordan warmly, and readily answered his questions about stolen horses. The idea of Comanche raids seemed to him an unlikely prospect.

Quanah Parker, he explained, led his people by example. To show them the white man's road, he had built a frame house near the foothills of the mountains. He sent his children to the agency school, and while some of the elders disagreed, he extolled the virtues of education. Yet no one, young or old, questioned his authority when it came to tribal matters. He acted as a magistrate in family disputes, and represented his people in dealings with the agency. He was still their chief, a warrior turned peacemaker, and stealing horses would undermine all he had accomplished for the Comanche. He would never allow it.

Halfway convinced, Jordan got directions to Quanah's

home. An hour later, on a rutted trace leading westward, he rode past a cornfield. Ahead, in the shadow of the foothills, he saw a large clapboard house with a spacious porch. Quanah emerged from the house, dressed in a linsey shirt, striped pants, and beaded moccasins. He stepped off the porch, moving forward into the yard as Jordan dismounted. A smile touched the corner of his mouth, his hand extended in friendship.

"*Hao,* scout," he said with a warm handshake. "You are long way from Palo Duro."

Jordan nodded. "I had business with the agent. Farming must agree with you, Quanah. You look well."

"Growing corn damn hard work. Not like old days."

"Agent Hazen tells me you have led your people onto the white man's road. He speaks of you as a 'peace chief.' "

"Got to be," Quanah said absently. "Peace good for Comanche, plenty food now. You here about cows?"

For two years Jordan had kept his promise. Ten cows were delivered every month to Comanche tribesmen at the eastern mouth of Palo Duro. "Here to see an old friend," he said, smiling at Quanah. "Comanche still get cows like always. I gave my word."

"Man's word important thing. Mebbe you stay night. We eat and talk."

Jordan saw two women watching from the doorway. Several children of varying ages, all of them dressed in store-bought clothes, shyly peered through an open window. He recalled that the Comanche often took many wives, and wondered how that squared with white missionaries, who preached monogamy. From the look of things, the old ways were not entirely dead.

"I cannot stay," he said, motioning off to the northwest. "Have cows on trail to Dodge City. Must join my men."

Quanah stared at him with a neutral expression. "Agent Hazen good man. He give you all you want?"

Jordan realized there was a question within a question. The Comanche way was to approach a thing in an oblique manner, rather than directly. "We talked of horses," he said, aware he'd been offered an opening. "Long time now, someone steals my horses."

There was a moment of deliberation. Quanah's eyes were solemn, probing, then he abruptly laughed. "You think Comanche steal your horses, huh? Good joke on you."

"Why would it be a joke?"

"Palo Duro many sleeps from this place. Any man gone that long, I know damn fast. People got no secrets from Quanah."

Jordan studied him. "While ago, you said a man's word important thing. You give your word this is so?"

"Hear me, scout." Quanah touched his mouth, swept his flattened hand away in a quick gesture. "Comanche not steal your horses. I have spoke."

"What about your friends, the Kiowa?"

"All the same, Comanche and Kiowa. Not raid *tejanos* like old times. Farmers now."

A short time later Jordan rode west into the mountains. He was somehow saddened by what he'd seen, horseback warriors yoked to a plow, red white men. But he believed Quanah, trusted his word, and felt gladdened that the Comanche were not behind the raids. All of which brought him full circle, and solved nothing. For the question still goaded him.

Who the hell was stealing the horses?

Jordan found the herd on the bed-ground south of the Cimarron. When he rode into camp, Deacon Walsh and the men greeted him as though he had never been gone. He got the feeling that the drive had suffered none at all by his absence. No one asked where he'd been for the last ten days.

Toward dark, as the men finished supper, the sky turned overcast. The air was still and sultry, with a warm, fetid smell, and Jordan wondered if a storm was brewing. Like all cattlemen, he wasn't ashamed to admit that it was the thing he dreaded most on a trail drive. A plains storm invariably meant trouble.

Still, other than keeping an eye on the starless sky, there was little to be done. Deacon Walsh, after consulting with Jordan, posted extra night guards and ordered the other men to picket their night horses close to camp. An hour or so later, with the herd scattered over the dark prairie, a sudden gust of wind swept through the camp. Every man in the crew was instantly alert, nerves on edge.

The longhorns clattered to their feet. Old Blue and the other steers turned their heads to the northwest, scenting the current. The wind dropped off a moment, only to be replaced by great bursts of hot air that struck like pounding waves, buffeting the men and the cows, and showering sparks from the campfire. Then, with an eerie suddenness, a dead calm settled over the prairie. The heat bore down with crushing force.

Jordan yelled for the men to get mounted. But even as they ran for their horses the herd started drifting south at a fast walk. A gust of cool air brought the smell of rain and ozone, and the atmosphere abruptly became charged with electricity. The darkened sky split apart with a blinding flash that illuminated the night in a blue-white incandescence. A great bolt of lightning struck the ground, gathering into a ball of fire that rolled across the prairie. An instant later the fireball exploded in a numbing blast that shook the earth.

The herd stampeded off to the south. The drumming of their hooves, mixed with their terrified bellows, sent a quaking tremor across the bed-ground. The electric air sparked luminous shafts of fire along the tips of their horns, and as they rumbled southward a wall of scorching heat clung in their wake. Jagged streaks of lightning split the clouds in every direction, sizzling into the earth with thunderous reports of an artillery barrage. The steady concussions, jolt after jolt, seemed to freeze the motion of men and cows in searing white brilliance.

The roar of the wind swelled to a deafening pitch. With

it came the rain, tearing and slashing as great torrents of water deluged the plains. The longhorns hurtled onward as the shriek of the wind and the stinging rain buried them in a fiery cataract. On the outskirts of the seething mass of cattle the trailhands quirted their horses savagely, barreling along in a blind, mindless fury. Nothing known to man could stop the longhorns from running while the storm hammered out of the skies. Their one hope lay in somehow keeping the herd in sight.

Ten miles, and what seemed a lifetime later, the raging torrent of Beaver Creek brought the steers to a halt. The crew quickly turned them back from the water and forced them to a milling standstill. Behind, on the soggy plains, lay a string of dead and dying longhorns, trampled under the hooves of those who had survived. Jordan and Walsh separated, circling the herd from opposite directions, and checked on the men. A streak of lightning lit the sky as they met at the edge of the creek.

"I count four," Jordan said. "How about you?"

"Three," Walsh replied, water pouring over the brim of his hat. "Lucky all we lost was cows."

"Looks like I got back just in time for the fireworks."

Walsh turned his face up into the pelting rain. His mouth curled in a sardonic grin. "Jesus Christ," he said with an aimless gesture. "Ain't it fun bein' a cowboy."

"Well, Deacon, it's got its moments. Tonight just wasn't one of them."

"Yessir, boss, you're right there. No barrel of laughs tonight."

They rode back toward the herd.

CHAPTER 40

On September 20 they sighted Dodge City. The stampede had cost them a day on the trail, and over a hundred steers trampled to death. The storm had also spooked the herd a day behind them, but the relay rider brought good news. None of the JA trailhands had been injured, or killed.

Deacon Walsh selected a holding ground a mile or so west of town. The point riders turned Old Blue and the lead steers, pivoting them in a slow turn, and milled the herd along the bank of the Arkansas. Upstream, and farther east, herds from Texas were bunched across the buff prairie.

Jordan found a clear spot along the river. He stripped, scrubbing himself clean, and washed his hair. By the time he returned to the chuck wagon, the cook had water boiling. He shaved with a straight razor and soap, and changed into fresh clothes he'd stored in the wagon. Unlike many herd owners, who left their men in camp and took quarters in the Dodge House, he stuck to a practice established years ago. The trail drive wasn't finished until the herd was sold.

The weather was comfortable, but warm. As Jordan strapped on his gun belt, he checked the angle of the sun, pegging the time around three o'clock. He still had no use for a pocket watch, relying instead on the plainsman's timepiece, the sun and the stars. After slapping dust from his hat, he mounted a sorrel gelding, one of his string caught fresh from the remuda and saddled by the wrangler. He waved to Walsh, who was still checking the herd, and rode out of camp. A tingle of excitement rode with him, for Dodge City was where all the hard work was converted into hard cash. He meant to make it a record year for the JA.

The South Side sporting district was packed with cowhands. Jordan never came to Dodge without marveling again at how vice operated like a magnet for men fresh off the trail. A modest drinker, and no patron of whores or the gaming tables, he was nonetheless intrigued by the wages of sin. The South Side had expanded year by year, and now covered several acres, all devoted to debauchery in one form or another. As he rode through the district, he calculated men and wages, and the amount of money squandered during trailing season. He thought the sporting crowd probably kept several banks in business.

Up ahead, Jordan crossed the Deadline, where the railroad tracks bisected the town. His attention was drawn to the cattle pens, on the far side of the depot, and he abruptly reined to a halt. A westbound train sat chuffing smoke, and saddle horses were being hazed up loading chutes into a string of boxcars. The Kansas Pacific had extended track to Denver, and he was accustomed to passenger trains, and freight trains, passing through Dodge City. But he'd never before seen horses being loaded for shipment west, and the sight aroused his curiosity. He made a mental note to inquire further while in town. Something about it bothered him.

Once across the Deadline, Jordan was struck as always by the dissimilarity to the vice district. Front Street bustled with activity, the boardwalks crowded with shoppers, and wagons loaded with trade goods trundling through the plaza. Twice a year, on his trips to Dodge, he was reminded of passing from a riotous carnival into a community concerned more with business than with pleasure. A ribbon of steel, and the town's peace officers, were all that separated tawdry whorehouses from sedate houses of worship. But then, as he threaded his way through a line of wagons, his thoughts turned to more immediate matters, the price of cattle. He left his horse hitched outside the Long Branch saloon.

Lloyd Meecham and Dave Thompson were by now an institution at the Long Branch. While other cattle buyers worked out of the Dodge House, or lesser saloons, they still held court at their regular table toward the rear of the room. After more than two years of dealings, Jordan considered them as much friends as business associates. He found them in a moment of leisure, Meecham reading the *Police Gazette* and Thompson perusing the *Dodge City Times*. Neither of them looked up as he approached the table.

"Must be my day," he said affably. "You boys don't appear swamped with business."

The men dropped their newspapers, startled by his voice. They clambered to their feet with surprised smiles, and each in turn pumped his arm with cordial handshakes.

"Good to see you, Jack," Meecham said, guiding him to a chair. "I take it you've just arrived."

"Hot off the trail," Jordan acknowledged. "How's things in the cattle trade?"

"Never better," Thompson said, signaling a waiter. "Let us treat you to a nice, cool beer. Wash the trail dust out of your throat."

"Hell, I wouldn't turn one down, Dave."

The waiter brought a schooner of beer. Meecham poured drinks for himself and Thompson from a bottle of rye on the table. He hoisted his glass in a toast.

"To old friends," he said amiably. "And Texas beef!"

"Palo Duro beef," Jordan amended. "Nobody grows better."

They drank on it, and Jordan wiped foam from his mustache. Thompson set his glass on the table. "Well, now," he said. "What have you brought us, Jack?"

"Nine herds," Jordan responded. "First one's here, and

the others are a day apart. Probably be a little shy of eighteen thousand head."

"Splendid," Thompson said, nodding to Meecham. "We'll take the lot, as usual."

The buyers never hesitated on Palo Duro herds. Jordan was one of the few cattlemen in Texas who conducted an advanced breeding program. With each trailing season, the infusion of the Hereford strain was more apparent in his livestock. Thompson went on to note that by the end of the fall season over half a million cows would have been shipped out of Dodge City. A record year, he observed, and no end in sight.

"Never saw anything like it," Meecham added. "Just when we think the market's peaked, the demand jumps again. We can use all you supply, Jack."

"Glad to hear it," Jordan said. " 'Course, I still expect to get top dollar. What's your price?"

"Standard range grade is going for thirty. As we have in the past, we'll still pay two dollars more a head for your stock."

Jordan sipped his beer, aware that they were watching him closely. Something in their manner, a vague sense of eagerness restrained, told him they would pay more. "Look here," he said. "You boys want quality, and I'm due all the market will bear. So let's not haggle among friends. I need thirty-four."

"Out of the question!" Thompson said stoutly. "We've always treated you right, Jack. For old times' sake, we'll go thirty-two and a quarter."

Jordan knew he had them. "Christ, why spoil a good thing, Dave? The market's changed, and we both know it. I'll let you off for thirty-three. Not a penny less."

"Now who's haggling? You're holding our feet to the fire."

"No, I'm just honoring our deal. You get all the JA beef, but only at the right price. Thirty-three's fair."

Thompson and Meecham exchanged a glance. Then,

with a resigned air, Thompson nodded. "Done," he said. "Thirty-three for the lot."

They sealed it with a handshake. Jordan was inwardly elated, for the deal guaranteed a record year. A quick mental calculation told him the JA would exceed the goal he'd set for 1878. Yet he kept a straight face, treating it as just another routine transaction. The idea was to leave them with the impression that they'd got the better of the deal. He casually moved on to other matters.

"Got a question for you," he said in an offhand manner. "On the way into town, I saw horses being loaded onto a westbound train. Where're they headed?"

"The High Plains," Meecham informed him. "These days, there's a big market up there for saddle stock."

"Well, I'll be damned. That's news to me. What brought it about?"

"For once, the army finally got it right."

Meecham went on to explain. Custer and the 7th Cavalry had been defeated on the Little Big Horn in June of 1876. A year later, after a massive military campaign, the Sioux and the Cheyenne tribes had at last been herded onto reservations. The result was a land boom, attracting ranchers to a sea of grass throughout Wyoming and Montana. By the summer of 1878, the demand for saddle stock had increased tenfold. Some horses were shipped west to Denver, and then on by rail to Cheyenne, Wyoming. Others were trailed overland to the High Plains.

"Supply and demand," Meecham concluded. "Whole herds of horses are being trailed from Texas to Dodge. From here, one way or another, they wind up on the High Plains. By the end of the year, over fifty thousand horses will have gone north."

"Lots of horses," Jordan said with an odd expression. "Guess they fetch a fair price up there?"

"I would say so!" Thompson trumpeted. "At least double what they bring down in Texas. Why, are you interested in trying the horse business?"

"Not just exactly," Jordan said. "But I'm damned interested in checking it out a little further. Somebody's stealing horses on a regular basis over in the Panhandle."

"I'm not surprised," Thompson said. "Wherever there's easy money to be made, thieves flourish. Horses are no exception."

"Who's the biggest horse dealer in town? Likely the brands have been changed, but it never hurts to ask. I might turn up a lead."

"Waste of time, Jack. Horse dealers are notoriously crooked, particularly with the demand so great. They turn a blind eye to altered brands."

"Dave's got a point," Meecham remarked. "Your best bet would be to talk with Sheriff Masterson. You'll at least get a straight answer."

Bat Masterson had been elected sheriff of Ford County in October 1877. His reputation was that of a tough but fair-minded lawman, one who seldom found it necessary to resort to gunplay. Over the years, on his visits to Dodge City, Jordan had become friendly with Masterson, as well as the assistant city marshal, Wyatt Earp. Unlike many Texans, he respected their no-nonsense attitude toward enforcing the law. He thought Meecham's suggestion was a good one.

"Appreciate the advice," he said now. "I'll have a talk with Masterson while I'm in town."

"Terrible thing, stealing livestock." Meecham shook his head. "If anyone can help, the sheriff's your man. We wish you luck, Jack."

"Indeed!" Thompson said. "High time someone taught these thieves a lesson."

"By God, I'll drink to that."

Jordan hefted his beer schooner. He thought Thompson's remark was dead on the money. High time the thieves were taught a lesson.

High time and long overdue.

Early that evening, Jordan rode over to the South Side. The contracts had been drawn that afternoon, and he'd signed the deal with Meecham and Thompson. At their invitation, he had taken supper with them at the Dodge House, discussing the future of the cattle market. But now, crossing the Deadline, his thoughts turned to horses.

Downstreet, he saw Bat Masterson and Wyatt Earp emerge from a cafe. They halted outside, and stood watching the throngs of trailhands along the boardwalks. As he reined in before the Lady Gay saloon, they turned and walked in his direction. He dismounted, looping the reins around a hitch rack, and stepped onto the boardwalk. Masterson saw him first.

"Well, look who's back in town. How's tricks, Jack?"

"No complaints," Jordan said, nodding to Earp. "Good to see you, Marshal."

"Likewise," Earp said. "When'd you get in?"

"This afternoon." Jordan jerked a thumb over his shoulder. "Just came from making a deal on my cows. Meecham and Thompson bought the whole bunch."

"You're a quick one," Masterson said jovially. "No sooner hit town than you've got a deal. Life must be sweet."

"Well, sometimes there's bitter with the sweet. Matter of fact, I was hoping to run into you gents. Thought maybe you could help me."

"How so?"

"From what I gather," Jordan said, "livestock dealers here are buying lots of horses. Understand there's a big market for them up in Wyoming and Montana."

"That's a fact," Masterson affirmed. "Why, are you in the market for horses?"

"Other way round," Jordan said. "Horse thieves are stealing us blind over in the Panhandle. Got an idea our stock winds up here in Dodge."

"Wouldn't doubt it," Masterson said. "But there's probably a thousand horses come through here every week. You'd do better lookin' closer to home."

"Closer to home?" Jordan gave him a puzzled squint. "I don't follow you."

Masterson glanced at Earp. "Dutch Henry?"

"That'd be my guess," Earp said. "He's within spittin' distance of the Panhandle."

"Never heard of him," Jordan said, looking from one to the other. "Who's Dutch Henry?"

"Henry Borne," Masterson replied. "Known as Dutch Henry because he's of German blood. Slickest horse thief ever to come down the pike."

"Best I ever saw," Earp added. "Not an Indian alive that could hold a candle to him."

Jordan's scalp tingled. "What makes you think he's raiding the Panhandle?"

"Simple," Masterson said. "Dutch Henry headquarters in No Man's Land."

"What the hell's No Man's Land?"

Earp laughed. "You ought to get a newspaper down your way. Tell him, Bat."

Masterson briefly explained. On the trail to Dodge, Jordan's herds crossed the eastern section of a strip of land that lay between the Panhandle and the Kansas Border. Technically a part of Indian Territory, the strip was an uninhabited wilderness, claimed by no one. Outlaws had adopted it as a sanctuary, and the newspapers had recently dubbed it No Man's Land. Dutch Henry Borne was rumored to headquarter in the western part of the strip, at a place called Wild Horse Lake.

"What do you mean 'rumored'?" Jordan demanded. "Does he headquarter there or not?"

"So we hear," Masterson said. "I've got no reason to go there. Out of my jurisdiction."

"How about federal marshals?"

Masterson and Earp seemed amused. "Not likely," Earp said. "Couple of marshals went there, and they didn't come back. Nobody's got the urge to try it again."

"See what I mean?" Masterson said. "That's why it's called No Man's Land."

Jordan questioned them at length. They told him all they knew, and what they had heard through the grapevine.

When they walked off upstreet, he stood there a moment considering what he'd learned. Though it wasn't much, it gave him a starting point, a place called Wild Horse Lake. And a name.

Dutch Henry Borne.

CHAPTER 41

Wild Horse Lake lay on the divide between the Beaver and the Cimarron rivers. Located in the western reaches of No Man's Land, it was less than ten miles from the southern border of Colorado. For centuries the Comanche and Kiowa had used it as a campsite during their fall hunts for buffalo. But the Indians came there no longer.

Jordan and his men approached from the northeast. Deacon Walsh rode at his side, and strung out behind were eight trailhands, all of them volunteers for the manhunt. Four days ago, where the Dodge City trail crossed the Cimarron, the other hands and the chuck wagons had been sent on to Palo Duro. Turning west, Jordan had then led his hunting party more than a hundred miles through a desolate land. He was searching for Wild Horse Lake.

The country they rode through was an isolated expanse of grasslands and raw wilderness. The Spaniards had called it *Cimarrón,* which loosely translated meant 'wild and untamed.' Yet there was nothing erratic or unruly about its borders. Texas and Kansas were separated by its depth of some thirty-five miles, while its breadth extended nearly two hundred miles from Indian Territory to the border of New Mexico. Through a hodgepodge of poorly written treaties, the land was now forgotten by man and government alike. No Man's Land.

Following the sketchy directions provided by Masterson, Jordan and his men came at last to the divide south of the Cimarron. The lake itself was actually a large basin, which trapped the spring melt off, and, somewhat like a deep bowl, served as a reservoir for thunder showers that came infrequently to the plains. Above the basin, sweeping away on all sides, was a limitless prairie where the grasses grew thick and tall. Wild things once came there to feed and water, but all that was in the past. Even mustangs no longer came to Wild Horse Lake.

The reason was quickly apparent to Jordan. After leaving the men hidden in the tall grass, he took the brass telescope from his saddlebags, motioning for Walsh to follow, and crawled to the edge of the basin. Far below, perhaps a quarter mile from their position, he spotted a crude log cabin on the north side of the lake. Across the way, on the opposite side of the lake, there was another cabin set back from the shoreline. Tendrils of smoke drifted on a brisk afternoon wind from the chimneys of both cabins.

Jordan extended the telescope. He scanned the nearest cabin and saw a man off to one side, splitting firewood. As he watched, the man dropped his axe, collected an armload of wood, and walked back inside. After a moment, he trained the telescope on the other cabin, and saw a man standing in the doorway, staring out across the lake. A short distance from both cabins were log corrals, with fewer than ten horses in each enclosure. The corrals were unusually large, and stoutly built, which struck him as odd. He collapsed the telescope.

"Looks deserted," he said. "Only one man at each cabin."

Walsh grunted. "Likely holdin' down the fort while the others are off stealin' horses."

"Likely so," Jordan observed. "What do you make of those corrals?"

"A mite big for so few head, aren't they?"

"Not if you're a horse thief. I'd say they're just right to hold fifty or sixty head."

"Makes sense," Walsh agreed. "You spot any brands

on them horses down there now?''

''None I recognize,'' Jordan said. ''Probably spares for Dutch Henry and his gang.''

''What d'you make of the two cabins? Figger there's more'n one gang?''

''That would be pure guesswork, Deacon. We won't know till we ride in there.''

Walsh looked at him. ''You aim to hit 'em now?''

''I think we'll wait—''

The drum of hoofbeats stopped him short. A string of some thirty horses suddenly topped the southern rim of the basin. Five outriders drove the herd down a weathered trail and pushed them across the basin floor, on the west side of the lake. The man in the nearest cabin hurried outside, running toward the corral, and swung open the gate. The riders hazed the horses into the corral.

Jordan quickly extended the telescope. He peered down at them, watching the riders dismount and hitch their horses outside the corral. He moved the glass from man to man, looking for some telltale sign of command and authority, the face of Dutch Henry Borne. The men walked toward the cabin, rolling cigarettes and laughing, clearly pleased with themselves. But none of them exhibited the mannerisms of a leader, or offered any clue as to who was in charge. They trooped into the cabin.

Across the lake, still standing in the doorway, the man in the far cabin appeared only mildly interested. Jordan swung the telescope back to the corral, and slowly inspected the horses milling around the enclosure. He saw that they were winded from a long run, burning with thirst, their hides coated with sweat. But then, focusing the glass on a horse stopped in the middle of the corral, he saw something more. He snapped the telescope shut.

''Bugbee's stock,'' he said. ''They're wearin' the Circle B brand.''

''Glory be,'' Walsh said in a keen voice. ''We done found the Panhandle thieves.''

''Well, there's five riders. We've been tracking three all

these months. But I'd still say they're our men."

"Any idea which one's Dutch Henry?"

"Hard to tell from the way they were acting just now. Could be any of them."

"Glad to see we got 'em outnumbered. How you plan to do this, boss?"

Jordan deliberated a moment. "You notice they haven't unsaddled. They'll probably wait a while and let those horses cool down. Then they'll drive them to the lake for water."

"Horses gotta have water," Walsh said. "So's that when we hit 'em?"

"We'll catch them out in the open, on foot. Just before they get to the corral."

"Do we go in shootin'?"

"What's the rule, Deacon?"

"Don't take no prisoners."

Jordan turned and crawled back through the grass. He gathered the men together and rapidly outlined the plan of attack. They were to hold their horses in readiness, and at his signal, ride forward with his mount. He would then lead them over the rim of the basin, spread out on line, and charge the cabin at a gallop. Any of the thieves who surrendered were to be disarmed and held. Those who resisted were to be shot dead on the spot. He asked if there were questions.

None of the men had questions. They began checking the loads in their pistols, and tightening cinches, as he walked away. A short distance ahead he dropped to all fours and disappeared through the tall grass. On the rim of the basin, he settled down to wait.

The one question unanswered, he thought to himself, was the one asked by Deacon Walsh. He wondered which of the men below was Dutch Henry Borne.

The sun tilted westward in a cloudless sky. Jordan estimated an hour had passed, and placed the time at around four o'clock. He began to revise his plan, for he'd seen no activity from the cabin, and a night attack was not an option. Given no choice, he would move on the thieves an hour before sundown.

As the afternoon wore on, a thought slowly formed in his head. The basin, more than he'd suspected, was a sanctuary where those who rode the owlhoot could retreat with no fear of pursuit. Masterson had told him that not even U.S. marshals dared venture into the isolated stronghold, and he saw now that a man on the dodge could find no safer spot. In the general scheme of things, Wild Horse Lake was the perfect hideout. A place where there was absolute immunity from the law.

All the more reason to hang them, Jordan told himself, for the law would never get the job done. He was still toying with the thought when the door of the cabin opened and the men stepped outside. From their loud laughter, and the slight hitch in their movements, he saw that they'd been celebrating over a jug of whiskey. He knew now why they had taken so long to water the horses.

On his feet, waving his hat overhead, he caught the attention of Deacon Walsh. The trailhands quickly mounted and moved forward, with Walsh leading his horse. He swung into the saddle, motioning them to spread out on line, and rammed hard with his spurs. As they came over the edge of the basin, he pulled his pistol and led them down the slope in a plunging charge. At the bottom of the grade, he gigged his horse into a headlong gallop, closing rapidly on the cabin. The outlaws were halfway to the corral, and they turned at the thudding sound of hoofbeats. Their faces registered drunken disbelief, stunned shock.

Jordan fired first, killing a man who fumbled at the pistol on his hip. The outlaws recovered, jerking their six-guns, dodging and darting as they snapped off shots at the onrushing horsemen. The gunfire became general, and Jordan saw another man fall, slammed backward by a shot from Deacon Walsh. An instant later, a third man went down, his shirtfront stitched with blood from four or five slugs. Then, as they were about to be overrun by the charge, the other three outlaws abruptly quit the fight. Their features etched in terror, they hurriedly tossed their guns to the ground. They raised their hands in surrender.

The JA crew brought their horses to a dust-smothered halt. Jordan was in the lead, and as he reined his gelding about, a flash of movement caught his eye from across the lake. Above the far cabin, he saw the man whipping a horse up the eastern slope of the basin. The distance was too great for a clean shot, even with a rifle, and he grudgingly accepted the escape of one thief. Turning back toward the corral, he did a quick head count and saw that none of his men had been wounded. The three outlaws stood rooted in their tracks, surrounded by horsemen. He rode forward.

"Listen close," he said, staring down at them. "I'm Jack Jordan, owner of the JA. You boys have been caught red-handed. So I'd advise you to cooperate."

The three men seemed transfixed by his stare. One of them, slightly older than the others, finally lifted his shoulders in a shrug. "You're gonna hang us anyway. Why should we cooperate?"

Jordan extended his Colt, thumbing the hammer, and fired. Horses snorted, dancing sideways, as the slug sizzled past the man's head. He flinched, ducking down, his eyes laced with surprise and fear. The men beside him were frozen in place, their eyes locked on the gun.

"You listening now?" Jordan slowly cocked the hammer. "Next time you'll lose an ear. Then your other ear, and if that doesn't do it, I'll start on your thumbs. Up to you how far I go."

The man swallowed, licked his lips. "What d'you wanna know?"

"For openers, point out Dutch Henry Borne. Or 'fess up if you're him."

"Dutch ain't here."

Jordan sighted on his left ear. "Not good enough."

"Wait!" the man screamed. "Honest to Christ, I'm tellin' you the straight goods. Him and the other boys are off somewheres in Colorado—stealin' horses.''

The panic in the man's voice convinced Jordan he'd heard the truth. ''When will Borne get back?''

''Week, maybe more. I ain't got no real idea. Him and McCoy sometimes join forces on long raids. Generally come back with a couple of hundred head.''

''Who's McCoy?''

''Pete McCoy.'' The man nodded toward the other side of the lake. ''Him and his bunch work outta that cabin over there.''

''Keep talkin','' Jordan said. ''How many men in both gangs?''

''Well, before today, there was nine of us in Dutch's bunch. McCoy's only got four.''

''Who buys all these horses you boys steal?''

''Fred Eckhardt,'' the man said. ''Livestock dealer in Dodge City.''

Jordan made a mental note of the name. He thought Bat Masterson would make good use of the information. His gaze was still fixed on the talkative thief. ''What's your name?''

''Bob Nolan.''

''Have to tell you, Bob, you boys are pretty slick. Every time you've hit the Panhandle, we lost your tracks at the Canadian. How'd you pull that off?''

Nolan managed a lame smile. ''Took to the river and swam the horses a mile or so downstream. Never brought 'em out till we found a rocky spot that wouldn't hold tracks too good.'' He shrugged. ''Horses can swim farther'n most folks think.''

''Yeah, you sure as hell fooled me.'' Jordan played a sudden hunch. ''When's the last time you saw Earl Stroud?''

''Long time ago. Must've been somewheres back in '76.''

''Whereabouts?''

''Why, right here,'' Nolan said, as though it was common knowledge. ''Him and Dutch got in a row, and he quit Wild Horse Lake. He wasn't no match for Dutch, and he knew it. Him and his boys just took off one night."

"What was the problem?"

"Earl heard you'd settled in Palo Duro, and he wanted to start rustlin' cows. 'Course, Dutch said cows was too easy to track, and wouldn't hear of it. Told Earl to stick with horses, or get out."

Jordan saw no reason to inquire further. Deacon Walsh and the trailhands were witness to the fact that Stroud was a horse thief turned rustler. He slowly wagged his head. "Well, Bob, I guess it's time to get on with things. You understand we've got a job to do."

"Jesus gawddamn Christ," one of the other men moaned. "You got back ol' Bugbee's horses, and we told you all we know. Don't that count for nothin'?"

"Shut your trap," Nolan muttered. "Don't turn crybaby just because you're gonna get hung. Take your medicine."

A lone oak tree stood between the cabin and the lake. Within minutes, the three men were bound, mounted on their horses, and positioned beneath a stout limb. When the horses were whipped from beneath them, they thrashed and kicked and finally strangled to death. The trailhands watched their struggles in brutal silence.

After it was over, Jordan found a scrap of paper and a pencil in the cabin. He wrote a terse warning in bold block letters. Outside again, he mounted, rode to the tree, and stuffed the piece of paper halfway into Nolan's shirt pocket. He stared up at Nolan's face for a moment, filled with some vague sense of regret that it had been necessary to hang the man. But the swaying bodies and the scrap of paper were meant to serve a purpose. Dutch Henry Borne would understand the message.

KEEP OUT OF THE PANHANDLE

Jordan ordered the cabin burned. Deacon Walsh and one of the hands rode to the opposite side of the lake, and torched the cabin there. By the time they circled the south end of the lake, Jordan and the other men were waiting with the string of stolen horses. They started up the trail to the top of the basin.

On the plains above, Jordan paused for a look back at Wild Horse Lake. The cabins were engulfed in flames, golden fire mirrored on the surface of the water. Three dead men lay on the ground, and three more hung by their necks beneath the distant oak tree. The scene was stark and cruel, and he took no great pride in the day's work. Yet it left the warning he intended.

Justice was swift and harsh, even in No Man's Land.

CHAPTER 42

Yellow leaves glittered like a sea of golden coins on trees throughout the canyon. There was a nip of frost in the air, and a bright October moon slowly ascended in an indigo sky dusted with stars. A phantasmal light sparkled off the rushing waters of the river.

Jordan and John Adair were seated in rockers on the porch. They were stuffed from supper, and lulled into that surfeited moment of silence which follows a good meal. A cigar jutted from Adair's mouth, like a burnt tusk, and he contentedly puffed thick wads of smoke. He stared out across the glimmering landscape as though mesmerized by the sight.

The Adairs had arrived late that afternoon. Their last visit had been more than a year ago, what seemed a lifetime. They had missed spring roundup, owing to the marriage of Cornealia's brother, and fall roundup as well. Nothing had changed in their absence, for Palo Duro itself was immutable, and yet everything had changed. Ethan was almost two and a half years old, and his sister, now four months, was a small bundle of amazement, the image of her mother. The log house they remembered, quaint and rustic in their memory, was now a home. A place of laughter and children, awaiting their discovery.

For Jordan and Rebecca, a visit by the Adairs was a festive occasion. Old friends, godparents to Ethan, the

Adairs were considered members of the family. Childless themselves, they were awed by Laura, marveling over her delicate features and her sunny disposition. But the center of attention was Ethan, a rollicking young hellion who kept things in a constant state of turmoil. Filled with mischief, a small keg of energy, the boy was like a lovable whirlwind, drawing laughs even as he left wreckage in his wake. Everyone breathed a sigh of relief when finally, after a stern look from his father, he allowed himself to be tucked in for the night. A calm descended on the house somewhat like the aftermath of a cavalry charge.

From the house, the sounds of Juanita cleaning up in the kitchen carried to the porch. Jordan and Adair, who wore their coats against the night chill, seemed content with a moment of quietude. What with the general conversation at supper, and an afternoon of watching Ethan's rambunctious hijinks, they had not yet broached the matter of business. Even now, gazing out across the moonlit canyon, their thoughts were elsewhere. Adair finally roused himself from the stupor of a heavy meal. He chuckled, shaking his head from side to side.

"Ethan certainly takes after his father, Jack. I've never heard one so young curse so well."

"Drives Becky to distraction," Jordan said. "She stays on me all the time about it."

Adair laughed, puffing his cigar. "The boy certainly gave Cornealia a shock. One of the few times I've seen her truly speechless."

In the course of the afternoon, on separate occasions, Ethan had let loose with a loud "goddamn" and a perfectly enunciated "sonovabitch." Rebecca had been mortified, scolding Ethan and apologizing to the Adairs. The look she gave Jordan would have blistered paint.

"Out of the mouths of babes," Adair said with a sly chortle. "The lad has an ear for pitch and inflection. I all but heard your voice when he popped out with 'sonovabitch.' "

Jordan grinned. "Wait till he catches some of the lingo

from the cowhands. Becky dreads the day.''

''Well, on balance, I'd not concern myself. By the Saints, a ball o' fire like Ethan and a bonny lass like Laura! Count your blessings, Jack.''

''Tell you the truth—'' Jordan's look was one of off-handed guile. ''I'm the luckiest *sonovabitch* alive.''

Adair rumbled a great belly laugh. ''I'll never hear the word but what I think of you and Ethan. You're two peas from the same pod, indeed you are.''

''Coming from you, I take that as a compliment, John.''

''And well you should. But enough tomfoolery for one day. I've gorged myself until it hurts to laugh. Let's talk of business, the ranch.''

''Laugh a minute there, too,'' Jordan said. ''I felt like a bank robber with the price we got on the fall drives. We're rolling in money.''

''No question of that,'' Adair agreed. ''The draft you sent through from Dodge City made our year. A princely sum, indeed.''

''Next year will be even better. Easterners love their beef, and there's no end in sight. The market just keeps getting bigger.''

''What of the ranch itself? Are you satisfied with the operation?''

''Guess I'm never satisfied,'' Jordan commented. ''There's parts of any operation that could be run better. What makes you ask?''

''Well, I know you, Jack.'' Adair idly tapped an ash off his cigar. ''You reached for the sun, and now that you've got it, you might have an eye on the stars. Have you expansion plans I've not heard of yet?''

''You talking land or cows?''

''Either.''

Jordan motioned into the night. ''We already own more land than most folks think decent. Hadn't given any thought to buying more.''

Adair nodded. ''And cows?''

''Cows are another story, John. We're getting top dollar

for our beeves, and that's mainly because of the breeding program. I'm of a mind to buy more Herefords.''

''How many?''

Jordan smiled. ''Five hundred bulls and a thousand cows. Now you're fixin' to ask me how much it'll cost.''

''You're a clever one,'' Adair said, wagging his cigar. ''Always a step ahead with your schemes. So, I'm waiting to hear. How much?''

''Quarter of a million ought to do it. We can take it out of petty cash.''

''Petty cash, indeed! You're talking most of our profits for the year.''

''No, John,'' Jordan said earnestly. ''I'm talking the future. One helluva future for the JA.''

Adair was silent a moment. He rolled the cigar between his fingers, studying the fiery coal on the tip. ''Well, why not?'' he said at length. ''What better investment than an investment in the future? After all, it's only money.''

''Where we're concerned, it's money on the hoof. We'll make it back tenfold. Maybe more.''

''Are you sure you're not Irish, Jack? I've never in my life met such a cockeyed optimist.''

''Hell, look in the mirror sometime. You're liable to surprise yourself.''

On that note, their mood light and jocular, they went back inside. Juanita had finished in the kitchen, and retired to her room at the rear of the house. Jordan and Adair shrugged off their coats, still laughing as they moved into the parlor. A stack of logs blazed in the fireplace, and Rebecca and Cornealia were seated on the sofa. They glanced up as the men entered the room, their curiosity aroused. Cornealia thought her husband had never looked so carefree.

''Aren't we happy, though?'' she said in an inquiring tone. ''Are you and Jack enjoying yourselves?''

''Oh, indeed we are,'' Adair replied with a zestful grin. ''We've just been discussing the correct way to pronounce 'son of a bitch.' Or is it 'sonovabitch,' Jack?''

Cornealia stared at him, not certain he was serious. Then, trying to suppress a smile, she heard Rebecca trying equally hard to smother a giggle. Suddenly, spontaneously, they all broke out laughing.

The next day was crisp and bright. In honor of the Adairs' long-delayed visit, Jordan decided to take the day off. He was enthused as well about showing them something they'd never seen. Half in jest, he termed it a riding academy for horses gone bad.

Early that afternoon everyone gathered outside the corral. The headquarters remuda had been put out to graze near the river, and two geldings, a roan, and a blaze-faced chesnut were tied beside the corral gate. Jordan, who held Ethan firmly by the hand, warned the Adairs to stay clear of the horses. He referred to them as outlaws.

Adair and Cornealia appeared puzzled, and Jordan went on to explain. For no apparent reason, he told them, a gelded horse, already broken and trained, sometimes turned outlaw. Perhaps the horse had been mistreated, or maybe, despite having been gelded, he still thought he was a stallion. For whatever reason, the horse reverted to the wild, adopting a hostile attitude, and became a danger to any cowhand who tried to step into the saddle. A horse of such temperament was dubbed an outlaw.

Buster Lomax walked down from the bunkhouse. The Adairs knew him for his skill at woodworking, recalling that he had built all the cabinets in their stone house. Jordan informed them that his nickname was one of unusual respect, earned the hard way. Lomax was the top broncbuster on the JA, unequaled in his ability to stay aboard a cyclone on legs. He was the only man on the payroll who tangled with outlaws, and today was a case in point. The roan had been returned from one line camp, and the chesnut from still another, and Lomax looked upon them as pupils. He intended to teach them good horse manners.

Lomax led the roan into the corral. He took a gunnysack hanging out of his hip pocket and tied it over the roan's eyes. Jordan explained that a horse denied sight was calmed by blindness, and rarely fought. Lomax collected a saddle blanket and saddle off the fence, and returned to the center of the corral. The roan trembled when he laid the blanket across its back, and snorted nervously when he slung the saddle into place. He waited a moment, allowing the horse to recover, then stooped low and caught the cinch band from the off side. He quickly threaded the latigo and snugged the rigging tight.

However unwilling, the outlaw was ready for its lesson. Lomax hooked a boot into the stirrup, swung his leg over the saddle. Everyone watched quietly as he jerked the blindfold loose and let it fall to the ground. For perhaps ten seconds the roan remained perfectly still, as though considering its new predicament. Then, with a faint smile, Lomax lightly feathered the horse with his spurs. The roan exploded at both ends.

All four feet left the ground as the horse bowed its back. With a bone-jarring snap, it swapped ends in midair and sunfished across the corral in a series of bounding leaps. Lomax was all over the horse, rolling with the gyrations, his boots rammed in the stirrups. Ethan screamed with delight, sitting astride Jordan's shoulders, as the roan veered away from the fence. A catlike turn brought the horse around, and it whirled and kicked, slamming the broncbuster front to rear in the saddle. His hat sailed skyward.

Lomax raked hard with his spurs. The spiked rowels whirred and the roan squealed a great roar of outrage. As though berserk, the horse reared, humping its back, then hit the ground and erupted in a pounding beeline for the corral fence. Jordan and the others scurried away, Cornealia clutching Adair's arm, as the roan barreled toward them. Lomax swung out of the saddle at the exact instant the outlaw collided with the cross timbers.

The roan buckled at the knees and fell back on its rump. Lomax nimbly scrambled aboard as the horse struggled to regain its feet. He gigged with his spurs and the roan jolted away in stiff-legged crowhops that lacked punch. But he sensed that the fight was gone, and he reined the horse around the corral in a turning maneuver. At last, satisfied with his pupil, he eased to a halt and stepped out of the saddle. The roan stood walleyed and heaving for breath, an outlaw no longer.

Lomax retrieved his hat. He jerked his thumb back at the spent horse. "Just needed the kinks ironed out. He'll behave himself now."

"Good work, Buster," Jordan said, lowering Ethan to the ground. "You ready to top off the other one?"

"I say." Adair stepped forward, motioning to the chesnut. "That looks like very fine sport, indeed. Would you mind if I had a try?"

Jordan and Lomax exchanged a quick glance. Before they could reply, Cornealia grabbed Adair's arm. "Are you mad, John?" she said in a shrill voice. "You'll get yourself killed!"

"Nonsense." Adair plucked her hand off his arm. "I'll thank you not to interfere."

"She's right," Jordan said with a slow smile. "Hell, John, I wouldn't get on that horse myself. He's too raw for me."

"Would you spoil a man's fun, Jack?"

"No fun getting stomped. You don't believe me, ask Buster."

"Mortal truth," Lomax said somberly. "Outlaws are plumb rank, Mr. Adair. You saw yourself what that fool roan pulled. Tried to commit suicide just to kill me."

"Here." Jordan passed the boy across to Adair. "Put your godson on your shoulders, and watch out for his heels. He'll give you all the ride you want."

Ethan laughed, wrapping his legs around Adair's neck. He grabbed a handful of hair, and began shouting "Horsey! Horsey!" Before Adair could object, Jordan took the reins of the chesnut and walked to the corral gate. He nodded to Lomax.

"C'mon, I'll give you a hand with the saddle."

Lomax fell in beside him. ''Godalmighty, boss, that was a close one. You likely saved his bacon.''

''Buster, I think we've just done our good deed for the day.''

CHAPTER 43

After supper, Jordan and Adair retired to the porch. A full moon rose over the distant battlements, casting a spectral sheen across Palo Duro. There was a brisk wind out of the north, and trees along the river fluttered brightly under a starlit sky. The muted wail of a harmonica drifted leeward from the bunkhouse.

Adair lit his evening cigar. He snuffed the match, tossing it off the porch, and puffed a pungent cloud of smoke. His eyes strayed to the corral, where the headquarters remuda now stood dozing, their rumps turned to the wind. The chesnut and the roan, awaiting return to their line camps, were clearly visible in the moonlight. He stared at them with a contemplative look.

"Tell me, Jack," he said without turning. "You recall when we first came here, do you? When you taught me to hunt buffalo?"

"How could I forget it?" Jordan observed. "You dropped that cow down there along the river. Damn fine shot."

"Well, you see, I was reminded of it today. Not long after we were through at the corral."

Adair had been unusually quiet during supper. Jordan thought he was sulking over having been denied a chance to ride a bronc. But this matter of the buffalo was an unexpected twist. He waited to hear more.

"You'll not tell Cornealia of what I'm about to say?"

"Fine by me, John."

Adair puffed smoke. "When you taught me to hunt buffalo from a horse, you were confident I could manage it. Is that a fair statement?"

"Yeah," Jordan said. "Wouldn't have let you try it otherwise."

"But today you believed I was overmatched with that horse?"

"Hell's bells, you saw it yourself. Buster got thrown what, three times? He had to ride that bastard into the ground."

"Exactly," Adair said. "There's no question that you saved me from serious injury, perhaps worse. I should have trusted your judgment in the matter . . . as I did with the buffalo."

Jordan wondered if it was an apology. He chuckled softly, rapped Adair on the arm. "Hard to admit you were wrong, huh?"

"Let's say it's something I would never admit to Cornealia. I trust you won't mention it to Rebecca, either."

"So far as I'm concerned, you never said it."

Adair laughed. "I still think it would have been good sport. Perhaps another time."

"John, we'll make a cowboy out of you yet."

Two riders materialized out of the moonlight. Jordan rose from his chair and watched as they circled the corral. He recognized John Poe and Luke Starbuck.

The men reined to a halt, stepped down. "Evenin', boss," Poe said. "Mr. Adair."

Adair knew of the stock detectives, though he'd never met Starbuck. Jordan quickly introduced them, then nodded to the men. "What brings you boys here?"

"Trouble," Poe told him. "You'll recollect this is our week to cover Palo Duro. We was headed here to spend the night."

"And?"

"We run across the night guard for the Rush Creek

camp. He was out on patrol and stumbled onto some rustlers. When the shootin' commenced, he took off. Figures they got away with forty, fifty cows."

Jordan frowned. "Stroud?"

"Gotta be," Poe said. "Tracks headed straight for Tierra Blanca. See 'em plain as day in this moonlight."

"Why didn't you follow them?"

"Figured you wouldn't wanna be left out. 'Specially where Stroud's concerned."

"You figured right."

" 'Course, you already know, we're gonna lose the trail in the badlands."

"Doesn't matter," Jordan said. "We've got proof that Stroud's a thief. I've just been waiting for him to pull another raid."

"Well, that is good news," Adair interjected. "How did you obtain the proof?"

"What the law calls a death-bed confession. One of my trail bosses and eight hands were witnesses."

"And the man who confessed?"

"A horse thief," Jordan remarked. "Gave us the whole lowdown on Stroud. Just before we hung him."

Adair arched an eyebrow. "A court might question the reliability of such proof. Is that a problem?"

"No problem for me, John. Damn big one for Stroud, though."

"Then I insist on coming along. Spare me any arguments to the contrary."

Jordan turned to the detectives. "Go over to the bunkhouse and get Dyer. Tell him I want five or six men, all volunteers. Have them ready to ride in thirty minutes."

Poe and Starbuck led their horses toward the corral. Adair followed along as Jordan went through the door of the house. Inside, Jordan took his gun belt off a wall peg and strapped it around his waist. Rebecca and Cornealia, who were seated before the fireplace, hurried from the parlor. Rebecca's eyes were filled with alarm.

"What's wrong?" she said. "Where are you going?"

"Tierra Blanca," Jordan said, reaching for his mackinaw. "Stroud's luck just ran out."

"Not a word!" Adair ordered, silencing Cornealia before she could object. "I'm going with Jack and that's the end of it. We'll have no discussion."

A half hour later the women watched from the porch as the men rode out of the compound. Cornealia's eyes glistened in the moonlight, damp with tears. Rebecca put an arm around her shoulders.

They stood wreathed in silence as the men forded the river.

The moon was suspended directly overhead. The metallic ring of horseshoes on stone echoed off the gorge walls. They rode in single file, ten men in all, their horses snorting puffs of frost. Somewhere around midnight they emerged from the shadowed ravine into Tierra Blanca.

Jordan wasn't concerned with tracks. He calculated the rustlers were at least three hours ahead, and no chance of overtaking them by first light. He'd led his men southwest through the night, on a direct line with the gorge that separated Palo Duro from Tierra Blanca. As yet, he had evolved no plan of attack, deferring any decision until he was able to scout ahead. He meant to gain, and hold, the element of surprise.

A short way into Tierra Blanca he signaled a halt. Ordering the men to dismount, he walked forward with Adair and scaled the outcropping that overlooked the canyon. The moon was at its zenith, flooding the landscape with silvery light that turned night to day. He expanded the small brass telescope, and slowly scanned the terrain ahead. He glassed the northern end of the canyon, then moved on to the dim outline of the cabin. There were no lights, and the distance was too far to make out the corral. He was about to collapse the telescope when movement caught his eye.

Off to the south, he saw a shadowy wedge in motion. He focused on the blur, staring intently through the glass, waiting for it to move closer. Then, suddenly, the blur came into range, and he saw the indistinct forms of horses and riders. He was unable to separate horse from man, but there appeared to be seven or eight riders in the group. Tracking them with the telescope, he watched as they turned toward the west wall of the canyon, and rode into the Rocking S compound. A few moments later the glow of lamplight abruptly blossomed through the cabin window.

Adair saw the flickering light as well. The distance was some three miles, but against the backdrop of the canyon wall, the lamp stood out like a tiny beacon. He looked around at Jordan. "What do I see out there, Jack? That speck of light?"

"Our boys just got home," Jordan said. "Somebody lit a lamp in the cabin."

"Where have they been all this time?"

"Well, they rode in from the south. I'd judge they drove our cows down there and tucked them away in one of those small canyons for the night. Probably aimed to put them on the trail for New Mexico tomorrow."

"Tomorrow?" Adair repeated. "I'd think they expect us to arrive on their doorstep at any moment."

"Not from the looks of things," Jordan informed him. "They had a good lead, and probably thought we wouldn't start tracking till morning. Likely figured they had time for a little shut-eye."

"Do you plan to trap them in the cabin?"

"That'd give them the advantage. No need to attack a fort unless you've got no choice. I think there's a better way."

Jordan scrambled down the outcropping, Adair a step behind. The men stood with the collars of their mackinaws turned up against the chill of the night. Dyer was talking with Poe and Starbuck, while the five cowhands waited nearby. He turned as Jordan and Adair walked toward them. His words formed cottony spurts of frost.

"What'd you see out there, boss?"

"Stroud and his gang are in for the night. All you boys gather around."

Jordan quickly outlined his plan. Based on past experience, he told them, the stolen cows would be put on the trail sometime before noon. He figured Stroud's men would sleep for five or six hours, then prepare to move out. That was when he planned to spring the surprise, just before they started saddling their horses. He wanted to catch them outside, on open ground.

With a stick, Jordan knelt and sketched a map in the dirt. The rough drawing, clearly visible in the moonlight, revealed the canyon floor, the west wall, and the cabin. He ordered Poe and Starbuck to take three men, circle across the canyon, and find positions in the rocks and boulders immediately south of the compound. Adair, Dyer, and the other two hands would accompany him, and take positions north of the cabin. The horses were to be secured somewhere to the rear, out of the line of fire.

The plan gave them the edge. Once outside, in the open, the gang would be caught in a cross fire from north and south. He would issue a single warning, ordering the rustlers to lay down their guns and surrender. Anyone who chose to fight was to be killed without hesitation. If anyone made it to the corral, their horses were to be shot, to prevent escape. Those who surrendered, or survived, would be hanged. He asked if there were questions.

"Just one," Poe said. "When do you want us in position?"

"Before first light," Jordan said, glancing at the moon. "You've got roughly five hours, no more."

"What if you're wrong?" Starbuck asked in a level tone. "Suppose they don't come out the way you figure?"

"Then we wait," Jordan said. "Whatever happens, you just follow my lead. We'll flush 'em out one way or another."

A moment passed while he awaited further questions. The men stared back at him, shuffling their feet in the cold, and no one spoke. He finally nodded, then turned toward his horse.

"Let's move out."

Not long after sunrise smoke billowed from the cabin's chimney. A short while later the smell of coffee and flapjacks drifted across the compound. First one man, then another, and finally four in all made trips to the outhouse. They hurried along in the brittle cold, rushing back to the cabin.

Jordan watched from behind a boulder. He was some fifty yards from the cabin, with Adair and Dyer and the other two men spread out around him. His hands were jammed in the pockets of his mackinaw, and a Winchester was hooked through the crook of his arm. Across the way, hidden in the rocky terrain, he occasionally saw movement from Poe's men. Everyone was trying to stay warm.

The activity from the cabin was much as Jordan had expected. An early breakfast, with men taking turns in the outhouse, was all part of the morning routine. He bided his time, watchful and alert, never once removing his hands from his pockets. As a Ranger, and later as an army scout, he'd learned that the element of surprise was often half the battle. He was unwilling to sacrifice surprise merely to waylay a man or two on the way to the privvy. He waited for the moment when at least four men were caught on open ground, with nowhere to take cover. Four out of eight would cut the odds in half.

By nine o'clock, with all of them still in the cabin, he started to have doubts about waiting longer. Then, without warning, the door opened and six men, wearing mackinaws and carrying saddles, walked toward the corral. Among them were Dave Reed and the two cowhands Jordan had fired from the Tule Creek line camp. A seventh man, attired in shirt and trousers, with a gun stuck in his waistband, moved to the corner of the cabin. He unbuttoned his pants and relieved himself with a splash that could be heard in the still morning air. Earl Stroud appeared in the doorway, watching as the six men trooped across the compound. His gun belt was cinched around his waist.

Jordan eased around the boulder. He brought the Winchester to his shoulder, sighting on Stroud, and yelled a sharp command. *"Nobody move! Surrender or get killed!"*

Stroud reacted instantly, stepping backward and slamming the door. Jordan levered three quick rounds, drilling holes through the door slightly below shoulder height. The man at the corner of the cabin dropped his pud, retreating toward the door, and pulled his gun. Adair's Winchester boomed, and the impact of the slug drove the man into the wall, the gun slipping from his hand. He slumped to the ground.

The six men near the corral dropped their saddles, wheeling in the direction of Jordan's voice. They clawed inside their coats, came out with pistols, their eyes darting between Jordan and Adair. Then, almost simultaneously, Poe and Starbuck, along with Dyer and the five cowhands, opened fire. The crack of eight carbines reverberated off the canyon wall, and a hail of lead sizzled across the compound. Five men went down as though their legs had been chopped from beneath them. The sixth man staggered, triggering a shot into the dirt at his feet. He slowly crumpled forward onto his face.

A moment of deafening silence fell over the compound. Then one of the horses crashed through the log corral, followed by the others, and bolted away at a crazed gallop. Jordan levered a cartridge into the Winchester, trained the sights on the cabin window. He called out in a loud voice.

"Give it up, Stroud! All your men are dead."

"You gawddamn asshole!" Stroud shouted. "I'm not gonna let myself be hung. Whyn't you come get me?"

"The party's over," Jordan yelled back. "You want me to set fire to that cabin? Come out or be burned out!"

There was a long moment of deliberation. "You win," Stroud hollered. "Tell your boys to hold their fire. I'm comin' out."

"No funny business, Stroud. Let's see your hands."

The door creaked open. Stroud stepped outside, his hands raised overhead. He paused, blinking in the sunlight, then walked toward the boulders. Jordan moved into the clear, the Winchester cocked, held at the ready. He saw that Stroud was still packing a gun.

"Hold it there, Stroud!" he ordered. "Drop that gun belt."

Stroud kept walking, his features blank. The distance closed to thirty yards, and his stride suddenly lengthened. Jordan roared a command. "Halt, goddammit! Halt!"

Stroud's arm moved, and the pistol appeared in his hand. He fired, still advancing, hurriedly thumbed off another shot. The first plucked at Jordan's sleeve, and the second whanged off the boulder. Jordan shouldered the Winchester, caught the sights, and fired.

The heavy slug dusted Stroud front and back. He lurched sideways, arms flailing in a nerveless dance, and dropped the gun. His knees buckled and he slowly collapsed, sprawled on the ground. One foot drummed the earth in a spasm of afterdeath.

The men walked forward. They stood in the sudden stillness, staring down at the body. After a time, Jordan glanced around at Dyer. "You once said he wasn't a quitter. Guess you were right, Leigh."

Dyer just nodded. His gaze went to the welter of bodies near the corral. "Three of them boys used to ride for us, over at the Tule Creek camp. You remember?"

"I remember," Jordan said. "Too bad they took up with Stroud."

Dyer snorted. "Damn fools should've picked better company."

"Have somebody find a shovel. I want all these men buried."

"I never knowed you to bury rustlers before."

"There's a first time for everything, Leigh. Let's get it done."

Dyer gave him a strange look, then walked away. Jordan turned, and found Adair watching him with a curious expression. ''Well, what do you think, John? Not like huntin' buffalo, is it?''

''No,'' Adair said in a bemused tone. ''I'd never shot a man before.''

''How's it feel?''

''Not all that bad, really. Particularly since he was trying to shoot me.''

Jordan thought it a telling remark. He looked down at Stroud and felt no qualms about today's work. There seemed to him a simple truth in the sightless eyes that stared back.

Some men lived their lives waiting to be killed.

CHAPTER 44

The men rode into the JA headquarters late that afternoon. As they dismounted, Cornealia hurried outside, her skirts flying, and threw her arms around Adair's neck. She kissed him soundly on the mouth.

Dyer and Poe, standing with Starbuck and the other men by the corral, watched with undisguised amusement. Their smiles broadened when Rebecca, who was only a step behind, peppered Jordan with kisses. Her eyes misted with tears.

''We were worried sick,'' she said breathlessly. ''Neither of us has slept a wink.''

''You shouldn't fret so,'' Jordan said, grinning down at her. ''I always come back.''

''Oh, I know. But I worry just the same.''

Jordan glanced over her shoulder. Cornealia clung to Adair as though he'd returned from the dead, and he seemed to bask in her attention. Juanita appeared in the doorway, the baby in one arm and holding Ethan by the hand. The boy broke away from her, jumping clumsily off the porch, and ran across the yard. Jordan scooped him up in his arms.

The men broke out laughing as the youngster's chubby arms clamped his father's neck in a tight hug. Jordan finally got himself untangled, and turned to face the men. ''You rowdies hold off a minute,'' he said, waiting until they quieted down. "I talked it over with Mr. Adair, and he agrees. You boys did a helluva job, and you deserve a reward."

There was an expectant hush. Jordan let them hang a moment, then smiled. "A hundred dollars to every man and three days off. Don't kill your horses gettin' to Tascosa."

The men roared their approval. They slapped each other on the backs, then surged forward to shake hands with Jordan and Adair. Ethan squealed his delight, struggling in his father's arms, as though he were riding to Tascosa with them. Finally, after another round of thanks, the men drifted off toward the bunkhouse. Jordan looked around at Adair.

"Let's celebrate ourselves," he said. "You and Cornealia come on over at suppertime. Bring your bottle of brandy."

Jordan wrapped his free arm around Rebecca, and walked away. Adair and Cornealia, arm in arm, crossed the compound and disappeared into their stone house. Rebecca uttered a low, lighthearted laugh.

"I hope John isn't too worn out. I think Cornealia has a special homecoming treat for him."

"Does she?" Jordan said. "Got any ideas of your own?"

She gave him a minxish look. "You might be surprised."

"I'll hold you to your word, Mrs. Jordan. I'm not the least bit wore out."

Juanita prepared a special supper that night. At Rebecca's direction, she caught a plump hen in the chicken coop and beheaded it with a hatchet. On a ranch, where beef was a mainstay of the diet, chicken was considered a delicacy, and served only on festive occasions. Rebecca willingly sacrificed one of her prized hens, for the occasion was not just festive, but a time of celebration. John Adair and her husband had returned alive.

After the children were in bed, Juanita served the

roasted hen. Adair and Cornealia expressed their compliments, and Jordan carved the bird. Cornealia was in a particularly effusive mood, and Rebecca suspected that she'd taken Adair straightaway to bed. She suspected as well that Cornealia had pried from Adair every last detail of the raid on the rustlers. Her normal practice was to ask nothing, for she found such stories to be gruesome in the telling. Yet she knew without asking, simply from her husband's carefree manner, that Earl Stroud had been killed. Later, at an opportune moment, she planned to casually extract the details from Cornealia.

Following a long, leisurely meal, Adair produced the bottle of brandy. Cornealia had brought brandy glasses from the stone house, and after he'd poured, Adair proposed a toast to the continued success of the JA. Everyone clinked glasses, and they sipped their brandy, with still no mention of the day's raid. A short time later, while the women helped Juanita clear the table, Jordan and Adair retired to the porch. The skies were clear, and Palo Duro stood out in bold relief under the glow of a full moon. They took seats in the rockers.

Adair lit a cigar. The meal, topped off with brandy, had put him in an expansive mood. All day, reflecting on a remark by Leigh Dyer, he'd wanted to ask a question. Instead, aware that Jordan was in many ways a private man, he had suppressed his curiosity. But now, perhaps because of the brandy, he decided no harm would be done. He puffed smoke into the cool night air.

"Would you satisfy a question that's nagged at me since this morning?"

"Fire away," Jordan said easily. "What's on your mind?"

"Dyer was surprised that you ordered those men to be buried. I recall him saying you'd never before buried a rustler."

"That's true."

"So tell me," Adair said. "Did you bury them because of Earl Stroud?"

Jordan looked at him. ''What makes you ask that?''

''I've an odd notion that you admired Stroud. Am I wrong?''

''Yes and no.''

''That's hardly an answer, Jack.''

''In the old days,'' Jordan told him, ''the Comanche seldom scalped an enemy who fought well. A man of bravery.''

Adair appeared confused. ''I don't take your meaning.''

''I didn't admire Stroud. I admired the way he went out.''

''Ahhh, I think I see. You're saying he died bravely.''

Jordan nodded. ''Stroud knew he was a dead man. But he chose his own way to go out.''

''He did, indeed,'' Adair said. ''And tried to kill you in the process.''

''I reckon that's all part of it. He went down still fighting. No quarter asked, none given.''

''You know—'' Adair considered a moment. ''I'm reminded of a saying I often heard as a lad in Ireland. ''Tis not enough that a man lived well. He will be remembered that he died well.' In the end, Stroud found respect in death.''

''Yeah, he did,'' Jordan said. ''Whatever else he was, he wasn't a coward. He had grit.''

''Not too different from the code of ancient times, Jack. Or the Comanche, for that matter. You Westerners have simply adopted it as your own.''

''Never heard it called a code before. But in a way, I suppose you're probably right. Every man measures himself against the same yardstick.''

''Quite so,'' Adair agreed. ''A standard of courage.''

''What's this about courage?''

They turned at the sound of Cornealia's voice. She and Rebecca stood in the doorway, woolen shawls thrown around their shoulders against the chilly air. Jordan and Adair quickly surrendered their chairs, and got the women seated. Rebecca's eyes were merry, her features animated.

"We thought the ladies should join the men for a change. We never know what you talk about out here on the porch."

"From the little I overheard," Cornealia said teasingly, "they were talking about courage. John tends to think of that as a manly virtue."

"Indeed not," Adair protested. "History records countless acts of courage by women. Joan of Arc would be an excellent example."

Cornealia laughed gaily. "See what I mean, Rebecca? The only woman he could think of was one who rode off to battle dressed in armor." She rolled her eyes in gentle mockery. "Men always equate courage with war."

A spirited discussion ensued. Rebecca joined with Cornealia, citing women throughout the ages, women whose acts of bravery had nothing to do with physical courage. Adair, who enjoyed playing devil's advocate, defended his position with droll good humor. Jordan listened, amused by their lively repartee, but his thoughts slowly wandered afield. His mind drifted off on another tangent.

The canyon, ablaze in a flood of moonlight, claimed his attention. His thoughts turned inward, prompted by the discussion of courage, and he recalled the day he'd brought Rebecca to Palo Duro. She had followed him into the wilderness, with nothing more than faith in his dream, and he recalled now that it was an act of unstinting bravery on her part. On occasion, half in jest, but knowing it was true, he had commented that she was a woman with sand. The passage of years had proved her to be far stronger than even he had imagined.

In time, his dream had become their dream. All he'd envisioned shortly became a shared vision, one she had held no less fiercely over the years. Together, one sustaining the faith of the other, they had transformed a raw wilderness into a sprawling empire. What he had once thought of as his legacy was now their legacy. Her courage, her indomitable spirit, had made it as much hers as his own.

A legacy beyond the dream, beyond the vision, even beyond time.

One day, Ethan and Laura would carry on in Palo Duro. Somehow, perhaps because they were of his blood, he knew that their bond with the land would be as strong as his and Rebecca's. No man was immortal, and the future he saw so clearly might not come to pass in his lifetime. But his children, and certainly their children, would live to see a Panhandle where there were towns and schools, a railroad, and a time when a man no longer needed to enforce his own law. Palo Duro would endure, and in time, the law would prevail.

Still, for all his musings, he saw no reason to leave a thing undone. The dream, and the legacy, were his to forge in whatever fashion he could manage. He planned to live a long time, and hard as it was to admit, the JA now operated pretty much on its own. The future was what a man made it, and sometimes *when* he made it. Never put off until tomorrow—

"Jack?"

Rebecca's voice broke into his reverie. He looked around to find her staring at him with an odd expression. She reached out from her rocker, touched his hand. "Goodness, where were you? We've been talking the longest time, and suddenly realized you hadn't said a word."

"Just thinking," Jordan replied, squeezing her hand. "What'd I miss?"

"A very scintillating conversation. What were you thinking about?"

"Well, one way and another, the future."

"Oh, honestly, Jack! Sometimes it's like pulling teeth. What about the future?"

Adair and Cornealia appeared amused by his discomfort. He lifted his hands in a shrug. "I got to woolgathering and an idea came to me."

"Watch yourselves now," Adair said with feigned apprehension. "When Jack Jordan gets an idea, there's danger afoot. I know the signs all too well."

"Pay him no attention, Jack," Cornealia said with an engaging smile. "We very much want to hear your idea."

Jordan gathered his thoughts. "Guess it just came to me out of the blue. Why wait for the future to happen? We can make it happen."

They stared at him, waiting. "And?" Rebecca coaxed. "Make it happen how?"

"Now," Jordan said vigorously. "We keep talking about towns, and a railroad, and our own county. But it's all talk, no action. Time to get off our butts."

Rebecca darted Cornealia an embarrassed look. "Pardon the crude language. Jack sometimes forgets he's in polite company."

"You're excused," Cornealia said wryly. "How do you suggest we get off our . . . *derrières*?"

"Take the bull by the horns. Raise such a ruckus that we'll be heard all the way to Austin. Let 'em know the Panhandle won't wait any longer."

"When you say 'them,' " Adair inquired, "are you talking about politicians?"

"Damn right," Jordan said forcefully. "Politicians, the railroads, the governor himself. Organize a lobby and put a bee in their bonnet. Don't take no for an answer."

"Jesus, Mary, and Joseph!" Adair ruefully wagged his head. "I've some small experience in politics, Jack. Do you know what such a lobbying effort would cost?"

"Who the hell cares?" Jordan said. "A railroad alone would double our land values. We can't lose."

"And we're to fund this ourselves, is that it?"

"Maybe the other ranchers will go half. But if they won't, what's the difference? We're filthy rich, John. We can afford it."

"By all that's holy, how do I let you talk me into these things?"

"Oh hush, John," Cornealia said sweetly. "How many times have you told me Jack has a genius for making money? Let him handle it."

Adair groaned. "I've no chance against the two of you."

"The three of us," Rebecca reminded him. "If Jack says it will work, then it will work. I just know it."

"Do you?" Jordan said. "You sound pretty confident."

"I would certainly hope so! After all, it's my dream, too."

"How would you like to go to Austin, Mrs. Jordan?"

"I think I would like that very much. When do we leave?"

"Before snow flies, sooner the better. I'll get to work on it."

A familiar sound attracted Jordan's attention. High in the sky, honking their way southward, a vee of wild geese was silhouetted against the moon. He stared at them a moment, then his gaze went out across the grasslands, the distant battlements of Palo Duro. He nodded, smiling to himself, certain of it now.

Some things last forever.